LEAVING THE BEACH

A NOVEL BY
MARY ROWEN

LEAVING THE BEACH

SECOND EDITION SOFTCOVER
ISBN: 1622535804
ISBN-13: 978-1-62253-580-4

Editor: Jessica West
Cover Artist: Kabir Shah
Interior Designer: Lane Diamond

EVOLVED PUBLISHING™

www.EvolvedPub.com
Evolved Publishing LLC
Butler, Wisconsin, USA

Printed in Book Antiqua font.

BOOKS BY MARY ROWEN

1. *Leaving the Beach*
2. *Living by Ear* (Coming Fall 2019)
3. *It Doesn't Have To Be That Way* (Coming Winter 2019/2020)

What Others Are Saying About "Leaving the Beach"

"This is an outstanding novel... Erin is a perfectly flawed heroine."
Semifinalist, 2017 BookLife Prize
(10 out of 10 in All 5 Categories Judged)

"...gracefully grapples with several important issues, including alcohol and drug addiction, loss, grief and sexuality... There are also many entertaining pop-culture references to offset the weighty themes... An intriguing novel that looks at the ways that people cope with the pain in their lives."
Kirkus Reviews

"I thoroughly enjoyed this unique and fast read. Erin Reardon is both typical and remarkable, flawed but likable. Readers need to hold on to hope as she makes mistakes. I didn't see the author's truly original finish coming, and that made the book an even better read!"
Book Club Mom

"Touching, first-person account of bulimia and the struggle to fit in, the struggles we face with addiction, the struggle to be loved. Also about the power of music."
Dave O'Leary, Seattle Author and Music Critic

"4.5 Unique, healing stars!"
Hazel Godwin, Craves the Angst Book Reviews

DEDICATION

For my children.
May you both grow in happy, healthy ways.

Chapter 1

Cambridge, MA, 1991

The dreamers were out in full force that windy March night. Someone had leaked the news about Lenny Weir's secret performance to the grunge community, causing fans from all over New England to swarm Central Square. Most didn't have tickets for the sold-out show, but still hoped for a miracle or at least a glimpse of the guy. "Feels like a giant family reunion, eh?" said Colin.

I nodded and shivered in my thin wool coat. But if we were at a family reunion, then I was an auxiliary member or something. Or perhaps a third or fourth cousin, or an in-law of the in-laws. I followed Colin and his friends through the hugging, high-fiving throng, feeling invisible one minute and painfully obvious the next. And why did no one else mind the cold? Even the waiflike teenager holding a sign that said MY FIRSTBORN FOR YOUR TICKET looked comfortable in just a t-shirt and jeans. Meanwhile, I could barely feel my fingers.

My original idea plan had been so much simpler: a box of ice cream, a package of cookies, maybe some Devil Dogs too. Then a couple of hours on the couch, eating and enjoying the latest issue of *The Boston Phoenix.* Basically the same thing I did every weekend night, and whenever I had free time. The reading material varied; the food, not so much. And the vomiting? Well, that always sucked.

But that afternoon, Colin had arrived home all rosy and breathless—ocean air and cigarette smoke steaming off his leather jacket—with an extra ticket *for me.* And how could I turn him down? Especially when he claimed to be skipping out on his first ever meeting with Suzanne's parents for the show. Not to mention the way Colin's Bono-esque brogue transformed me—plain old Erin Reardon—into *Aerin,* a Celtic princess, and turned my insides to mush.

"Plenty of people'd give their left arm to see Lenny, Aerin," he said with a wink. "Just never breathe a word of this to Susie, okay? She thinks the boss needs me down at the bar. Emergency situation, you know? Massive party. All hands on deck."

Secret shows are usually a win-win. The artists are psyched to try out new material with a live audience, and their superfans get to hear the stuff first. Aerosmith occasionally plays them in Boston—using fake names, of course—and the Stones gave a legendary performance at some dumpy little club in Worcester a few years back. The bands spread the word through loyal friends and trusted industry people only, making the best shows cozy, intimate affairs. And although I'd bet some hardcore Winterlong fans would've considered sacrificing an arm to see Lenny play solo that night, none of the lucky folks holding tickets seemed interested in trading them for severed limbs.

Lenny Weir's show at the Middle East was a particularly big deal because he'd recently been released from drug rehab and clearly struggled with his newfound fame. About a year earlier, he'd been arrested for opiate possession, and the police had made several trips to his California home during the fall of 1990 for domestic disturbances. Nevertheless, Winterlong found themselves preparing for a European summer tour, and Lenny had chosen Cambridge as the city for his first public performance in months. Which made sense, because Cambridge was a mecca for the type of students, musicians, and artists who appreciated Lenny's work.

What did they hear in it, though? That really puzzled me. I mean, it sounded sloppy, discordant, and inaccessible. And Lenny—the guitarist and lead singer—didn't like showing his face for some reason, so he kept it covered with long hair most of the time and refused to be photographed unless he was wearing dark sunglasses.

"C'mon, let's cross," said Colin, leading Jimmy, Dan, and me across Mass Ave. When Colin had invited me to see Lenny with him, I'd assumed it'd just be the two of us, but as it turned out, his friend Mark—who worked at the alternative radio station WFNX—had given him four tickets. Jimmy and Dan worked with Colin at the pub. They were Irish too, but their accents weren't nearly as sexy as Colin's.

I reached into my coat pocket to check on the little notebook and pen I'd brought along. Because why not write a review of the show and try to get it published? I needed a new job anyway, and I could string together a few words well enough. That's how Lester Bangs got his start. He wrote an unsolicited album review for *Rolling Stone* back in the 60s, and they hired him on the spot. And since this Lenny Weir concert was such a big secret, I figured most of the established local critics wouldn't have tickets. Worth a shot, anyway. I'd send my review to the three major Boston papers—*The Globe, The Herald,* and *The Phoenix*—and see if anyone bit.

The temporary office work I'd been doing for several years—ever since things went bad with Elvis Costello in Geneva—got really old, really fast. I was sick of working in new situations each week, meeting new people all the time, and eating lunch alone. So yeah, becoming a newspaper critic might be the perfect fresh start. Maybe it'd even help me stop puking, because I'd have to work lots of nights and weekends.

Not to mention that I was fed up with the bullshit other writers constantly spewed about Lenny and Winterlong in the various music rags. A reviewer at *New Musical Express* had recently called Winterlong "the American heroes singlehandedly kicking down barriers established by poser groups like Guns 'n' Roses and Poison." *Rolling Stone* had credited Lenny with "ushering in a whole new era in rock & roll." And *Spin* crowned Winterlong "the band of the century." What the hell? Surely Winterlong's record label *paid* those magazines to generate propaganda. The band of the century? Had they forgotten the Doors? I mean, Winterlong was a refreshing change from the pretty boys, drama queens, and formula-rock posers of the late 80s, but the adulation had gotten out of hand. Someone needed to put things in perspective.

"Hey Colin!" called a girl on the crowded sidewalk, but Colin just waved and said something about needing a beer. Then he pulled open the door of the Middle East and motioned for Jimmy, Dan and me to follow. I'd never been to the legendary nightspot before, and couldn't believe how much it resembled a 'normal' Middle Eastern restaurant.

"Where do the bands play?" I shouted to Colin over the din of voices, laughter, and silverware. An experienced local club goer would've known that three separate musical venues lurked within the building: an upstairs room that held about two hundred people, a small adjoining café where acoustic acts and belly dancers often performed, and a large, converted bowling alley in the basement with a capacity of about six hundred.

"Lenny'll be downstairs later," said Colin. "But let's have a black-and-tan up here first. Hey, look, there's Mark over by the bar. I'll get the first round."

It didn't take long for me to start resenting Mark. Sure, he'd supplied us all with tickets, but he also struck me as a serious asshole. He kept his pale gray eyes glued to the door—even while Colin introduced us—and his mouth turned down in distaste when he shook my hand. I already felt self-conscious about my appearance, and Mark just made it worse.

Every other female I spotted had dressed their slender bodies in variations on the grunge uniform: flannel shirt, ripped jeans, and Converse sneakers. None carried handbags or wore visible makeup—other than eyeliner—and all walked with the confidence of women who knew their way around the Middle East and probably nightclubs in general. Not me, though. I slouched on a barstool, clutching my purse and coat, and hoping my black miniskirt, black wool tights, and sensible pumps blended into the darkness of the room. Even worse, I had caked foundation makeup and pressed powder onto my poor blemished face—all that puking takes a real toll on the skin. I was a chunky Madonna wannabe, ten years too late.

Just focus on your newspaper review, I scolded myself, mussing up my hair. Lester Bangs didn't get famous for his appearance.

Colin caught the attention of the busy female bartender right away, and ordered up five black-and-tans: a mixture of Guinness and IPA. But even though the beer was strong and potent, I couldn't relax. Twenty-seven years old, and I felt ancient. I hadn't hung out in a bar with four cute guys since Europe, and never without other girls in the group.

Colin pointed his glass in the direction of a dark-haired man talking to a woman in a plaid shirt and said, "Brett Milano. As you'd expect."

"That's Brett Milano from *The Globe?*" I asked. "The music critic?"

"Uh huh. He writes that nightclub column for *The Phoenix* too. The girl there with him's Kim Deal. From the Pixies, you know?"

Well, yes, I knew about the Pixies, but *shit.* Brett Milano critiqued all the best Boston rock shows. So if *he* was there, he was covering the concert either for *The Globe* or *The Phoenix*. Possibly both. Something inside me dropped. But wait. What about *The Herald,* the city's most conservative newspaper? Surely none of their reporters had been invited. Okay. Change of plans. Rather than send my review to all three papers, I'd give *The Herald* an exclusive. And unlike other writers who fawned over Lenny Weir for inexplicable reasons, I'd be brave enough to tell my truth. The spirit of Lester Bangs lived on.

"Hey, Colin," said Mark, nodding toward a scruffy guy smoking a butt at a corner table, "check out Peter Wolf."

"He's always here," said Colin. "Probably lookin' to sing a duet with Lenny later on."

I opened my mouth to ask if the dude in the black wool hat was *that* Peter Wolf—the guy from the J. Geils Band who sang "Centerfold" and that song about the wooba-gooba with the green teeth—but stopped before any sound came out. Because *of course* he was *that* Peter Wolf. I wasn't in my bedroom, eating junk food and fantasizing anymore; I was out on the real Boston music scene. Elvis Costello had derailed me for a few years, but I'd bounced back.

"You okay, Aerin?" asked Colin. "You're lookin' tired, girl."

"Just a little." I wished I could tell Colin how much I liked *his* looks. Maybe someday.

He reached over and patted my shoulder. "Ah, don't worry. Lenny'll give you a second wind."

I couldn't help sighing. I mean, why the hell was Colin dating Suzanne? They'd been together over a year, and I knew they had good sex—our apartment had very thin walls—but she didn't understand his *soul*. Unlike me, she never stayed up late with him when he played guitar on the porch, and she didn't help him write lyrics either. Suzanne liked drinking tea, watching sitcoms, and padding off to bed with her fashion magazines around 11 o'clock. Sometimes, she'd sit and listen to one or two of his songs, but her long lashes and expertly plucked brows couldn't hide the boredom in her eyes. The way I saw it, she liked being a musician's girlfriend, but didn't appreciate good music.

So I waited patiently for Colin to come to his senses and realize he'd chosen the wrong roommate. Sometimes, when we'd both had a few beers and the moon was glistening on the ocean, I'd expect him to look straight at me, then drop his guitar and lead me down to the cool, dark beach. Other times, I'd wake up in bed, still quivering from the way he'd touched me in a dream, or feeling the weight of his lanky body on top of me. Once, I even woke myself calling out his name in my sleep, but I don't think anyone heard. And how great would it be when I didn't have to hide my feelings for him any longer?

"Drink up, girl. We gotta head downstairs soon."

I rubbed my chin, which was still throbbing from a zit I'd popped earlier, and forced a smile. "Okay. Just gimme a minute."

In the club's cavernous basement, a forgettable local band was massacring an Aerosmith song. The smells of bygone beer, old cigarettes, and ancient body odor mingled comfortably with fresh sweat, new smoke, and something resembling bad breath. I couldn't even estimate the number of people in the large room—since most huddled around the bar or in the dim corners—but the place seemed far less crowded than you'd expect for such a special show. And everyone was ignoring the band on stage.

"Poor guy," said Colin, glancing at the guitarist. "That's a hard-workin' man. If I see him around later, I'll buy him a beer."

He knows what it's like, I thought. Colin's punk band played a lot of after-hours parties—in private homes—and occasionally at fundraisers or backyard barbeques. They hoped to get a deal with an indie record label, but they'd never even been booked in a club like the Middle East.

"Speakin' of beer," said Jimmy, "I got the next round. C'mon, Danny, gimme a hand. Budweiser okay with everyone?"

Mark, Colin, and I nodded, and Jimmy and Dan headed off toward the bar. The band finished the Aerosmith song and the guitarist unplugged, bitterly bidding the crowd a good night before stomping off stage. The other musicians shrugged—they'd obviously expected to play longer—and began disassembling their shabby equipment.

"Bravo!" shouted Colin, whistling and clapping. "Joe Perry'd be honored!"

I wasn't so sure about that, but whatever. "Should we go stand up front?" I suggested.

"Good idea," said Colin. "Place is startin' to fill up. But don't expect to see much o' Lenny, no matter how close you get. Guy doesn't like showin' his face in public."

"Yeah, what's up with the hair and the sunglasses?" I asked. Finally, after two full beers—and the Xanax I popped before leaving the house—I felt more chill.

"Don't know," said Colin as Mark lit a cigarette and exhaled in a noisy, exasperated way. "If you want my opinion, Lenny's a bit like Steve Miller."

"Steve Miller?" I asked. "'Big Old Jet Airliner' Steve Miller?"

Colin nodded. "Exactly. Everyone knows Steve Miller, right? But you wouldn't recognize him if he walked through that door, would ya? That's 'cause he never put his picture on the record jackets. Wasn't comfortable in the spotlight. Same thing with Lenny. I've heard he has bad acne too—"

"Total bullshit," interrupted Mark, blowing smoke in my face. "Bullshit rumors, bullshit tabloids. Lenny did an interview at FNX last year and his skin was fine. He's an introvert. End of story. People need to give him some fuckin' space."

Colin looked amused. "Easy there, Marky boy. We're just friends talkin' here. No need to bite my head off."

"Sorry," said Mark. "But I'm fuckin' sick of people who think they know Lenny."

And you do? I thought.

But the conversation ended there, because Jimmy and Dan had returned with plastic cups of beer for everyone. I accepted mine, promising to get the next round, despite the fact that I'd probably had enough beer already. My empty stomach growled, and combining alcohol with Xanax is never a great idea.

A few roadies began dragging new musical equipment onto the stage. They stacked Marshall amps, plugged cords into outlets, tested microphones, tuned guitars, and arranged the instruments in silver stands. Fans started pouring into the place too, and the air grew thicker, warmer, and smokier.

My heart beat with cautious excitement, and I shivered. But when I reached up to scratch my chin, I touched liquid. *Shit!* The freaking zit was bleeding again. "Be right back," I muttered to Colin and headed for the ladies room.

But cleaning up a zit in that environment would've been impossible. All three stalls were full of women chatting and smoking pot, and a pack of grungy teenage girls dominated the sink and mirror area. Some smoked butts while others chatted drunkenly about Lenny and some new Winterlong video they'd seen on MTV. *Fuck, fuck fuck.* I needed space and privacy. Fast.

Darting back out into the dark club, I almost crashed into a cocktail waitress. "Excuse me," I said, "but is there another bathroom? Somewhere? I have a little emergency." I pointed to the blood on my face, hoping she'd understand.

The waitress looked me up and down. Thin and angular, she was probably about forty years old, with deep lines around her mouth. But the sight of the zit softened her a bit. "Over there," she said in a gravelly voice. "Down that hallway, keep goin' straight. Ignore the *STAFF ONLY* sign. Anyone asks what you're doing, say you got lost. Got it?"

"Okay ..." I tried to thank her, but she scurried off with her tray of drinks before I could say anything else.

In the dimly lit hallway, I found two little bathrooms: one with a WOMEN sign on the door; the other labeled MEN. No one was around, so I scooted into the women's room and went straight to work on my face.

Then, just as I patted on some pressed powder, heavy footsteps approached. *A manager?* I rehearsed the waitress's advice in my head: *Oh no! This isn't a public bathroom? I'm sorry. I got lost. I'm leaving now ...*

But when the door opened, I realized I wouldn't need any excuses because the man who entered was barely conscious and clearly not an authority. Drunk, stoned, or both, he sported a huge, untrimmed mustache and beard, and all of his clothing—wrinkled and dirty, like the rest of him—swam on his thin frame. Unlike the cute grunge guys out in the club—with their clean flannel shirts and low-slung corduroys—this guy's ragged attire barely passed for clothes. His tattered black hi-tops lacked shoelaces. Probably homeless.

I inched away from the sink as he stumbled toward a stall, his elbow bumping mine.

"Sorry," he mumbled. "You Dave's girl?"

"Uh, no, I'm Erin, and I'm outta here. But you might wanna use the men's room. This is the women's. Just sayin'."

It took a second for that to register with him, but when our eyes met, I saw a brief flash of recognition—like he knew me, or wished he did. "Erin," he repeated. "Erin the Beautiful."

Oh well, I thought, scooting out the door. *He's a mess, but he's harmless.* The only person the guy seemed capable of hurting was himself.

The crowd had grown much denser, and I didn't reach the front, where Colin and his friends waited, for about fifteen minutes. I thanked everyone who allowed me to pass, but most people ignored me.

"Where you been, girl?" asked Colin, handing me another beer. "I thought you'd abandoned us."

Before I could answer, though, Jimmy smacked Colin's arm. "There's the man!" he shouted as the room exploded in whistles and applause.

"Holy shit!" said Colin. "Holy shit, there's Lenny!"

But his surprise couldn't hold a candle to mine. Because stumbling around onstage was the man I'd just seen in the bathroom. He'd donned a pair of large, dark sunglasses, but everything else remained the same.

"*That's* Lenny Weir?" I asked.

Colin shot me a suspicious glance. "I'd say so!" he shouted.

I wanted to tell him about recent my encounter with the dude, but the noise of the crowd drowned out every other sound. Not to mention that my heart was pounding in my ears like an amplifier on reverb. People around us were screaming Lenny's name, and a very drunk girl appeared to be having some kind of nervous breakdown.

Lenny, however, remained unfazed as he shuffled over to a wooden stool and picked up an old acoustic guitar. Something about the way he carried himself—his stooped posture under the ratty sweater—reminded me of my dad when I was young, when he'd first started having sciatica problems.

"Hi?" said Lenny to the crowd, his mouth too far away from the microphone. "You guys okay?" He slurred every word, but his voice was sweet, almost innocent.

A roadie ran out and adjusted the mike while the crowd responded enthusiastically to Lenny's question. "Good," said Lenny, re-tuning a guitar string and sounding slightly jealous. "Good to hear."

"I love you Lenny!" hollered the nervous breakdown girl.

Lenny flinched and peered into the audience through his dark glasses. "Okay," he said. "I'm gonna do somethin' mellow, okay?"

Some people clapped, but a few booed too. Lenny Weir wasn't known for his mellow songs. Poor guy; he was doing his best. *This is like Dylan plugging in at Newport,* I thought, *only backwards.*

The man on stage, however, didn't appear to be making any kind of Dylanesque political statement; I think he just wanted to stay upright. He plucked a few strings, then stopped abruptly, tapped lightly on the guitar, and began playing a vaguely familiar melody. But it wasn't until his damaged voice—something between a crackle and a moan—kicked in that I recognized the song. It was Bob Dylan's "Tangled Up in Blue."

I gasped in disbelief. I'd just been thinking about Dylan and then ... wow. Lenny and I were on the same wavelength. But Lenny's rendition of "Tangled Up" bore little resemblance to Dylan's. I mean, it's not the happiest song to begin with, but Dylan keeps it slightly optimistic. Not Lenny, though. The pain in his delivery was almost unbearable. I reached into my bag for the notebook, but decided to just listen for a while instead. I had to *process* this shit.

Which wasn't easy. By the time Lenny reached the line about everyone he'd once known being nothing but an illusion now, the nightclub had become a church, with Lenny Weir presiding as the darkest, most miserable prophet ever. Only his long, graceful fingers looked comfortable on that stage. Every other part of him seemed intent on burying itself beneath hair, glasses, or clothing. But I saw through it all because I'd seen his eyes in the bathroom. And he'd seen mine too. Nobody else in that audience could say that. *Erin the Beautiful.* Something had happened between us, and I needed to talk to him again. Maybe we could help each other.

Now, I'd had similar feelings about other rock stars, but this was different. Totally different. Lenny and I had *spoken*. Privately. And I knew where to look for him after the show.

The next song he attempted—which I'd heard on the radio—was an edgy rocker called "Shaded Mind," but Lenny didn't switch to an electric guitar. Instead, he clung to the acoustic and stripped the song bare.

Sleepless angel, tarnished pillow,
Membrane opens as you lie
Cripple growth and cripple beauty
Counting backwards, pain subsides.

He stopped singing at that point and strummed a sad-sounding chord. Then he played it again. And again. And again. His head began to nod hypnotically, in sync with the strumming, and his eyes focused on something no one else could see. I couldn't look away throughout the entire, terrifying ordeal. Nobody could. How long did it go on? I'm not exactly sure. After a while, Lenny just hung his head to one side and started singing again.

Muffled silence, needle glisten
Swollen eyelids, cannot see
Shaded mind it cannot listen
Dirty powder, set me free.

He tried shrieking those last few words, but his voice came out hoarse, tormented, and far more forlorn than it'd ever sounded on the radio. A blazing guitar solo should've followed that verse, but Lenny ended the song abruptly after the word *free*, and the crowd burst into relieved applause.

"Thanks," he said, struggling to light a cigarette. "Um, you mighta heard I was... sick."

People nodded and mumbled.

"Yeah, it sucked. But I wrote some songs. I, uh—" He interrupted himself by sneezing, then laid his lit cigarette on the stage floor and started digging in his sweater pockets, as if he forgot he was performing. Eventually he found what he'd been looking for—a tissue—and carefully blew his nose. "Awright," he said, the cigarette still burning on the floor, "this one's called 'Cracked.'"

Eyes darted around and people shifted their weight uneasily, like horses before a storm. "I think *he's* crackin'," whispered Jimmy. "Or smokin' crack."

But Lenny was more than just cracked. That long hair, the sunglasses, the layers of clothing: they served as camouflage but also held him together. Somehow, they made it possible for him to survive.

And the wire-bound notebook? It never left my purse. The tragedy playing out on stage mirrored my own desperate story, leaving me weak, confused, and unnerved. I touched my neck and imagined Lenny's fingers there. If only he could hold me like he held that guitar.

Instead, he started to leak. He slipped into another trancelike series of minor chords, and I swear I saw blood pouring down his face. It may have been sweat, but it sure looked like blood. And like everyone else in the club, I stood stonelike, helpless, watching the whole world hemorrhage out of that elegant, wretched body.

A terrible beauty is born. I didn't know where I'd heard that phrase before; it just popped into my head and hung there. Later on, though, I remembered it came from a Yeats poem I'd learned in high school. *Such a terrible beauty.* A perfect description of Lenny at the Middle East that night.

I turned away for a second, and that's when I heard the thud. Looking up, I saw the guitar bounce off the stage floor.

"Oh god," Lenny moaned into the microphone. "I ... where ... heron?" Then his body went limp and collapsed into a heap of yarn and wrinkled khaki.

For a split second, the room fell silent. Then roadies swarmed the stage and carried Lenny away, a small, frail creature in their arms. Sickening memories of my dad after his accident flooded my mind. His stained white neck brace ... the perpetual smell of urine ... that hollow, gape-mouthed face, like a rotting jack-o-lantern. And his eyes, so empty and lifeless until they'd land on me. Then they'd glimmer oddly. "See, Erin, he loves you," my mom would say. But I knew the truth: my father blamed me for everything. And I deserved it.

"Thank you, everyone, for coming out tonight," said a clean-shaven guy in a black t-shirt who'd replaced Lenny onstage. His voice sounded measured and confident, but he kept clasping and unclasping his hands. "I'm Lenny's tour manager, and I apologize for the abbreviated show. I'm sure he'll be fine after some rest. He's just ... exhausted. And dehydrated. So ... have a good night. And ... drive safe."

As the overhead lights flashed on, someone in the audience began to clap. Others joined in slowly, as though awakening from a dream. Lenny had taken us all on a tour of his private hell, but the harsh florescent lighting dropped us rudely back in a Cambridge nightclub.

And yes, the show was over.

"I think Lenny said somethin' about heroin at the end there," muttered Colin as Dan drove us home to Winthrop. "Any of you hear that?"

"Yeah," said Jimmy. "So much for his rehab."

But their voices were white noise in the back of my brain. I stared out the window at the taillights of the cars ahead of us in the Callahan Tunnel, knowing that Lenny had called out to me, Erin. His *Erin the Beautiful.* He needed me. He wanted me. And someday soon, the two of us would reunite. I just needed to figure out how to make that happen.

Chapter 2

All the rock stars in my life have been thrilling men. Dazzling guys, capable of emptying their souls in a three-minute song, tossing back a little beer, and doing it again. And again. Jim Morrison. David Bowie. Bruce Springsteen. Elvis Costello. Lenny Weir. Their musical skills surpassed only by a supernatural ability to mainline songs straight from vinyl into human veins. My veins. Even over the airwaves. You call that a drug? Well, yes.

Freddie Mercury was my first. But despite what people say about that first high, that it's always the best and can never be duplicated, I disagree. Addicts, after all, are eternal optimists.

Winthrop, 1978

The wind was already dropping hints of fall. Teasing or threatening, depending on personal taste. Once or twice a day, I'd catch a whiff of the oily bluefish that schooled near shore in late August, and the gusts blowing off the ocean at sundown carried an unmistakable chill. Still, most townies chose to ignore it all; they went right on living as if summer might last forever that year. But not me. For the past two months, I'd been obsessing about one thing and one thing only: my first day of high school. And I wasn't psyched. But what could I do? I turned up the kitchen radio.

"It's a bo-da-cious afternoon, folks, so shut off those soap operas and come join us here on the Boston Common right now. You don't wanna miss this opportunity to meet the entire RKO van crew, including yours truly. But hurry up, 'cause we're only here a few more hours. And what're you waiting for, anyway? We've got the hottest RKO t-shirts, bumper stickers, and pins that'll get you noticed by all the right people. All free. I can't think of a better way to spruce up your back-to-school wardrobe for no dough at all. Hey, you might even get lucky. What's that, you say? You wanna hear some music?

Okay, okay, here's Nick Gilder with 'Hot Child in the City.' Oooh! This song makes me sweat!"

I cut my fluffernutter sandwich in half and considered asking Dad to let me take the T downtown. I mean, it sounded like fun. Meet a real DJ, get a free shirt, maybe even request a song, which, of course, would be Helen Reddy's "Angie Baby."

But the more I thought about bringing my father into the situation, the more my stomach ached. Because if he said yes, I'd have to go. He totally wouldn't understand me wimping out at the last minute and staying home. *Why'd I have to turn fourteen?* I wondered. *I liked thirteen just fine.* I definitely didn't want to stay a kid forever, but full-on teenagerhood terrified me.

"What're you doin' in the house on such a nice day, Erin?" Dad's croak jerked me right out of my little daze, and I winced at the stale, sweaty alcohol odor pouring out of him. "How come you're not down the beach with the other girls?"

Ever since his sciatica got bad enough to qualify him for disability, Dad had been sleeping most days 'til noon. His pain meds made him super tired, and drinking whiskey every night sure didn't help.

"I'll go out soon," I promised. "My stomach's hurting again."

Dad squinted, then shuffled over and grabbed my sandwich. "Well, stop eatin' then. What's this, marshmallow? You're puttin' on weight, kiddo. Maybe you should go on a diet."

"But I'm *hungry.*" I loved him like crazy, but he was turning into such a bastard. He was constantly kicking me out of the house during the day, and poor Mom had to work all the overtime she could get at the phone company to keep up with the bills. It wasn't fair, and Dad acted like he couldn't care less.

"Well then, eat and get outta here before your girlfriends come ringin' that doorbell. I don't need kids runnin' around the house today. My back's killing me. When does school start, anyway?"

My stomach tensed. "Wednesday after Labor Day." Less than two weeks of freedom remained. Even worse, my friends couldn't wait for high school. Almost magically, they'd grown more graceful and sophisticated over the summer while I'd just increased in size. Sometimes I felt like everyone except me had been taught critical lessons in maturity—perhaps on a day I'd been absent from school—and now they spent their afternoons flitting around the seawall like newly-hatched butterflies, while I would've been happier at home listening to the radio.

Hidden under my mattress was a notebook I'd filled with thoughts about various pop songs and the feelings they evoked in me. Their lyrics transported me to places I'd never been, and drew me into stories of beauty, heartache, and loss among people like the forlorn fiancé in "Billy Don't Be a Hero," and the guy who loses his horse in "Wildfire." I secretly mourned for them all, especially Brandy, the girl who waits in vain for her sailor boyfriend to return from the sea. Gosh, I wished she lived in Winthrop so I could comfort her.

But my ultimate favorite song was "Angie Baby." It creeped me out for sure, but I spent hours trying to understand what Angie, the 'touched' girl, had done with the neighborhood bad boy who'd snuck into her bedroom and disappeared. Angie's parents thought their friendless daughter spent her days alone, but according to the song, a secret lover kept her satisfied. Which made no sense, but I was fascinated. I mean, if the boy was alive, then how did he eat and go to the bathroom? And if Angie had killed him, then why didn't his body stink? Right? Whatever the answer, I was proud of Angie. She was no dope, and maybe not insane at all.

"Erin! Hurry up!" called Patty from the porch. "C'mon, it's prime tanning time."

Shit! She'd seen me. Now I couldn't hide in my room. Patti and I had been best friends since kindergarten, but she'd been pulling away from me—hard—all summer. She still stopped by to get me on her way to the beach most days, but more often than not, she treated me like luggage someone made her drag around.

I understood why, too. Patty had grown so wild-eyed, so itchy, so restless. I could practically smell the hormones burning through her coconut suntan oil, and sometimes I imagined the florescent flowers on her bathing suit bursting into flames. Everyone stared at Patty; they couldn't help it. Girls, boys, adults. Her skin was tanned golden like the Coppertone girl's, and her long, dark hair reminded me of Cher's. Every time Patty walked past a guy, I could tell he wanted to touch her.

And me? Well, forget Cher; I strove to look like Kristy McNichol, and missed by a mile. No guy in his right mind wanted to touch my embarrassing little nub breasts, which were too small for a real bra but too chubby to ignore. So, I compromised with one of those stretchy training bras. Everything about my body was fleshy, like turkey burger. Mom called me solid, but *solid* implies firm, like solid chocolate. I was a pale, five-foot-ten, hundred-and-sixty-pound turkey burger.

"My stomach hurts," I told Patty through the screen door.

She shrugged her shiny brown shoulders. "Prob'ly cramps. The sun'll help. C'mon, let's *go*. Hey, where's your bathing suit?"

I felt a sudden urge to cry. "Well, the weatherman said something about thunderstorms ..."

"Oh, for god's sake!" said Patty. "Look out the window. Not a cloud in the sky."

"Okay," I conceded. "I'll change and meet you guys on the seawall in ten minutes."

But Dad wanted me out. Through a haze of Lark smoke, I saw his eyes roll. "Erin, you're bein' rude. Go get your suit on and go with your friend. What's the matta with you today?"

"Down here, guys!" called Cindy from the wall as Patty and I rounded the corner onto Shore Drive.

The afternoon sun was blazing, and my flip-flops kept sliding off my sweaty feet. "Wait *up*, Patty," I whined, and she stopped just long enough to glower at me. I'd wasted twenty minutes changing into my flowered, two-piece bathing suit with its apron-like curtain in front, and another ten pinning up my hair. *What's so great about tanning, anyway?* I thought. *All you do is grease up your skin, then lie around on a concrete wall – in public – almost naked.*

And yet, tanning on the seawall was the prime summer activity for Winthrop teenagers. The surfer boys hung out at the lower end, down by the rocks. Sure, the waves hardly ever got big enough for real surfing—and in the late 70s, the off-shore Deer Island sewage outlet polluted the water terribly—but the surfers didn't care. They'd still gather out there almost every day with their wetsuits and zinc oxide, waxing their boards, watching the ocean, and incessantly calling each other *man*. Sometimes, they'd even catch a wave or two, but usually they'd just hang around, bullshitting and listening to WBCN, a new FM rock & roll station that played everything from Fleetwood Mac to the Ramones to Dylan and the Who. Patty loved strolling past the surfers to ask what time it was or if the tide was on the way in or out, but I couldn't bear to make eye contact with them. They were so gorgeous and comfortable in their lanky brown bodies that I considered them almost superhuman.

About ten yards north of the surfers—and even more beautiful—lounged the girls they dated and slept with. Blessed with smooth skin, soft hair, and easy smiles, these beach princesses in impossibly small bikinis—their limbs glistening with Bain de Soleil—chatted lazily and sang along with songs like Peter Frampton's "Baby I Love Your Way" on their transistor radios. I couldn't fathom leaving the house in nothing but a few stitched-together triangles of stretchy fabric—didn't they worry about their breasts falling out or their pubic hair showing—but their demeanors didn't reflect any of that. Yeah, if anything, the princesses seemed even less human than the surfers.

I related more to the burnouts in their denim cutoffs and black t-shirts. For starters, the burnout kids were goofier, and they all hung out together—unsegregated by gender—smoking butts, drinking Southern Comfort out of soda cans, and occasionally getting high in broad daylight. They cared a lot about music too: no wimpy transistor radios for the burnouts. Instead, they'd blast Skynyrd, Zeppelin, and Black Sabbath tapes on their car stereos with the windows wide open. One guy, Johnny Palmese, killed the battery in his old army jeep at least once a week because he couldn't resist playing *Dark Side of the Moon* at top volume. Then he'd go jogging up and down the beach, shirtless, until he found someone to give him a jumpstart. Johnny was a few years older than us, with deep dimples and a skinny body like Mick Jagger's, and sometimes I'd close my eyes and imagine kissing him. His smile was sweet and he didn't appear to have a steady girlfriend, but he never spoke directly to me.

After the burnout section, the seawall became more of a hodgepodge: a few jocks and nerds, a smattering of daytrippers from nearby towns, plenty more fledgling teenagers like us. "Where were you guys?" asked Cindy. "I've been waiting here for, like, an hour." Her shoulders were pink from the sun.

I adjusted my bathing suit to cover as much of my butt as possible, and spread my thin towel on the hot wall. "I had to do stuff at home," I said.

Patty rolled her eyes and sighed.

I took a blue container of Noxzema out of my beach bag and offered it to Cindy. "Want some of this on your shoulders? The sun's wicked hot today."

For some reason, my friends and I considered Noxzema to be a sunscreen, perhaps because it was white. "I'm fine," said Cindy. "I wanna good tan for starting high school."

I shrugged, opened the lid, and slathered some of the cool cream onto my arms and legs. On the radio, Elton John was begging Kiki Dee not to go breakin' his heart, and I did my best to let the music sink into my muscles along with the Noxzema's menthol. But just as I started to relax, a surfer named Derek whistled shrilly up the beach.

He whistled a second time and waited until he had everyone's attention. Then he shouted something. Patty, Cindy, and I couldn't decipher his words, but they seemed pretty urgent. And since nobody had anything better to do, kids transmitted the message up the wall from one group to the next: at one o'clock, tune your radios to BCN and crank it!

Most of us assumed something serious was gonna be announced—like the Beatles getting back together or KISS breaking up—so we speculated like crazy for the next ten minutes. Then, just as the bell on the local church chimed once, the most amazing thing happened: the voice of a DJ named Mark Parenteau boomed up and down the coastline. "Hey, all you sun worshipers soaking up the rays down there on Winthrop Beach! Today's a no-underwear day for sure. And we've got a special, post-lunchtime request for Derek, who tells me he's waiting on the perfect wave. Here's hopin' you catch it, dude."

As the DJ uttered those final words, the angelic *a cappella* voices of Queen—wondering if life was real or just a fantasy—wafted up over the wall, the beach, the water. The whole planet, as far as I was concerned.

Now, I'd heard snippets of "Bohemian Rhapsody" before, but never the whole song from start to finish. The top AM pop station in Boston—WRKO—usually stuck to shorter, catchier numbers, and most of the other sunbathers didn't seem to know it very well either. Everyone just gazed around for a minute or two, trying to process it all: the volume and the harmony.

But by the time Freddie Mercury—poor misunderstood Freddie—stopped playing piano to proclaim that he needed to leave everything behind and face the truth, some of the surfers had begun playing air guitar, and a few bikini girls were up and dancing a bit. I wanted to dance too, but felt paralyzed, overcome with emotion.

Then Freddie's voice turned tougher, and in his operatic way, he chastised someone planning to throw stones at him and spit in his eye. The operatic ballad had morphed into a full-on rocker, complete with power chords.

A whole bunch of burnouts leapt into the back of a pickup truck, some stomping their feet and pumping their fists. Patty and Cindy pointed and laughed, but all I could do was smile. I felt my body inflating like a giant balloon; then, before I knew what was happening, I rose up over the scene. I don't recall ever feeling so calm. As I floated down the beach, I high-fived Johnny Palmese—who'd temporarily halted his search for jumper cables—and, for the first time ever, his dimples flashed just for me. Debbie Geraldo, one of the bikini girls, waved as she swayed to the music, and Derek, the cutest surfer by far, reached out and pulled me into his strong brown arms. "You'll catch your wave some day, Erin," he whispered. His warm skin smelled clean and salty, and I longed to stay in that place forever.

But Brian May's guitar was skillfully guiding the song down to its coda. Freddie quietly assured us that nothing really mattered, and Derek gently released my body back into the air. I closed my eyes and drifted a little further; then a sea breeze tickled my tear-soaked cheeks, and when I reopened my eyes, I'd returned to my original spot on the wall.

It doesn't matter, I realized. *You can be beautiful and popular, or shy and overweight, or tanned, or pale, or stoned. Everyone's cool. Everyone's okay.*

For the first time in my life, I felt linked to the universe and completely tuned in. Is it any wonder, then, that I ended up a rock & roll junkie?

Chapter 3

Winthrop, 1991

Two weekends after the Lenny Weir show, Colin accompanied Suzanne to her childhood home in Connecticut and met her parents. I spent most of Saturday and Sunday expecting him home early. I mean, a cool guy like him would *have* to come to his senses and break up with her. But on Sunday night, the two of them burst through our door acting all tired and silly. "Check it out!" said Suzanne, flashing a small but sparkly diamond ring in my face.

I managed to utter some lame words of congratulations, then Suzanne clobbered me again. "Oh, and we should probably say this now too. Colin and I wanna try living on our own. Just the two of us, you know?" She turned to him for support and added, "Right, Col?"

Colin couldn't look me in the eye. "Yeah, but we're not kickin' you to the curb or anythin', Aerin. Take all the time you need. I'll ask around the pub too. Perhaps someone there's lookin' for a roomie."

I blinked hard, most likely in shock. "Oh no. No worries. Really. I'll find something." But my guts felt like they'd been vacuumed out. Even though I'd recently realized that Lenny Weir—not Colin—was my *true* soulmate in this world, I'd planned to stay close with Colin. We were pals, after all, and I didn't have many friends. And now he was booting me out to please that sniveling little Suzanne.

"Oh yeah, you'll be fine," she said. "C'mon, Col, let's go crash."

For half a second, the pained expression on Colin's face made me think he might reconsider everything. But when Suzanne took his arm, he followed her to their bedroom without a word.

If you look at a map of Winthrop, you'll see that it's shaped roughly like a male's sex organs. I grew up in the section of town called the Highlands, which is approximately where the pubic hair would be. The town center—where Colin and Suzanne lived—makes up the testicles, and the peninsula of Point Shirley is the long, flaccid penis. Jeff and Pete rented a place on Point Shirley.

From a boat in Boston Harbor, the densely-packed, multi-colored houses on the Point appear randomly flung on top of each other, like a sea monster's forgotten Lego project. But up close, they comprise a complex maze of cottages and multi-family homes, many adorned with anchors, buoys, and other nautical décor to mask their weathered faces. When I was a senior in high school, our teacher assigned us a poem called "Point Shirley" by Sylvia Plath—another former resident of Winthrop—and I'll always remember Sylvia's line about the sea steadily eating away at Point Shirley. And you know, it can feel that way at times. But the Point's a scrappy one. She's not gonna let herself go down without a fight.

Anyway, the ad in the *Winthrop Sun Transcript* stated that Jeff and Pete sought a "peaceful, independent M/F to share cozy space with a quiet male couple." The rent was three hundred dollars a month—a little less than I'd paid at Colin's—and after meeting Jeff and Pete, I was ready to move in. Not only were they thoughtful and kind, but also gay, and I figured that would keep me from trying to start romantic relationships with them. And because they lived only a mile away from Colin's, Suzanne lent me her car for a day. I'm sure she just wanted me out as fast as possible, but I was glad I didn't have to rent a moving truck. The only thing that really concerned me was the word *independent* in their newspaper ad. That's one adjective I'd never used to describe myself.

Especially not in the spring of '91. A year earlier, my mom and her boyfriend Edward had sold our house in the Highlands and bought a mobile home in Harlingen, Texas. For them, it was a great adventure—starting over together in a whole new environment—but as a result, I was left a struggling renter with a major puking problem. At twenty-seven years of age, I absolutely should've sought professional help, but my fear of psychiatric hospitals and medication—a fear I'd developed as a teenager—still held me captive. Not to mention that I had no health insurance, and my paychecks from the temp agency barely covered rent and bills. As a result, I lived day-to-day, hoping the puking would simply cease at some point.

"Lemme give you a hand," said Jeff as I hauled a Hefty bag full of clothes through his front door. Two old bicycles leaned against the hallway wall, and a wide array of boots, shoes and sneakers lay strewn around the entranceway. A strong sea breeze blew through the open windows, but it wasn't strong enough to hide the scent of marijuana in the house.

"No, I'm good," I replied, trying to sound confident. I'd agreed to rent the apartment's "second bedroom," which was really just a section of the living room cordoned off with a heavy curtain. The landlord, who apparently never came around, wouldn't be informed of my existence.

Jeff had just showered, and his dark, curly hair glistened in the afternoon light. I allowed myself to admire him for a moment, noting the way his biceps bulged under the sleeves of his tight black t-shirt. He exuded a Lou Reed vibe, and I think he knew it. Pete was a lucky guy.

Then again, Pete possessed his own brand of charm. Smaller, heavier, and shaggier than Jeff, his smile won me over in about thirty seconds. The two men had met while training to be waiters at Legal Seafood, and, according to Jeff, they'd fallen in "love at second sight."

"Second sight?" I asked. "What happened the first time?"

"My lips are sealed," said Jeff while Pete blushed. "Let's just say I'm glad we got another chance."

Jeff and Pete were incredibly happy as a couple. Every night after work, they'd go out for a nightcap and a snack, then return to the apartment around midnight, wanting only to smoke a joint and crawl into bed together. Although if I happened to be up watching TV, they'd gladly share that joint with me, and always made a point of asking about my temp job and the various co-workers I dealt with in my wacky, itinerant "career."

On weekday mornings, as I got ready for work, Jeff would often start a pot of coffee then run out to the local bakery for bagels or pastry. I adored my roommates and they liked me too, but I'm also certain they savored having the place to themselves when I was gone.

I, however, despised being home alone during the day, and Jeff and Pete left at three o'clock every Saturday and Sunday afternoon to work the dinner shift at the restaurant. As the door closed behind them, a deep chill would settle in my gut. *Nine hours,* I'd think. *I've gotta find something constructive to do before it's too late.*

I'd consider walking the beach or going into Boston to buy art supplies. I'd never learned to draw or paint well, but how hard could it be? Sometimes, I'd even change into my good jeans and a nice blouse. But that was usually about as far as I got. I swear I had the best intentions, but I couldn't stop the tastefully erotic coffee table books in the living room from winking at me. Or I'd use the bathroom and get temporarily lost in the provocative black-and-white Mapplethorpe prints on the wall. *Sex.* It lurked everywhere in that apartment, but I had no one to touch. It was maddening. And as my need for stimulation intensified, I'd quickly lose interest in exercise or shopping in Boston. First things first. And since I couldn't have sex, then sugar, starch, and total control would have to do.

Just a little ice cream, I'd decide. *Maybe a quart. Then, after I puke it, I'll go for a walk and do some writing.*

I'd never gotten around to reviewing the Lenny Weir concert, but I still had time. Especially since the press had essentially buried the news about the poor guy passing out at the Middle East. "Dehydrated," said the *Boston Globe.* And a reporter from *The Herald* speculated that Lenny had been fighting a virus. So perhaps one of the music magazines would appreciate a more honest, in-depth explanation from someone who'd been there. Hell, maybe they'd even pay for my work.

But once I made it to the supermarket and chose an ice cream flavor, a demon would possess my arms and legs, and I'd find myself walking down the cookie aisle like a zombie, practically drooling as I grabbed a package of Oreos. My brain would scream, *Put it back!* but the demon was too strong. Sometimes, it even forced me to open the package right there in the aisle and eat a cookie. Then I'd *have* to buy them.

For the entire twenty-minute walk home, I'd keep my eyes on the ground, dreading the thought of running into anyone who might ask what I was doing. I'd also try like crazy to abort my self-destructive mission. After all, my health was surely more valuable than seven or eight dollars worth of junk food. But no matter how many trashcans I passed, the demon wouldn't allow me to ditch the grocery bags.

Sometimes, my hands would shake so badly, I'd have trouble unlocking the front door. But once I got in, I'd run to the kitchen for a spoon. Then, I'd draw back the curtain that served as my bedroom door. After that, nothing could stop me.

I'd position myself on the futon so I could stare straight into Lenny Weir's crotch. Or, to clarify, straight into the crotch of the grainy black-

and-white Lenny poster on my wall. I loved the way his jeans fit in that picture—all loose and low and worn—and I'd tear into the ice cream like a feral animal, savoring the first few creamy spoonfuls before letting them slide down my throat. It felt good, like exciting foreplay. Oh yeah. Yeah.

Inevitably, reality would remind me of its presence, perhaps in the form of a booming car stereo outside or even people chatting loudly on the sidewalk. The source of interference didn't matter, but the results were consistent: my sad container of melting ice cream would momentarily feel like a torture device.

But I couldn't turn back. Not at that point. Once the ice cream was gone, I'd go straight for the cookies. A twinge of tension in my thighs would warn of future regrets, but I'd rip the package apart, the aroma of chocolate and Crisco too rich to resist. Twisting open a cookie, my lower teeth would scrape the sugary frosting, my tongue dredging the velvet graininess. There was no food in the world more seductive than Oreos, and I had an entire package in my lap.

"Hey there, Erin," Lenny would whisper from the wall. "Erin the Beautiful."

"I'm here, baby." I'd swallow the frosting and start sucking another cookie, and something inside me would let loose. Then I'd close my eyes and Lenny would be on top of me, his hands massaging my neck, my breasts, my legs.

Yes. And as long as I had cookies, things remained good. I'd make the most of each one, keeping my eyes closed. Lenny's hot skin blanketed me; my blood pounded into him. *Another cookie.* Against my inner thigh, I'd feel the pressure of his cock while his lips nibbled my neck—gently, then hungrily. Sometimes, he'd stay totally silent and intense; other times, he'd tell me how much he loved me, how easily he could relate to me, how sexy I was. Warm currents would swirl in my pelvis as I clawed at the package of cookies, craving more sugar, needing his mouth against mine, aching for more.

But always, always, just before I climaxed, the cookies would be gone. And everything else too. My eyes would pop open, and I'd collapse on the bed—my teeth caked in chocolate, my guts packed with poison. *Why?* I'd ask, sometimes out loud. *Why did I do this again?*

I couldn't even make eye contact with Lenny, back up there on the wall, two-dimensional once more. And I couldn't go to sleep either. Not in that condition. There was only one thing to do, and it was gonna hurt.

In the bathroom, I'd tie back my frizzy brown hair and pull off my sweatshirt to minimize the mess. The fat on my belly disgusted me, but I needed to act quickly if I didn't want more. Inside me, food was already digesting. Sometimes, I'd think about sophomore year in high school, and Mrs. Doogan, my health teacher, who'd spent several classes lecturing us kids about anorexia and bulimia. Maybe she'd known someone with an eating disorder—or had one herself—because she'd almost cried when she talked about those diseases damaging your liver and kidneys, messing up your electrolytes, and wrecking your teeth. During our last health class in that unit, she gave us copies of a magazine article about models in California who'd ruptured their stomachs and died of heart attacks because of eating disorders.

I guess I should've paid more attention. At the time, though, I couldn't stop thinking about my dad's recent death and his burial in the town cemetery. Because of me. No one else knew it, but his accident had been my fault. And now I needed to purge.

Hanging over the toilet, tears flowing down my face, the food would start coming up. Slowly at first, then faster. Rivers of ice cream, ribbons of Oreos, undigested grapes from lunch, putrid liquid, chunks of whatever. I'd sweat, pant and convulse, and sometimes my throat would bleed. But I'd keep going until my head spun. Sometimes, I'd lie down on the tile floor, and several times, I passed out. No two times were identical, but as I staggered off to bed—after washing the puke and toilet water off my ravaged face—I'd make the same promise as always.

Never again.

Lenny most likely returned to rehab after collapsing at the Middle East. And he must've employed some great publicity people too, because the mainstream press pretty much left him alone for several months. Unfortunately, the tabloids remained as vicious as ever. They went on printing unverified stories about Lenny's drug use and the horrific fights he and his on-again-off-again girlfriend, Violet Chasm, allegedly had on a regular basis. Violet, the lead singer of an all-female grunge band called Funspot, was becoming a star in her own right, and lots of "alternative" radio stations were playing Funspot in heavy rotation. Some Winterlong fans contested that Lenny actually wrote the Funspot songs, but I don't know. I mean, they had plenty in common with Winterlong's music--lyrically and musically—but Violet struck me as a woman who could be creative on her own.

Then, in late April, right before Winterlong headed to Europe for an anxiously awaited summer tour, they canceled more than half of their scheduled performances, including all the ones booked in large auditoriums and outdoor venues. In fact, the only shows they kept on the schedule were in small-to-medium-sized nightclubs. Ticketholders were devastated and/or enraged, but also powerless. Apparently, Winterlong was determined to lay low and perform only in front of small audiences, regardless of what the public wanted.

Unfortunately, that attitude didn't sit well with the American music press, which had already given the band several months to pull their act together. Then Winterlong's management took things a step further, issuing a press release stating (among other things) that, "No members of our organization will engage in interviews or photo sessions with print, radio, or television sources for the foreseeable future."

That was the breaking point. I mean, the media had been involved in a symbiotic relationship with Winterlong for over two years. In fact, the band may never have "made it" without the fawning of MTV VJs and magazines like *Rolling Stone.* And media outlets of that caliber aren't inclined to simply allow their darlings to walk away for no apparent reason. So, they doubled down on Winterlong, sending teams to actively stalk band members in Europe. They were going to get their stories, one way or another.

Like the night in Amsterdam when Lenny—high on something—stumbled out of his hotel room to buy cigarettes, and was caught on camera by a reporter who'd been waiting in his hallway. The guy snapped a few shots of the disheveled rock star before Lenny realized what was happening, knocked the camera to the floor, and whipped a Zippo lighter at the dude.

It shouldn't have been a big deal—the lighter didn't even hit the guy—but variations on the incident made *MTV News* for days. Poor Lenny. The more he tried to be left alone, the more he was harassed. And that only made him angrier.

In Brussels, he unleashed a series of obscenities on a tourist he mistook for a *paparazzo* because the guy was taking pictures of people on the street. And a few days later, when a well-known American journalist approached Lenny in a London pub and asked how he was doing, Lenny stormed out of the place and drunkenly informed a police officer that the journalist had threatened his life.

Obviously, the man needed medical attention. But no one with any authority over him seemed willing to seek help. Meanwhile, the thousands—maybe millions—of rebellious teenagers worldwide who considered Lenny a role model only idolized him more. The misunderstood kids were too naive to understand that Lenny was fighting the international media machine while they were just pissed off at their parents. In their eyes, anger was anger and they could relate.

And me? Well, no matter how much I despised the media's vampiric feeding frenzy on Lenny, I couldn't look away. And I obsessed over every tidbit of Lenny information I could find: a blurry photograph in a supermarket tabloid; a fifteen-second clip on *MTV News;* a blurb in the *Boston Globe*. I also started frequenting the local library to pore over back issues of *Rolling Stone, Spin,* and *Melody Maker.* I bought rare Winterlong imports at second-hand record stores, and stayed up late watching MTV at night. And when I read the papers on my lunch break at work, I paid no attention to the headlines. Instead, I turned straight to the entertainment pages, hoping to learn something new and encouraging about my man. But he remained in Europe all summer.

Things didn't improve much when Winterlong returned home either. The band's management claimed that Lenny was resting and writing songs at his California home, but in March of '92, he was rushed to the hospital twice for "exhaustion." Then, early that summer, Violet Chasm attempted suicide by swallowing a handful of pills.

Every time a picture of Lenny appeared in the press, his face grew paler, his hair wilder, and his sunglasses bigger. One MTV VJ nicknamed him *Animal* because of his resemblance to the drummer on *The Muppet Show,* while another joked about Lenny borrowing eyewear from Elton John. I guess Lenny's dismissive treatment of the media had turned many professionals against him. Despite it all, his fans loved him more than ever.

"I can't explain it," said a doe-eyed girl being interviewed outside the MTV studio in New York City. "Lenny's just so ... interesting. I mean, that *pain* in his voice. It's sad, but he makes it all, like, beautiful, you know?"

"You fucking moron!" I shouted at the screen. "You don't know the first thing about Lenny's pain!" I was aware of the fact that I sounded a lot like Colin's asshole friend Mark that night at the Middle East, but I didn't care. Because Mark had never been alone with Lenny and had never seen Lenny's eyes. Lenny had never called him beautiful.

I listened to Bob Dylan's "Tangled Up in Blue"—the song Lenny had played so tragically on our special night—each morning as I dressed for work, and it filled me with hope. And if I drank enough white zinfandel while listening to Winterlong records at night, I could feel Lenny's spirit in the splintered fragments of energy that streamed through the atmosphere. I simply *had* to believe he'd come looking for me some day, just as Dylan resolved to get back to that mysterious woman in his song.

He'd recognize me instantly when we made eye contact again, and everything would fall into place. Lenny and I, walking Winthrop beach, breathing the salt air and healing together. He'd kick heroin and I'd kick bulimia while the rock critics and fans wondered where the hell he'd gone. But when we were both ready, we'd reemerge as one, like Bowie and Iman, Springsteen and Patti Scialfa, John and Yoko. Soulmates, supporting each other to the end.

Chapter 4

Winthrop, 1978

"They built that wall to contain hurricane force waves," the Winthrop police chief explained to my mom, his cigar smoke polluting the air normally reserved for Dad's cigarettes. Chip Gartside, a decorated Korean War vet, squinted like Humphrey Bogart when he talked. "Even a giant Buick like Ben's doesn't stand much chance against it. That cement doesn't have a lotta *give.*"

The room was uncomfortably warm, but neither Mom nor I had opened the living room windows that sunny Sunday morning in September. Even the drapes remained tightly drawn. Mom clutched a cup of coffee in her stubby fingers while I lay on the couch, sobbing into a velveteen throw pillow that smelled like Dad's hair.

"But Chip," said Mom, "Ben's been drivin' that road since high school. How could he miss the turn?"

The cop took a long puff on his cigar and let the smoke roll out of his mouth. If we hadn't been discussing my dad's near-fatal accident the previous night, I might've laughed. I mean, Chip easily could've been a character on a cheesy cop show. "Carol," he said, lowering his voice, "the ambulance guys smelled booze on his breath. We won't mention that in the report, but alcohol coulda had somethin' to do with it."

"No way." Mom hadn't colored her hair in a while, so her long gray roots made the fading reddish-orange dye look extra fake. But that was the least of my concerns. I wanted to wake up and discover the whole morning was fake. "Look," said Mom, "we all know Ben likes a drink or two, but he doesn't drive drunk. Isn't that right, Erin?"

I nodded as Chip opened his mouth, then closed it again. "Right," he finally said, flicking an ash into a clamshell on the coffee table. "And neither one o' you saw him before he went out last night? You're certain about that too?"

"Absolutely," said Mom, clearly struggling to remain patient. Neither of us had gotten any sleep. "Like I said, they called over to Papa Luigi's to tell me. I was eatin' suppa with the girls." She wiped her eyes—smudging what was left of her mascara—and blew her nose into a crumpled tissue. "You try an' have a little fun an' look what happens. I just wish I knew where he was goin' at that hour."

The police chief turned his squint on me. "He didn't say a word to you before he left?"

"No. I told you. I was sleeping in my room."

"Sorry, honey. Sometimes I hate this job."

"Well, I think you're done," I growled, pushing myself off the couch and standing shakily. I'd never spoken to any adult—other than my parents--in that tone, let alone the town police chief. But I was mad at him for sitting in my dad's chair, asking those terrible questions. Why wouldn't he leave us alone?

Mom didn't reprimand me for being rude. She just shook her head at Chip and said, "This feels like a bad dream."

"Well, at least he's breathin'," said the cop with a sigh. "That's always a good sign."

But based on what the doctors had told us about Dad's injuries, I wasn't so sure about that.

According to Mom, Dad had been a very handsome teenager. "He was a looker, Erin," she'd bragged when I was little. "A real lady slayer, with those big blue eyes and that wavy blond hair. All the girls wanted to date Ben Reardon, but we got him. You an' me, Erin. We got him all to ourselves."

I'd blush when she talked that way. Somehow, I could sense her insecurity, even back then. Mom had plenty of friends and a big, generous personality. But she hated her body, which was just plain big.

But I don't think Dad cared about her size at all; at least not in those early days. My memories of life as a preschooler were pretty happy. We cooked on the grill, read stories after dinner, and sometimes walked over to the penny candy store a block away. And regardless of the weather or the season, we could look out our living room window and watch the never-boring ocean: that giant body of water that stretched all the way from Logan Airport in the east to a peninsula called Nahant in the west. Dad would let me look into his binoculars so I'd have a better view of the cargo barges sailing into Boston Harbor and the planes taking off and landing over the water.

But I never realized they went any farther than Nahant. In other words, on a clear day, I believed I could see the whole world.

But my innocence ended abruptly one Friday evening at the Showcase Cinemas. Mom had taken me up to Revere to see *Born Free* for a last-day-of-second-grade treat. We both loved the movie, but on the way out of the theater, we spotted Dad in the ticket line for *The Godfather*. And facing him—standing way too close—was Natalie Cotechi, a small, stylish woman who'd gone to high school with my parents. Natalie looked like she wanted to kiss Dad, and she was rubbing the curly hair that sprouted at the neck of his blue t-shirt. I was only seven years old, but my stomach shrank in horror.

For at least a year after that, Mom answered every question Dad asked her in the smallest possible number of words, and Dad began sleeping on the couch. If I asked, he'd claim it helped his sciatica, but he never looked very comfortable lying on it.

Even worse, my parents had frequent nighttime whisper-fights when they thought I was asleep. I couldn't make out most of their actual words; they just sounded like cats hissing at each other. But every once in a while, they'd accidentally speak loudly enough for me to catch a few scraps of their conversation.

"Donna told me she saw you down on Yirrell Beach with some—" Maybe Mom didn't finish that sentence, or maybe she dropped her voice at the end.

"Donna Murphy?" said my dad, his voice *definitely* pushing the limits of whispering. "You're gonna trust a broad who oughta be payin' rent at the packie?"

"Takes one to know one."

"Oh for—" Dad slammed a door and stomped into the kitchen. I heard the hinges of the liquor cabinet creak, then nothing. I hated the silence more than their fighting.

Other times, he'd try a gentler approach. "Come on, Carol. I've apologized a hundred times. When you gonna forgive me?"

But Mom wasn't backing down. "Never," I heard her say once. "And if you ever cheat on me again, I'll divorce you and take every last thing we own.

She wouldn't have absconded with much. We lived in a "winterized beach bungalow," a former summer cottage updated with a boiler, radiators, and fuzzy pink insulation designed to seal in the heat during cold weather. My parents bought the place in 1963, intending to live there only until they saved more money and had another kid. But when neither of those things happened, we stayed put. Happily, I thought, until the fateful Natalie Cotechi incident.

After that day, Dad pretty much stopped going out for beers with his buddies and started drinking heavily at home. By the time I entered middle school, his lady slayer sword had grown tarnished and rusty. The only things seducing him on a regular basis were "handles" of Canadian Mist and twelve-packs of Schlitz, all of which he slayed like a champ.

But as his social life died, so did the flirty guy who'd once been the half-in-the-bag dancing king of every neighborhood cookout. Ditto for the man who'd earned the nickname "Mr. Mistletoe" at his company's Christmas party, and the one who could make every female bank teller, supermarket clerk, and waitress laugh at his goofy jokes. I never learned the details of my father's extramarital affairs, but as I grew older, it became apparent that Natalie hadn't been the first.

And although I've heard of men who get caught cheating and totally turn their lives around for the better, my dad turned into a miserable drunk. Taking out the trash became my least favorite chore; the sound of his bottles clanging in the bag haunted me night and day. But Dad kept sucking down the booze as though he believed that ingesting alcohol could cure his despair.

Mom, on the other hand, thrived in spite of—or perhaps because of—Dad's dramatic lifestyle changes. While he aged prematurely, she started looking younger and healthier, even pretty sometimes. Not Cheryl Tiegs pretty, but maybe Penny Marshall pretty. I'm sure she hated his drinking, but at least he wasn't out chasing other women, and neither of my parents had the energy or money to hire a divorce lawyer. Instead, they settled into a routine of watching TV in different rooms, listening to different music, and sleeping separately.

It frustrated the crap out of me. Sometimes at the dinner table—the family still ate dinner together almost every night—she'd smile the way she used to smile before Natalie Cotechi, the way she must've smiled when she and Dad first fell in love as teenagers. Her eyes would turn all dreamy and romantic, and her cheeks, neck, and chest would flush. *Look at her, Dad!* I'd want to scream. *Look how beautiful she is. Now go over there and give her a hug. Show her you still love her!*

But he never did. He'd go right on chewing his pot roast or whatever, raising his eyes only to reach for the salt or the butter dish. I actually began to wonder if Natalie Cotechi could've stolen my father's soul that night at the movies; maybe she'd yanked it out of his chest during that heart-stopping moment when she'd recognized Mom and bolted out of the theater.

"Well, of course he's a little depressed," said Mom when I told her I was worried about Dad. He'd been out of work for months, and although he blamed everything on the sciatica, it seemed more like mental pain to me. "He doesn't feel good. The doctor told him to walk more."

But Dad didn't exercise for the sake of exercise. He'd been a blue-collar laborer all his life, and like many of his peers, he scoffed at the joggers, power walkers, and "fancy fellas" who worked out in gyms. "Country's goin' straight to hell," he'd say every time a sweaty runner passed the house in shorts and sneakers.

So, I considered it a positive sign when he'd take the Buick out for a little spin. I mean, he couldn't drive the beast without walking to the end of the driveway, and that was a start, right? Sometimes he'd "go down the Elks" for a drink or two; other times, it'd just be the convenience store for butts and lottery tickets. But occasionally—on summer nights—he'd cruise up to Kell's Cream on Revere Beach for a soft-serve twist. He enjoyed eating it on the seawall up there, especially when he ran into old friends also treating themselves to ice cream or perhaps scarfing down sandwiches or fish plates from the famous Kelly's Roast Beef a few doors down. On those nights, Dad would come home reasonably sober and in a decent mood.

But how I wish I'd tried to stop him the night he crashed the car. Yes, I knew he was drunk, but *Love Boat*—my favorite show at the time—was on TV, and I was in no mood to be yelled at—or worse—by a boozed-up guy. Besides, he always swore he was fine and went out anyway. And the one time I'd actually grabbed his keys, he'd shoved me against the doorframe and held me there until I handed them over. Dad was stronger than me, and Drunk Dad didn't take no for an answer.

But I'd always wondered what ran through his mind when he lost control of the Buick. And when he went through the windshield, did he wish I'd taken his keys? Or did he even know what was happening? Perhaps he'd simply been anticipating a creamy, chocolate-and-vanilla soft-serve on a beautiful September evening.

All my anxiety about feeling awkward as a high school freshman temporarily vanished after Dad's accident. By the second week of September, 1978, everyone in town knew about my father and his totaled car, and no one expected me to act normal after something like that. All the kids—and I mean *all* the kids, even surfers and cheerleaders—treated me kindly, and Patty and Cindy waited patiently on my porch each morning, no matter how long I took to get ready. I think escorting a suffering person to school elevated their social status, and I actually began to wonder if the sympathy of the other students could somehow make me a popular girl. Did the mattress of Dad's hospital bed hide a silver lining? But if such a lining existed, it quickly rotted and disintegrated, like everything else in Dad's life. Including him.

Weeks passed, and new, more interesting dramas soon consumed Winthrop High: a well-liked math teacher suffered a heart attack; the football team trounced their archrival; two girls in the junior class were visibly pregnant. Meanwhile, nothing in my dad's case changed. Day after day, he remained the same, boring, motionless guy. And by default, I became boring too.

Kids didn't invite me to parties. I'm sure they considered me too sad to have fun. Which was true for a while, but by the time I started accepting my new family situation, most of the student body had conveniently forgotten me. No one asked if I'd be attending the Harvest Dance, and no boys showed any interest in dating me. In a way, it all made sense, because drinking and smoking weed were instrumental to the high school social scene, and everyone knew Dad had been trashed when he hit the seawall. Chip was true to his word about leaving that detail out of the official report, but since both my parents were Winthrop townies, the facts of Dad's accident hit the rumor mill hard.

And with each passing day, I felt additional responsibility for his fate. Confiding in Mom might've helped, but she and I had been functioning more like teammates than parent and child since the car crash, and my fear of risking our newfound closeness was too strong. If Mom turned against me, I'd be completely alone, and I needed her. We needed each other.

Nighttime sucked, though. I slept fitfully, and had terrifying dreams about losing all my teeth. I still managed to get up each morning and go to school with normal, happy, hormonal kids. I'd sit in class, doing my best to learn about Charles Dickens, Lyndon Johnson, and Gregor Mendel. And I developed a huge crush on another misfit named Todd Eldridge.

Todd sat near me in study hall, but I'd never spoken to him directly. He and I had lots in common, though: weight issues (I was overweight and he was skeletal), bad hair, acne, and few friends. But Todd also had an underappreciated gift: he played lead guitar in the school's jazz band. No respectable jock or burnout had any use for the jazz band, and everyone referred to its members as "band fags." But when Todd Eldridge and his cohorts entertained at school assemblies, electricity surged through my body. With his eyes closed and his greasy head nodding to the rhythm, Todd quickly became the most gorgeous creature I could imagine. I had no interest in learning to play an instrument; I just loved the way I felt watching him.

Sometimes, I'd try to catch his eye as I waited in the lunch line, but then Patty or Cindy would come along and ask how my dad was doing. And no matter how many times I told them that Dad wasn't expected to improve much, they'd reply with some cheesy comment like, "Don't give up, Erin," or, "Miracles happen every day, you know."

Oh yeah? I'd think, watching Todd and his band friends goofing around at the next table. *Well, they don't happen to everyone.* In fact, one of Dad's doctors had mentioned miracles *specifically* the day he'd informed Mom and me that Dad was being transferred to a nursing home. His exact words were, "We can't perform miracles here." But Dad was only thirty-nine. Couldn't someone help? I felt sick when I thought about the way his body was deteriorating so rapidly. Especially his feet, with their toes all curled up like dead baby shrimp.

All of Todd's friends were high school geeks too, and a few were in my advanced-level classes. So, every day at lunch—as I listened to Patty, Cindy, and the other girls discuss cheerleading and cute boys—I'd fantasize about walking over to Todd's table with a question about the English or history homework. Then Todd would join the conversation, and after some back and forth, we'd become a couple. I mean, that's how people in movies got together, right? I just needed to wait for the right moment.

Chapter 5

July 1992

As a twenty-eighth birthday gift, my mom and her boyfriend Edward gave me an old white Honda station wagon, and they agreed to pay the insurance on it, "for a couple years, anyway." They'd come back to Winthrop from Texas to visit with family and friends for a month, and had found the car at a dealer on the Lynnway. The body was in great condition, but the dude had sold it to them for only a thousand bucks because of "a minor overheating issue."

"You need more independence, Erin," Mom declared as she handed me the keys in my driveway. "It makes me crazy, knowing you travel all over creation on buses and trains. And I don't like you bummin' rides off those roommates of yours, either. They seem like nice guys, but—" She grimaced and cut her eyes in the direction of Pete's dented Corolla with the LEGALIZE IT bumper sticker on the back. "Yeah, I'll feel a helluva lot better with you drivin' yourself around. Just make sure to keep a jug o' water in the trunk in case it overheats. Especially on warm days like this."

I had a driver's license, but had never wanted my own car. They were complicated and expensive, and I liked the MBTA. "What do I do with the jug of water?" I asked, my voice trembling a little.

"Oh, you know," Mom replied, displaying a new set of boxy dentures. "Just ... pour it in the little hatchy thingy under the hood. Where the water goes, you know?"

The car had more than a "minor" overheating issue. It ran hot—way too hot—whenever the temperature outside reached over sixty degrees, which was pretty much every day in the summer, and at least half the spring and fall. I took it to a mechanic who, for a hundred bucks, informed me that oil was leaking from somewhere (possibly a hairline crack in the engine), and that the head gasket was most likely damaged. Extensive diagnostic work would be necessary if I wanted to learn more, and the cost of repairs would be in the thousands.

"But it still runs *now*," I said, reeling. I mean, *thousands*? For a thousand-dollar car?

"Yup," he said with a shrug. "And keep drivin' it if you want. But trust me: it's a ticking time bomb."

"Like, it might explode?"

He shot me a strange look. "Um, well, probably not. It'll probably just shit the bed one day. Hopefully not when you're miles from home and alone at night."

I considered all that, but no way could I afford to fix it. So, the guy showed me how to add oil to the engine and water to the radiator. He also said to run the heat all summer long.

"Wait. What?"

"Oh yeah. That's the only way to keep it cool. And *never* run the air conditioner. Ya hear me? You'll destroy the engine in minutes." He sighed. "Just open all the windows and pretend you're in Alaska."

Oh well. The Honda was for emergency use only. Better than nothing.

Linda, my boss from the temp agency, usually called on Fridays to discuss potential jobs for the following week. So, it was no surprise to hear her voice on the phone that evening in late July. I'd just completed a five-day stint at an insurance company in Everett. "Hey, Erin, here's a doozie. A two-week gig up in Gloucester. You interested?"

"Gloucester?" I asked, opening the box of Twinkies I'd picked up on my way home. "Isn't that, like, the other end of the earth?"

"Nope. Just about an hour north of Winthrop. And the job sounds decent too. Some t-shirt company needs a girl to take orders over the phone. And get this: it *has* to be a girl. It says so right here on the paper: *no men*."

Isn't that illegal? But Linda didn't always play by the book. I laughed instead of saying anything. "Where is it, the Playboy Mansion?"

"Beats me, honey, but it pays fifteen an hour plus commission. Not too shabby."

"Commission?" I said. "C'mon, Linda. You know that means telemarketing, and I don't do that." I'd tried telemarketing once—

selling vitamins—and it'd almost killed me. "Besides," I added, "my car sucks. I doubt it'll make it to Gloucester two days in a row, let alone two weeks."

Linda ignored my concerns about the car. "Nope. It also says *no telemarketing*."

"Yeah. I've heard that one before—"

"Oh, be a sport, Erin. I'm thinking this'll be a nice change for you. Get you outta the hot city. They've got gorgeous beaches up in Gloucester, and you could use a change of scenery. How 'bout you give it a try?"

"But my car—"

"Erin, your car'll be fine. And truth be told, it's the only job I've got for you now, and I'm guessing your rent's due first of the month."

Ugh. Why couldn't Linda just *start* with the truth? I mean, she had a tiny agency, so of course, she didn't always get offered the best jobs. But she refused to admit that; Linda believed you had to act like a big company if you ever wanted to become one. Her half-truths irritated the crap out of me, but I also wanted to get off the phone and start my Twinkie binge.

"All right," I said with little enthusiasm. "Sign me up."

Come Monday morning, though, my enthusiasm had dwindled to the point of non-existence. "Don-Wash," I said out loud, dumping water into the Honda's radiator with the help of a funnel. "What a fucked-up name for a company." I'd overslept, my skin looked especially puffy, and my eyelashes were clumped together with hastily applied mascara.

Still, I assumed I'd make it to work on time. Then I reached Route 128 and hit *insane* traffic. What the hell? I mean, everyone knows getting *into* Boston's a challenge in the morning, but I was going the opposite direction. Between the heat and humidity of the day and the car's heater blasting, I started pouring sweat, and by 8:30—when I should've been arriving at work—I was still twenty miles south of Gloucester with a soaking dress. But I couldn't just go home. Linda would murder me.

Finally, wet, smelly, and stressed, I pulled into the parking lot around nine o'clock. A man—perhaps a maintenance worker—sat reading the *Boston Herald* on the steps of a structure that looked like a cross between a converted trailer and a modular home. "Hey!" he called. "You the new girl?"

"Uh-huh," I answered, hauling myself out of the Honda and attempting to smooth my damp dress.

"Well, welcome to Don-Wash," said the guy, extending his hand. "I'm Don Washburn."

Don Washburn? The company's owner? A sickening cloud of Drakkar Noir hung in the air between us as I shook his damp hand. "Oh, hi. I'm Erin Reardon. Sorry I'm late."

Don ignored my apology. "C'mon inside. You'll love the new digs. We've been here a week now. Big improvement over the last place."

I followed him and his cologne up the stairs. Tall and thin, his face gave off an orangey hue, as if he'd applied some sort of self-tanning cream. His thinning brown hair looked dry, and his dark polyester slacks and white button-down shirt were both too tight. But based on the way he walked and looked me up and down, he obviously considered himself sexy as hell.

The only other people in the room—two young blond women chatting over coffee at a folding table—looked up as Don and I entered. Both wore fake nails, and one wore a see-through black blouse that exposed her entire bra. The other woman's eye makeup was so smudged that I wondered if she'd slept in it. All the furniture was plastic and mismatched, and the air conditioner made random sputtering sounds for no apparent reason. The entire place smelled like Latex paint too, but somehow Don's cologne was stronger.

"Hello again, ladies," Don addressed the women. "As promised, we've got a new girl with us today. New Girl, meet Amy and Tara, our salesladies. You'll all be working together."

I wasn't sure which woman was Amy and which was Tara, so I just said hi.

"Hi," they said in unison.

An awkward silence followed. Don's eyes were focused on my legs, and I couldn't tell if he was spacing out or assessing them. "Sorry I'm late," I said a second time. "You wouldn't believe the traffic on 128."

"Oh, you're not late, honey," he said, shooting me a sly grin. "You're right on time. Didn't I tell your boss—what's her name, Linda—to get you here by 9:15?"

I glanced at the clock, which read exactly 9:15. "Um, I'm pretty sure she said 8:30."

"No, no, no," said Don, turning to Tara and Amy. "Ladies, what time do people at Don-Wash report to work?"

The woman in the peek-a-boo blouse raised her hand like a schoolgirl.

"Go on, Tara. Tell her," said Don.

He's a weirdo, I thought. The whole scene felt like an outtake from a bad TV show.

Tara's tone implied that she'd answered the question more than once. "Don doesn't care what time we get in," she said. "As long as we give him a full eight hours."

"Perfect, hon," said Don. "Love your attitude today. But what's up with you, Amy dear? You don't look tip-top."

The smudged-makeup woman shook her head and said nothing.

"Amy had a rough night," explained Tara, "so we're all gonna be extra nice to her today. Okay?"

Don nodded and winked. "Okie doke. As long as I get full details later."

"I need a butt break," said Amy, grabbing a pack of Newports and heading out the door.

Don watched her go, then turned to me. "That make sense, New Girl? I don't care *when* you work, as long as you put in eight solid hours a day. Come in at ten, take an hour lunch, go home at seven. Show up at eleven, skip lunch, still go home at seven. It's all good. There's always work to be done here."

I looked around the room and wondered what he meant by work. All I'd seen so far were people chatting, drinking coffee, smoking, and reading the paper. And what kind of boss would allow a *temp* to set her own hours?

"Are you sure?" I asked. "'Cause I live in Winthrop and it'd be great if I didn't have to be here right at eight-thirty, but I'm just a temp and—"

"Did you hear me, honey?" Don asked. "Oh, and tell me your name again."

"Erin. Erin Reardon."

"Right. Now, listen up, Erin Reardon. Gimme eight solid hours a day for two weeks, and we'll discuss permanent employment. How's that sound?"

"Good," I said, trying not to appear freaked out by the words *permanent employment*. I'd pretty much given up on getting hired by one of my temp bosses. For some reason, Linda's clients rarely considered me anything other than a short-term replacement for employees on vacation or maternity leave. Only once before had I been offered an interview at an office where I'd worked for a week, but the job sucked so badly—answering the phone at an overbooked pediatric dental practice—that I'd almost laughed. But maybe there was more to Don-Wash than met the eye.

"All righty then," said Don. "Let's set you up." He directed me toward the back of the room, where two functional desks peeked out from under a pile of phone books and magic markers. "You'll be sitting back here with Claire, who's apparently late again today." He cleared his throat and frowned. "She's always late."

"But I thought you didn't care what time—"

"Claire's different," he snapped, cutting me off.

"Oh. I'm sorry." I looked across the room to Tara for help, but she was absorbed in a fashion magazine at her folding table. Amy, who'd been on butt break for at least fifteen minutes, was nowhere in sight.

As Don adjusted the waistline of his too-tight pants, the smell of cologne swirled around us. Back in college, I'd hated the scent of Drakkar Noir—I'd associated it with scumbag guys in clubs looking to get laid—but on Don, a man in his forties wearing a wedding ring, it struck me as ludicrous.

"All righty," he said. "Your job is to take incoming orders and generate sales leads for Tara and Amy. In other words, the girls up front handle the outside sales, and you and Claire hold down the house. Make sense?"

"Sort of ..."

"Here. Siddown and I'll explain again. It's really very simple."

Obediently, I sat on one of the black plastic chairs, and tried to breathe through my mouth to avoid smelling his cologne. Don dumped a few phone books on the floor to clear some work space. "Okay, so we have a whole bunch of clients who buy our t-shirts on a regular basis. Sports teams, schools, small businesses, amusement parks, you name it. They call in orders, then you and Claire take down the info. You ask all the right questions. You make sure they're ordering enough too, if you know what I mean. Encourage 'em to get plenty of extras. People always need more t-shirts than they think. Then, when everything's all set, you fax the order over to the factory in Everett. Which, coincidentally, is down in your neck of the woods. You live in Winthrop, right?"

"Uh huh."

Tara turned the pages of her fashion magazine as if they contained classified world secrets.

"And that's it?" I couldn't imagine an easier way to make fifteen bucks an hour. Could Don-Wash be a front for something else? And if so, what did they actually do?

Don shrugged. "Pretty much. Although when the phone's not ringing, you can't just sit around, right?"

"Right," I said, getting an uneasy feeling.

"So, when the phones are quiet, you identify *new* clients. We need new clients to survive in this market. Make sense?"

"Um, I guess so, but—" If he mentioned telemarketing, I was outta there.

"But what?"

"Um, I'm not sure where you're going with this."

Don's eyes flashed. "Listen. It's part of your job to help grow the business. Every one of my girls does it. I do it too."

"Donny?" called Tara from across the room.

"Yes, honey?"

"My computer's all screwy again. It won't turn on."

"Just a minute," he replied. "I'm training the new girl."

Tara pouted and stood up in her extremely high heels. *Knock-me-over-fuck-me-shoes,* the girls at Danforth would've called them. "All right," she answered, still pouting. "Then I'm makin' my coffee run. Who wants Dunkie's?"

Don said he'd have a medium with four creams and four sugars, and Amy requested hazelnut with skim milk.

"You want anythin', Erin?" asked Tara.

"Oh no. I'm fine." I would've appreciated some caffeine, but didn't feel comfortable asking her to buy me coffee on my first—and possibly last—day at skeevy Don-Wash.

"Poor Tara," whispered Don. "This computer stuff really frustrates her. But you should see her in front of customers. Stick o' dynamite. Amy too. No one can resist those ladies with their flares firing."

He chuckled a little while I sat there trying to visualize what the hell he meant. I mean, the company sold t-shirts, right? "All right, let's try a call or two. You'll be amazed at how easy it is."

No. I would not let him trick me into telemarketing. "You know," I said, "I'm thinking this isn't the right job for me. I mean, it seems like a great company and all, but I can't telemarket. I just can't."

"Telemarket?" said Don, blinking a few times. "Who said anything about *telemarketing*? We don't *telemarket* here. We do straight up corporate *sales*, and if you don't know the difference between the two, that's your loss."

"Okay," I said, gathering my courage. "I guess ... I don't."

Don sat up straight, folded his hands, and drew a deep breath. "Telemarketing, my dear, is making call after call, with your only objective being a sale. At the end of the day, all that matters is the bottom line. Telemarketers don't care if every single one of their customers falls off a cliff and dies, as long as the credit cards go through. Correct?"

I didn't know what to say. "Um ..."

"Yes," he said.

"Okay."

He stared straight at me and squinted. "Bottom line. That's it. But corporate *sales* is about building *relationships*. Establishing *trust*. Making *friends*. My girls take great pride in their work. Great. We're family. And I promote from within. So, if you choose to stay, you could be in Tara's shoes someday. Or Amy's. It's up to you. Your life. But please don't ever insult me like that again. Telemarketing. Please."

Wow. I hadn't intended to hit a nerve like that. But despite feeling a bit guilty, I also wanted to laugh. I mean, everything about Don-Wash was so pathetic, especially Don. And I'd never wear shoes like Tara's. "Look, I'm sorry," I said. "I didn't mean to offend you, but—"

"No apologies," he said. "It's shit or get off the pot here. Now, lemme explain how the numbers work. You get a twenty-dollar bonus for every good lead you generate. That's twenty bucks on top of your fifteen-an-hour base, *every* time you book one of the salesgirls on an appointment. Okay? I challenge you to go out and find a telemarketing job that offers that benefit. I challenge you."

I couldn't argue with him there. I mean, I'd never even made fifteen dollars an hour before, let alone with a bonus incentive. "Wait a minute," I said. "You're saying that if I call someone up at say, Raytheon, and they wanna book a meeting with Tara or Amy, I get twenty extra bucks. Just like that. And I still get fifteen an hour?"

"What are we, in an echo chamber?" said Don. "But slow down a minute. Raytheon's a big company. They handle government defense contracts, that sorta thing. Probably a little too big for us. Unless you know someone over there, of course. You got connections at Raytheon?"

"No."

"Then don't bother with them. If I were you, I'd start out focusing on schools, smaller companies, startups, that sorta thing. And don't waste your time on the *tiny* guys. No mom and pops. Forget 'em if there's less than ten employees. Those folks'll nickel and dime you to death."

From behind me, a deep, sarcastic female voice joined the conversation. "Don't waste your time? Don! You're advising this woman not to waste her time? Wow. She better get her ass outta here, pronto."

I whirled around in my chair to see a petite woman holding a Styrofoam coffee cup. Everything about her was short and dark: her hair, her body, her black tank dress. Even her nostril was pierced with a tiny onyx stud. The other thing I noticed immediately was her striking resemblance to Lenny Weir's on-again, off-again girlfriend, Violet Chasm. But while hollow-cheeked Violet gazed out at the world through heroin eyes, this woman glowed with health.

"How nice of you to show up today, Claire," said Don. "I trust you'll be working late this evening?"

Claire shrugged. "I dunno. I assume you expect me to train the new employee?" She smiled kindly at me, though, and I caught a fleeting whiff of baby powder and cigarettes. "So, if my boss would get his ass out of my seat, I'll get started."

"Watch the mouth, Claire," snapped Don, his cologne smelling stronger. "Or you'll be taking the week off."

"Ooh," said the woman. "I could use a vacation." But when she turned to me again, her tone softened. "You seem nice. And since my boss has the social skills of an orangutan, let me introduce myself. I'm Claire Terelas."

Don shook his head in disgust.

"I'm Erin Reardon," I replied. The interaction between Claire and Don felt a little dangerous—and, therefore, exciting—but the office contained way too much bad chemistry. I needed to escape before I got sucked into the mix. And since the wall clock said it was 10:00 a.m., I realized I could skip lunch and leave by 5:15. Then I'd go home and never come back. Linda would understand. I'd get paid for one full day, and maybe Linda could find me something else for the second half of the week.

Claire smiled again, revealing a mouth full of perfect little teeth. "Nice to meet you, Reardon. And don't let old Don scare you. The good news is, he travels a lot, so we don't have to see him every day."

"I told you to watch it, Claire," said Don. But this time, his voice was gentler. He reminded me of a burnt-out middle school teacher who'd just realized that his students were winning. "You and I can talk later." Then, standing up, he walked off without another word.

"Fucker," muttered Claire, fanning her hand in front of her nose. "Ugh. What a stench."

I giggled nervously. In all the years I'd been temping, I'd never seen an employee treat a boss the way Claire had just treated Don.

"So. What'd Salon Don tell you about the job so far?" she asked.

"Salon Don?"

She shrugged. "The tan? Although seriously, I think he just buys that cream at the drugstore."

"Oh. Yeah." I wanted to laugh, but also didn't want to get tossed out in front of everyone. "Well, he said we take orders—"

"Yeah," said Claire, "forget about that. Forget everything he said. Let's start from scratch."

Now, I didn't want poor Claire wasting her time and potential commission training me. After all, I was planning to quit. "No, it's okay. I got the basic stuff. Maybe I can just watch you take some orders. But ... when do the phones start ringing?"

Claire chuckled to herself. "See," she said, "that's why I wanna start from scratch. 'Cause we hardly ever take orders."

"But—"

"I know. Don's a filthy liar. Let me guess—he gave you the impression your job's ninety percent answering the phone."

"Uh huh."

"Think about that a second. If you were a Don-Wash customer, wouldn't you call your *sales rep* to place an order?"

"I ... guess so."

She nodded. "Yeah. You would. And that's what our customers do. They call Tara and Amy."

"So, what about us?"

"What d'ya think? We make cold calls. All day long. We look for new suckers. We're telemarketers."

"But—"

"I know. I've heard it a million times. Building relationships, growing the company, making friends. Yada yada." She pressed her lips together and closed her eyes for a second. When she opened them, she said, "Reardon, Don's a moron. An IROC driving moron. Although certain women consider him attractive. Fuck knows why." She glared over at Tara and Amy, who were both on their phones.

I couldn't understand why anyone as intelligent as Claire would work in such a depressing place. "Don drives an IROC?" I asked.

"Yeah, you musta seen it out there in the lot. Tacky black thing with chrome wheels? And let me just add that in Don's case, *all* the cliché acronyms apply. 'Nough said."

"Wow."

Claire took a deep breath. "Yeah. But now that that's off my chest, whatdaya say we do some dialing for dollars, Reardon?"

"Okay." It occurred to me that she might've misunderstood when I told her my name, because she kept calling me "Reardon" instead of "Erin," but I was a little afraid to correct her. Besides, what did it matter? I'd only be staying six and a half more hours.

"So, as you can see," she said, motioning toward the various stacks of phone books lying around, "you'll never have to worry about screwing up or saying the wrong thing on the phone, 'cause we've got an endless supply of people to call. Don doesn't make us keep a log, and he doesn't care how many people say no or hang up. It's all about the number of appointments we schedule each week. Don't believe anything else. Here. I'll make a few calls. You'll catch on fast. It's not brain surgery. But if you're good at it, you can make decent cash."

During the next hour, I watched in awe as Claire booked two appointments, and promised to send catalogs to two other people who requested follow-up calls in a week or so. Then she decided we needed a cigarette break. I told her I didn't smoke, but she said I should get some fresh air anyway. "Besides, you'll probably *start* smoking if you stay here long. This place would be intolerable without butts."

It definitely felt good to get out of that stuffy trailer. Don-Wash was a couple of miles from the ocean, but even on such a humid day, the sea breeze found its way into the parking lot. As I watched Claire light up, it occurred to me that Gloucester actually had some basic stuff in common with Winthrop: both were working-class coastal communities that managed to retain their blue-collar identities. Most other Massachusetts beach towns had become magnets for the wealthy, but Gloucester and Winthrop remained somewhat gritty and proud.

"This place reminds me of Winthrop," I observed. "I like the smell of the ocean."

"Oh yeah. Inlanders don't get it, but the ocean changes your perspective on life. On everything, really."

A chill shot up my back. Usually when I temped, my coworkers treated me civilly, but when lunch or break time rolled around, they'd slip off with their pals, leaving me on my own. Which made total sense. I mean, why would they invest time and energy in someone who'd soon be gone? But Claire behaved as though she genuinely liked me. Or maybe she was just bored. Maybe she chatted with temps for the same reason she smoked: to make her days at Don-Wash bearable.

"So why aren't you selling software, or pharmaceuticals, or something?" I dared to ask, as she took a drag of her cigarette. "I mean, you just made fifty-five bucks in an hour, right? You could probably make millions in New York or something."

She held out her arm and observed the way the smoke curled around the little Yin-Yang tattoo on her wrist. "Ya think so?"

"Yeah," I answered. "I really do."

She took another drag and blew a few smoke rings. "Well ... I guess it's about flexibility. Lifestyle choices, you know? I love my boyfriend, and he lives here, with me. Plus, I hate professional clothes. And ironing. My boyfriend's the same way. He's in a band and does landscaping to pay rent. We do shit jobs so we can hang out in clubs at night. No one cares if we show up at work stinking or looking half dead. Ya know?"

But her boyfriend was in the band, not Claire. I wondered if she was sacrificing her chances at success to accommodate him. "Hmm," I said.

"Now, what about you, Reardon? What makes *you* tick?"

No one had ever asked me that before. But if I told her about my dream of getting together with Lenny Weir, she'd write me off as insane. "I don't know. I like writing. I mean, when I have free time. And get inspired." *What the hell? Why did I just say that?* I'd barely written anything since college.

But Claire wasn't fazed at all. I think she actually believed me. "Cool! Short stories? Poetry?"

"Um ..." My face heated up with embarrassment. "Well, mostly music stuff, actually. And I read a lot too. I love books about musicians. And articles about them. In magazines and newspapers." *Stop babbling! You sound like an idiot.*

Claire exhaled more smoke and looked straight into my eyes. She didn't seem to care about my weight, my bad skin, or the sweat soaking through my blue cotton dress. "So, you're saying music makes you tick? Reading and writing about music?"

"I guess so. And listening to it, of course. That's my favorite thing." I couldn't stop. Claire's attention had me under some sort of spell.

She nodded. "Well, I'm with you there. Bobby—that's my boyfriend—and I love seeing bands. We're in Boston a few times a week."

"Huh. Have you ever gone to the Middle East? In Cambridge?"

She flicked her ashes. "Of course. All the time. Bobby knows the guy who books their bands: Dave something. Do you hang out there too?"

I choked up a little. "No, not really. But I saw a great show there last year."

"Oh yeah? Who?"

"Um, Lenny Weir? From Winterlong? He played solo and—"

"Get outta here!" she shouted. "You're shittin' me! Tell me you're joking. The show when he passed out?"

Don stuck his orangey face out the window. "Girls, that's been a long butt break. C'mon. Back to work."

"Chill out, Don," said Claire, extinguishing her cigarette against the building. "We need a minute." But when she turned back to me, she lowered her voice. "Did you really see Lenny? Lenny fuckin' Weir?"

Claire was the only person, aside from Colin and his friends, I'd ever told about the show. "Yes. I wouldn't lie about that."

"But how'd you *know*? Even Bobby didn't hear 'til it was too late, and he's in on all the rumors."

For the first time in months, I thought about Colin, and wondered how things were going with him and Suzanne. "Oh, a friend told me. An old friend."

"You bitch!" said Claire, clearly in awe. "Oh my god. Did you cry?"

"A little," I admitted. "It was sad, you know?"

Claire looked like *she* might start crying. "I can only imagine. Did you write about it?"

I stared at her. Did she know me better than I knew myself? "Not yet," I said. "I mean, I've tried, but ... I get emotional. It's hard to put that stuff into words."

"Oh yeah. I'm sure. But you're a writer. You'll figure it out. I know you will."

Don's face popped out the window again. "Warning number two, girls!"

"Yeah, yeah, yeah," said Claire.

But as we headed toward the building, Claire took my arm and whispered, "Don's been fucking Tara for a year, and his wife's good friends with my sister. That's why I get special privileges at this shithole. He knows I'll rat him out if he pushes too far. Don may be scum, but he doesn't wanna be divorced."

Damn it, I thought. Why did I meet Claire here? At the worst company on the planet? And if I quit, would I ever see her again?

Chapter 6

April 1980

I lay on my bed beside the radio, staring at the Kmart flyer and trying not to cry. Which wasn't easy when the sky outside was bawling. Fifteen minutes earlier, I'd called and asked Todd Eldridge to the Sophomore Spring Fling and he'd said no. No explanation, no excuse, just no. Then he hung up.

Almost all the girls from my school lunch table had found dates for the dance, and were now focused on gowns and shoes. Patty and her mom had paid over a hundred dollars for a dress at some fancy mall store, which set the bar pretty high. But my mom didn't have that kind of money.

So, when the Kmart ad featuring a gorgeous, pale green, spaghetti-strap dress for $29.99 arrived in the mail, I'd been elated. Some kids called Kmart cheesy, but the green dress was anything but. It was classy, sophisticated, and altogether mesmerizing. Perfect for dancing all night with Todd Eldridge.

All week long, I'd been studying the flyer in a weird little way. I'd start with the front cover and turn each page slowly, pretending to care about the men's pants, and the spring handbags, and the bras, and the cute kids' clothes. And then ... even more slowly ... I'd flip over to page twelve ... and there ... would be ... the dress! The dress that actually shocked me with its beauty every time I saw it. That pastel color—like apple-flavored taffy—and the glamorous, chiffon skirt that just grazed the floor. The model wearing it looked like a movie star, and I'd envision myself in her place, with some pink blush on my cheeks, and my hair pinned up like a ballerina ...

But no. Todd Eldridge, the love of my life, shut me down with one cold syllable. I couldn't believe it.

Dad had died five months earlier, right after Thanksgiving. Many details from that time period had already been obscured by muddy brain puddles. I'd start recalling a particular situation or event, but only parts of it would rise to the surface while the rest would sink into deep, murky holes. I guess it was my body's way of protecting me from too much pain, and I was grateful for that. But certain things still haunted me, like the shiny brown lid of Dad's closed casket, the undertaker's wiry black eyebrows, and the dry leaves crunching under people's feet as we left the cemetery. Especially the leaves, because my dad's body would soon be just like them: rotting its way back into the earth. Even his eyes, which had silently accused me of murder ever since the accident.

But although my grief sometimes made it hard to breathe, I also couldn't deny my tremendous sense of relief. Now, he'd never be able to tell Mom I'd been awake and watching TV when he left the house that final time. My secret was safe forever. But I was so messed up.

After they lowered him into the ground, the funeral party drove over to the Winthrop Elks Club for a breakfast reception. Because that's what a teenage girl wants to do after burying her father, right? She wants to sit at a table in a dingy building where her dad used to drink, pushing lukewarm eggs around on a plate, while a bunch of locals swilled cocktails before noon and claimed to be really, really sorry. I tried, though. I listened as Dad's sister Jean rambled on about the trouble she and Dad got into as kids, and nodded politely when his high school math teacher told me he'd been one of her favorite students. But Patty and Cindy strutted over to my table—both wearing new, high-heeled leather boots—and Patty said she understood how I felt.

"Thanks," I answered before returning to staring at my eggs. It was my father's funeral breakfast and I could be antisocial if I wanted.

"We'll always be here for you," said Cindy in her best *After-School Special* voice.

I'm not sure why it was Cindy's melodramatic sorrow that sent me over the edge; all I knew was that I couldn't act any longer. "You know what?" I said, standing and shoving my chair back on the squeaky floor. "You guys don't understand *shit!* And if you're always there for me, then why don't you ever invite me *anywhere?*"

Patty jumped back and said, "Whoa," but I stormed past her and out of the Elks Club. My shoes were a size too big, but I walked all the way home in them and didn't feel the blisters until later that night when they really swelled up.

We hadn't planned on Dad dying so soon. His doctors had been brutally honest with us about his condition and the fact that dead brain cells don't regenerate, but they'd expected him to hang on for five more years or so. Yes, his limbs were paralyzed and most of his nutrition came through a feeding tube, but he'd also been taking a little food orally each day and his brain showed clear signs of activity.

So the early morning phone call was a huge shock. The doctor explained to Mom how unexpected things often happened to people like Dad, and that he'd probably suffered a stroke or heart attack in his sleep. We could order an autopsy if we wanted more details, but Mom said no. Why chop him up when nothing could be done anyway?

I held her hand throughout the conversation, and wept with her for hours afterward, but still couldn't believe he was gone. "Are they sure, Mom?" I asked late that afternoon. "Are they sure he's not still a *little bit* alive?"

Mom let me stay out of school for a week after the funeral, and she didn't go to work, either. We cried, watched soaps and game shows, and cleaned out Dad's closet and drawers. Neighbors brought casseroles to the door, and we ate whenever we felt like it, paying little attention to the time of day or taste of the food. We wore sweats and pajamas, didn't bathe or shower much, and spoke few actual words. But the house refused to be silent. Constantly, it whispered memories of Dad: good, bad, neutral. All bittersweet.

Then, on Sunday afternoon—exactly one week after Dad's death—Mom declared it was time to return to the real world. "We gotta start combin' our hair again, Erin. And brushin' our teeth before they fall out." Lead settled in my bowels when she spoke those words, but she was right. We couldn't be dirty hermits forever.

But how could I walk into school after all that'd happened? I mean, it was bad enough before, when people could cling to some phantom hope that Dad would get better. Not to mention that my hysterics at the funeral breakfast had certainly been analyzed and dissected in the lunchroom and beyond. So how would people treat me now? Would they swamp me with sympathy or ignore me even more? And what would be worse?

As I tossed and turned in bed, I suddenly remembered a girl in my elementary school named Lisa Overend. Lisa was a pretty normal kid until fourth grade, when her father drowned in a pool over spring break. I never learned the details of his death, but when poor Lisa finally returned to school, she was fragile and traumatized. She'd obviously seen things that children—and maybe even adults—shouldn't see, and her pale gray eyes didn't focus the way they'd done before. It's a cruel thing to say, but the new Lisa was scary, and most kids in our class, including me, avoided her as much as possible.

Then, one day, for no apparent reason, she ran out of the classroom and locked herself in the school bathroom. The teacher pleaded with her to come out, but she stayed put until the janitor broke the lock with a special tool. Lisa's mom arrived and brought the girl home, and we never saw her again. Through the grapevine, I heard that the family moved away, and I think all the kids were relieved. We wanted to help Lisa, of course, but what could we do? Better for everyone that she start over again somewhere else.

And now, I thought, *I'm the new Lisa Overend.* But Mom and I couldn't just move. I'd have to figure out a way to survive at Winthrop High, and I sure didn't want the other kids feeling freaked out and stressed around me. I just wanted to be plain old Erin again.

Eventually, I fell into a fitful sleep, and awoke around 4:00 a.m. with a fantastic idea: I'd march into Winthrop High School like a warrior, and I'd *fight* Lisa Overend syndrome. Better yet, I'd be the *anti*-Lisa Overend. No crying, no acting glum, no locking myself in any bathrooms. No sir. I'd earn the respect of my classmates by staying strong. And if I needed a role model, I'd think about Jackie Kennedy, who held her head high through tremendous suffering. She walked proudly at JFK's funeral, and went on living the way she wanted to with dignity and class.

Could I do that too?

Yes. Yes, I could.

So when the sun's first orange rays appeared over the December ocean, I gathered up the dead leaves of my grief and buried them someplace deep inside me. I took a long, hot shower, washed my face with cold water, and pulled on some clean jeans and a fuzzy blue sweater. Then I blow-dried my hair, spruced up my face with a little foundation makeup and blush, and applied some black mascara.

Mom seemed happy to see me so fresh and chipper at breakfast. "Good girl, Erin," she said as I devoured a large bowl of cereal and poured a second glass of orange juice. "You're makin' your daddy very proud."

That last comment threw me off for a second, but it provided a good opportunity to practice my new act. "Thanks, Mom," I answered. "I know Dad's proud of you too. Wherever he is."

Unfortunately, nobody at Winthrop High was prepared for the shiny, cheerful Erin Reardon who showed up that day. Some kids handed me sympathy cards in the hallway, and the girls from my lunch table had chipped in and bought me a little fern plant. But when they presented it to me at my locker, I accepted it with a big smile like I'd won a beauty pageant or something.

"I'm sorry, Erin," said my English teacher, a motherly woman who hugged me when I entered her classroom.

"Oh, it's okay," I replied, squirming out of her arms in the nicest possible way. "It was for the best. He's better off now."

And when my geometry teacher asked me to stay after class, I laughed nervously. "How are you, Erin?" he asked.

"Pretty good," I said between giggles, "although now I've gotta catch up on all the work I missed. I guess I'll be busy."

A stunned expression crossed his face, but I held it together. I mean, he'd been expecting Lisa Overend and he was getting Jackie O, so of course he'd be surprised. He'd get over it soon enough. It never occurred to me that anyone would consider my sunny attitude far more disturbing than tears. But when I arrived in Spanish class, the teacher told me that Mrs. Hess, the guidance counselor, needed to see me immediately.

"How's your personal support system, Erin?" asked Mrs. Hess after expressing her sympathy. "I know you're an only child, but do you have good friends to talk to? Cousins maybe?"

"Oh yeah," I answered, proud of my emergent acting skills. "I've got lots of friends."

Mrs. Hess leaned across the desk, her smudged purple lipstick making her pale face more corpselike. Her breath smelled faintly of mildew. "Well, whatever you tell me is entirely confidential. You don't have to pretend you're fine. You've suffered a serious tragedy."

Tears filled my throat, but I fought them hard. It might be nice to tell her about my sadness and guilt, but what if she talked to my teachers? Or Mom? Or anyone? "I'm not pretending," I said. "I'm really okay."

She sat back and sighed. "Well, I think it might be good for you to speak to a therapist. What's a good time to reach your mother?"

"Oh, please don't call her," I said, my voice breaking a bit. "She's got enough to deal with now."

Mrs. Hess smiled with those purple lips, revealing lipstick on her front teeth too. "Erin, you're *both* dealing with a lot. And everyone needs a little help sometimes."

Don't cry. You can't cry. If you do, she'll know you're falling apart. Instead, I focused on her stained teeth. "Yeah, but I've already got a therapist. A really good one. I saw her the other day."

Mrs. Hess looked surprised but pleased. "Oh. That's ... great, Erin. Who're you seeing, if you don't mind my asking?"

"Um, she's in ... Everett. Her name's Doctor..." I looked down at the thin gray carpet on the floor, "... Carpeta. She's really nice."

"Doctor *Carpeta*? Is that C-a-r-p-e-t-a?"

"Uh huh."

Mrs. Hess scribbled the name on a piece of paper. "Hmm. I definitely don't know her. Does she specialize in adolescents?"

I hadn't planned on telling such a blatant lie, and my mouth felt dry. But I continued in my calmest voice. "I don't know. But she's great."

Mrs. Hess nodded and sighed again. "Erin, you've got so much potential, but I'm not sure *you* believe that. All your teachers have told me how bright you are, but your self-esteem could use a boost. I hope your therapist helps you appreciate your inner beauty."

Inner beauty, my ass. No one in high school gave a shit about inner beauty. "Hey Mrs. Hess, would you mind if I went back to class now? I've got a lotta work to catch up on."

She pressed her purple lips together and assessed me. "Sure, go ahead. As long as you're seeing someone."

I stood up. "Thank you."

"But ... wait a minute." I could tell she was going over our conversation in her head. "I just wanna make sure ... I mean, do you believe Doctor Carpeta's the best person to help you?"

"Oh yeah," I said in my strongest voice. "She's worked with hundreds of kids with dead parents." Did that sound over the top?

Mrs. Hess smiled. "Okay, then. But Erin, my door's always open. You can come back anytime."

"I know," I said. "But I'm good."

I was better than good; I was ecstatic. I mean, if I could fool a guidance counselor, I could probably fool anyone. My confidence grew, not as Erin Reardon, but as the actress *portraying* Erin Reardon. Maybe my performances weren't Oscar caliber, but People's Choice Awards caliber for sure. I'd just force myself to remain unnaturally optimistic and agreeable in school. I didn't complain about stuff that bothered other kids—homework, teachers, rainy weather, stomachaches—because I didn't want anyone to sense my misery, and I dreaded the thought of another visit to Mrs. Hess's office.

But being on stage all the time was draining. And exhausting. So exhausting that I failed to notice my entire audience walking out the door.

That's why Todd Eldridge's stark refusal to be my date for the dance was such a shock. I mean, wasn't he at least flattered by the invitation?

Alone in my bedroom, I allowed tears to roll unobstructed down my cheeks. *Why was life so hard, and why did no one care? And would things ever improve?* Mom had some Valiums in the bathroom that she took when she couldn't sleep—she'd stolen them from Dad's hospital room—and I was pretty sure they'd kill me if I swallowed the whole bottle. But how would it feel to die? Would I just go to sleep and never wake up, or would it hurt? Would I know what was happening, or would everything just go black?

And did I actually want to *die*? I mean, would I be able to watch the kids at school crying for me? And if so, would seeing Patty and Todd Eldridge sobbing at my funeral—wishing they'd been nicer—be *worth it*? Because they'd still be alive, and I'd be ... dead. People would forget about me after a while; grass would grow over my grave, and ... yeah. But life sucked, too. I needed to do something fun.

The April wind blew another gust of rain against the bedroom window, and I shivered as the model in the green dress went on smiling her vapid Kmart smile, blissfully unaware that her store would be selling one less dress that year. Down the street, a bus rattled by, and I glanced at the clock. It was almost 4:30, and Mom had mentioned something about getting out of work early that day. So I turned up the radio, just in case. I didn't want her to walk in and hear me crying.

The DJ was interviewing some guy who'd coauthored a book called *No One Here Gets Out Alive* about Jim Morrison, the singer from the Doors. The author said the book was a must-read for anyone who cared about music history because it provided real insight into the life of a poetic genius and true rock legend.

Rock stars fascinated me. I couldn't understand how they walked out on stage and exposed their souls to the world, night after night. Especially guys like Simon and Garfunkel. I mean, "The Sound of Silence" is such a personal song, but they sang it all the time, in front of thousands of people. Then there was James Taylor, who wrote "Fire and Rain" about a friend's death. How could he sing that in front of *anyone* without crying?

"All right," said the DJ to the author, "everyone remembers Jim Morrison as the Lizard King, swaggering around in those snakeskin pants. But in the book, he seems quite vulnerable. Almost timid at times."

The author agreed. He claimed that Jim Morrison was extremely shy beneath his leather and snakeskin armor.

"I don't know," said the DJ. "Morrison never struck me as a shy dude."

But the author wasn't backing down. He suggested paying close attention to the lyrics of "People Are Strange," because they demonstrate Morrison's true alienation.

With nothing better to do, I closed my eyes as the music began to play. I didn't know much about Jim Morrison, but he sure sounded like my kind of guy. And that day, with my head full of tears and the rain pounding against the windows, the song went straight to my gut. It started out almost like circus music, but when Jim Morrison's voice joined the instruments, the circus became a sinister, lonely place, where faces were ugly, women were wicked, and people forgot your name.

I'd been to that circus too. Looking out my window, I swear I saw Dad's face in the rain—just for a split second—before he disappeared into the storm. Then I caught a glimpse of Patty and Cindy, laughing wickedly in their fancy boots at Dad's funeral.

None of it made sense in a linear way, but poetically, Morrison's words nailed my sadness perfectly. If only I could talk to him, but he was dead. Once again, I thought of that Valium in the bathroom.

Then the DJ asked the author why Morrison's death, allegedly in a Paris bathtub, still evoked so much mystery. The author replied that only a couple of people—all of whom were also dead—claimed to have seen Jim's body, and their accounts of his death didn't exactly add up. He also reminded the DJ that Jim loved playing pranks on people, and that several of his songs and poems—"Moonlight Drive", "Yes, the River Knows"—focus on his obsession with drowning.

"I see," said the DJ dramatically. "So you're implying that Morrison is still playing his biggest prank ever. On the world."

The author cleared his throat. "No one can say for sure. But we can't rule out the possibility that he never actually died."

The cover of *No One Here Gets Out Alive* seized me the way Farah Fawcett's bathing suit poster had seized millions of others a few years earlier. I obsessed over Jim's intense eyes, his sculpted cheekbones, his pillowy lips. His sexuality oozed in every direction, and his Christlike arms stretched wide, waiting impatiently for me to fall into them. My breathing faltered, and a foreign wetness struck between my legs. And I was still in the bookstore.

When I got home, I ran straight to my room, locked the door, and studied every page of that orange-and-yellow paperback like a guidebook for the rest of my life. And you know what? Maybe it was.

That cover photo was striking for sure, but the pictures inside were even better. Jim, bare-chested, a strand of beads flung rakishly around his neck ... Jim on a beach in tight leather pants ... Jim in a poet shirt holding a wineglass, his wild hair resembling the curls of an angel. Even the more disturbing shots, like the one of him sprawled on a stage floor—almost passed out but still clutching a microphone, still trying to sing—elevated him to superhuman status in my book.

I stayed up reading most of the night, and by morning, I'd been transformed. Until that moment, I'd associated liquor and drugs with losers, danger, and (of course) car accidents. But Jim partied *romantically*. His drinking was *glamorous*. He didn't get wasted and crash a car into a seawall; he used alcohol and drugs to blow peoples' *minds.* Chemicals *unleashed* him; they made him *brilliant.* Reality was too boring for Jim. And come to think of it, it was too boring for me as well. After all, what would I do with a plain old high school boy like Todd Eldridge? I needed Jim. And if he was alive on this planet, I'd find him.

The following Saturday, when Mom and I took the bus and train into Boston, I scanned every guy in sight for resemblances to the Lizard King. Because Jim couldn't just run around in those snakeskin pants anymore, right? No. He needed to lie low, wherever he was.

Since he'd "died" ten years earlier at age twenty-seven, I tried to imagine how he'd look at thirty-seven. And how would he choose to disguise himself? *Probably with lots of facial hair.* That'd be the best way to hide his strong jawline and sexy lips. I'd learned from *No One Here Gets Out Alive* that after leaving America for Paris, he'd grown a big beard, which had enabled him to stay unrecognized by most people overseas.

Mom and I had planned the Boston shopping trip as a reward for surviving the winter without Dad. She'd decided we deserved some fun new spring clothes, and Filene's Basement in Downtown Crossing was our favorite place to bargain hunt. Every time we went, we found amazing stuff among the unfolded items strewn on tables and on the automatic markdown racks, where discounts could run as high as ninety percent.

"Look at these pants, Erin!" shouted Mom, paying no attention to the people around her. "They'd be so cute on you!"

"Mom, they're filthy and too small." I rolled my eyes at the white Chic jeans in her hand. They must have been rescued from a fire or something. Both legs were marked with random gray smudges, and everything on the table smelled faintly of smoke.

"Well, try 'em on, Erin. I think they're big enough, and they're only five bucks. They just need a good washin'."

I'd never owned a pair of jeans with a designer label before, unless Levis count as designer. "Here," said Mom, "go behind that rack. I'll make sure no one peeks."

That was another unique thing about Filene's Basement: it had no dressing rooms. Customers needed to stake out secluded areas of the store for trying stuff on, all the while keeping an eye out for creepy dudes and nosy kids. I never understood why they couldn't put up a curtain or something, but getting undressed in public added a whole new level of anxiety to the shopping experience. Luckily, the low prices and quality of the clothes made it all worthwhile.

And the pants zipped! They were skintight, but I could walk and sit down in them. "See what I mean?" said Mom with a satisfied smile. "You're thinnin' out, Erin. You've got a beautiful figure."

No one with a beautiful figure wears size fourteen, I thought. But I didn't say it because Mom was significantly bigger. Instead, I asked, "Hey, would you mind if I ran over to Stairway to Heaven? Just for a little while?"

She couldn't disguise her disappointment. "Oh, you're not gonna spend the whole morning lookin' at records, are you, Erin? This is our day together."

"No. I'll be back in time for blueberry muffins at Jordan Marsh. Half an hour. I promise."

Reluctantly, she agreed. But as the escalator carried me up toward street level, I glanced back and barely recognized my own mom from that angle. She'd been too tired to dye her hair since Dad's death, but when had the roots changed from salt-and-pepper to pure salt? And when did she start slouching like that? Her stomach pooched over the top of her stretchy pants, and one of her wide bra straps drooped lazily on her bare upper arm. If I'd had more time, I would've run back and fixed it for her, but my clock was ticking.

Outside on the crowded street, the oily smell of roasted nuts hung heavy in the late morning air, but I swallowed my hunger and jogged across Washington Street and up Winter to Stairway to Heaven, Boston's best and most famous record store/head shop. I don't know if Stairway made more money selling albums or weed-smoking accessories, but they were obviously doing something right because the place was always packed.

Entering Stairway intimidated me a bit, but I loved sifting through the album bins and browsing through t-shirts and posters, especially the velvet ones that turned fluorescent under black light. That day, a bunch of tough-looking punks in black t-shirts and camouflage pants milled around the imported 45s while over by the checkout, two boys wearing skinny ties and eyeliner chatted with a cute girl in a vintage prom dress about a local band called Human Sexual Response. I envied kids with enough courage to walk around that way, but took comfort in knowing that most Stairway customers were more like me; we went there with our pimples, dirty jeans and corduroys in search of the records that would someday define us.

And wow, what a stash I left with. Three Doors albums, all second-hand, and only a few bucks each: *The Doors, Strange Days,* and *Waiting for the Sun.* The pictures on the jackets thrilled me almost as much as the promise of the music inside, and I didn't even bother to examine the actual vinyl for scratches. I just paid as fast as I could and ran back to meet Mom for breakfast.

A few hours later, I dropped my stash from Filene's Basement—in addition to the jeans, I'd picked out a couple of shirts and some underwear—on the kitchen table, and disappeared into my room with the albums. Finally, I could be alone with those new pictures of Jim! I ran my fingers over the close-up of his face on the cover of the Doors' first album, paying special attention to his stellar cheekbones and magnificent lips. Sadly, *Strange Days* didn't feature any photos of that caliber, but *Waiting for the Sun* provided a full body shot of the whole band. At first, the picture didn't grab me because Jim looked drab and pale, and he wasn't wearing his traditional leather, just normal clothes. But then I noticed the sun on the horizon, and realized his frustration came from *waiting.* Waiting for daylight, waiting for happiness. Waiting, perhaps, for someone like me.

He stared straight into the camera too, hands over his crotch, and I couldn't help imagining what lay beneath those hands. Penises sort of grossed me out—maybe because a guy on the beach had flashed me when I was young—but when I studied Jim's beautiful face, I knew *his* private area couldn't possibly be as ugly and hairy as that flasher's. My cheeks heated up with shame and anticipation as I kissed the record jacket, first on Jim's mouth, then on those hands covering his crotch. It was only cardboard, of course; still, I felt the slightest bit of disappointment when I pulled away from that cool, lifeless surface.

The music, however, was far more encouraging. The first few songs on *Strange Days* skipped badly due to deep scratches in the vinyl, but when I coaxed the needle ahead, I fell in love with "Unhappy Girl," the fourth track, which could've been written specifically for me. In it, a girl has somehow locked herself in prison, but Jim tells her she can escape if she tries. He says she can cut through her bars and free herself, maybe even *melt* her cell away. *Could I do that too?* I mean, I certainly hadn't locked myself up, but I desperately longed for freedom.

Next, came a confusing poem called "Horse Latitudes," followed by the best Doors song of all time, "Moonlight Drive." I'd been dying to hear how it sounded because it'd been discussed so much in *No One Here Gets Out Alive*. But even though I'd memorized all the lyrics, nothing could've prepared me for the song's musical intensity. Jim Morrison's voice plunged me straight into the ocean with him as he swam to the moon and climbed through the tide. And when he moaned about *penetrating* the evening with me, I collapsed on my bed in a puddle. Until that afternoon, I'd never thought much about the word *penetrate*. But after listening to "Moonlight Drive" a few times, I wanted Jim to penetrate me in every possible way.

Chapter 7

August 1992

Thanks to Claire, my two weeks temping at Don-Wash flew by. I only managed to set up one appointment for Tara and Amy—adding a whopping twenty dollars (minus taxes) to my paycheck—but Don claimed to be impressed, and when he called me into his office and asked me to stay on as a real employee, I said yes.

The hour-long commute each way in my shitbox car? Oh well. The Honda still ran after two weeks, so maybe it'd keep going for years. *Working in a dingy, trailer-like building with a broken air conditioner?* Hey, September was right around the corner, so things would cool off soon enough. Hanging out with Claire was so much fun, and I loved her stories about Bobby and his band. Most of the time, I'd just listen and comment, but every now and then, I'd imply that Colin and I had been romantically involved. I hated lying to Claire, but feared she'd stop confiding in me about Bobby if she found out I'd never had a real boyfriend.

And Claire shared *a lot* of her Bobby issues with me. One thing that really upset her involved a song he'd written a few years earlier about an ex-girlfriend who still lived in the Boston area. According to Claire, the song—a fan favorite—was driving a wedge between Bobby and her. "You know," she said one day at work, "everyone expects me to be all cool about it, but it makes me wanna fuckin' scream. It's called 'Lizzy' and it's about how he loves this chick so much but 'can't touch that part of her that needs touching' or some shit like that. And I'm supposed to stand there smiling like an idiot, as if I have no feelings. It ... I don't know. Sometimes I seriously think about taking a break from Bobby."

"Would you really do that?" I asked.

She shrugged. "I don't know. I mean, I don't want to. I love him like crazy and we talk about having kids, and ... the whole thing. It's just ... sometimes he doesn't respect my feelings."

"Hmm," I said. "That's a tough situation."

"No shit. It's fuckin' ridiculous." She paused and took a breath. "What would you do, Reardon? You know, if you were still with Colin and he humiliated you like that?"

My heart raced. I had no idea, but I loved it when Claire sought my advice. "I don't know. I mean, Bobby's obviously an awesome guy. What does he say when you talk to him about the song?"

She replied with a wince. "First time I heard it, I told him it made me cringe, and he yanked it right off the set list. I didn't hear it again for like two years. If someone at a show requested it, Bobby'd act like he didn't hear 'em. But then he got really hammered one night at Green Street, and when someone yelled out, 'Lizzy,' he told the band to play it. And they did."

"What'd *you* do?"

"Well, considering that Bobby couldn't remember anything about the performance the next day, I let it go. Everyone makes mistakes, right? But about a month later, they played it again. I got so pissed, I stayed at a friend's place that night, and then all of a sudden, 'Lizzy' was back on the regular set list. And Bobby says they're gonna leave it there now 'cause it brings in the crowds."

"Crowds?" I said. "Shouldn't Bobby be more worried about pleasing *you* than crowds?"

Claire was quiet for a few seconds, and I thought I'd overstepped. But then she smiled. "You're right, Reardon. I need to talk to him again."

Hearing those words convinced me—at least for a few hours—that I'd never binge and purge again. *I don't need that shit any more,* I decided. *I have a good friend, and I don't wanna lose her.* But that evening, as I headed home, I stopped into the Cape Ann Market. My plan was to buy something healthy for dinner and maybe a *little* ice cream for dessert, but when I entered the store, my self-control walked straight out. By the time I arrived at the cash register, I'd acquired a day-old cake covered in greasy frosting, a half-gallon of cheap, store-brand ice cream, and a box of Captain Crunch. Then I spent a painful evening at my apartment with Lenny and Winterlong, eating, vomiting, and promising to quit the very next day.

When Tara, Amy, and Don traveled to sales meetings with customers, Claire and I had the office to ourselves. And although we still got our work done, we also snuck in plenty of gossip about our coworkers. Since Claire had gone to high school with the Don-Wash salesgirls, she knew firsthand that they drank for free at every bar in Gloucester. "In a nutshell," she said, "their bodies are more familiar than fish to the local fishermen."

"But they sell so many t-shirts," I countered. "And they're at work bright and early every morning. That's pretty impressive."

"Yeah. And you know what's not impressive? Having an affair with Dirty Don. *Pathetic*'s the word for that."

I knew she was referring to Tara's thing with Don, but my stomach twitched anyway. "She seems happy enough."

Claire stared straight at me like she was trying to assess my sanity. "Reardon, I don't care if she's happy. Nor do I care if she bangs a million guys. But I fucking *hate* the way Don lets her treat us like slaves because she sucks his smelly dick. Someday, I swear I'm gonna call up that dipshit wife of his and tell her exactly what's going on around here. I don't care if I get fired. It'll be worth it to see Don get tossed out of his house."

"Oh, come on! You wouldn't really do that, would you? You'd lose all your job flexibility. Plus, I couldn't handle Don-Wash without you."

She sighed. "Yeah, but this is a toxic environment, Reardon, and it's not cool. Not to mention that it's illegal to screw your employees. We should report him to the cops. He's worse than Clarence Thomas."

I smiled and picked up the phone, hoping to end the discussion right there. Discussing Don's sex life was a real sore spot for me. Because Don and I had a few secrets of our own.

It'd all started innocently enough. One afternoon, shortly after being hired, I'd been walking out of Don's office when his hand apparently slipped off the doorknob and onto my ass. "I'm glad you work for me, Erin," he said calmly, the hand unmoving, his eyes targeting mine like grinning lasers.

"Me too," I answered, before bolting back to my desk. Luckily, Claire was on the phone with Bobby, so I had a couple of minutes to freak out privately.

But after that, the butt-touching became a habit. Sometimes Don would sneak up behind my desk when Claire was in the bathroom to give it a pat; other times, he'd rub me discreetly at the water cooler, or slip in a squeeze when he passed me in the narrow hallway where we stored the office supplies. And although I knew I should've been angry and indignant, I actually felt a little thrill every time it happened. I guess I was relieved to know that someone considered me attractive.

When I think back on my Don-Wash days, I imagine someone pressing the *play* button on a boombox. Which makes sense in a literal way, because Claire and I would blast our Winterlong tapes on the office boombox whenever Don traveled out of town with Tara and Amy. But the other button getting pushed was deep inside me. For the first time ever, I had a real job, a cool girlfriend, and a flesh-and-blood guy fondling me. All day long, as the Erin Reardon tape played, I'd feel alive. But as I headed back to Winthrop, the tape would slow and fade with each passing mile. By the time I reached home, I'd be back on pause, and on nights when I felt particularly weak, I'd worry about stopping for good.

One sunny August evening, Claire and I drove over to Good Harbor Beach to eat pizza on the sand and sip red wine from her Thermos. The waves were higher than normal, and a bunch of cute surfer guys were taking advantage of the situation. Most of them said hello as they strutted past with their boards, and I swear a couple actually checked me out. Of course, they checked Claire out too, but still. I couldn't help blushing.

"You're one voluptuous chick, Reardon," said Clair after her second—or third—paper cup of wine. "Guys must love your ass."

I thought about Don and smiled inside, even though our boss didn't qualify as a guy in Claire's estimation. "Yeah right. Everyone loves fat girls with zits." I had a long drive home ahead of me, so I was drinking way slower than Claire.

Claire frowned and tapped her skull with her index finger. "Reardon, you're whacked. Do you know how many skinny girls would kill for your curves? And those eyes of yours? You look like a painting by, like, Raphael or something. And who gives a shit about a couple of pimples? Pimples are natural. If you want my advice, you should flaunt your gifts you've got. Seriously. Confidence is everything."

I stared at Claire, lounging there on the beach—not even five feet tall and probably about a hundred pounds—in a tight black t-shirt and little denim cutoffs that somehow made her look like she belonged on

Mick Jagger's arm. Claire didn't spend much money on clothes, but she was an expert thrift shopper. "Whatever you say," I replied.

"Good. 'Cause I know what I'm talkin' about. Women are all just arms and legs and tits and vaginas. The trick is believing that *your* arms and legs and tits and vagina are special. Once you do that, everyone else'll agree."

I smiled and played with the sand. "Okay."

"You think I'm kidding? Reardon, I was a total dork in high school until I decided I was sick of being overlooked. You have to start loving yourself. For real."

"Hmm." I wasn't in the mood for one of those *pretty on the inside* talks, so I nodded. "Hey, it's getting dark. I better hit the road."

"All right, but let me take you shopping after work tomorrow."

"No way," I answered immediately. But when I saw the hurt look on her face, I backpedaled. "I mean, where would we go?"

"Ha! That's *my* secret. Just make sure you bring extra cash with you, 'cause the place we're going doesn't take credit cards."

"I don't have a credit card," I said.

"Awesome," said Claire. "Neither do I."

The next day, we ate lunch at our desks and left Don-Wash at 4:30. And somehow, in a dark and funky little consignment shop in Rockport, Claire convinced me to buy a pair of vintage bellbottom jeans that looked like they'd been teleported straight out of 1972.

"Don't worry," she said when I hesitated. "New Englanders haven't quite rediscovered bellbottoms yet, but *everyone* in New York's wearing 'em. By next spring, they'll be huge here. Trust me. Bellbottoms look amazing on curvy girls."

The jeans fit pretty snugly, but I brought them home and tried them on again in my bedroom. And after a while, I glimpsed a tiny fragment of Claire's vision. No, I didn't feel amazing in the bellbottoms, but they did sort of balance out my tall, wide body.

Jeff and Pete expressed their approval by saying things like *smokin'!* and *badass!* So I snipped off the tags from the store and hung the pants in my closet. Then I made a grilled cheese sandwich, poured a glass of wine, and didn't vomit. I didn't even want to.

I'm gonna be okay, I thought as I fell asleep. *I'm gonna beat this thing.*

But a week later, the worst Friday in history happened.

I woke up hungover and sweaty, with the DJ on the radio warning people to be careful if they needed to be outside during the day. The thermometer already read ninety degrees, and the humidity was increasing by the moment. We didn't have air conditioning in the apartment, but I considered calling in sick anyway. I felt like shit.

Lenny Weir had been scheduled to appear on *The Tonight Show with Jay Leno* the previous night, but he hadn't shown up for the taping. At the start of the program, Jay had announced the comedian who'd take Lenny's place, but I'd watched the entire broadcast, hoping my man would miraculously appear. Besides, I'd already popped the cork on a bottle of white zinfandel.

It wasn't my best decision. The comedian sucked, and I ended up drunk, angry, and frustrated. I didn't sleep well either, and my head was throbbing. But I also realized I should rally and go to work because Don had the day off, and Claire hated being stuck in the office with Amy and Tara.

So I pulled on my lightest sundress and dragged my sticky butt out the door to dump water into the car's radiator. Then I opened all the windows and turned on the heater. The Honda had been running poorly over the past couple of days, but what could I do? With some luck, things would improve after the heat wave. Driving through Revere, the needle on the temperature gauge plunged into the red zone, and I tasted vomit. *Cheap fucking wine,* I thought.

Hoping the DJs might have an explanation for Lenny's failure to appear on the *Leno* show, I switched on the local "alternative" radio station, but they were too busy spewing sports drivel. "I think you could fry an egg on Mo Vaughn's stomach today," said one of the DJs, referring to the overweight Red Sox player. "You know why the Sox haven't won a World Series in all these years? They're all frying eggs on Mo Vaughn's stomach. Dude, did you see how *slow* that guy moved last night? Too many eggs, man. Too many eggs."

That didn't even make sense, but the other DJ laughed anyway. "Well, I don't know from eggs, but I know it's hot out there. Word on the street is we might hit a hundred this afternoon. Whassup with that?"

"Global warming," the first DJ said matter-of-factly. "Haven't you heard about that? Or else Rodan's just really pissed off, and this time, he's taking no prisoners."

"Ohmigod, tell me you're not blaming the heat on *Rodan!*" The second guy launched into a fit of hysterical, fake laughter. "Is that where your mind's at, dude? *Creature Double Feature?* 'Cause that explains a lot about you. A *lot.*"

"Hey, at least I'm not into the Spice Girls," countered the first guy, "like some people I know. But let's not mention any names." The other guy tried to protest, but the first one talked right over him. "All right, all right. Let's play some music. How 'bout a little something from Sublime?"

The needle on the car's thermostat rose a bit higher. "Shit!" I shouted, pulling into the breakdown lane as poor Bradley Newell sang about getting high and having a Dalmation, and I burped up a mouthful of stomach acid. Using every foul word I knew, I turned off the engine, staggered out onto the scorching pavement, popped the hood, and waited for the car to cool down enough for me to remove the radiator cap and add more water. Then I stood back, panting and trying to avoid the intense heat coming off the engine block. I had a bad feeling about the day, but I was more than halfway to Gloucester. It made sense to keep going.

"... yeah, gotta love them Chili Peppers," mused the lead DJ as I started the car again twenty minutes later. "I remember seeing 'em in New York when they used to wear nothing but socks on stage. Those were the days, huh? Although I never did understand how those socks stayed on. What d'ya think they used? Duct tape?"

"Ouch!" said the second guy. "Maybe Velcro?"

"Oh, shut the fuck up!" I screamed, punching the radio off as the heater blasted my face. "What a bunch of fucking *morons!* Get a real job!"

I felt so sick, I thought I might have a panic attack, but somehow, I pressed on in angry, anxious silence. By then, my only goal was to arrive at work without the Honda totally croaking. So in that regard, I was successful.

"Fuck!" I whispered, slipping into my seat beside Claire. At first, I thought she was napping because her head was down on the desk. The office air conditioner had quit completely, and whole place smelled like a blend of sweat and Don's cologne. His cologne constantly lingered in the building. "Ohmigod, this place reeks! Did someone call Don about the AC?"

But when Claire sat up, all I saw was mascara running down her cheeks. "Didn't you hear?" she asked through her tears.

"What?"

"Don't you ... listen ..." She couldn't finish the sentence.

"Claire! What happened?" A chill ran up my spine in the hot room.

"He's gone," Claire blurted. "He caught on fire and he's dead. Lenny's dead."

Chapter 8

October 1980

Like so many other high school girls, I broke up with my first boyfriend because of jealousy. *No One Here Gets Out Alive* turned out to be one of the best-selling paperbacks in history, and by fall of 1980, half the kids at Winthrop High worshipped at the Church of Jim Morrison. You couldn't walk through the outdoor smoking area without spotting at least one *Doors* t-shirt or pin, and every other locker in the school seemed to have a photo of Jim taped inside it. Morrison even made the cover of *Rolling Stone,* despite the fact that he'd supposedly been dead for ten years.

Even worse, lots of burnout girls had begun wearing their hair long and straight with bangs, like Jim's former girlfriend, Pamela Courson. And they were all so much prettier than me! No amount of cream rinse could turn my thick, frizzy hair smooth and glossy like that.

But I didn't give up right away. For a while, I clung to the hope that some other rock star—perhaps one who was *undeniably* alive—would somehow overshadow Jim in popularity at school. But when Patty walked into the lunchroom one December day sporting silver hoop earrings and a tight black t-shirt with Jim's face on the front, I had to step back. I mean, Patty and her cheerleader friends usually listened to Pat Benatar, REO Speedwagon, and Bob Seger. So if *they'd* turned into Doors fans, I had no hope.

Of course, no one else understood Jim the way I did, and none of the other kids at school wanted—or needed—to break on through to any other side. Not to mention that they'd never *begin* to comprehend the agony of the swimming horses in "Horse Latitudes." But Jim had become a commodity—like Elvis Presley—and I'd have to wait for the hype to settle down. It wasn't easy having a rock star for a boyfriend. Especially when he couldn't be seen in public.

I continued to act happy and carefree throughout junior year, but the teachers may have sensed my struggles because I skipped numerous assignments but still got A's and B's for final grades. And although I didn't participate much in class, teachers rarely busted my balls or gave me a hard time. On the surface, then, I was having a decent academic year.

I probably appeared to be doing well socially too. Certainly, I had no enemies, and with my well-rehearsed smile, I managed to blend into the day-to-day tapestry at Winthrop High. I perfected the art of staying just a few shades murkier than invisible.

Kids I knew waved to me in the halls, but no one stopped to chat. Acquaintances who sat nearby in class would make small talk when the teacher stepped out for a moment, but didn't initiate meaningful conversations. And while I continued to eat at Patty and Cindy's lunch table, nobody sought out my emotional support. I never got invited to peoples' homes *after* school either, or to beach parties down on Point Shirley, or on shopping trips I'd overhear other girls planning. When groups of kids went to the movies, or ice-skating at the local rink, or into Boston for all-ages rock concerts, no one asked me to join them.

And for a while, I let myself believe that I *would've* been part of those activities had there been more room in the car, or if I was a bigger fan of the band the kids were seeing, or if I could skate better. But by Christmas of junior year, I began to lose hope. My only real chance of a social life at Winthrop High revolved around the possibility of a new kid moving to town and befriending me. Otherwise, things had gone too far; my father's blood had left me with an ugly, permanent stain. No one was more surprised than I when I found a new pal in my very own home.

Every weekday, I walked home from school, let myself in with a key, and watched TV or did homework until Mom got out of work. When Dad had been alive, Mom wouldn't drink until dinnertime, but after his death, she'd mix up a gin and tonic before even taking off her shoes. "Heaven," she'd say—almost like a prayer—before indulging in a long sip and collapsing in a chair.

She now worked more hours than ever before, but also knew she was lucky to remain employed. Operators all over the country were getting laid off, and as the phone company automated more and more of its systems, it was only a matter of time before her job became obsolete. In the meantime, her daily responsibilities grew more challenging, and the social aspects of her job—once a major benefit—were now almost non-existent.

Maybe that was why she anesthetized herself so thoroughly each evening. She'd polish off at least one more gin-and-tonic during dinner, then move on to the jug wine. I quickly learned to relay any important news or information to her the minute she walked in the door, because if I waited until later, she'd forget by morning. I hated seeing my mother drunk, but was strangely jealous of her too. Sure, alcohol compromised her abilities, but unlike me, she had a way to temporarily escape her pain.

The liquor cabinet had fascinated me since I was a little kid. Back then, Mom would let me remove all the bottles and line them up on the kitchen floor on rainy days. I'm not sure how many existed then—at least thirty—but most were older than me and hadn't been opened in years: relics from the days when my parents entertained with cocktails and onion dip. Bailey's Irish Cream, Galliano, triple sec, crème de menthe, crème de cacao, Kahlua, several types of schnapps, and more. I loved the colors of the liquids, the shapes of the bottles; they reminded me of fancy perfumes. But I had no interest in *drinking* them.

That all changed, however, after *No One Here Gets Out Alive*. Suddenly, the bottles began jingling seductively each time I passed the liquor cabinet. And I knew Mom didn't take regular inventory. She trusted me, and the only bottles she monitored closely were her gin and jug wine. When either of those hit the half-empty mark, she'd replace them at her next opportunity.

Now it did occur to me that some of those ancient liquids might have rotted with age, so I went to the library to research the shelf life of alcohol, and concluded that none of them would poison me—at least not immediately. One afternoon, after finishing my homework, I twisted the cover off a sugar-crusted bottle of peach schnapps and got buzzed for the first time. It didn't take much either—just a few sips. The whole experience was sort of magical; I felt like *Alice in Wonderland,* except I didn't shrink. I just got numb. And I *loved* it.

I established an entire new after-school routine. Now, instead of lingering at my locker hoping someone might invite me to a party, I could scurry home to my own party! I developed an immediate preference for Kahlua and Bailey's, but soon recognized the importance of treating all the bottles equally so as not to arouse Mom's suspicion. Underage alcohol thieves can't be too picky.

Anyway, once the buzz set in, I'd wipe up the counter and return the bottle *du jour* to its designated spot in the cabinet, then head to my room and turn on the radio. By then, the WBCN DJs had become my closest friends and favorite teachers. They were always there, and always willing to share their extensive knowledge about music and rock history. And they loved introducing students like me to new bands and artists breaking onto the scene. Of course, I'd discovered Queen and Jim Morrison on BCN, but it was also the first place I heard the Cars, the Clash, the Police, Roxy Music, U2, Tom Petty, Blondie, and the Pretenders. BCN's airwaves quivered with restlessness and camaraderie, and listening to the station made me feel like a vital part of the exciting new wave rocking the music world.

Everything's gonna be okay, I'd think, lying there with the radio beside my liquored-up head. And when you're a sad, lonely girl who gets her kicks from stealing her mom's semi-rancid booze on a daily basis, it couldn't get much worse. But most days, my eyes were fixed on a prize dangling less than two years in front of me: college. I couldn't wait to get to that place—far away from Winthrop—where I'd begin life all over again, fresh and clean.

Then there were the afternoons—when I drank more than usual—when I'd dream of jetting off to an exotic island with a rock star like Bono or Bryan Ferry. In those fantasies, I'd bypass higher education altogether and go straight for the glamour. But the three core principals remained the same:

1. *Life for me would soon change dramatically.*
2. *The transformation would begin with my escape from Winthrop and its seawall of death.*
3. *Once away, I'd make lots of friends and fall madly in love.*

Inevitably, though, the alcohol would start to wear off, and doubt would rush in to replace my fantasies. I mean, how could Mom afford to send me away to college? Most likely, I'd end up taking the T to one of local commuter schools, where I'd get a two-year degree in something practical and boring. And what would Bono or Bryan Ferry want with a loser like me? My doubt would turn to full-on depression, and I'd hurry back to the kitchen for a few more gulps of something sticky and warm. Then I'd climb under the covers and doze until dinnertime.

As you might guess, my private, booze-fueled rollercoaster became less thrilling after about a month. But I'm glad I stayed on it, because a new twist—in the form of Mr. David Bowie—was about to change everything.

I'd actually been introduced to Bowie about eight years earlier, in 1972. Even now, the scene remains clear in my mind. I was in second grade, reading a Nancy Drew book on the back porch while my father flipped absentmindedly through the latest issue of *Newsweek*.

Dad and I often spent summer afternoons together during the post-Natalie Cotechi days. He'd drink a beer or two, and we'd read and talk about stuff like school, Mark Spitz, or my favorite TV show, *The Odd Couple*. Sometimes he'd ruffle my hair when he walked past, and would occasionally mutter, "I love you, kid," even though his eyes would water when he spoke those words. But on that particular day, Dad totally alarmed me by letting out a groan and slamming his magazine shut.

"What's the matter, Dad?" I asked.

His forehead knotted in anger, but he turned his pale blue eyes toward the sea. "Nothin'," he said, tossing the magazine aside.

How could I resist investigating further? Later on, when my parents were both asleep in their respective spots—Dad on the couch, Mom in the bedroom—I snuck back onto the porch and snagged the magazine. And it didn't take long to figure out the issue.

I actually felt a little upset too, but also couldn't help staring. There, on the glossy pages normally reserved for stories about Nixon, Vietnam, cancer, and Skylab, were photos of a man dressed up like a crazy-looking woman. But the guy clearly wasn't trying to be funny, like when Flip Wilson performed as Geraldine. No, even though this guy—whose name was David Bowie—looked completely bizarre, I could tell *he* thought he looked *good*. In one picture, he wore a tight, powder-blue pantsuit, silver high-heeled boots, earrings, and a shade of blue eye shadow popular with teenage girls. He also had bright red hair—cut in a short, womanly way—and a shy, boy-next-door grin on his face. It may have been the strangest thing I'd ever seen.

I mean, why would anyone do that? His tight pants left no question about his manhood, so why was he was on stage in front of an audience, smiling and singing as if it were all perfectly normal? On the next page, he strummed a blue guitar in a leopard-print suit and shiny leather lace-up boots in one picture, and let his butt cheeks peek out from beneath the hem of a woman's blouse in another. But the weirdest photo of all was the one of him kneeling in front of another man playing electric guitar, and sticking out his tongue like he wanted to lick the strings. But the article claimed that David Bowie was married to a *woman* and had a son with her.

What the hell? I thought. I mean, what the *freaking* hell? My stomach felt queasy, but I also wanted to keep the magazine. Unfortunately, I couldn't do that, because Dad would know it was gone. So I put it back where I'd found it, and the next day, Dad cleaned up all the newspapers and magazines in the house and put them out for the trash truck.

By May of '81, I'd learned to mix my booze with various juices and sodas to make them more palatable, and quickly started draining the bottles under the kitchen sink. I wasn't sure what I'd do when they went dry. Certainly, I'd need a new source of alcohol, because it was my only escape from the drudgery of daily life.

I hated Mondays at school the most. All day long, I'd overhear gossip in the hallways about the various events that had happened over the weekend: who'd hooked up, broken up, or gotten really fucked up. It was torture. My peers lived exciting, sexual lives, while at almost seventeen years of age, I'd never even kissed a boy.

But the end of the week sucked too, because as the weather got warmer, more and more kids got drunk or stoned *before* school on Thursdays and Fridays. Talk about feeling left out. Even school was starting to feel like a party I hadn't been invited to, and I couldn't believe how many teachers appeared not to notice all the intoxicated students cruising around the building. In fact, according to rumors I'd heard, some of the younger, hipper teachers actually smoked weed with kids from time to time. Then, someone would run out to buy snacks to munch on during class.

You might assume I was psyched for summer vacation, but you'd be wrong. Because the only thing worse than feeling like a ghost all day at school is waking up in the morning with absolutely *nothing* to do. If I hadn't landed an awesome waitressing job at the Sand Dollar, I might've done something desperate.

I'd wanted to work at the Sand Dollar since I was about five. I loved its blueberry pancakes and syrupy smell, and couldn't wait for the opportunity to *serve* people. It may seem weird, but the idea of waitressing struck me as very romantic. And, of course, if Jim Morrison ever stopped in for breakfast, I'd recognize him immediately.

But I didn't start work until July, so as junior year drew to a close, I began making my afternoon cocktails even stronger, and napping more soundly. Hence, getting up to eat dinner with Mom became a serious challenge. Some days—when I was too out of it to face her—I'd lie and tell her I was dieting. Which Mom seemed to consider a great idea.

Of course, I'd wake up starving a couple of hours later. So I'd struggle through my homework and wait for Mom to go to bed. Then I'd tiptoe out to the kitchen and cook myself some Kraft macaroni or a can of SpaghettiOs.

"You feelin' okay, Erin?" called Mom one night from her darkened bedroom.

I'd just finished writing a paper titled "Thoreau, Emerson, and the Transcendental Movement." Or maybe I shouldn't say *written*, since I'd really just paraphrased a bunch of bullshit from a library book. But my English teacher wasn't the type to bust people for plagiarism.

"Yeah, Mom! I'm fine. Just grabbing a snack."

"Okay, honey," she said. "But get to bed soon. It's 11:30 and you've been lookin' tired lately."

I definitely wasn't looking my best. My face was puffy and pale, I got lots of headaches, and all my jeans were too tight. "It's this diet I'm on," I muttered.

"What's that, honey?"

"Nothing, Mom. Go back to sleep." I opened the fridge and cringed at a plastic container of leftover beef stew with congealed fat on top. But what else could I eat? Ketchup, mustard, old deli meat, butter, Aunt Jemima maple syrup, orange juice, a few slices of Wonder Bread, milk. Mom would probably grocery shop the next day, but I needed food immediately, and the beef stew looked *way* too gross.

The milk was fresh, though, and I'd been rationing the Kahlua in the liquor cabinet because it tasted so good. I took one more look at the beef stew and decided to go with a Sombrero. Light on the Kahlua, heavy on the milk. It might actually be healthy.

A few minutes later, I was back in my room, feeling quite Hemingway-esque. The radio played softly by my side as I sipped and edited the shoddy English paper. *Oh well,* I thought as I closed my notebook, *it's good enough.* Not to mention that the drink was delicious.

"And now it's time for the Classic Album at Midnight, or what we like to call the *CAM* here at WBCN," announced the smooth-talking DJ. "And tonight, we've got a very special treat for you: David Bowie's *Ziggy Stardust* album. As always, the Classic Album at Midnight will be played in its entirety, completely commercial free."

I didn't normally pay much attention to the CAMs, because the late-night DJs tended to feature a lot of old Cream, Moody Blues, and Canned Heat. But I needed to finish my drink, and had always been curious about the *Ziggy Stardust* record. So I plugged in my headphones and slipped them over my ears just as the broken-sounding drumbeats of "Five Years" began pulsing through.

The rhythm grabbed me instantly; it was sad and urgent at the same time, like a diseased heart trying to keep beating. Then Bowie's distinctive nasal whine crept up over it, singing about someone trudging through a market square in the rain. Mothers were sighing, and a newsman announced that the world would end in five years. Then all kinds of terrible, freaky things happened. A girl beat up some tiny children, a cop knelt and kissed a priest's feet, and a "queer" vomited. But the main character—the guy trudging through the market square in the rain—kept thinking about someone he wanted to kiss.

Whoa. I'd never heard a song like that before. It sounded like poetry, but not the boring stuff we read in school. I thought about the pictures of Bowie I'd seen in *Newsweek* as a kid, and my English notebook slipped onto the floor.

The next song had a funkier vibe, but also revolved around themes of sadness and lonely people, like a mom kneeling at her son's grave. Then Bowie mentioned something about loneliness evolving, and I almost cried. *Yes,* I thought. *That's exactly what loneliness does.* People grow and change, but our loneliness evolves with us.

It'd never occurred to me that a guy like David Bowie—a man wacky enough to wear all those women's outfits and makeup on stage—could feel isolated. Or that his coy little smile camouflaged his sorrow. But that night, I understood. Crawling beneath the covers, I found myself wishing he could be there with me in my dark room. The record played on, but I paid little attention to the slicker, more upbeat songs. I wanted to hear more of Bowie's insecurity; that was the stuff I related to. I swooned when his voice wavered, when I could feel his vulnerability.

He obviously questioned his sexuality too, especially in "Lady Stardust," a torch song about a boy in bright blue jeans watching a drag queen sing on a stage. But partway through, the song changed from third-person to first, and suddenly, Bowie was that boy: the skinny kid watching from afar, sighing, and *wanting* the drag queen so badly. Maybe that was why David dressed like a woman onstage: to let people know it was okay, that they weren't alone. He knew firsthand how it felt to have to hide your true self.

But why was the world such an unfair place? My shoulders trembled as I sobbed into my pillow, my tears warming then cooling the fabric. I thought about Todd Eldridge and his new girlfriend, a quiet clarinet player in the marching band who constantly chewed her pencil in study hall. What did Todd see in her? And why didn't he talk to *me*? What was *wrong* with me?

I felt like the drag queen in "Lady Stardust," a person so strange that others only watched from a distance. Were they afraid of me? Disgusted? Unsure? And did they realize I was human like them? A lonely human who got buzzed on her mother's liquor every night just to feel temporarily okay?

Now, the *Ziggy Stardust* album was released nearly ten years before that night in 1981; David Bowie had even "killed" the character of Ziggy Stardust onstage in 1973. Since then, he'd changed his musical style and style of dress multiple times. But I chose not to acknowledge any of that because I liked Bowie as Ziggy. Maybe I even loved him. In any case, I wasn't ready for any of his other incarnations. Not yet, anyway.

Suddenly, I felt unnaturally warm and took off all my clothes. Normally, I hated being naked—I only undressed completely for the shower—but nothing about that night felt typical to me. I was drunk and not feeling at all like myself. The last thing I recall before falling asleep was Bowie reminding me I wasn't alone in the song "Rock 'n'

Roll Suicide." Which made sense. Because how could I be alone when I had David?

I awoke a few times during the night, drenched in sweat. But when I got up in the morning, my head throbbed with a combination of pain and excitement. There'd be no more drinking alone and going unnoticed at school for me. It was time for a brand new strategy.

Chapter 9

August 1992

Death enveloped me for weeks. Everywhere I looked, everything I read, everything on TV: it all related to death, and all led back to Lenny Weir. Lenny died. *My* Lenny. On August 27, 1992, this story made the front page of the Boston Globe.

The apparent remains of Lenny Weir, lead singer, guitarist, and principal songwriter for the grunge band Winterlong, were discovered yesterday outside the musician's Van Nuys, California home. According to a report released by local police, a badly burned body believed to be Mr. Weir's was discovered by his agent, Robert Kousakis, early Wednesday morning.

Kousakis told police he became concerned when Weir failed to appear at a taping of The Tonight Show on Tuesday evening. Kousakis made repeated attempts to contact the troubled musician throughout the night, and on Wednesday morning, drove to Weir's residence, where he found a body in the back yard. Police added that a "disturbing" note was discovered on Weir's kitchen table, but did not reveal its contents. An autopsy has been ordered, but foul play is not suspected at this time.

Nothing more. I watched multiple news reports and read every article I could get my hands on, but uncovered no additional information. The police wouldn't even confirm that the body in the yard was indisputably Lenny's. "It's all under investigation," said a detective during an MTV interview.

The entertainment media, of course, made a huge effort to talk with people close to Lenny—family, friends, band members, Violet Chasm—

but no one seemed interested in commenting. MTV threw together a retrospective on Lenny's career, then ran it about fifteen times a day. Meanwhile, all the major music magazines, plus *Time* and *People,* featured sentimental cover stories about him.

But I grew increasingly frustrated because the articles revealed nothing I didn't already know. They discussed Lenny's unremarkable boyhood as a shy Californian, his parents' divorce when he was ten, and how he dealt with the stress of being a teenager by playing guitar in his bedroom with the amp turned up to "eleven." They repeated (and repeated) the tale of Lenny dropping out of college after only one semester, reportedly telling his roommate, "School's for people who've already given up on life."

Another popular story dealt with Winterlong's early days. The band went through three drummers before discovering Shay Trochman, and actually started out with a different lead vocalist—a guy named Paul Wake—before Lenny summoned the courage to sing his own lyrics. But once Lenny started singing, the band kicked Paul out—not only because of his inferior voice, but also because he desperately needed help for his drug addiction. Unfortunately, Paul died of an overdose just a few weeks later, and Lenny never got over that loss.

Finally, after those stories had all been played out, several music magazines explored the rumor—circulated among Winterlong fans—that Lenny's only sibling had died during childhood. But although several reporters had questioned Lenny on the existence of such a sibling, he'd categorically refused to discuss the topic, and even walked out on one interview with a major newspaper when the question was broached. Still, he peppered his music with references to early death, and one song in particular—"Little One Gone"—did nothing to dispel the speculation.

But I *knew* all that. Every Winterlong fan did. We wanted to know what'd happened during Lenny's final days. Like why he hadn't shown up for *The Tonight Show* taping. And how he'd ended up burned past the point of recognition in his own backyard.

I anxiously awaited the release of the police report, and when it finally came out—in mid-September—the official cause of death was "suicide or accidental incineration." Which meant *nothing*. I mean, was it an accident or did he kill himself? The Van Nuys Police Department admitted they didn't know. In many ways, it appeared to have been suicide, but then again, they'd found camera equipment close to the body, and Lenny had recently told his band he wanted to make a video about fire's contribution to humanity. So he *may* have been working on his concept and screwed up royally.

Then, a day or two after the report's release, the police revealed the contents of the "note" found in Lenny's kitchen.

Deliver me down where I can breathe.
Fame gleams, but night reveals the hollow.
No more now, I cannot borrow
Another day, escape invades
Only your face could save me now.

Most people considered that to be Lenny's unique way of bidding a final farewell to the world. But others—like me—thought it sounded more like lyrics to a new Winterlong song. I mean, aren't suicide notes usually a little more direct? And don't people normally say things like *goodbye* and *I'm sorry* in them? In other words, the note didn't give me much closure.

Not that it made a hell of a lot of difference, because dead was dead. And the more I thought about it, the sadder I got. I mean, was it possible that Lenny was talking about *my* face in those final words he'd ever write? Had he been working on a song for me, the beautiful girl he'd met in the Middle East bathroom?

All over the world, people held ceremonies in Lenny's memory. They lit candles, said prayers, and sang his songs while weeping and hugging. In Central Square, Cambridge, where I'd seen him perform just five months earlier, fans planned an all-night vigil outside the Middle East nightclub.

But I didn't attend. Claire invited me to go with Bobby and her, but I said no, I'd be too upset. Which was true. But I also feared resenting certain fans so badly that I wouldn't be able to mourn Lenny in a respectful way. I mean, just the thought of hearing complete strangers sharing their Lenny stories freaked me out. They'd never spent any time alone with him or looked him straight in the eye. The way I saw it, vigils like the one in Cambridge were for the masses, not people who'd actually known Lenny Weir.

Early in October, Winterlong's bass player, Max Lee, went on *The Arsenio Hall Show* and informed the world that Lenny and Violet Chasm had broken up (for perhaps the fifth time) a few days before his death. According to Max, Lenny went storming out of Violet's place and barricaded himself inside his modest home in Van Nuys. He'd then informed his bandmates that he didn't want to be disturbed for any reason, claiming he'd require total solitude in order to work on his new music.

"I've known Len since high school," Max told Arsenio, "and when that dude went into his solo phases, no one could touch him. He'd lock himself down, man. Wouldn't answer the phone, wouldn't go out. Nothing. I was used to it. That's how he did all his songwriting." He sighed. "Lenny's depression wasn't pretty, but it totally fueled his creativity. Winterlong wasn't known for its upbeat tunes, you know?"

"You weren't worried about him?" asked Mr. Hall.

"Look," said the bass player, "it's like this—everyone worried about Lenny. Especially us in the band. But there was only so much we could do. We couldn't have the fire department breaking down his door every time he locked himself in the house, right? Do I wish I'd gone over there *that* night and done something? Hells, yeah. But hindsight's always twenty-twenty. It's tough, but we all gotta forgive ourselves."

Oh really, Max? I thought. You're saying that you and all the other band members had no clue that Lenny was in such a bad state? Not even when he didn't make it to the taping of The Tonight Show? Wouldn't that have been an appropriate time to call the cops?

It was all too weird. I mean, how could someone like Lenny Weir—an international icon—be left to die alone, like my dad? Wouldn't *someone* have checked on him after he missed the taping of a major TV show without even a phone call to explain his change of plans? The story didn't add up, and I couldn't help thinking that some people weren't coming clean.

In regard to Lenny's physical remains, little discussion was necessary. A morgue worker—who spoke with the press on the condition of anonymity—told a California newspaper that a blackened skeleton had been identified with dental records and transferred to a crematorium, in accordance with the wishes of Lenny's parents. The funeral was private, and the grief-stricken family made no statement to the press. According to Max Lee, Lenny's family felt as though the media had already taken far too much from them.

It took a while for true Winterlong fans to accept Lenny's death. But by late October, many of them—even Claire—were doing better. The media moved on to more current stories, and alternative radio stations like FNX in Boston began featuring a new crop of crappy, copycat bands attempting to take Winterlong's place. But they all sounded fluffy and clichéd, and their lyrics reminded me of poetry written by middle school kids.

Music, once my primary source of hope, now felt like a sham. The great Freddie Mercury had died of AIDS a year earlier, and although I'd handled his loss fairly well at the time, it came back to haunt me that fall. Freddie, the ultimate showman, and Lenny, the reluctant rock hero: both gone way too soon. Driving to work one day, "Bohemian Rhapsody" came on my car radio, and I wondered how I'd ever considered the song inspirational. I mean, Freddie's lyrics were all about dying and tragedy, and they ended with the conclusion that nothing really matters. *Nothing matters?* Then why live at all? "Bohemian Rhapsody" was the saddest thing ever written.

Ever since I began working at Don-Wash, I'd been stopping at the supermarket in Gloucester almost every evening to buy sugary food to eat on the drive back to Winthrop. Then I'd get home, vomit, and swear never to abuse myself like that again. And in my weakened state, I'd actually believe myself. By that point, I'd been making myself throw up for over ten years, and the damage to my body was palpable.

My teeth ached, my throat felt scratchy most of the time, and I was always tired. Each morning, then, as I left for work, I'd commit to a puke-free day. Because if I could do it once, I could do it again, and again, and again. Before long, I'd be normal.

But around four o'clock most afternoons, something antsy would start squirming in my gut. I'd go on making phone calls, but the squirmy thing persisted. And the longer I neglected it, the more attention it demanded. *Don't give in!* I'd chide myself. *You can beat this.* I couldn't, though, and as soon as I reached my eight-hour target, I'd bid a hasty goodbye to anyone still working and head straight for my car. I'd always make a final, lame attempt to stay on the road and avoid a binge, but at the entrance to the Cape Ann Market, the Honda would take that well-worn left turn all by itself.

Control? I had zero.

Then, one October morning, I woke up extra early and couldn't fall back to sleep. So I jumped in the shower, dressed quickly, and was on the highway before seven. The traffic at that time was super light, and cruising up 128, I imagined all the work I'd get done while alone in the office. I'd clean my desk, organize files, maybe even attempt a few calls to potential customers I'd never been able to reach later in the day. But when the supermarket plaza came into view, I noticed that the grocery store was already open. And oh god, I wasn't prepared. I'd never actually puked at any job before—common sense, right—but the antsy thing in my gut had no use for common sense that day. It sat up and roared, and I surrendered.

I'd crossed a new line. Achieved a new low. *How did I get here?* I wondered, entering the store with Billy Joel's "Uptown Girl" assaulting my ears. I knew from experience that the market played the same ten or twelve perky songs constantly, but that morning, with the place virtually empty, the music was so much louder. As I hightailed it to the freezer section—ignoring the whiny voice in my head begging me to leave and go to work—UB40's "Red, Red Wine," started playing on the soundtrack. It felt like a weird choice so early in the morning, but then again, better that than "Rat in the Kitchen." Right? Ooh, and ice cream sandwiches were on sale.

One box, I decided. Just one. Then I'd eat them fast and be done puking and brushing my teeth before anyone else arrived.

Little did I know, though, that I was developing a new routine. The next day, I tweaked it slightly by stopping at a supermarket in Revere *before* hitting the highway. That way, I could binge on junk food on the ride *to* work and vomit the minute I arrived at Don-Wash. I may have been destroying my health, but damn it, I was smart.

Claire almost caught me once, but I handled the situation pretty well. She'd arrived at work earlier than usual one morning, and when I stepped out of the bathroom—all red-faced and disheveled—she was right outside the door at the water cooler. "You okay, Reardon?" she asked.

"Oh yeah," I answered, wiping toothpaste off my lips. "Fine."

She squinted and cocked her head to one side. "You sure? It sounded like you were puking in there."

I scanned the room. No one else was there yet, but Don was due any minute. "Well actually," I whispered, "I'm a little sick. My friend Colin had a party last night and I had one too many margaritas." Of course, I hadn't seen Colin since the day I'd moved out of his place, but he'd been on my mind lately.

"Ohhh," said Claire, her concern changing to mild amusement. "Colin? Anything good happen?"

I pressed my lips together and shook my head. "Uh uh. He's pretty serious about his fiancé these days." I could feel the lies heating up my face.

Claire looked at me skeptically. "Interesting. You're blushing, you know."

"No, Claire, I'm not. Really. But I gotta sit down."

"All right, then. Take it slow today, okay? You want some Advil?"

"No. I'll be fine."

She smiled and shook her head. "Whatever you say, Reardon. You crazy girl."

A greatest hits album titled *Winterlong: Seasons of Winter* was released around Halloween with maximum hype. The record label spent millions promoting it, promising that it would electrify both old and new Winterlong fans. Claire and I remained cynical until the day it hit stores. Then, like everyone else, we were blown away.

For starters, the record was really, really good. Rather than just taking the best tracks off old albums and sticking them together on one, the producers had dug deep to uncover live and remixed versions of songs that'd never been heard by most people. But that's not what caused the real commotion. No, the truly shocking part of the album was the final song, which was brand new, disturbing, and endlessly controversial. Every rock critic, DJ, VJ, musician, and fan of the band seemed to have a slightly different take on the meaning of that last track, called "Weeds."

The theories, however, fell into three major categories. The first—and most popular—was the presumption that the eponymous weeds somehow referred to Lenny's heroin addiction. Almost all Winterlong songs contained veiled drug references, so that totally made sense. Second was the idea that "Weeds" further supported speculation about Lenny losing a sibling during childhood. Which was also reasonable, given the song's cryptic lyrics and overall dark tone. But the most interesting theory of all—and most far-fetched—asserted that Lenny had faked his death.

"It's another Jim Morrison situation," joked a well-known DJ on my car radio one morning. "I mean, who saw the body? Like three people, right? A couple cops and some shifty medical examiner? Please. Of course they got paid off to keep their mouths shut. End of story. The whole thing was suspect from the start, and now we've got a song to explain it all. Thank you, Lenny Weir. We hope you're happy wherever you're hiding, and when you get bored, by all means, come down to the station and hang out. We've got plenty of beer in the fridge."

The DJ clearly didn't believe that, though. He was just goofing around, trying to get listeners mad enough to call the station and argue with him.

But me? I was legitimately confused. I mean, of course I wanted Lenny to be alive, but everyone who subscribed to that theory seemed nutty. Not to mention that the "Weeds" song was pretty ambiguous. It started off slowly, with only a cello and Lenny's deep voice whisper-singing:

Under water, under oceans
Under voices, under you.
Tangle Pisces, tangled lovers
Mangle kisses, mangle blue.

At that point, the guitars, bass and drums kicked in, and Lenny started screaming at the top of his lungs:

Tangle children, tangled gardens
Cripple horses, mangle monsters
Crumble lightning, mangle blackness
Tangle thunder, cripple madness.

Next came a long, frenzied instrumental break, with the band launching into a calamitous jam session that approached musical anarchy. Then, just as it began to feel like something truly dangerous might happen, all the instruments stopped, and the cello resumed its dirge-like rhythm. After several measures, Lenny's quiet voice crept back in to finish the song:

Into the weeds you traveled
You made me go there too
You let them take you under
You took me in with you
But when my eyes were opened
I couldn't find you under

They made you disappear
They made you disappear.
I couldn't disappear.

Then, with no musical accompaniment at all, Lenny whispered:

Turn around. I'm standing here.

I couldn't listen to that last line without major goosebumps. Some reviewers slammed the record producers, accusing them of doctoring the song for shock value and maximum profit. And if that was the case, well, they'd succeeded. *Seasons of Winter* sold more copies in two weeks than all other Winterlong albums combined, ever. Meanwhile, stores like Newbury Comics started selling bumper stickers and t-shirts declaring LENNY LIVES!

Some people found the shirts funny, while others, of course, wore them with genuine hope and conviction. But I never bought one. I worried about people laughing at me, and also understood—firsthand—the danger of raising my hopes too high about one of my heroes. After the Elvis Costello debacle, I feared that another crash might kill me.

Chapter 10

June 1981

Bowie's *Diamond Dogs* was spinning on my turntable the Saturday I shaved off my eyebrows. I hadn't planned such a drastic move, but after plucking both sides with tweezers for almost an hour, I'd hit my frustration limit. The freaking things were still uneven, and I'd drawn blood several times. Finally, then, I just grabbed a razor and solved the problem in thirty seconds. Boom. I painted on some skinny new brows with liquid eyeliner and was good to go. In my opinion, I looked quite sophisticated.

Next, I hit the drug store and made a beeline for the hair dye section. Because one thing was clear: my plain brown mop wasn't working. I mean, what would Bowie think of such a boring color? For a minute or two, I considered going bright red like Ziggy Stardust—or even jet black—but when I spied a shade called Platinum Dream—with a sassy Marilyn Monroe look-alike on the box—my search ended. I'd heard people say that bleaching can make your hair dry and frizzy, but what did I care? I was about to turn seventeen and I wanted attention. In other words, the more drama, the better. Plus, my hair was already frizzy. What harm could a little bleach do?

Unfortunately, Mom didn't share my enthusiasm. She hated the painted-on eyebrows even more than the platinum hair, and said I looked like a floozy from the Combat Zone. That hurt. I mean, I felt radical and punk and badass: the opposite of cheap. Mom didn't understand, but people my age would.

The next thing I needed was a new wardrobe. And since I was broke, I did something I'd read about in *Seventeen:* raided the attic for Mom's old seventies clothes, and transformed them into new fashions. I chopped long, gauzy skirts into unhemmed minis, turned turtlenecks into "vests" by cutting them down the front, made a jacket out of a button-up dress, and used leftover fabric scraps for belts. And punk alterations were so easy with safety pins! Suddenly, no piece of clothing was too unique for Erin Reardon. Looking in the mirror, I saw a young Bowie in training, and felt certain he'd be impressed with my creativity.

I don't have any pictures of myself from those days, but can say with confidence that any neighbors who saw me heading off to school that Monday must've done a double take, and I sure got a lot of stares in school. No one said much, though. A few kids told me they liked my new hair color, but that was about it. No one asked where I'd gotten my clothes, or why my style had changed so radically. At the very least, I'd expected some of the funkier dressers to give me a thumbs-up or something, but no. Basically, people who'd never acknowledged me continued in that vein, and the ones who'd been moderately friendly were a little less friendly. I still sat at Patty's lunch table, but she and I had already reached the point of hardly ever speaking, and after my transformation, we spoke even less frequently. As for Cindy, I couldn't tell if she found my new look amusing or if she was worried, but every time our eyes met, she'd just frown and shake her head. Meanwhile, Todd Eldridge went on dating his shy clarinet player and ignoring me.

But I wasn't discouraged. I figured people just needed some time to adjust. Based on what I'd read, Bowie hadn't been an overnight sensation either.

Of course, I was no match for Bowie. Not yet anyway. Seeing his gorgeousness sprawled across the covers of records I bought at Stairway to Heaven only made me realize how much further I needed to go. He was so magnificent in his freakiness, so convolutedly sexy, so cool, so provocative. And no matter how long I studied him in that hippie dress on the jacket of *The Man Who Sold the World,* I remained confused. I mean, how could he look so pretty and feminine with that man's razor stubble?

I'm not sure why, but *Station to Station* became my favorite Bowie album. At first, I didn't love it because some of the songs—particularly "Stay" and "TVC-15"—sounded a lot like disco, and everyone knew disco sucked. But the more I listened, the more the record grew on me, especially the title song. I can't say I understood the lyrics, which jumped from the dart-throwing Thin White Duke, to dredging the ocean, to the side effects of cocaine, to the European canon, whatever the hell that meant. But something about the track made me want to play it over and over again. Eventually, my drunken needle-dropping scratched the vinyl and it started skipping in a few spots, but I kept playing it anyway.

Which isn't to say I ignored Bowie's other music, because I didn't. I loved every song he'd ever written, and every one of his characters. The mousy-haired girl in "Life on Mars," the poor, sad "Man Who Sold the World," Major Tom who tragically lost touch with ground control. But the song "Station to Station" just *killed* me, and over time, it mingled with my DNA or something. I'd be walking down the street, or taking a math test, or just going to the bathroom, and it'd start playing in my head. Then, as soon as I could get to my stereo, I'd play it for real. Skips and all.

On the last day of my junior year, the hallways buzzed with news about all the house parties happening in town that night. And although I kept my shit together as I traveled from classroom to classroom—making cheerful small talk with kids and teachers about summer jobs and vacation plans—I blinked back tears when no one was looking, and spent my lunch hour sobbing in a bathroom stall. I couldn't help it. It was the last day, goddammit, and no one—not *one* kid—had even *suggested* that I join them at a party. No one wanted to hang out with me. I'd run out of excuses.

It hit me hardest when the final bell rang, and everyone streamed for the doors in groups. I couldn't bear to be seen leaving the building alone on a day like that, so I snuck back into the bathroom to cry a little more. Then, when my emotions were temporarily under control, I washed my face and tiptoed down the hall. I felt certain that all the kids were gone, but didn't want any teachers seeing me looking like such a loser either.

Even the teachers were gone, though. Probably off someplace partying together, for all I knew. Only the janitor's truck and the school librarian's station wagon remained in the parking lot. Tears filled my eyes again, but this time, they were angry tears. Which scared me, because I hadn't allowed myself to get mad in years. *What's wrong with people?* I wondered, half out loud. *Can't anyone see how much I'm hurting?* I looked down at my chunky body, safety-pinned into one of my mother's old yellow halter dresses. I'd cut the skirt diagonally on purpose, making it knee-length on the left side and thigh-length on the right, and lots of threads hung from the bottom because I hadn't sewn a hem. On my feet were cheap silver sandals I'd snagged at a yard sale, and my hair was so dry from bleaching it a second time that a few clumps had fallen out.

Fuck! Trying to blend in hadn't worked, but neither had dressing outrageously. My situation in Winthrop was hopeless. And I was stuck there for another year. I didn't have enough money to run away from home, and besides, I'd never do that to Mom. I was trapped.

Never in my life had I swilled alcohol like I swilled cheap vodka that afternoon. I drank straight from the bottle and didn't even bother to wipe up when some dribbled down my chin. Then, I tore through the kitchen cabinets until I discovered a brand-new bag of Lay's potato chips, which I hauled off to my bedroom along with the bottle. Hey, what could Mom do if she noticed the missing vodka? If she asked about it, I'd say I had no idea.

Bowie's *Hunky Dory* album was sitting on the turntable, so I dropped the needle on it and collapsed on my bed, tears pouring down my cheeks. I'd done all I could, and it hadn't been enough. I'd failed. Every girl at Winthrop High had friends and boyfriends—or ex-boyfriends, or soon-to-be-boyfriends—but I had *no one.* Not even a good friend to call on the phone.

I took another swig of the innocent-looking vodka, wincing as it burned down my throat, and tore open the bag of chips. Fuck 'em all! I didn't need those Winthrop assholes. Better friends waited for me out there in the world.

Lay's had been Dad's favorite snack, and their crisp saltiness transported me back to the lazy summer Saturdays of my childhood, when a bag of chips, a pot of Campbell's chicken noodle on the stove, and a can of Schlitz meant lunch for my father. Who would've guessed I'd someday be sentimental about a time when Dad could feed himself? Life was a fucked up thing.

I'm not sure how long I sat there reminiscing with the vodka and chips, but after a while, my lips stung from the salt, and my stomach really started to ache. Next to me on the bed lay the flaccid yellow-and-white Lay's bag, empty except for a few crumbs. I took another swig of vodka, hoping it would break up the greasy lump of starch in my belly, but it didn't.

I sighed and rested my head on the pillow as Bowie sang about being on the eleventh floor of a hotel, watching people cruise on the street below. "Queen Bitch" is such a cool song because even though the guy in it gets ditched by his lover, he's not whining. He may be upset, but as he tosses the bitch's bags down the hall and calls himself a cab, his tone is flippant and defiant. He doesn't lie on the bed stuffing potato chips in his face.

Attitude, I thought. That's my problem. I need to stop acting like a fat, grinning doormat, and start living for me.

Standing up shakily, I caught a glimpse of myself in the mirror. Ugh. The chips bloated my gut, and the vodka distorted my face. I wanted that crap out of me. *Immediately.* I needed to be sharper. I needed an *edge.*

And that's when it hit me: Stick your finger down your throat, Erin! Make yourself puke! You don't have to stand here like a dolt, accepting your situation. Changing your hair and clothing was a start, but you've gotta take control of your mind and body too.

Of course, I didn't want to end up like those bulimic models I'd read about in the fashion magazines. I just wanted to trim down a little.

Chapter 11

April 1993

Don made his first real move on a day when Amy and Tara were on a sales call in Connecticut, and Claire was home sick with a stomach bug.

"Just you and me today, huh, Erin?" he said, coming up behind me and laying a large hand on my shoulder. His cologne smelled stronger than usual.

I opened the Yellow Pages and picked up the phone. Don had been touching my ass for almost a year, but always on the sly, when other people were within earshot. For me, the possibility of getting caught was part of the thrill.

But being alone with him was totally different and kind of scary. "I guess," I replied, ducking behind my hair. "I've got tons of follow-up calls to make."

He nodded and massaged my neck, his "tan" a sickly shade of post-winter tangerine. "Umm. That's what I like to hear." Moving his massaging hand down to my shoulder, his fingers brushed the top part of my left breast and I shivered. "What'd you think about your last paycheck?" he asked. "Not too shabby, huh?"

It'd been my biggest paycheck ever; after taxes, I'd cleared almost six hundred dollars in one week. Setting up sales appointments for Tara and Amy got easier by the day. "It was great," I replied. "Thank you."

"Oh no. Don't thank me. Thank yourself. You're a little hustler, Erin. You know, if you pulled in that much dough every week, you'd make over thirty grand a year. Cha-ching!"

I smiled with self-conscious pride. Yes, the job sucked, but I did it well.

"So you wanna have lunch later on?" he asked. "My treat?"

"Lunch?" Even as the single syllable left my mouth, I heard the tension in my voice. Normally, Don ate lunch with Tara and Amy, and if they weren't around, he ate alone. "Oh ... I ... brought a bagel today. I, uh, actually need to leave a little early for a dentist appointment." That last part was a lie; I didn't even have a dentist. I had visited one a few years earlier, but she'd scared the crap out of me. She said my tooth enamel had deteriorated to a dangerous level, and that I should get most of my teeth crowned. The enamel damage probably came from vomiting, but since I had no money for crowns, I'd ignored her advice.

"Not a problem," Don answered calmly, appearing somewhat amused by my discomfort. "What time do you need to be outta here?"

"Um ... pretty early. Like, 4:30."

He made his thumb and forefinger into the shape of a pistol and clicked his tongue. "You got it. Four-thirty, you're out the door. No questions asked. But let's grab a quick bite together around noon. We'll call it a working lunch. I wanna discuss something with you."

I nodded and winced. The thought of eating with Don terrified me, but he was the boss.

"The fried haddock at this place is absolutely fantastic," Don announced for at least the third time as we entered a seedy looking restaurant on the Gloucester waterfront. The air in the parking lot smelled like a combination of raw and fried fish.

"Hey Donny!" said the hostess. "I gotta window seat for you today!"

Most of the booths and tables were occupied by casually dressed, middle-aged people who looked like office workers and retirees. "Best kept secret on the North Shore, this place," Don commented. "Fantastic haddock."

I wondered how many more times he was going to mention that haddock. The jeans I'd bought at the thrift shop with Claire over the summer felt a little too tight, and they pulled across my thighs when I sat down. My head spun, probably from all the coffee I'd swilled earlier.

This is no big deal, I reassured myself. We're just two professional people eating lunch together.

The waitress came over, and Don ordered the haddock plate. I asked for a tuna sandwich. "No haddock, Erin?" he asked.

I wasn't really a fan of fried haddock. "No thanks. Not today."

"Okey dokey," said Don with a shrug. Turning to the waitress, he said, "Bring over a couple beers, too, all right? Heinekens." He raised his eyebrows and shot me a sly grin. "You'll drink a beer with me, wontcha, Erin?"

It'd never occurred to me that Don *drank* when he went out to lunch, and I wondered if the alcohol would make me too sleepy to work later on. "Two Heinekens?" asked the waitress, and I nodded, sitting up straighter.

"You're quiet today," said Don. "How come?"

I folded my hands and looked down at my thighs. "I don't know."

"Well," he said with a wink, "if you were this quiet with a *customer* you took out to lunch, you'd have a hard time closing the deal."

What an odd thing to say. Still, I forced a smile. "I guess that's why I don't take customers out to lunch. I'm much better on the phone."

The waitress dropped off our beers, and Don grinned widely enough to provide a full view of the gold crowns on his back teeth. "Oh, I doubt that," he said with half a wink. "I'll bet you're great in the flesh."

The hair on my forearms stood up. I mean, had he just made a sexual innuendo?

Thankfully, he laughed right away. "Hey, I'm sorry, Erin. That came out all wrong. I'm used to Amy and Tara's humor. The girls and I can get a little crude sometimes. Pressures of the job, you know." He took a big gulp of beer and I followed his lead.

"It's okay," I said. But my heartbeat increased and my breathing grew shallower. I hoped the food would hurry up and arrive so we could eat and get back to the office as soon as possible.

Don let out an exaggerated sigh. "Oh good. I'm glad you understand. Especially since you and I might start spending more time together soon."

"Why?" I asked, much too quickly.

"Why what?"

I took a sip of beer and avoided his gaze. "I mean, why would we spend more ... time together?" Don's ass touching had been happening more frequently, and I'd actually developed a sick kind of crush on him. Sick because he was Don. Salon Don. *Dirty Don.*

He raised his eyebrows again. "Erin, I'm seriously thinking of moving you into an outside sales position. Tara and Amy can't handle all our customers alone anymore, and who's better for that job than you? You're a great little saleslady, and you always rise to a challenge. Don't you?"

Some of the beer from my stomach found its way back into my mouth. "But what about Claire?" I couldn't fathom the possibility of being promoted ahead of her. Claire had worked at Don-Wash much longer than I had, and her sales ability far exceeded mine.

"Oh no," said Don. "This discussion isn't about Claire. It's about *you*. Let's stay focused."

"Yeah, but—"

He raised his hand to stop me from saying any more. "No. I shouldn't even say this, Erin, but for the record, Claire doesn't have the necessary skills for outside sales. If she did, I'd have her out there on the street right now, as we speak. She does well on the phone, but in person, she comes across sloppy and bored. Like she's got better things to do. There's no hunger in her eyes. But you've got that, Erin. Hunger. And I like it."

I laughed nervously as the waitress placed a thick tuna sandwich in front of me. "Well, believe it or not, I'm not very hungry today." I actually felt like I might vomit. The whole situation was too much.

"Not hungry," said Don with a chuckle. "Good one. But you know I didn't mean it literally, right? I meant hungry *hungry*. Hungry for a bigger paycheck. Hungry for the good things in life."

I shrugged. "Oh. I see."

"But I liked your joke. You're quick-witted, Erin. And that's important for a salesgirl."

Quick-witted? Ha! In high school, I'd been odd and quiet; in college, just plain odd. In Europe, most other young tourists had treated me like a naive adventurer, and the workers at my temp jobs before Don-Wash considered me a short-term replacement part. Jeff and Pete legitimately cared about me, but also considered me sweetly pathetic. But quick-witted? Did Don really think of me that way? Gosh, he was messed up.

He also had Claire all wrong. Sure, she wore funky clothes, but that's because she worked in a freaking trailer, and she was anything but sloppy. And of course, she'd dress more professionally if she got promoted. I think Claire intimidated Don and probably made him jealous too. After all, how would it look if he made her a salesperson and she sold more shirts than him?

He took a big bite of his haddock, and dribbled some tartar sauce on his chin. "Are you dieting?" he asked as he chewed, "'cause you've been looking good lately, Erin. Thinner."

I'd actually gained a few pounds that winter, and all the puking had caused my skin to break out pretty badly. "Thanks," I said, polishing off the beer. I didn't know what else to say.

"Atta girl," he continued, wiping his mouth and snapping his fingers to get the waitress's attention. "Two more Heineys when you have a chance, dear."

I shivered and checked the clock on the wall. We'd been at the restaurant for almost an hour. I was ready to get back to work.

"Chilly?" asked Don as two new frosty glasses appeared on the table.

"Yeah," I said, "I'm not feeling great today."

He sighed. "I'm sorry, honey. Maybe you should take the sandwich in a doggie bag. But the beer's good for you. Drink up!"

Back at work, I poured a big glass of water. At Don-Wash, there was always a random collection of cups and glasses on a table near the water cooler, none of which ever looked clean. Normally, if I needed one, I'd scrub it with soap and hot water in the bathroom, but that day, I didn't care. I checked the clock, saw I had three more hours of work before going home, and put my head down on my desk. With a little luck, Don wouldn't notice if I took a nap.

But a few minutes later, I smelled cologne and almost jumped out of my seat. "You left this in the car," said Don, holding the brown paper bag with my uneaten tuna sandwich inside. "And feel free to relax. Drinking beers at lunch is an acquired skill. You gotta work up to it." He had that amused grin on his face again, as if he could see something secretly funny.

"And hey," he continued, "why dontcha join me in my office, honey. We never finished our talk." I saw something flicker in his eyes, and when he breathed, I caught a whiff of toothpaste.

He'd called me "honey" plenty of times before, but that afternoon, it sounded more ... lovey-dovey. Reaching out, he took my hand in one of his. Then he put his other hand on my butt.

I knew exactly what was happening, but went with him anyway. His breathing grew harder and faster as he led me down the hallway and closed the office door behind us.

"Don," I said.

"It's okay, Erin. I promise. It's okay."

I'd never had fully conscious sex before, and couldn't deny my excitement. "Okay," I said as his hand slipped down the front of my jeans. A thrill went through me, and not just because his fingers were in my vagina. It was also exciting to realize that his entire hand *fit* inside my jeans. And my fly was still zipped! He squeezed one of my nipples, and when I looked down, I saw that he'd somehow gotten his pants off. His penis was bigger than I'd expected, and it was sticking straight out.

"Touch it, Erin," he whispered, and I did. It felt like velvet. Closing his eyes and sighing, he took off his shirt and lifted me up by the butt. "Can we do it in my big leather chair?" he asked, his voice shaky and wet.

I couldn't believe how turned on I felt. I mean, sure he was Dirty Don, but he seemed pretty sexy when he was naked and holding me that way. "Yeah," I agreed. He kissed me then, and I kissed him back—hard—like I'd practiced in private with Jim Morrison and the others. Don had obviously just brushed his teeth, but I could still taste a little haddock in his mouth.

It felt so natural, though, and I actually enjoyed holding his hips as he thrust himself into me. Even his cologne smelled better than usual. I could tell how much he liked my body, because he moaned like I'd never heard anyone moan before.

After he'd finished (and I let him come inside me because my period had just ended), he stroked my clitoris until I had my very first orgasm with another human. Then he kissed me again on the mouth and called me a sexy bitch. Which I didn't really believe, but also didn't mind hearing.

CHAPTER 12

June 1982

By the time I graduated high school, puking was my best pal and confidante. I could be pouring coffee at the Sand Dollar (I'd gone back there to work for a second summer), watching TV, or taking the bus into Boston to shop for records, but one thing remained constant: my secret sidekick reminding me to eat and puke. Not that I would've forgotten. After all, food was cheap, comforting, legal, and delicious, and toilets were everywhere.

Vomiting at home worked best. Once Mom got accustomed to living without Dad, she started socializing more. Much more. I'd hear her telling people she needed to stay busy because sitting around the house depressed her, but she was also having a damn good time. A group of townie women she'd known since high school got together for dinner every couple of months, but the *single* ladies in that crowd formed a smaller subgroup that went out more frequently, and drank a lot more alcohol.

But Mom felt sorry for me too. Sometimes, she'd even invite me to join her group of girls for a night out, and a few times, I almost went. But I never did. Instead, I learned to invent stories about the things I'd done with my "friends" to make her feel better. I remember sitting with her at breakfast one Sunday morning, telling her—in great detail—about a movie I'd seen at the cinema the previous night when I'd really just read the review in the paper.

My only hope came from knowing that college waited at the end of August. Of course, Mom assumed my plans for higher education involved studying and book learning, but she couldn't have been more wrong. Sure, I'd ended up with a decent high school GPA, and had done well on the SAT too, but my priority for college was reinventing myself as a fun party girl.

The waiting sucked, though, so I went on puking. I knew all about the dangers of bulimia, and the magazines at the supermarket checkout seemed to feature a new story on eating disorders every week. Still—as

I stood in line waiting to spend my Sand Dollar tips on ice cream and Doritos—I somehow convinced myself that I wasn't like those magazine girls. I mean, it was obvious, right? They were all skinny and gorgeous, and they starved themselves or puked to get jobs as models or actresses. But I wasn't talented or pretty. I just liked food. It comforted me, gave me something to do, and made me feel better in the short term. And since I didn't want to be obese, I vomited.

Ever since that morning after the vodka and Lay's chips—when I stepped on the scale and saw that I was down three pounds—I'd been sold on the value of purging. But once I lost a few more, my weight plateaued and I couldn't figure out why. None of the articles I read mentioned that bulimics rarely get thin—in fact, they often get heavier—because their bodies can't vomit *all* the food they eat; some of it still ends up getting digested and absorbed. I only knew that I was eating pretty much anything I wanted, and not gaining *too* much. Which to my messed-up brain felt like a luxury.

Every once in a while, though, I got scared. Some vomiting sessions were particularly painful and difficult—certain foods had a way of sinking to the bottom of my stomach and sticking there—and the effort involved in getting them up left me shaky, dizzy, and exhausted. Afterwards, I'd lay on my bed with my heart beating so fast it felt like it might give out. During those times, I'd admit—or at least consider the possibility—that I had a problem.

The next morning, then, I'd wake up and vow never to abuse my body like that again. I'd resolve to take a long walk on the beach after work, pick up a new book at the library, or find a good movie on TV. Not to mention that I'd get my body in great shape before college. And things would start off well. I'd arrive at the Sand Dollar and eat a bowl of fresh fruit and a slice of toast with my coworkers in the break room. (Joe, the owner, allowed the staff to eat whatever we wanted while at the restaurant, so most people arrived early and stayed a bit late in order to get two free meals.)

But once the morning rush was over, I'd start noticing how *juicy* the blueberry muffins looked, or I'd catch a whiff of pancakes coming off the grill. But while other staff members might mention feeling hungry, I'd find myself craving the food in a totally unnatural way. My customers needed—and got—my attention, but I couldn't help counting down the minutes until my shift ended.

Of course, nobody would know what to think if I made a habit of chowing down half a dozen muffins or a giant stack of pancakes for lunch in the break room, and I'd feel too weird doing that anyway. So while I completed my side work—vacuuming the rug, filling the ketchup and syrup bottles, cleaning the coffee pots—I'd grab a couple of muffins when no one was looking and stash them in an apron pocket. Then, a little later, I'd do the same with a few coffee rolls, and maybe some doughnuts too. We workers were a fairly tight bunch, and sometimes when I punched out, someone would ask why I never had lunch at the Dollar. But I'd lie and say I had stuff to do. Then, I'd sneak across the street to the grocery store to round off my binge with a bit more junk food, rush home, eat, vomit, and spend the afternoon sleeping.

If Mom went out for the evening, I'd often binge and purge again, making do with whatever food we had in the house. But if she stayed home, I'd eat dinner with her, then mix up a screwdriver after she went to bed. By then, I'd figured out how to acquire my own vodka: I'd take the bus to a liquor store in a nearby town and ask young dudes to buy for me. Some would refuse, but most really didn't seem to mind, especially since I'd offer an extra five bucks for a bottle. Anyway, once I'd made a nice drink, I'd settle in on the living room couch and watch MTV.

The same stupid videos came on every night—The Rolling Stones's "Start Me Up," Duran Duran's "Hungry Like the Wolf," John Cougar's "Jack and Diane," Billy Idol's "White Wedding," and Pat Benatar's "Shadows of the Night"—but I didn't care. They were more interesting than anything in my actual life, and unlike the pictures on my Bowie album jackets, the images on MTV *moved*. None of the video characters held a candle to David, of course, but they all became guests in my home with a simple touch of the remote control. And when they appeared, they looked straight at me, pouting, flirting, and coming on to me in ways I could only imagine David doing. The videos were instructional too, since they prepared me for the *real* sex I planned to have as soon as I got to college. I absolutely couldn't wait to lose my virginity.

So yes, my expectations for college were pretty warped, but I had no idea. I'd chosen to attend a small private school in Providence called Danforth, which fulfilled my two major requirements: it was far enough away from Winthrop to keep my mom from visiting regularly, and it offered a nice chunk of financial aid.

When I arrived at Danforth, I quickly discovered that nobody cared if you displayed bottles of alcohol in your dorm room, even if you were underage. And as an added bonus, the liquor store across the street from campus would sell to *anyone*. The store didn't seem to have a real name, but the words BEER AND WINE stenciled on the side of the building in red paint sufficed. Ha! My days of asking men to buy my booze were over.

On a more disappointing note, I also learned that most freshmen at Danforth actually *cared* about their grades. In other words, they went to classes and studied! That confused me. I mean, college kids on TV and in the movies didn't do much of that. *Maybe these Danforth kids are a little naive,* I decided. *They probably need some time to loosen up.*

But my third major discovery was even more unsettling. At first, I tried to overlook it and focus on the positive, but it was everywhere. *He* was everywhere. Inescapable. Impossible to ignore. *Bruce Springsteen.*

I felt personally betrayed by the school's admissions office. I mean, my interview with the dean had lasted half an hour, and the guy hadn't said *a word* about Bruce, even when I'd asked what types of music Danforth kids were into. He'd told me—with a straight face—that they liked all types, but that was an outright lie. Because I swear nine songs out of every ten that got blasted from the school's dorm windows were by Springsteen and his horn-heavy band. And what about that glossy brochure Danforth sent out to thousands of prospective freshmen, including me? It'd contained pictures of red brick buildings, green lawns, and students studying in the library, but *none* of Bruce. Not one. And yet, on campus, he was a god.

How could that be? In what universe could a twerpy little dude who looked like a gas station attendant—or maybe a clerk at Beer and Wine—inspire hundreds of perfectly normal-seeming college girls to swoon all over him? And who in their right mind would attend one of his four-hour concerts padded with long, meandering stories about growing up in New Jersey? Not to mention boring songs like "Born to Run" and "Tenth Avenue Freeze Out." Back home, I'd always changed the station when those songs came on the radio, but at Danforth, I didn't have that choice.

There was a rule on campus about stereos, stating that they needed to be kept at low volume between eleven at night and ten in the morning. And for the most part, the school enforced it. But Bruce obviously had special privileges, because I'd hear him belting out his tunes until at least one in the morning on weekends, sometimes even later, and no one complained. It was as though the RAs couldn't hear him. But the one time I tried blasting Bowie's "Station to Station" out my dorm window on a Saturday afternoon, a girl from downstairs knocked on my door and asked me to lower the volume because she was studying.

It was bad. But even worse than *actual* Bruce music were the Springsteen *cover* bands that ruined so many Danforth mixers and keg parties. Like the pathetic band from Providence called The River, and a bunch of guys from southern New Hampshire who went by the name Jersey Girl. The *ultimate* worst, though—by a long shot and for so many reasons—were Danforth's very own Spike and the Asbury Rockers. Spike Walker, the lead singer/guitarist/moron, was in his junior year at the school, and a rumor on campus claimed that he was actually related to Bruce. During the time I spent at Danforth, I never once saw Spike without his black leather motorcycle jacket and his hair all slicked back with grease. I hated his singing voice, his guitar playing sucked, and in my opinion, he looked like a jerk.

Very few other people, however, shared my sentiments, and Spike and his ridiculous band performed all over the place. Why? I couldn't begin to guess. They played too loud, they were always drunk, and their instruments were often out of tune. They also played nothing but Springsteen covers. Obviously, I avoided Spike and the Rockers whenever possible, but do have a distinct memory of watching hundreds of students dancing to their music on the lawn at a house party one rainy September night. Everyone was muddy and soaked to the skin, but the band—which was on the porch trying to keep their equipment dry—kept banging away while Spike screamed "I Came for You" at the top of his lungs like a real rock star would. But he was no star.

"So, so shallow," said Toni, as she and I hurried past the party under her umbrella. "This whole school's the shallowest."

"Yeah," I agreed. "It's so sad the way they treat a fake band like the real thing. Especially when the real thing sucks so bad too."

Toni was my brand-new best friend, and every night when I crawled into my lumpy dorm bed, I took a moment to feel grateful for her. She and I were different in many, many ways, but as roommates, we clicked.

She came from one of those fancy suburbs in Westchester, New York, and wasn't much of a rock music fan. In fact, on the rare occasions when she turned on her clock radio, it was set to the soft pop station that played stuff like Air Supply and REO Speedwagon. But she hated Bruce and his copycat bands as much as I did, and like me, strongly preferred drinking to studying.

In fact, on the very first day of classes, the two of us decided to skip the afternoon session so we could attend happy hour at a local bar. "The teachers won't teach anything the first day, anyway," said Toni. "They just wanna say hi and meet the students." Which was total bullshit, but I'd already been to two morning classes and was tired of taking notes. I figured I deserved a break.

Don't get me wrong, I had no desire to flunk out of Danforth, and I definitely wanted to make friends and date boys. But I assumed I was smart enough to handle my schoolwork without much effort, probably because the teachers in Winthrop had gone so easy on me after Dad's death. Toni, on the other hand, only got into Danforth because her father, an alumnus, had begged them to accept her; she had *zero* interest in earning good grades. According to her, her older brother had started college as a total fuck-up, but cleaned up his act second semester and graduated with a 3.5 average. So her parents assumed she'd do the same. "My 'rents are so stupid," she told me. "I mean, yeah, I'm not gonna take a shit in a dorm closet like my brother, but I'm also not gonna waste any precious time studying."

"Your brother shit in a closet?"

"Uh-huh. And now he's married with two kids. To a woman he met at college. Go figure."

Danforth was a preppy little school, and I quickly realized that the clothes I'd hacked out of Mom's vintage stuff weren't gonna cut it there. At least not if I wanted to fit in, and I desperately did. Luckily, Mom had taught me how to shop for bargains, and the East Side of Providence—home to Brown University and RISD—featured some of the best consignment shops ever. Even better, they were chock full of fair isle sweaters, Izod shirts, corduroy pants adorned with whales, and every color turtleneck imaginable. From what I could gather, kids from Brown and RISD put their preppy clothes on consignment so they could buy artsy, new wave stuff, and Danforth kids like me would snap up their castoffs in an attempt to look Ivy League.

But Toni didn't dress artsy *or* preppy. She preferred Guess and Girbaud jeans—considered very unique and European at the time—and silky, sexy blouses. When the weather cooled down, she switched over to tight cashmere sweaters, scarves, high-heeled Italian boots, and chunky jewelry. She said she loved shopping in New York with her mom. Sometimes, they even paid a woman at Saks to help them choose outfits.

"Saks Fifth Avenue?" I asked in disbelief. "Isn't that store, like, really expensive?"

But Toni just rolled her eyes. "My mother doesn't care."

I never learned exactly what her dad did for work, but it had something to do with Wall Street. And he must've been pretty successful, because Toni was the only kid I knew with her own Visa card. Technically, the account belonged to her parents—since they paid the bill—but she could use it whenever she wanted, and her parents never seemed to question any purchases she made with it. Maybe they were trying to teach her responsibility, but it sure wasn't working.

Anyway, she and I spent our first couple of weeks at Danforth checking out the campus scene. We went to keg parties and neighborhood dive bars, and met lots of classmates. If anything, my expectations for college were being exceeded. Everyone accepted me at face value, and no one assumed I'd been a high school loser. I developed a crush on a sweet boy in my English class named Phil Sanders, and he seemed to like me too. He hadn't asked me out or anything—not yet, anyway—but we'd chatted and joked around a few times, so I was optimistic. Yes, sometimes I drank too much, and sometimes I woke up in the morning unable to remember every detail of the night before, but I trusted Toni to take care of me. For the first time since middle school, I felt like a normal girl.

But Toni grew more frustrated with each passing day. Every morning, she'd lie in bed ranting about all the geeks and losers at Danforth. Then, one Friday night we went to an off-campus party where the drink of choice was grain alcohol punch. The Squeeze album *Singles-45's and Under* was playing on the turntable, and everyone was dancing and having fun until a girl ran outside to barf on the lawn. Then another girl started heaving and stumbling toward the bathroom, and a skinny guy who'd been half asleep for about half an hour suddenly leaned over and hurled all over the rug. "Let's blow this joint," shouted Toni, over the music. "This is amateur hour!"

I hadn't binged and purged once since arriving at Danforth—I was hardly ever alone, and all the girls on my floor shared one large bathroom—so seeing all those other people throwing up gave me a weird sense of déjà vu. I guess I also felt a bit superior to the pukers: a veteran soldier surrounded by a bunch of new recruits. Some kids acted like they'd never seen vomit before, but I wasn't the least bit fazed. "It's okay, Toni," I said. "The worst should be over now." Phil Sanders had arrived about fifteen minutes earlier, and I'd been waiting for a chance to talk to him.

But just then, a big jock named Doug started retching over by the keg, and a bunch of girls screamed.

"That's it," said Toni. "I'm outta here."

I heard a gurgling sound behind us and turned to see Phil Sanders spitting into a red plastic cup. He looked unnaturally pale, and his eyes were watery and red. "You okay, Phil?" I asked.

"Yeah," he said, sounding both angry and embarrassed. I wanted to help, but wasn't sure what to do.

"Disgusting," Toni said loudly. "Let's go, Erin. I've seen enough amateur douchebags for one night."

I didn't understand. I mean, we were college freshmen, not middle-aged professionals. And drinking was more fun with friends. We were bonding, forming relationships, all the stuff I'd dreamed about doing after high school. And hanging out with Toni was usually a blast. Why did she want to leave the party so badly?

Still, I followed her out the door. "I'm so done with this frat-boy bullshit," she declared. "We go to school in a city, for god's sake."

"And?" I had no idea where she was going with that line of reasoning. Danforth didn't even have frats on campus.

"And the clubs are downtown. Let's check some of them out tomorrow night."

I'd never been to a nightclub before, and the cover of the *Saturday Night Fever* album popped into my head. Then I remembered something. "Oh no. We can't tomorrow. There's that party at The Pit." The students who lived in The Pit—a legendary three-story, off-campus house—were having their first twenty-kegger of the year. Everyone from my dorm would be there, and probably Phil Sanders too.

But Toni just laughed. "Up to you, Erin. I'll be skipping that clambake."

On Saturday morning, Toni bought the newspaper so she could check out the club listings. "Are you really going out *alone*?" I asked.

"Not if you come with me," she answered without looking up.

I was curious, of course, and I adored Toni, but a twenty-kegger at The Pit? With four-dollar admission, and unlimited beer? "How 'bout we go downtown *next* weekend? 'Cause I'm totally broke now, but I get paid Thursday." My financial aid package included a work-study job in the school cafeteria, and I made about twenty-five bucks a week.

"Erin," said Toni, holding up her wallet, "I'll buy you drinks all night. Top shelf. Whatever. Sky's the limit." She pulled out her Visa card for extra emphasis. "Just come with me. We'll have a nice night out. With cocktails and real men."

Once again, I thought about *Saturday Night Fever* and guys who looked and danced like John Travolta.

"And you know," Toni continued, "people say The Pit parties get better as the year goes on."

I'd heard that too, and was also really worried about letting Toni go downtown by herself. Providence wasn't the safest—or cleanest—city in the 1980s.

So I blew off The Pit and my new campus friends, and went with Toni. Then, the following weekend, she convinced me to go again. I didn't exactly enjoy the clubs we visited—they were all dives, and the guys we met were far sleazier than anyone at Danforth—but we were exploring a seedy new world, and in that world, I got fancy drinks for free.

I also have to admit that after so many years of feeling inferior and being marginalized by Patty and Cindy, hanging out with a beautiful, socially experienced girl like Toni didn't suck. She knew how to start conversations, men were naturally drawn to her, and I got to be part of it all. The trouble didn't start until our third weekend downtown, when Toni went home with one of those guys on Friday night. Then, on Saturday, she left a different club with a different one.

What was going on? What did Toni want? I mean, Danforth was crawling with cute, clean-cut boys, most of whom seemed kind of innocent and probably STD-free. But the nightclub guys were older and often sort of scummy. Also, if two Danforth kids had a one-night stand—or a "scoop" as we called it—they'd still have to face each other on a regular basis for the duration of their college days. So students tended to be careful about actually having sex with one another. But Toni's one-nighters were with complete strangers, and she had all kinds of sex with them. Even worse, none ever seemed interested in seeing her a second time. "Scooping" sounds sort of cute, but "dredging" was a more accurate description for what Toni was doing.

Looking back, I realize I should've confronted her about her self-destructive behavior. And I definitely should've recommended that she talk to a counselor. Why didn't I? Fear of losing her, I guess. I couldn't stand the thought of pissing her off and being alone again.

Instead, I rationalized: Toni was an adult and could make her own decisions. But deep down inside, I must've known something was very wrong. I mean, how could she possibly believe the claims of all those guys who swore to be doctors, lawyers, and corporate bigwigs? I had no proof of their occupations, of course, but none of it rang true for me; their stories contained too many obvious holes, especially when I questioned them about specific things.

Toni, on the other hand, asked no questions. For an intelligent woman, her brain seemed to evaporate in those nightclubs. The first time she contracted gonorrhea, I expected her to start being more careful, but she didn't slow down at all. "One shot of penicillin, and I'm back in action," she crowed the second time she got it. "Gotta love that."

Love it? I didn't. But by the time I realized that going out with Toni was no fun for me—and almost always left me scrambling for a way home (alone) late at night—I'd pretty much cut myself off from the other freshman girls on my floor. They'd grown so accustomed to Toni and me heading off campus on weekends that they'd stopped asking if we wanted to join their more traditional college adventures. One Friday evening, as I washed my face in the dorm bathroom, I considered asking a girl named Ellen if I could tag along with her crowd that night. But just as I opened my mouth, another girl opened the door to tell Ellen that a cute Danforth guy was on the phone for her. "Oh my god!" said Ellen, turning and running out of the bathroom without saying goodbye.

It felt like high school all over again. Different circumstances, same problem. Once again, my peers had forgotten me. I'd become invisible to them. My chin quivered, and my eyes filled with tears. But right then,

Toni strolled into the bathroom in a tight sweater and black leather miniskirt she'd bought in New York over Thanksgiving break. "What time will you be ready to go?" she asked, giving my sweats and dirty t-shirt the once over.

I desperately wanted to say I was staying in, but couldn't summon the courage. "Um, I'll need, like, an hour?"

"Cool," she replied. "How 'bout I meet you in the room at seven? I'm gonna go grab a quick beer down the street."

Since neither of us owned a car, Toni and I would take the bus or the "thumb train" downtown together. But late at night, when the Providence buses had stopped running and taxis became scarce and expensive, the thumb train (our slang term for hitchhiking) often became my best option for returning home. And let me just say for the record that most of the men—because I never got a late-night ride home with a woman—picking up hitchers in the city at that hour terrified me. Many smelled so strongly of weed that I feared they'd fall asleep at the wheel or drive off the road. Other times, they'd do creepy things, like touch my legs or suggest we have sex, and most took offense when I refused. One really messed-up dude grabbed my face and kissed me in a truly disgusting way, and another one pulled over on a main drag, unzipped his pants, and offered me the privilege of jerking him off under a flickering streetlight. But somehow, I always managed to stay strong and keep my shit together until they dropped me at the Danforth gates. Then, once they were gone, I'd freak out. Sometimes, my legs would shake so badly I could barely make it across campus and up my dorm steps.

I know most people wouldn't have stood for Toni's treatment for more than a night or two, and I shouldn't have either. But having a pal like her trumped everything for me. Sure, I hated being dumped in downtown bars night after night, but at least I wasn't spending weekends in my room alone. And as an added bonus, I'd temporarily stopped puking.

In my opinion, then, college was fulfilling most of my dreams. All I needed was a boyfriend (preferably a rock star, but a regular guy would do too) and I'd be all set.

One Saturday, I woke up unable to stand my frizzy, bleached-out hair another minute. So I showered and took the bus over to the East Side, where I'd seen a salon offering discounted haircuts from intern stylists.

The guy assigned to me had long blond bangs and tight black jeans and looked like a member of Duran Duran. Or maybe A Flock of Seagulls. "How much do you want me to take off?" he asked, running his fingers through my hair.

"A lot," I said as the Cure's "Boys Don't Cry" on the salon stereo instantly infected my heart with new wave fever.

"A *lot* lot? Cause your hair's really damaged, girl. You wanna go short like me?"

I hadn't considered going anywhere *near* as short as him, but the dizzying atmosphere of the place made me feel a little crazy. "Yeah ... I mean, if you think it'll look good. I need a serious change."

"Oh, you do!" He seemed so confident and skilled for an intern. "And I know the perfect cut to bring out your pretty eyes." Then, without another word, he grabbed an electric razor and got to work.

When I returned to the dorm, Toni rolled over in bed and propped her head up on her elbows. She'd gotten home in the wee hours, and the smudged black mascara around her eyes told me she'd been crying at some point. "Wow," she said.

"I look like a dude!" I squealed, rubbing the back of my head, where the hair was only about half an inch long.

Toni coughed a weird cough and covered her mouth. "No," she finally said. "You look like a cool punk girl. You'll just have to start wearing a little more makeup."

By the time I got home for Christmas break, my new wave "do" had progressed to the short-and-puffy stage. But no matter how much hair gel I used—Toni bought me a tube of expensive European stuff called Tenax—I still looked like a man. A hard look in the bathroom mirror could depress me for hours.

Then the envelope from Danforth arrived in the mail, and I intercepted it before Mom made it home from work. I'd earned straight C's and D's, along with a letter from the dean stating that if things didn't improve second semester, I'd lose my scholarship money. That freaked me out slightly, but I mixed myself a screwdriver, tossed the letter in the trash, and vowed to do better. I'd gotten used to screwing up in school and staying afloat, so I didn't really worry.

And my work did improve when I returned for second semester. Winter in Providence is a cold, raw thing, and I actually enjoyed some classes and teachers enough to buckle down and study. I even skipped a few weekends of clubbing with Toni.

But spring struck early in 1983, and the allure of keg beer—combined with the smell of barbeque blowing across the quad—proved too strong for me. Like the Springsteen songs blasting from dorm windows at all hours of the day and night, my willpower took flight, and I surrendered to the party life on and around campus.

I did, however, accomplish one of my main college goals that April: I had sex with a man. But not the way I'd planned it. Not even close.

Being from Winthrop, I knew all about the Boston Marathon and Patriots' Day in Massachusetts, but the holiday isn't formally celebrated in Rhode Island. All my life, I'd had it out of school, but Danforth was business as usual.

"Yeah, but who's gonna go to class on Marathon Monday?" said Toni the previous Friday.

"Um, most people, I think. Why wouldn't we?"

"Duh. 'Cause the Marathon's an all-day party. I'll charge two bus tickets to Boston, and we'll leave Monday morning around nine. That'll put us in a bar by the time the first runners hit the finish line."

I'd watched parts of the Marathon on TV over the years, and didn't find it particularly exciting. "Nah. I can't. Midterms are coming up."

"Suit yourself," said Toni.

But that night, she raised the issue again with dialed-up intensity. "It's one freaking day! And you meet *so many* cool people. You'll never forgive yourself if you don't come, Erin."

My grades had begun to slip—I had two C minuses and three D's—so I needed to stay focused. "Hmm. Maybe next year."

"Next *year*? We could all be dead next year. Besides, you're a fucking *Bostonian*! People fly from all over the world to party in your city. You need to be there too."

I took some deep breaths before speaking again. "Toni, it sounds really fun, but I can't. I just can't."

Tears filled her eyes and her chin quivered. "Oh Erin. I ... I want you to come with me so bad. Please. I've been depressed lately. You have no idea." She flopped on her bed and cried into her pillow. "You're my best friend in the whole world."

She'd never said anything like that before, and as her sobbing grew harder, I went and sat beside her. I rubbed her back and hugged her awkwardly, and eventually, she sat up and wiped her eyes. "Erin, please, please, please come. I can't tell you how much this means to me." Then she wrapped her arms around my neck and hugged me harder than anyone had ever hugged me before.

One day, I decided. I can miss one day of school. As long as I'm back Monday night and get to all my classes Tuesday.

The bartender poured our first beers around 11 a.m.—our fake Danforth IDs clearly worked well in Boston—and by two o'clock, I was trashed. Like, barely able to keep my head up trashed. Runners in colorful shoes and clothes kept crossing the finish line on TV, but I couldn't identify any of them, and had no idea who'd won the races, or ... anything. Was it fun? I guess, but I couldn't help wondering why we hadn't just stayed in Providence and watched the race there, because we could've saved a lot of money.

The answer to that question came in the form of two guys about our age—one very cute, the other pretty average looking—who'd been checking out Toni and me from across the bar. Suddenly, they were standing behind us, asking where we went to school and if we enjoyed running. "Ha!" said Toni. "Yeah, we run from our dorm to the local bars."

"Sometimes we hitchhike," I added drunkenly.

Toni rolled her eyes and the guys laughed. The cute one had curly blond hair and high cheekbones; the other had a flat nose and dull gray eyes. I can't recall much about what we discussed—marathons, mostly, I think—but I definitely remember being introduced to a sweet, green drink called a Pearl Harbor. The guys insisted on buying a round, then another. But when the bartender cut us all off, the cute guy pointed to some middle-aged men eating lunch at a nearby booth. "Put it on their tab," he said. "They're the bosses."

The bartender nodded slowly. "So you fellows are with the hockey team too?"

"Yup," said the cute guy.

At that moment, one of the men in the booth looked over and waved at the bartender. "Yes, they're ours. Have fun, boys!"

I don't remember much after that, although I definitely had trouble walking out of the packed bar. Someone may have carried me. I also remember Toni asking the guys about hockey, and someone saying they played for a semi-pro Canadian team. I recall two people (probably the hockey players) holding my arms and helping me as I struggled to walk over cobblestones, then the very bright lobby of a fancy hotel, an elevator, and a dimly lit room with a big bed. Then, nothing until a sharp pain stabbed me in the vagina while a guy moaned.

Next thing I knew, sunlight was streaming through the open blinds, and someone was peeing loudly into a toilet. Looking down, I saw my body, completely naked on a strange bed with bloodstained sheets. Little shards of the previous night pierced my consciousness, and I deduced that the guy with the dull gray eyes was the person in the bathroom. I covered myself with part of the bedspread, my head throbbing.

Then—miraculously—I heard the shower start, and recognized my opportunity to flee. *I'm in Boston,* I remembered, *not too far from Danforth.* So I pulled on my clothes, grabbed my purse, ran out of the room, and headed down on the elevator. I had no plan at that point, but Providence was about an hour south.

"Congratulations!" said Toni as the elevator door opened in the lobby. "I've been looking for you!"

"Who were those guys?" My stomach wretched and my mouth filled with vomit. Toni grabbed my hand and dragged me out into the harsh sunlight, where I puked all over the cobblestones. "Toni, what happened last night?"

"Who cares?" she answered breezily, looking far too chipper. "You're in the club now. C'mon, let's go find the bus station."

A week later, the dean sent Mom a letter informing her that I'd been placed on academic probation. Then Toni missed her period, and for the first time ever, I saw true concern in my roommate's eyes.

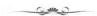

Chapter 13

November 1993

The black wool coat wasn't nearly warm enough. Twenty-nine years in New England—almost my whole damn life—and I still hadn't learned to properly prepare for winter. But why not? Why hadn't I bought that toasty, down-filled parka on sale for forty bucks at Filene's Basement in the spring? Hadn't I believed winter would eventually return? Was I following in the footsteps of other Winthropites who got so attached to their beaches each summer that they thought they could stave off the cold with mind power? Or had I just been so wrapped up in life at Don-Wash that I hadn't planned ahead for more than a week at a time?

In any case, I'd screwed up royally. Because if I'd known the Honda would die an ugly death on the side of the road—engulfed in flames like poor Lenny Weir—I would've done lots of things differently. Starting with buying that warm jacket.

The sleet turned to rain as I buttoned my damp wool collar over my chin and trudged toward the Route 145 intersection, my coffee mixing with icy precipitation. The paper cup from the convenience store slowly disintegrated in my hand, but I needed caffeine and intended to keep sipping until the thing fell apart completely. I felt like a character in a movie, in one of those critical scenes when she realizes she's really screwed up and needs to change her entire life.

But in those movies, the character is usually aware that she's making bad decisions and goes on making them anyway. In my case, I felt somewhat blindsided. I mean, I'd been driving up to Gloucester the previous week when my oil light went on, but that was why I kept a bottle of oil in the trunk. I pulled into the breakdown lane and popped the hood. Yes, the engine felt extra hot as I unscrewed the cap and started pouring, but concern never entered my mind.

Who knew that a few drops of oil spilled on a sizzling hot engine block had the potential to ignite? But a second later, the thing was ablaze. I panicked and screamed, and within moments, firefighters arrived at the scene. Thankfully, the car didn't explode, but it never started again either.

I didn't actually cry, though, until the tow truck guy told me that not only was the dear old Honda destined for the junkyard, but that I'd have to pay fifty bucks to dispose of it. Talk about bad luck. I'd been saving what little I could for a year, hoping to trade the Honda for something more reliable, but in matter of minutes, my trade-in was gone. In order to buy another car, I'd need to work harder, save more than ever, make even more sacrifices.

Number one on that list was cancelling my Thanksgiving trip to Texas. Meaning I'd have to spend my first big holiday alone. I wondered how that would work out as I slogged on through the freezing rain. In some ways, it felt unimaginable, but on the other hand, I'd avoid the risk of Mom hearing me puke Thanksgiving dinner down the toilet. She spent days preparing that meal, and I hated the thought of breaking her heart. *A thin silver lining*, I thought.

But aside from silver linings: how would I end this illness? Because it had to end. I didn't want to die of bulimia. Meanwhile, every day in the *Boston Globe*, I'd see ads for resorts where people with eating disorders could go to recover. Some of those resorts even had horses to ride. Part of me wished I could afford such things, while another part doubted their treatment could possibly help. I mean, I'd been puking—and hating it—for well over ten years, so what chance did horses have of stopping me? I mean, seriously.

So, I went on screwing Don and vomiting. At least I had Claire and Jeff and Pete. Three real, true friends who loved me.

Approximately thirty-five miles separated my house and Don Wash, and the commute involved three major highways and more side streets than I could count, all of which made hitching quite a challenge, but it was still quicker and easier than the alternative. Because to get to work via public transportation, I had to take a bus to the subway, the subway to the commuter train at North Station, that train (for over an hour) to Gloucester, then a bus that stopped a few blocks from Don-Wash. In other words, to be at work by 10:00 a.m., I had to leave my house at 6:30, which was ridiculous. And the trip home was even worse. If I left Don-Wash right at 7:00 p.m., I couldn't make it home until almost midnight.

And so, for the past few days, I'd been walking up to the intersection and sticking out my thumb. Yes, it was dangerous, embarrassing, and scary. But if I got lucky with rides, I could be at work in an hour and a half. And if I promised Don a blowjob at my house, he was happy enough to drive me home. It wasn't even a huge imposition for him, since the t-shirt factory he used was in nearby Everett, and he liked stopping in there to check on the outstanding orders.

I was soaked to the skin when I reached the 145 intersection, and with no one else to turn to, prayed silently to my angels in heaven. *Oh please, Jim* (Morrison), *or Freddie* (Mercury), *or anyone else up there watching over me, please send a ride soon. A good, long ride, so I can warm up a little. Please.* I squished what was left of the coffee cup and stared up at the gray November sky. But as I faced the traffic and raised my thumb, the reality of my situation overwhelmed me. I mean, I was risking death for a dead-end job, and depending on dead rock stars to get me there. I needed a *life.*

Not that anyone seemed to care. Cars kept speeding past, splattering me with gunk from the road, while little rivulets of rain streamed down my nose. Some drivers slowed a bit, apparently checking to make sure they weren't hallucinating. *Yes!* I felt like screaming. *Yes, I'm a woman hitching in the rain! Big fucking deal! Keep moving if you're not gonna help me!* But I kept my mouth shut and my face as optimistic as possible. Even though I couldn't feel my fingers, I knew no one would stop for an angry hitchhiker.

Finally, a shiny black Range Rover with tinted windows pulled over a few yards ahead of me. I was accustomed to older, more banged-up vehicles stopping; I think some people with nice cars worried about hitchers stinking them up or something. Suspiciously, then, I jogged up to the open passenger window. A bald guy about my age, wearing aviator sunglasses and a worn leather jacket, sat behind the wheel. "Where ya headed?" he asked in a deep, even tone. Something about him felt vaguely familiar. Was he one of my old customers from the Sand Dollar? Or maybe someone I'd worked with at a temp job?

"Gloucester," I said, my teeth chattering. "But I'll go anywhere in that direction. Anywhere north." Honestly, at that point, I might've gone south just to get out of the icy rain.

"No shit," he muttered. "Well, get in. I'm headed there too."

"You're going all the way to *Gloucester?*"

"Yup."

I couldn't believe it. *One ride?* That was a first. Usually it took three or four to make it all the way. I opened the heavy door and climbed in, my numb body collapsing against the leather seat. The heater blew hot air against my cheeks, and I peeled off my dripping gloves.

"Thanks for stopping," I said, noting that the guy wasn't dressed for the weather either. His old motorcycle jacket looked more suited to spring, and he wore red Converse hi-tops. "I was just about to go back home and call in sick."

He didn't respond right away. Instead, he focused his sunglasses on the road, saying nothing until he'd eased back into the flow of traffic. "No problem. You work in Gloucester?"

I'd definitely heard that voice before, but couldn't place the guy. At least my fingers were thawing out, and I rubbed my hands together. "Yeah, unfortunately."

"Sucky job?" he asked, assessing me briefly.

Yup, I thought. But I didn't feel like discussing my career—or lack thereof—with this stranger. So I turned and looked out the window, my blue eyes gazing back at me from the exterior mirror. "Nah. Just a sucky commute."

He regarded me with new interest. "You don't bum rides every day, do you?"

I wasn't about to answer that question honestly either. For all I knew, the guy was a serial killer or something, one of those dangerous people Claire kept warning me about. "No. My car's just in the shop. I should be getting it back tonight." *Okay, time to change the subject.* "So, why are *you* headed up to Gloucester today?"

His upper lip twitched a little. "Uh ... I'm sorta visiting a friend."

"Oh," I said, but my stomach tightened. How do you "sorta" visit a friend? Especially in this weather? Oh god, is this whole thing too much of a coincidence? Is he actually gonna bring me to work? Or will I never be heard from again?

I forced myself to stay calm, though, and breathe normally. After all, I'd taken rides with weirder people in Providence—at night—and had survived. But I did glance at the door to take note of where the handle and lock buttons were. A woman who'd driven me up Route 1 a few days earlier had advised that my best defense against a male attacker was a punch or kick to the balls, then a quick escape.

The guy drove on in silence, going the same way I would've if I'd been behind the wheel, and I relaxed a little. He checked his watch frequently and kept stretching his neck, but seemed more uptight than sinister. I wondered what kind of work he did to afford such a fancy car, especially since he didn't appear to be working that Monday morning. Maybe he worked nights. Maybe even as an artist or musician. I could only hope.

"What's your job?" he finally asked. I couldn't tell if he cared or was just making conversation.

"Oh, I sorta sell t-shirts." Sorta, I thought. I sorta sell t-shirts and he's sorta visiting a friend.

"Hmm," said the guy. "You work in a store?"

"Um, well, no. It's more like corporate sales, you know? Like for sports teams and businesses?" I rubbed my hands together again, even though they were quite warm by then. Part of me was being vague for personal safety, but I wasn't proud of my telemarketing career either.

"Cool," said the guy.

My outside sales job at Don-Wash had turned out disastrously. The real stress started when I learned that Don's t-shirts cost *way* more than comparable ones on the market, and that most customers only bought from his company so they could spend time with his fun-loving "salesgirls." During my training sessions, Tara happily demonstrated how she modeled the product for customers: she'd excuse herself to use the bathroom, then return wearing nothing but a t-shirt. Amy had been more reluctant to share her sales secrets, but did invite me to her annual customer appreciation party at a dive in Gloucester. The party reminded me of nights in Providence clubbing with Toni: excessive booze-swilling in air clouded with cigarette smoke and sexual innuendo.

But that stuff made me sick. So I tried selling in more conventional ways—laying out shirts on conference room tables, talking about the quality of their stitching—but Don's price point was simply too high without Tara and Amy's fringe benefits, and I sold next to nothing.

Eventually, then, I chose to "demote" myself and return to working with Claire.

Which was where I belonged. Not only because I enjoyed her company so much more than Don's, but Claire was also having issues with her boyfriend, Bobby. He'd been getting home late a lot and blaming it on traffic, but Claire had her doubts. She loved Bobby, of course, and wanted to trust him, but other guys had lied to her in the past and she knew where that led. I couldn't share any real dating experience with her, but I listened and provided what seemed like sensible advice. Hence, our friendship was developing into a genuine give-and-take thing.

The Range Rover guy turned on the radio, which was set to WFNX, the "alternative" station I'd been listening to for a few years. But by 1993, the term "alternative" had grown pretty murky. I mean, with mainstream stations focusing heavily on Smashing Pumpkins, Porno for Pyros, INXS, and Stone Temple Pilots, how could you call those bands "alternative?" The way I saw it, *alternative* had died with Lenny Weir.

"Radio sucks these days," said the guy. "I'm thinking of putting a CD player in the car. Although I hate CDs too."

CDs were still relatively new in late '93, but most people considered them superior to tapes and record albums, and even Claire was slowly updating her music catalog to CD. But I secretly hoped they'd go away; I wanted someone to find a fatal flaw in them or something. Because they were killing vinyl records, and I loved vinyl. I loved the big, square album jackets, especially ones that opened up like books. I loved the pictures too, and the liner notes, and I loved reading lyrics when artists chose to share them. Even though David Bowie had been one of the first major players to embrace CDs, I couldn't imagine replacing my beloved Bowie albums with those little silver discs and plastic boxes. Nor could I afford to. If I spent my money on a CD player, I'd have nothing to play on it. "What do you hate about CDs?" I asked the guy.

"Everything," he said in his familiar voice. "I hate the whole music business, if you want the truth. They've got everyone by the balls. Right now, everyone's switching over to CD, but as soon as that becomes the industry standard, they'll be ready with something newer and better. Just wait. There's always something newer and better. Trust me. I know from experience." He winced. "And honestly, every time they make a so-called *improvement*, they make things a little worse. No CD will ever duplicate the sound of a vinyl record. They lose the warmth when they digitalize it."

My stomach dipped like it was on a carnival ride and for a second, I felt like I was back in high school, watching Todd Eldridge play guitar. *Chill out, Erin!* I scolded myself. *Don't be stupid enough to fall for this guy. He could be a psycho.* But I agreed with him a hundred percent. And he knew about the music industry from experience! "I'm a big vinyl fan too," I told him, "but maybe that's because it's all I've got right now."

The guy pulled into the left lane to pass an old white K-car going about forty miles an hour, and I saw a man with white hair behind the wheel, singing to himself with a sentimental smile on his face. He looked fearless, despite the fact that he was heading up Route 128 in bad weather.

"Well, there's nothing wrong with being happy with what you've got," said my driver, his eyes lingering on the old man. "Look at that dude."

I smiled and relaxed a little more. "Yeah." He couldn't be a killer or a rapist; he seemed more like an old friend. We drove a few miles without speaking. Every once in a while, the guy would check his watch and stretch his neck, and I wished he'd take off his sunglasses for a second so I could see his eyes. But no. We listened to radio commercials for Giant Glass and some new nightclub, then a bunch of stupid DJ banter and songs by Screaming Trees and Pearl Jam.

Then the opening cello notes of Lenny Weir's posthumous "Weeds" came on, and sadness descended on me. Every time I heard the song, the sky seemed to darken, even on sunny days. And at nighttime, the lights in the room would dim. Always, I'd think back to that evening at the Middle East, and wish I'd known the man in the bathroom was Lenny. Maybe then, I could've helped him. On the radio, he began to sing.

Under water, under oceans

The speakers in the guy's car were definitely high end—far better than the ones in my crappy old Honda—and Lenny's naked voice sounded more vulnerable than ever against that mournful cello. *If only I hadn't been so wrapped up in Colin,* I thought. *If only ...*

Slam. The guy's fist pounded the radio's power button, silencing poor Lenny in mid-sentence. I felt like I'd been shot.

"Winterlong," he said with contempt. "I don't know about you, Erin, but I've had enough of that Weir asshole for the rest of my life."

My eyes widened. *Weir asshole?* Calling Lenny an asshole was, in my book, an offense punishable by death. Maybe he was exaggerating? But wait. *Wait.* Had he just called me *Erin*? Because I was pretty sure ... And no, I didn't tell him my name. Or did I? By accident? No. No, I never would. I mean, every hitcher knows you don't give drivers your real name. But I'd been semi-delirious with cold when I'd first gotten in the car. I tried to reconstruct our initial conversation, but couldn't.

Suddenly, way too much stuff was swirling around in my head. Part of me wanted out of that car immediately, but we were also pretty close to Gloucester and I needed to get to work.

"Have I ... have we met before?" I asked when I felt capable of keeping my voice steady.

"I don't think so," said the guy from behind his sunglasses. "But you never know. You meet a lotta people in this world."

Neither of us said another word until we reached the second rotary in Gloucester. I couldn't decide whether I should make an excuse and bail out—in which case I'd have to start hitching again in the freezing rain—or just sit tight and let the guy bring me to work. Finally, I decided to have him drop me somewhere *near* Don-Wash but not quite *at* Don-Wash. Better safe than sorry.

"You can let me out anywhere around here," I said. We were about a mile from where I needed to be.

"Seriously?" he asked. "You wanna get out *here*? At the lights?"

I didn't really, and the rain had gotten harder too. Suddenly, I remembered the industrial park just down the road from Don-Wash. I'd never been in the park, but it housed a big company called Cyrk. "Um, well, do you know where Cyrk is?"

The guy thought for a second. "Oh yeah. Yeah. You work *there*?"

"Right near there. That's a great place to drop me."

He looked confused for a second, then sighed and said, "Oh sure. You got it." He knew I didn't trust him.

I was embarrassed, but also relieved when he pulled over and stopped at the entrance to the Cyrk park. "Thanks so much," I said. "This is awesome." Maneuvering my fingers back into my wet gloves, I opened the car door as winter air rushed in and chilled me all over again. *Maybe he didn't actually call me Erin,* I thought. *Maybe I misunderstood.* But he'd definitely called Lenny an asshole.

"No problem," said the guy, handing me my purse. "So your car's getting fixed today?"

"Yeah. That's the plan anyway. Thanks ag—"

"Cause if it's not ready, I can take you again tomorrow. I'll probably drive back up here in the morning."

The same mix of fear and gratitude I'd felt earlier came surging back. "Back to Gloucester? Really? Why?"

The guy's mouth twitched. "Friends, you know? Visiting."

A car blasted past, sending slush in all directions. "Well," I said, "if you see me hitching ..."

"I'll stop," he said with a smile. "Or if you wanna gimme your address, I can swing by your place. Do you live in Revere?"

"Um ... no. Winthrop, actually. Hey, I gotta go. Maybe I'll see you at the rotary?" I slid off the seat and stepped out into the rain.

He nodded behind his sunglasses. "Winthrop. Cool. The original hometown of Little Steven."

"Little Steven?" I asked. "Isn't he from Jersey?" My head was getting soaked again, but I'd never heard anyone say Springsteen's guitarist was from Winthrop. It couldn't be true.

"Nope. He lived in Winthrop when he was little. Look it up."

"Wow," I said. "That's ... wow."

He looked at his watch again. "All right. Take care. And good luck with your car. I'll keep an eye out for you tomorrow."

I watched him drive away, noting that he was careful not to splash me. When he was out of sight, I crossed the street and walked the short distance to Don-Wash.

CHAPTER 14

May 1983

Toni quit Danforth a week before finals, and I never saw her again. To this day, I regret the way I wasted freshman year, allowing myself to participate in her fucked-up adventures weekend after weekend. I guess she never really considered me a friend; I was more of an escort, paid in cocktails.

The night before she left to go home for good, I walked in on her in our dorm room, talking on the phone to her mom. She was all hunched over on the bed—her hair uncombed—sobbing into the receiver like a child. Even her voice sounded babyish as she said things like, "I don't know, Mommy," and "I'm so, so sorry," and "yeah, she *is* a bad influence." I was confused. I mean, since *I* was the only girl Toni ever spent time with, who was this "bad influence?" And if she could apologize so passionately to her mother, didn't she owe *me* an apology too? After all, she'd ditched me in every dive in Providence. But when she hung up the phone, she said she was too sick to talk, pulled the covers over her head, and turned out the lights. I was forced to change into my sweats in the dark, then try to sleep, despite the fact that it was only ten o'clock on Saturday night.

The next morning, Toni's father showed up in slacks and a sport jacket. I was still in bed when he knocked on our door, but my roommate was already showered and dressed in clean Girbaud jeans and a preppy peach sweater I'd never seen before. Her dad assessed my flattened "new wave" haircut and wine-stained sweatpants with unabashed disgust. I said hello to him, but he acted like he hadn't heard me.

"I talked to Aunt Dolores," he told his daughter. "She made some recommendations."

"For a therapist?" asked Toni.

"Yeah. For ... everything. C'mon. Let's get outta here. We'll talk in the car."

He grabbed two of Toni's suitcases, and Toni picked up the other without a word. Not knowing what to do, I followed them down the stairs and out to where her dad's Saab was parked. The trunk was open, and her dad tossed the suitcases in.

"Bye, Erin," said Toni as her father started the car and she opened the passenger-side door.

"Bye?" I answered, barely able to speak. I felt like a fish being gutted alive by the person who'd caught me. "That's it?"

Toni shrugged and came sulking back to give me a quick hug while her dad drummed his fingers on the steering wheel. "I'm doing the right thing," she said, picking a strand of my hair off the sleeve of her sweater. Then she laughed a strange, nervous laugh and stepped into the car.

I'm not sure I've ever felt as alone as I felt that morning. Toni had two parents who'd help her reboot her life after the abortion, and she was already planning to start college again in a semester or two. At a different school, of course. With a different roommate. And a clean slate. But what about me? Who was going to help me?

At that moment, I experienced a small epiphany. Looking out across the manicured lawns and brick buildings that made Danforth such a quaint New England campus, I realized I'd have to help myself. I didn't love the school—I didn't even like it—but the thought of returning to Winthrop as a college failure was even worse. I had a week. One week to get ready for finals.

It took hours just to locate the various syllabuses for each of my five classes, but once I did, I started reading immediately. I also asked two girls from my hallway if I could Xerox their class notes, and when they hesitated, I played the poor-fatherless-girl card until they handed over their notebooks. Sure, I felt bad, but what else could I do?

And since I needed every potential hour for studying, I drank gallons of coffee and experimented with No-Doze—the latter making me miserably sick—but no matter how much reading I got through, I remained at the bottom of a mountain. So I scheduled meetings with four of my professors and begged for mercy. As I'd done with the girls in my dorm, I talked about the pain I'd felt after losing my father, and the depression that'd kept me from attending classes at Danforth. And you know what? I think I actually started believing myself after a while. "I'm not asking you to do anything unfair," I told the professors earnestly, "but I'd really appreciate you taking this stuff into consideration when you grade my finals."

None of them guaranteed anything, but I felt their sympathy. My psychology teacher even gave me extra time to prepare for her exam, which was really nice. Sure, it meant I'd have to stay on campus two days longer than the other freshmen, but I didn't mind. And although my stomach was a mess when I handed my final blue book to her, I knew I'd answered most of the multiple-choice questions correctly. I felt okay about the short answers too, and was pretty certain the bullshit in my essays was high-quality bullshit.

Once I returned to my quiet dorm hallway, though, I felt really ill. The moldy beer smell rising from the carpets had intensified over the past couple of days, since the school had instructed students to close and lock all windows before leaving for summer break. I wanted to crawl into bed and cry.

But Mom was coming to get me in a couple of hours, and I had to clean out my room. Tears streamed down my face as I carefully took down the posters of Ziggy Stardust and Jim Morrison, realizing—as the walls grew bare—that this space that had once held so much promise for Toni and me would soon be just another generic dorm room again. Perhaps next year's occupants would achieve more; maybe they'd accomplish things I'd attempted but failed at so miserably. Like making good friends, going on dates, doing stuff they're proud to talk about with people back home. How had I ...

"Hey Erin! Is that you?" I didn't recognize the woman's voice coming from down the hall.

"Yeah?" I answered, placing Jim Morrison on the bed. "Who's that?"

"Down here. We're in 318."

My room number was 303, and I didn't know anyone at that end of the hall. They were all juniors and seniors, and most didn't interact with freshmen. But the voice had called me by name, so what could I do? I wiped my eyes and headed that way.

"Hey," I said, peering into the darkened room. The shades were drawn, but I could make out the forms of two girls sitting beside each other on a bed. A cigarette lighter clicked, and the flame momentarily illuminated their faces. I recognized them from around campus, but we'd never spoken. The room smelled like old pizza, burnt popcorn, and tobacco smoke. On the stereo, a record played, but I couldn't identify the singer. His voice sounded like Bruce Springsteen's, but with no horns, no drums, and no electric guitars. Just acoustic guitar and harmonica.

"Was that you playing *The Man Who Sold the World* this morning?" asked the dark-haired girl with the cigarette.

My cheeks heated up. "Oh, I'm sorry! I was getting psyched for a test. I thought the whole floor was empty."

"Pssh!" said the other girl, her blondish ponytail swaying back and forth as she smiled. "We're not complaining. We love that old Bowie shit. We were just surprised. We thought *we* were the only ones left on the hall. Hey, where're you living next year?"

I didn't even know if I'd be back at Danforth. The day after Toni went home, I'd thrown my name into the general housing lottery. Meaning that if my final grades made the cut, I'd receive a letter over the summer informing me of my new roommate situation. If not, oh well. "It's complicated," I said.

"I'll bet," said the dark-haired smoker. "Sucks that your roommate Tina got knocked up."

"Toni," I said quietly.

"Huh?"

"Her name's Toni."

The girl shrugged. "Toni? Tina? It still sucks for you. That's why we were thinking you might wanna move in with us." She shrugged again. "Totally your call, though."

Live with them? *These* girls? *Why*? My eyes had adjusted enough to identify several Springsteen posters on the walls and a carton of Doral cigarettes on one of the desks. A large jug of red wine held the door open, and an empty pizza box served as an ashtray on the floor. I realized my mouth was hanging open, and snapped it shut.

"What's wrong? Do we smell bad?" asked the girl with the ponytail.

"No!" I said. "It's just ... well ... I don't even know your names."

The ponytail girl giggled while the other one smiled wryly. "Fair enough," she said. "I'm Janet and this is Beverly. And we both like Bowie. A lot. What else you wanna know?"

"Um, I don't know," I answered, feeling slightly silly. "This is just ... sudden."

Beverly looked concerned. "Well, I love Bowie, but not *Let's Dance*."

"Yeah," agreed Janet. "Me too. *Let's Dance* sucks."

"Me three," I said. Honestly, I couldn't believe Bowie had even been *capable* of making an album as bad as *Let's Dance*. It sounded like it'd been written for pop radio, and all the Top 40 stations were playing the hits from it like crazy.

"Whadya you think happened to him?" asked Janet.

"I don't know," I said, suddenly realizing I needed to get back to my room and finish packing.

"Well, at least it's better than the new Bruce," she said, nodding toward the turntable. "This is *total* shit."

"Wait. This is Springsteen singing now?" I asked, slightly proud of myself for recognizing his voice earlier, but still stunned. I mean, what the hell had happened to *Bruce*? He sounded sad. Maybe even humbled.

"I guess he's been experimenting," said Janet with a sarcastic smile.

"The album's called *Nebraska*," added Beverly. "He recorded the whole thing in his bedroom. "

"Yup," said Janet. "Sounds that way too, huh?"

"I guess so," I said, although Bruce's lyrics distracted me from the conversation. And for the first time ever, they interested me. He was singing about being a little boy, going with his dad to test-drive a used car. Then, in the chorus, the boy dreams of someday winning the lottery and buying a brand-new car.

"This *totally* doesn't sound like Bruce," I said. "It sounds like one of my dad's old Johnny Cash records or something."

"Yeah?" said Janet. "Well, maybe your dad would like *Nebraska*. Feel free to bring it home to him. Unless you want it, Bev."

Beverly looked slightly unsure. "Nah," she concluded. "I'll never listen to it. Take it, Erin."

"My dad's dead," I said.

Both girls expressed sympathy simultaneously. "We had no idea," said Janet.

"Don't worry, it's fine," I assured them. "Really. He died a couple years ago."

Bev got off the bed and opened the blinds, letting in some gray light. "My grandma's dying," she said. "It sucks."

"Yeah, it always sucks," I agreed. "I'm sorry about your grandma." Then, to change the subject, I said, "But you know, this record's actually kinda cool. I'm not ... uh ... I'm not necessarily the world's biggest Springsteen fan."

It's hard to say what shocked Janet and Bev more: the news of Dad's death or hearing that I wasn't crazy about Bruce. They exchanged eye contact, then nodded somberly. "It's okay," said Janet, "and if you're into it, we'd still like to live with you next year."

They were really sweet. But what did two almost-seniors want with me? "I'd love to," I blurted. "But the truth is, I might've flunked out this semester. I'm not sure I can come back."

Once again, the girls looked at each other before responding to me. "But you don't know yet?" said Janet, raising her eyebrows.

"No. Not 'til grades come out. I guess in a few weeks?"

Bev smiled and Janet said, "Cool."

I didn't understand. "What's cool about that?"

"Well," said Janet, "we applied for one of those mini-suites on the top floor. But our third roommate sorta pulled a Tina on us the other day. Toni, I mean."

"She got pregnant?" I asked.

Bev chuckled. "Nah. She left Danforth for another reason."

"But if we don't find a third roomie today, we lose the suite and end up in the housing lottery," said Janet. "Bottom line is, we need you, Erin. So say yes. *Please.*"

"*Please?*" echoed Bev.

I was truly flattered, but a little scared too. "What if I flunk out?"

Janet smiled. "One thing at a time. But if you do ... I think it'll be too late to take the suite away from us. The housing people want everything settled this week. That's what they told us anyway."

"So you two would get a suite all to yourselves."

"Maybe," said Janet. "Who knows? But for now, let's just say the three of us are living together next year. Okay?"

"Okay," I said.

Bev clapped her hands. "Yay! And Erin, the suite's amazing. It's got a little kitchen where you can plug in a hotpot, and its *own* bathroom. No more gross community toilets and showers."

"Wow," I said. "I hope I get to live there."

Janet smiled and walked over to the record player. Without a word, she picked up the needle, pressed her hand against the black vinyl disk until it stopped spinning, and lifted it off the machine. Then she slipped the album into its jacket and wrote a phone number on the outside in pen. "Here's your door prize," she said, batting her lashes just a little. "And that's my phone number. Lemme know what happens with your grades, okay?"

"Thanks," I said. "But I gotta run now. My mom'll be here in a few minutes."

I'd had no TV at Danforth, so it wasn't until I got home to Winthrop that I got to see the full extent of David Bowie's transformation from eccentric, androgynous genius to pop star. And although I tried *really* hard to remain supportive of him, one hot day in June—as I watched the "China Girl" video on MTV—I gave up.

All those images of David and his glowing white skin, kissing a pretty Chinese woman and throwing a bowl of rice over his head. It was too much. Ridiculous. Why would he beg for the general public's acceptance when mainstream acceptance was the *antithesis* of Bowie?

Luckily, I knew enough about David to know how much he loved trying out new styles of music and clothing, so I felt certain he'd ditch the pop star thing soon. But I couldn't join him on his shiny, happy trail.

On the other hand, that song on Springsteen's *Nebraska* record—the one I'd heard in Janet and Beverly's room, about the dude buying a used car—haunted me from beneath my bed, where I'd stashed the album. One night, I even dreamed about it. But I couldn't bear to play the thing. I mean, Erin Reardon didn't listen to Springsteen. Hating Bruce was a big part of my identity. Not that anyone in Winthrop would know or care about my musical choices, but *I* cared. I had principals about that kind of thing.

Instead of giving in, I focused heavily on the new wave music getting commercial airplay in 1983—the Cure, Squeeze, Eurythmics, the Police, Culture Club—and liked them all. But all those bands lacked the one essential element I craved: a strong, gorgeous, male singer to idolize and obsess over. Sting from the Police probably came closest, but he was married, not to mention too serious and intellectual for a girl like me. I couldn't quite get a handle on the Cure's Robert Smith—with his smudged red lipstick and hairspray—and although Boy George was awesome, I didn't get the sense he'd want to hang out with me. *I guess I'll go it alone for a while,* I decided.

Besides, I'd started puking again, and that kept me occupied. Returning to my disgusting habit made me feel like a failure, but I'd quit once, and I could quit again. The second time would probably be easier, too.

Right?

Then came the night Mom called to say she wouldn't be home until morning. She claimed to be out with the girls and too tired to drive, but I could hear the liquor in her voice.

"Mom, what girls are you with?"

She hesitated a minute before answering, "Just Joanie and Louise. Hey, honey, I gotta run. I'll see you tomorrow. Love you." In the background, a man laughed softly, and Mom giggled. Then she hung up.

So Mom was sleeping with a guy. *My* mom. I didn't know if it was the first time since Dad's death or the hundredth, but it didn't matter. What mattered was that she was out having sex—and fun—while her nineteen-year-old daughter sat at home, mixing up a post-vomit screwdriver. I felt sick.

I poured more vodka into my glass and thought about that Springsteen song again. Meanwhile, on the radio, Men Without Hats sang "The Safety Dance," one of the dumbest songs ever. *Oh what the fuck?* I decided, pulling *Nebraska* out from under the bed and studying its stark black and white cover.

The photo featured lots of ominous clouds with something dark and shiny beneath them. A lake, perhaps? But on closer inspection, I realized the picture had been taken through the windshield of a car—or truck—driving on a road in the middle of nowhere. The ground was speckled with snow, but no signs of life appeared anywhere, and the words "Bruce Springsteen" and "Nebraska" appeared in the color of blood. Flipping the jacket over, I was disappointed to see nothing but a blood-red list of songs.

Compared to the busy, colorful *Let's Dance* album cover—with its photo of blond, bare-chested Bowie in boxing gloves on the front—*Nebraska* looked threatening. If *Let's Dance* was an invitation to a funky nightclub, *Nebraska* was the funeral home across the street. Just the same, I longed to hear it. All of it, just once. Then I'd get it out of my system and could stop thinking about it.

My palms sweated as I slipped the vinyl disk out of its sleeve and placed it on the turntable. Just seeing Springsteen's name in my bedroom made me feel like I was cheating on someone. I mean, how many times had Toni and I made fun of the Danforth people listening to Bruce? But I calmed myself with another sip of the cocktail and a shot of the truth: *I didn't buy the album. It was a gift I couldn't refuse.*

Then a lonely harmonica wailed, and Bruce began singing about a young girl spinning a baton on her front lawn. I turned up the volume. In the second line, he says he took the girl out for a ride, then ten innocent people were killed. He was narrating the song in the voice of a murderer! Pretty much the opposite of Tenth Avenue Freeze-Out.

The entire album went on like that. The next song was about someone called the Chicken Man, who got blown up—killed, I assumed—while another guy kept trying to convince his girlfriend to put on some makeup and take a bus with him to Atlantic City. The guy had no job, and planned to do something illegal for money. Plus, he kept talking about death, with that sad harmonica and acoustic guitar in the background. In other words, the trip to Atlantic City wasn't gonna be a good time.

I couldn't believe the irony. Bowie, the voice of outliers everywhere, had gone commercial, while American Jersey Boy Bruce had turned so bleak that even longtime fans like Janet and Bev had given up on his new record. I swallowed more vodka and lay there listening to one mournful story after another about wasted dreams, desperate people, messed-up Vietnam vets, and cops who didn't know the difference between right and wrong. Then I must've fallen asleep, because I awoke the next morning with the turntable still spinning and the needle gliding back and forth across the smooth ribbon of vinyl at the end of the record. My head ached, and Mom still wasn't home.

Maybe if I'd known that the guy she'd slept with the previous night—Edward—would end up being her boyfriend for decades, I would've felt less stress. But I had no idea, and wasn't sure what to do. I wasn't scheduled to work at the Sand Dollar that Sunday, so I showered, washed my hair, and cleaned my room. I considered taking a walk on the beach, but my stomach felt hollow. Instead, I decided to make a pot of coffee and listen to more Springsteen.

But rather than start at the beginning of the record, I laid the needle on the second-to-last song, called "My Father's House." It reminded me a little of "Used Cars," because it's about a man looking back on childhood. He's thinking about the house where he grew up, and the comfort he once felt in his father's arms. But then bad stuff happened, and the guy and his dad parted ways and stopped communicating. Now, as an adult, the guy wants to resolve things. So he drives back to his old home and walks up the steps only to find a stranger living there, with no info about his dad. And so the guy stands outside, realizing he'll never talk to his father again. His sins will forever remain unatoned.

Unatoned. I lay there on my bed, recalling all the unresolved issues I had with my dad, and how I'd never even tried to apologize for letting him drive drunk. Did something similar happen between Bruce and his father? It must've, because why else would someone write a song like "My Father's House?" I shivered and wondered if maybe I'd been wrong about this Springsteen dude. Was it possible that he had some talent after all?

The first week of July, my grades showed up in the mail and I screamed out loud when I saw that I'd earned straight Cs for second semester. Not even one D. I'd been taken off academic probation, at least for a while.

It's a reason to believe, I thought. Not so coincidentally, "Reason to Believe" was the title of the final track on *Nebraska,* which I'd been listening to quite a lot. And as reluctant as I was to admit it (to myself, of course), I'd also been getting acquainted with the albums *Born to Run, Greetings from Asbury Park,* and *The River.* At first, I thought maybe I'd lost my mind or something, but eventually I realized that I'd simply never given Bruce a fair chance. For some reason, I'd *wanted* to hate him, which was very sad. Especially since he was so beautiful and depressed.

Anyway, once I actually paid attention to the lyrics of songs like "Lost in the Flood" and "Meeting Across the River"—I heard the same darkness, the same doubts and pain, the same sad ironies I loved on *Nebraska.* Then, when I forced myself to listen to some of his slicker tunes—the ones I'd found completely intolerable during my freshman year at Danforth—I discovered that most of *them* were okay too. Underneath all those horns and splashy keyboards lay heartfelt stories about ordinary, working-class people trying to live decent lives.

Bruce also inspired me to consider socioeconomics for the first time. Growing up in Winthrop, most of my peers came from blue-collar backgrounds like mine, and although Toni obviously had more money than me, I'd never thought about the fact that she and I belonged to different social classes. Naively, I'd thought all Americans were basically the same. But although Bruce identified with the working class, he understood that rich people—like the folks in his song "Mansion on the Hill"—were different. They didn't struggle to buy used cars; they hosted parties in fancy houses surrounded by iron gates. They were wealthy, but weird too. Some were also corrupt.

Bruce had no use for people like that, either. He desired working-class girls: waitresses and factory workers, with names like Sandy, Cherry, Mary, and Rosie. Some hung out on the boardwalk drinking beer on summer nights, while others got their kicks at local carnivals. Some hid on the backstreets, sleeping in abandoned beach houses. Still others danced alone on their front porches, or huddled in cars with their boyfriends, dreaming of something better. Like me, they desperately wanted to leave their hometowns—full of losers—behind and start over someplace else. And Bruce made it all sound so romantic.

He believed in a Promised Land too, right here on earth. I wasn't quite sure what that meant, but I knew I wanted to go there with him. I wanted to wrap my legs around his velvet rims ... and ... yeah. I wanted to do everything he sang about doing in "Born to Run," and "Thunder Road" too.

And he lived nearby! Just about a thousand miles down the Atlantic coast. My hair was growing out all dark and natural again, so I'd just need to quit puking, get into shape, and spend some time lying on the beach. I'd become the beautiful, tanned, working-class girlfriend Bruce obviously needed.

Of course, if I'd had any idea that he'd already begun work on *Born in the USA*—the full-scale, E Street Band album that would yank Bruce out of his depressive *Nebraska* phase and transform him into an A-list American icon just a year later—I never would've allowed myself to get so attached to him. But I couldn't see into the future.

So I formulated a plan: I'd save my tip money from the Sand Dollar and head down to the Jersey Shore in August. According to a story I'd read in *Rolling Stone*, Bruce often played at a bar in Asbury Park called the Stone Pony, so I'd go there and introduce myself after a show. Never did it occur to me that hundreds of other people might have had the exact same idea. As far as I was concerned, Springsteen was mine for the taking.

Chapter 15

November/December 1993

After he'd driven me to work three weekdays in a row, I inquired about his name. "You look familiar," I said. "I'm not sure why, but I feel like I've met you before. Someplace."

"Huh," he said, keeping his eyes on the road. "I don't know. My name's Luke. What's yours?"

"Erin."

"Cool," he answered. "Nice to officially meet you, Erin." Nothing in his tone indicated that he was hiding anything, so I decided I'd imagined him calling me *Erin* on that first ride up to Gloucester. I mean, what other explanation could possibly make sense?

A few days later, I told him the garage had called with bad news. My car was totaled.

"Oh wow. What're you gonna do?"

"Keep hitching, I guess. I can't afford another one right now."

He sighed. "I hear you. Well, anytime I see you on the road, I'll pick you up. I drive to Gloucester a lot."

Clearly, he did. And it was making my life a lot easier. But although I'd begun sharing more information with him, he revealed very little about himself.

The Range Rover crawled past the fake cows outside the Hilltop Steak House on Route 1. Due to an accident on the road ahead, traffic was backed up at least a mile.

"You ever eat at that place?" asked Luke.

I nodded, wishing I had a coffee. I usually stopped at the convenience store before hitting the road, but had overslept that day. And now, because of all the traffic, I'd missed Tara's nine-thirty Dunkin Donuts run, and Claire had recently switched from coffee to herbal tea. In other words, I wasn't getting any caffeine until lunchtime. "Oh yeah," I told Luke. "My family loved the Hilltop. Their steaks always tasted so much better than steaks everywhere else. Sometimes we'd wait an hour—maybe even two—for a table."

Luke chuckled. "So you'd hang out there on the lawn with all those plastic cows, then go inside and order yourself up some beef?"

"Yeah," I said with a shrug and a smile. "Everyone did. Didn't you?"

He laughed again and his lip twitched. "Hell no. I'm not from here. Besides, I don't eat meat."

That may have been the most personal thing he'd disclosed yet, but despite—or maybe because of—his mysterious nature, I found myself developing a serious crush on Luke. I loved the sharp angles of his face: his hard jawline, those high cheekbones, the deep cleft in his chin. I'd also glimpsed his hazel eyes for one brief second—when he removed his Ray Bans to clean them—and had seen intelligence and kindness in there. I believed I could trust those eyes.

"Where *did* you grow up?" I asked, hoping that didn't sound too nosy.

His mouth twitched. "Oh, all over. My family moved a lot when I was a kid."

"Hmm. But you've been in Revere a while?"

"Yeah, I guess you'd say that," he answered, his neck muscles tensing as he swallowed. "Hey, could you look in the glove box for some tissues? I think I'm getting a cold."

He didn't seem sick to me, but I found a napkin and handed it to him. "Thanks," he said, blowing his nose.

Another thing that puzzled me was Luke's baldness. The guy obviously shaved his head regularly, because on days when he *didn't*, his hair would start growing in. Then, a day or two later, it'd be gone again and he'd have razor nicks on his scalp. But unlike many men who rock the cue ball look, Luke didn't appear to be losing his hair. In other words, when he had stubble, it covered his *entire* head, and his hairline wasn't receding at all. Why would a man with a full head of hair *choose* to shave it off? Especially in the winter.

The traffic remained stalled. Far ahead, I could see flashing red and blue lights, but how long we'd sit there was anyone's guess. Luke turned on the radio, and I got the distinct sense he didn't feel like talking any more. With a glance at the clock, I thought about how pissed Don would be when I arrived at Don-Wash.

Our nasty little "affair" was still going strong, or at least as strong as a sexual relationship between a thirty-year-old woman and her married boss could be. Don and Tara had "broken up" (she'd met a new guy at a dance club), so I'd inherited the role of Don's number one office girl, and he was still bringing me home to Winthrop every night. But when I worked late, he'd be late for dinner with his wife too. And although he hadn't mentioned anything about it to me, I knew he was worried. I mean, how could a person be married to Don and *not* suspect something was up?

And speaking of suspicion, Claire didn't trust Luke at all. "He's gotta be some kinda perv," she said one afternoon at work. "Driving you all the way up here every day? It's not normal. And why's he so secretive? What's he hiding?"

"Probably nothing. We just don't talk much. I hardly tell him anything about me either."

She shook her head. "C'mon, Reardon. You're a woman and he's a guy. You're the passenger and he's the driver. What's he got to lose? But you? You've got everything. He could be one of those creeps that makes snuff films or something." Her eyes widened. "Actually, now that I think about it, he's probably a drug dealer. You know Gloucester has, like, a record number of heroin users, right? And he drives up here every day? Think about it. I can't believe you told him where you work. You're looking for serious trouble."

It was true that after a couple of days of getting dropped off at the industrial park, I'd started letting Luke bring me directly to Don-Wash. It seemed silly to keep my work address a secret since at least one other person was always in the office with me. And Luke was so sweet.

"He's just shy, Claire," I assured my friend. "I'm pretty sure he's no drug dealer. And I really like him."

"Yup. And you like Don too. So excuse my bluntness, but I question your taste in men." Claire had figured out I was having sex with Don the day she overheard him asking if I had condoms at my house. Although he'd asked the question so loudly that I think he *wanted* her to know.

"I don't *really* like Don," I said. "But he's nice to me and he drives me home, and believe it or not, he's very gentle—"

"Stop!" said Claire, shutting her eyes and shaking her head. "I don't wanna hear a word about your sex life with Don! Ugh!" She sighed and blinked a few times. "Listen, Reardon, I'm sorry. You know I love you, but I'm worried you're gonna turn up dead. 'Cause your choices? I mean, what the fuck? Maybe it's got something to do with your dad dying when you were young, but you gotta wake the fuck up. Like, for real. You need therapy. Okay?"

"Okay," I replied quickly. "I'll think about it." It wasn't the first time she'd made that suggestion.

"No. No more thinking. Do it. Call the number on your health insurance card *today*, and ask for their list of therapists. I know I already told you how that shrink I saw when I lived with Fergus literally saved my life, but I'm saying it again. She's the reason I'm alive today."

"Do you think you'll go back to her to talk about Bobby?" I asked. Bobby had admitted to hanging out with his ex-girlfriend Lizzy from time to time, but claimed it was all platonic. Claire wasn't so sure.

"Maybe. But right now, we're talking about *you*, Reardon. And you need serious help."

Part of me loved the idea of lying on a couch with an intelligent, caring professional who'd listen to me and provide advice about men. But wouldn't a good shrink also know the telltale signs of eating disorders? And if I got "outed," I'd probably get sent to a hospital and be forced to quit. Which I couldn't handle. Not yet. I mean, I hated being bulimic, but also wasn't ready to surrender my "freedom." Of course, that freedom enabled my destruction, but I couldn't see that.

Besides, I'd been cutting back on my puking, mainly because of logistics. With Luke driving me to work each morning, and Don driving me home, it was almost impossible to get to the supermarket on workdays. Some evenings, after Don left my apartment, I'd walk down to the convenience store and buy some junk food, but everything there was so expensive. I also hated standing in the checkout line with a gallon of ice cream and a family-sized bag of Doritos when everyone else just wanted cigarettes and lottery tickets. Even worse, sometimes the owner—a sweet, motherly woman—would ask how I managed to pack away all those calories. I'd usually laugh and tell her I had guests coming over, but she'd give me a funny look. After all, who feeds guests ice cream and Doritos on a regular basis?

So a lot of the time, I'd just scarf down a bowl of cereal or a peanut butter sandwich for dinner, and digest it normally. Then I'd crack open a beer or pour a glass of wine, and watch TV in the living room like a healthy person. If my roommates got home early enough, we'd watch *Leno* or *Letterman* together.

Those are the nights I choose to remember when I think about that phase of my life. I never grew tired of hearing Jeff and Pete's stories about the annoying customers at their restaurant, or their crazy, funny, creative coworkers. And when I got to witness how much my roommates loved each other—how considerate they were, and how they never seemed to get under each other's skin—I'd dream of having a real partner someday. Then I'd go to bed wishing Luke could sleep beside me.

As winter weather settled into New England, I stopped wondering why Luke drove up to Gloucester every morning. I mean, what did it matter? He was never rude, and we got along great. Some days, I actually wondered if he *had* been sent to me by Freddie Mercury.

Then, two weeks before Christmas, Luke turned to me and said, "I'm taking a vacation."

"When?" I asked, trying not to sound too rattled. I'd grown accustomed to riding in his warm Range Rover, and had naively assumed that my days of hitching to work were in the past.

"Pretty soon," he answered, his eyes glued to the road. We were at the rotary at the end of Route 128, meaning that we'd arrive at Don-Wash in a few minutes.

My stomach knotted up. I mean, lots of people take vacation during the holiday season, but Luke's news caught me by surprise anyway. He just didn't strike me as the type of guy who made a big deal out of holidays; Thanksgiving had come and gone without him ever mentioning it. "Are you ... going to see family?" I asked.

The twitching around his mouth started immediately. "No. I'm just going down to Miami for a while."

A while? Pretty soon? I needed more specifics. I'd already taken a bunch of days off that year, and Don wasn't going to let me take more just because my morning driver wasn't available. He liked having sex with me, but also needed me at my desk making phone calls. "Oh. Okay. You mean like *tomorrow*?"

Luke shook his head and let his breath out heavily. "No. Not tomorrow. Listen, Erin, I know this is weird, but I don't know exactly when. But it'll be soon."

"O ... kay?"

"Yeah," he answered, scratching his bald head. "And I promise I'll give you more info when I have it. Until then, I can keep driving you to work. But you should probably think about getting that new car. You know?"

For the first time, I wondered if Claire might be right. I mean, could Luke be a drug dealer anticipating some sort of trouble? "I've been looking at cars," I lied. "I just haven't found one yet."

"Yeah. Good ones are hard to find." He laughed humorlessly. "In all aspects of life."

He pulled into the Don-Wash parking lot, and my eyes filled up. "Yeah, that's true." I fumbled to unbuckle my seatbelt, which seemed trickier than usual.

"Erin, are you all right?"

"Yeah. Of course." I knew it wasn't fair to make him feel bad, but I couldn't help getting emotional either. And it was all my fault. What kind of idiot would fall for a guy who drove her up the highway every day but barely spoke at all? I grabbed my purse and opened the door.

But he reached over and laid his hand on my forearm. "Don't worry, Erin," he said, focusing those Ray-Bans on me. "We'll work something out. I won't be leaving for at least a week. Okay?"

"Okay," I blurted, startled by his touch and practically jumping out of the car. "Thanks. Thanks for everything."

The next morning, when he met me at the intersection, his nose was running, and he yawned twice in a row. "Sorry, man, I caught that cold bad. Didn't sleep all night." He yawned again. "I gotta get some coffee."

Man? Luke had never called me *man* before. Nor had we ever stopped for coffee together. He'd told me he only drank one cup a day, first thing in the morning. But the guy obviously needed something—possibly more than caffeine.

I assumed we'd start heading north and stop for coffee on Route One, but Luke had a different idea. He did a U-turn and drove down a side street to a Brazilian convenience store in Revere.

"How do you take it?" I asked, opening my door and hopping out. Buying Luke's coffee was the least I could do, since he never accepted the gas money I offered.

"Black, six sugars," he replied with another yawn. "Extra large."

Six sugars? Whatever. I had to wait in a short line for the coffee, and when I returned to the Range Rover, I found Luke slumped over the wheel. His sunglasses had fallen to the floor, and he was actually snoring. "Luke?" I said, tapping his shoulder. "Luke, are you okay?"

"Umm, yeah. Just tired." I could tell by the way he smelled that he hadn't showered.

"Uh, are you gonna be able to drive?" I asked.

He didn't respond.

"Luke, can you drive?" I started to panic. I mean, I couldn't leave him there alone, but I needed to get to work.

"No. You gotta do it."

Oh, holy shit. I'd never driven anything as big as a Range Rover, and Luke's car was practically brand new. "Are you sure?"

But he'd gone back to sleep. It occurred to me that I should try to get him home. Don would be pissed, but Luke needed help.

"Luke," I said, "I think you need to rest. If you tell me where you live, I can bring you there."

Those words rallied him. Grabbing the steering wheel, he pushed himself back into a sitting position. "No," he said, his eyes still closed. "You gotta get to Gloucester. Just drive. Please."

I had no idea what would happen when we reached Don-Wash, but at least the Range Rover had an automatic transmission.

"Okay," I said. "Can you slide into the passenger seat?"

Cruising up 128 behind the leather steering wheel, I gazed down at the cars below and smiled a little smile. The SUV was pretty easy to drive, and I felt a bit like a movie star. Or a drug dealer.

Of course, I kept glancing over at Luke, hoping he'd wake up and start acting normal. But he remained totally crashed out until we reached Don-Wash. Sighing, I parked at the far end of the lot and nudged him again. "We're here," I said. "Do you wanna come inside with me and rest for a while?" Don-Wash didn't have a couch or anything, but at least the building had heat.

He opened his eyes partway, obviously confused. "No. No. Just grab me the blanket. It's in the back."

Sure enough, I found a heavy wool blanket stashed in the back of the truck, along with a deflated rubber raft, a hard-shell guitar case, an air pump, and a spiral notebook with no cover. On the exposed page were lots of illegible words—written in longhand—and I knew just enough about music to know that the letters printed above the words were guitar chords. *So he is a musician!* I thought. *Maybe that's why he's going away. Maybe he's going on tour or something.*

The outdoor temperature was about thirty-five degrees—above freezing, anyway—so I covered Luke with the blanket as well as I could. I did notice a clump of damp beach sand stuck to it, but didn't pay that much attention. I just hurried into the building, making a mental note to check on my friend in a little while.

An hour later, he was rustling around under the blanket, and I felt his forehead with my palm. He had no apparent fever, and didn't seem chilled either. From what I could deduce, he was actually fairly comfortable, and since people go tent camping in much colder weather, I figured he'd be all right for a bit longer. Claire had been at the dentist all morning, but was expected in soon, and I wanted her advice on what to do with Luke.

"Are you okay?" I asked him, my face close to his.

"Tired," he whispered. His breath smelled rancid, as if he hadn't eaten in a while.

"Okay," I said. "Hang in there."

But just before I shut the heavy door, Claire's blue VW Rabbit pulled into the lot.

"What're you doin' out here, Reardon?" she called, climbing out of her car. Then she took a hard look at the vehicle beside me and came running over. "What the fuck?" she said. "Is he dead?"

"No! Just asleep. He's got a bad cold so I drove up here today. Whatdya think I should do with him?"

Claire assessed Luke quietly. "He's kinda cute. At least with his eyes closed."

"Well, let's not wake him. Not yet anyway."

"How long's he been out here?" asked Claire. "I heard on the news it's gonna get really cold this afternoon."

"About an hour."

She looked across the lot at Don's IROC. We both knew our boss wouldn't be kind to Luke if we brought him into the office. *Why didn't I just take the poor guy home?* I thought.

Suddenly, Luke's eyes popped open. "Shit!" he said. "What the fuck?"

I laid my hands on his shoulders. "It's okay, Luke. You're at my work. You weren't feeling so great earlier. But it's chilly out here. Maybe I'll take you down to Dunky's?"

He shrugged, pulled away from me, and retrieved his sunglasses from the floor. Shoving them back on his face, he said, "No. I'm okay. Shit."

"Maybe you should go visit your friend in Gloucester?" I suggested. "You probably don't wanna drive very far."

"Mmmm," he said, shivering and pressing his fingers against his temples. "Gimme a minute."

Claire, who'd been standing behind me, stepped into Luke's field of vision. "Excuse me," she said, "but I agree with Erin. You can't drive in that condition." For once, she didn't call me Reardon, and I was grateful.

Luke drew his head back. "Violet?" he blurted, sounding slightly terrified.

Claire smiled smugly. "You wish." In my opinion, she did try to look like Lenny Weir's ex-girlfriend, Violet Chasm. I mean, she resembled Violet anyway, but it wasn't just coincidence that Claire cut her hair in the same jagged style, wore mostly dark clothing, and lined her eyes in black, like Violet did. "Sorry to disappoint," she said, "but I'm just plain Claire. I work with Erin."

Luke examined her more closely and yawned. "Ugh. Sorry. I'm not myself today."

"I hope not," said Claire, "'cause you're a mess. Erin, why don't you bring your friend here down to that little cafe in the industrial park and buy him a sandwich? If Don asks, I'll tell him you had to run an errand."

"Guys, I'm fine," said Luke, his voice getting stronger. "Really. Just leave me alone. I'll be on the road in ten minutes."

I started to protest, but Claire beat me to it. "Ten *minutes*?" she said. "Seriously? Dude, you're not fit to drive for *hours*. In fact, if you attempt to drive anywhere in this condition, I'll call the cops and have them hunt you down. I've already got your license plate memorized."

Luke's lower lip fell open and he held up his hands in defeat. "Okay, okay. I'll go see a movie ... or ... two. Okay? Can you girls drop me at the cinema?"

Claire looked at me and nodded before addressing Luke again. The movie theater was a couple of miles from Don-Wash. "Sure. Erin'll drive your car and I'll follow. But I mean it, Luke. You better not get behind that wheel until you're sober. Even if it means staying in a hotel up here tonight. I need your word on that."

"You got it," said Luke. "Last thing I need's trouble with cops."

"Yeah," said Claire. "I bet you know a thing or two about that, dontcha?"

Luke acted like he hadn't heard her.

"Still think he's a creep?" I asked Claire as she drove us back to Don-Wash.

"Not necessarily," she said slowly, "but he's a serious druggie. No question about it."

"Oh, c'mon, Claire. I've known him for weeks, and he's always been fine. He's got a virus or something."

Claire rolled her eyes. "Sure he does. Believe what you want, Reardon. But I'm telling you now, you take your life in your hands every time you let that man drive you around."

CHAPTER 16

September 1983

Bruce was promising to prove it all night for me with every ounce of sweat and muscle in his body, but I couldn't stand to listen anymore. I yanked off my headphones and jammed the Walkman into my purse. It was too painful to hear him sing about the hunger no one could resist, because it'd been *my* hunger—hunger for food and its subsequent purging—that'd kept me away from him all summer.

Every day, I'd woken up determined to quit; to get my act together so I could head to the Jersey Shore as soon as possible. *No more vomiting!* I'd vow. *Stop spending your tip money on junk food or you'll never meet Bruce.* But the urge—that insatiable urge—to eat just a *little* something unhealthy would hit me, and a couple of hours later, I'd be flushing a pound or two of food down the toilet.

So sitting there in the passenger seat of Mom's car as we pulled onto the Danforth campus for sophomore year felt pretty bleak. Knowing I'd have Janet and Beverly for roommates was fine, but I wanted to be in Candy's room with Bruce. I wanted him to want me the way he wanted Candy in the song, and for him to see the sadness hidden in my face. I wanted to show him the hidden worlds in *my* darkness. So much *want,* and none of it involved Danforth or college.

"Such a beautiful campus," said Mom, pulling up in front of my dorm. She knew nothing of my thwarted plan to run off with Bruce, and couldn't understand why I wasn't more excited.

I grunted and began unloading the garbage bags full of clothing—my "luggage"—and stared up at the brick building, which seemed to have grown taller and uglier since spring.

"Hey, look, Erin! I think I see your friend Toni over there."

My eyes darted across the quad and landed on a pretty blond girl who definitely wasn't Toni. "No, Mom," I said, unable to keep the impatience out of my voice. "Toni's taking a year off, remember?" Of course, I hadn't told her about the pregnancy or any other negative stuff; I'd just said Toni needed a break from school. "But I think you'll like my new roommates even better."

She and I climbed the stairs to the fourth floor slowly, each carrying a Hefty bag. When we reached the top, Mom stopped to catch her breath while I went ahead to the room. I felt a little guilty at the time—I mean, it would've been nicer to wait for her—but when I opened my door, I was glad she wasn't right behind me. I was so stunned that I didn't even have the presence of mind to shut the thing. I just stood there, staring.

"Ever hear of knocking?" asked Janet, jerking her head away from Beverly's. "Because I think we should all get in the habit of knocking. Don't you?"

My mouth still couldn't form words as my roommates unwound themselves from each other; Beverly's fingers were tangled up in Janet's long, dark hair. Unlike our previous meeting, this time, the room was filled with natural light, so I saw everything quite clearly. At least they were both fully clothed.

"Okay, okay, show's over," said Janet, climbing off the bed and steadying her thin frame. "At least we don't have to have 'the talk' now, right? A picture paints a thousand words."

"Yeah, I guess," I answered, feeling dizzy. I'd never known any gay women before, at least none who admitted it. Sure, David Bowie was bisexual, but he was a guy. "I'm gonna go get the rest of my stuff," I blurted. Then I bolted out of the room and ran down all four flights of stairs.

I didn't know what to do. I mean, I couldn't *live* with lesbians, could I? It was 1983, a full fourteen years before Ellen DeGeneres came out to the world on TV. At my high school, girls rumored to be gay had been described by other kids—both male and female—as "gross," "weird," and "freaky." But I'd agreed to share a mini-suite with Janet and Beverly for a year. My head spun.

When I returned to the room, Mom asked if I had everything, then glanced at her watch. Part of me actually wished I could head back to Winthrop with her—write the whole college thing off as a bad experiment and figure out something else to do with my life—but I just nodded and said, "Yeah."

She smiled. "Oh, you girls are so lucky! Maybe someday I'll go to college too. Whadya think? Would I fit in in a dorm like this? Or a suite, I guess they call it?"

"Of course!" said Beverly. "Just stay here with us now. We won't tell the RA."

Mom chuckled. "I wish. But someone's gotta pay the tuition." That made me feel worse, but she didn't appear to notice. "Well, I'd better get going. I hate drivin' in the dark. My eyes get worse by the day."

"My mom's the same way," said Janet, the little gap between her front teeth adding to the tomboyish charm of her round face. "She doesn't go anywhere unless she can be home before sunset."

"Well, I'd love to meet her," said Mom. "Hopefully I'll get invited to the parent party this year. Last time, I didn't hear about it 'til it was over."

That was true, and also entirely my fault. Toni had begged her folks not to attend Parents' Weekend—she made up some story about needing to study, but really just didn't want to sacrifice two nights of clubbing—and persuaded me to keep it a secret from my mother. And honestly, I was fine with the whole scam until I returned to campus alone on Saturday night—after another shitty night downtown with Toni—and ran into a couple of classmates strolling across the quad with their moms. Then I'd run up to my room and cried for an hour.

"This year will be better, Mom, I promise," I said. "Everything'll be better this year."

I walked her out to the car and said goodbye, then slunk back upstairs and knocked loudly on the suite's door. "Come in!" shouted Beverly, sounding like Florence Henderson on *The Brady Bunch*.

My roommates sat on separate chairs, waiting for me.

"Okay," said Janet. "You're right. We shoulda said something earlier."

"I didn't say—"

Beverly cut me off. "But it's true. You didn't deserve that."

"Well, it's just, like ... you guys surprised me, you know? And I'm sorry for surprising you too."

Janet shook her head. "Not your fault. We all live here and we all have rights." She laughed a bit sheepishly. "At least we coulda locked the door."

"But I should've knocked, and—"

"Stop it, Erin," said Janet. "And we'll understand if you wanna move out. Bev and I have ... sorta been getting closer over the past couple years. And this summer ... well, we spent a *lotta* time together. But we're still confused about a bunch of stuff, and no one here at school knows we're a couple. Yet, anyway. Except you, now."

"Okay," I said.

"Please don't say anything," said Beverly. "'Cause we're not freaks. I promise. And we're both tryna quit smoking too."

I smiled. "Well, that's good." I considered telling them I didn't really mind cigarette smoke because it reminded me of my dad, but didn't feel like bringing him into the conversation.

"So what'dya think? Can we still be roommates?" asked Janet. "If we promise not to do anything ... you know ... in front of you?"

I got a lump in my throat. They were so sweet, and they trusted me with their secret. "Yeah," I said. "Of course."

"Awesome!" said Beverly, running over and high-fiving me. "And guess what? We've been thinking about throwing a room-warming party. If you're up for that."

"Um ... sure," I said, my stomach rumbling with nerves and hunger. Toni and I had never thrown a party in our room. In fact, I hadn't hosted a party since sixth grade. "When?"

Janet smiled, the gap between her teeth more pronounced than ever. "Tonight!" she said. "Like, in an hour!"

"But all my stuff's still ..." I motioned toward the bags full of clothing. "And we haven't made the beds, and you guys aren't unpacked, and ..."

"Best time for a party," Janet pointed out. "People can't spill drinks on your shit if it's packed away."

She made sense, but I couldn't get my head around the idea. "Yeah, but who will we invite? And we don't have any food ... or ... beer."

Beverly seized a pack of Dorals and lit one. "Our friends'll come," she said, "and we don't have to buy a thing. We'll just make it BYOB."

We moved my bed into one of the back corners of the room, then walled it off as much as possible with my desk and bureau. But Janet and Bev left their twin beds on separate sides of the main living area. I couldn't help wondering if they planned to push them together at night—or possibly share just one—but that was none of my business.

Beverly retrieved a bottle of rum from her suitcase, and Janet ran down to the lobby to buy three cans of Diet Coke from the vending machine. Then, we mixed ourselves some cocktails. "To a great year!" proclaimed Janet, taking a gulp then adding more rum to her soda can.

But twenty minutes later, when I emerged from my private bed-nook in a red-and-blue striped rugby shirt and my trusty white Chic jeans—which looked pretty gray after so many washings and wearings—Bev's face fell. She'd teased her blonde hair up with a ton of hairspray, and painted her lips cotton-candy pink. I guess she was going for the Madonna/video vixen look. "Erin," she said slowly—and I could hear the rum in her voice—"I think you should try dressing more *fun.* You do wanna meet guys, right?"

"Yeah." The only guy I *really* wanted to meet was Bruce Springsteen, but I'd probably have to settle for Danforth boys for a while.

"Well then," said Beverly, "I have an idea."

Janet returned carrying a few bags of ice. "You guys ready to party?" she asked.

"I am," said Beverly. "But I'm gonna lend Erin some clothes. Don't you think that's a good idea, Jan?"

"Sure," said Janet with a shrug. "She looks okay to me, but you're the fashion police." Janet was dressed in plain old black jeans and a maroon t-shirt, but Beverly said nothing to her about dressing more "fun."

"That's right," said Beverly, opening one of her duffle bags and digging around until she pulled out a short denim miniskirt made from a faded pair of Levi's. "Phew, I'm glad I packed this! Try it on, Erin. My big sister Coleen made it in college in the seventies."

"Get outta town!" said Janet, darting over and snatching the skirt from Beverly's hands. "*Coleen* wore this?"

"Yup," said Beverly, her face glowing from the rum. "Seriously. She used to be a hippie." She turned to me. "You should see her now. Suburban queen. Three kids, station wagon, PTA, everything."

"Well, it's cool," I said, "but too small for me. Maybe one of you guys should wear it."

"We're already dressed," said Beverly. "Besides, this'll make you look *sexy*. Like Pat Benatar or Joan Jett. And if you can zip it, it fits."

I felt my face get hot. I was pretty sure I wasn't sexually attracted to my roommates, but their kindness overwhelmed me. Especially compared to the dismissive way Toni had often treated me.

And the skirt zipped, too! Just barely, but it did. Still, I walked out of the bathroom protesting. "Guys, my legs are huge. I can't wear this."

"Oh, Erin," cooed Beverly, "you look like a model. Now let's get some makeup on you."

"Wowza," said Janet. "I'd ask you out, but I'm already with Bev."

Beverly gasped and Janet cracked up laughing. "I'm kidding, Bev! Lighten up, for god's sake. Have another drink." She gave Beverly a quick peck on the cheek and squeezed her arm, but Beverly still looked hurt.

"Look, Bev," said Janet, "you're the one gettin' Erin all dolled up. I'm just saying she looks nice."

I stood there, frozen.

"Hey," said Janet to me. "Don't let our shit get to you. Bev and I are a little crazy these days. Right?" She looked to Beverly for confirmation.

"Yeah."

Janet nodded. "See? And wear the skirt, Erin. Definitely wear the skirt."

I hadn't shown my thighs in public since I was about thirteen, but when I looked in the mirror again, I decided my legs weren't *too* chubby, and they *were* nice and straight. In the tight, jagged skirt, I had to admit I felt a little like a rock star. "Okay," I said, pulling my rugby shirt down as far as it went. "I just hope I don't split the freaking thing in half." Right then, my stomach let out a huge growl.

"Was that your gut?" asked Janet.

"Uh huh. I didn't eat lunch."

"So let's call Andrina's and order a pizza," said Bev. "I'm starving too."

She went looking for the phone number, but just as she found it, the phone rang, and Bev started yakking away with a friend in another dorm. Janet dumped one of the bags of ice into a bucket, and all thoughts of pizza—as well as my makeup—apparently vanished from their minds. If Bev hadn't been on the phone, I would've called Andrina's myself, but since that wasn't an option, I did my own makeup, then ran downstairs and bought a package of crackers and cheese from the vending machine. *Oh well,* I thought, making my way back up the stairs munching crackers, *it won't kill me to skip dinner for once.*

An hour later, the mini-suite was filled to capacity with people and booze. More of the latter than the former, I think, and everyone but me looked like upper classmen. Bev hadn't been kidding about the BYOB thing, and a group of guys had actually smuggled in a beer ball of Budweiser and dropped it in our ice-filled bathtub. They were hooking up the tap when I asked, "What happens when people need to go to the bathroom?"

"It'll work out," said one of the guys with a wink. "It always does. By the way, I'm Mike."

Mike wasn't really my type—he was short with a crew cut—but he seemed okay. I liked all of Janet and Bev's friends. So far, anyway.

"Don't forget," said Janet, mixing up a pitcher of rum and Cokes on the windowsill, "Bev and I haven't told anyone about, *you know.*"

It made me sad to see my roommates hiding their relationship while heterosexual couples paraded around everywhere, holding hands and kissing openly. But I also believed they were making the right choice. Danforth was a pretty traditional place. "Don't worry," I said, making a zipper sign across my lips with my finger.

But as I did, Janet turned pale, and a glimmer of fear flashed through her eyes. Following those eyes to the doorway, I saw a squat, lumpy guy standing there, apparently trying to decide whether or not to enter the room. Something about him frightened me too; he had the red, wrinkly face of a giant infant—but his small, dark eyes were almost hawk-like. "Who's that?" I asked. "He's a little scary."

"He's not," said Janet. "He's just ... Charlie Fuller. He graduated a few years ago."

"Oh," I answered as if that explained everything. I finished off the plastic cup of beer I'd been drinking and cracked open a cold can of Bud, keeping an eye on the Charlie guy, who was signaling to someone out in the hallway. Then another guy stepped into the room. A much cuter one. In many ways, he was Charlie's polar opposite.

"Oh wow," said Janet. "Andrew's here too. C'mon. Let's go say hi."

From a distance, I found Andrew intimidating. Lanky, blond, shaggy, and tanned, he looked like a Winthrop surfer in white painter's pants. But after shaking his hand and watching him pour a vodka and grapefruit juice, I noticed that Andrew lacked the self-assurance I associated with those wet-suited hometown heartthrobs. He wasn't particularly graceful either, and his teeth were unusually small and pointy. But those flaws didn't bother me; in fact, I appreciated them because they made him more *attainable.* The room spun a bit as I smiled and decided to slow down on the alcohol. I'd already downed five or six drinks in the past couple of hours.

Looking around the room, I waved at Mike, who'd been swilling Budweiser outside the bathroom with the other beer ball guys. They'd been super friendly all night, but this time, Mike didn't wave back. Instead, his whole group just watched Charlie, like cowboys in an old Western, waiting for a shootout to start.

Charlie sighed and spoke softly to Andrew. "I gotta get outta here. Those asswipes are under my skin."

"Oh, c'mon, Charl," said Andrew. "They're just jerks. Ignore 'em."

But Charlie's eyes grew darker and smaller. "No. They're human pollution." Turning to Janet, he said, "Thanks for the invite. We'll see ya around."

"Charlie," said Andrew cautiously, "I'm gonna stay a bit longer. I wanna tell Janet about last night."

For the briefest second, the corners of Charlie's mouth slipped up into a smile. "Oh," he said. "Yeah. Yeah, that's a good story."

"What?" said Janet. "What happened? Tell me, Charl!"

"Andrew can do the honors," said Charlie as he walked out the door.

Janet looked concerned. "Poor Charlie."

Andrew shrugged. "Mmmh. I think he's tired."

"I guess," said Janet. Then her face brightened. "All right, spill it."

"Oh, you won't believe it," said Andrew, looking back and forth between Janet and me.

"What?" said Janet. "You're killin' me!"

Andrew's crystal blue eyes narrowed. "Well, you know the Stone Pony ..."

Janet smacked herself in the face. "Oh, fuck me."

Andrew kept smiling. "Uh huh. He showed up."

"Who?" I blurted. But even in my drunken state, the pieces were coming together in my mind. The Stone Pony was the bar in New Jersey where Bruce sometimes played.

"You know Springsteen?" Andrew asked me.

My limbs went numb. "Yeah?"

"Yeah," said Andrew. "Well, he jumped up on stage with some no-name band and played for like twenty minutes."

"Fuck!" shouted Janet. "Why do I miss him every single time? It's not fair!"

Andrew started talking about the set list, but I zoned out for a second. I mean, it felt like a dream. This guy, Andrew, had seen Bruce at the Stone Pony. Just one night earlier. *Bruce.*

But Beverly, calling Janet from the other side of the room, brought my head back to Danforth. Bev had been playing bartender all night and sampling way too many drinks. "Janet! I keep screwinup the blackrussians."

"What?" said Janet.

"I think she said she's screwing up the Black Russians," offered Andrew.

"Ohhh." Janet rolled her eyes. "Hang on! Help's on the way!" She wasn't exactly sober either, but Bev was a mess. "I'll be back to hear the rest of this, Andrew," said Janet before heading in Beverly's direction.

Andrew's eyes twinkled. "What time did *Bev* start drinking?"

I had no idea, especially since time had pretty much stopped for me. "It's my dream to see Bruce at the Stone Pony," I said.

He raised his eyebrows. "Really? Janet's too. I guess I'm just lucky. I've caught him there a few times."

I finished my can of beer and saw black for a second. "Whoa," I said. But I couldn't pass out. I needed all the information I could get. "Do you live on the Jersey Shore?"

"Red Bank. It's pretty close. I went to high school with Janet."

In the insanely hot room, I shivered. "Have you ever *talked* to Bruce?"

Andrew clearly enjoyed the attention. "Well," he said, running his fingers through that shaggy blond hair, "not exactly *talked,* but I think he might ... recognize me. Not by name, but as a fan, you know. There was this one time, a couple years back, when I bought him a beer at this bar in Sea Bright, and he waved and said, 'Thanks, man.' So I think he remembers. I get the feeling he does."

I couldn't process it all. I mean, earlier in the day, I'd been so depressed about self-sabotaging my summer plans to hook up with Bruce on the Shore that I hadn't even wanted to return to Danforth. But there I was, just a few hours later, talking to a guy who'd once bought

Bruce a beer. A guy Bruce had *spoken* to. A guy Bruce *recognized.* And even more importantly, a guy I could probably date. Then, he'd bring me to the Stone Pony.

Suddenly, the door to the room opened and a woman yelled, "Hey!" really loudly. Everyone stopped talking at once as the RA—a fresh-faced grad student in a navy blue sweat suit—stood up on a chair and said, "Listen up! I know you're all excited to be back at school, but some people in this building need sleep. There's classes tomorrow, remember? So let's break it up. Now!"

"Okay," said Janet, walking over to the RA and addressing her politely. "Got it. Party's over."

Beverly looked stunned. "Were we noisy?" she asked from the makeshift bar.

"Yes," said the RA. "Very, very noisy. Here's the deal. I'm gonna take a five-minute walk, and when I come back up here, you all betta be gone. Understand?"

Everyone nodded as she left the room. RAs at Danforth had the power to fine students fifty dollars for disturbing the peace on campus, and nobody wanted to start the year off like that.

If I'd been a little less drunk, I probably would've asked Andrew for his phone number, or at least given him mine. But I was on alcohol-fueled autopilot, and the lyrics to "Prove It All Night" were throbbing in my head again. Particularly the line about wanting it bad and having to pay the price.

"C'mere," I whispered to Andrew as he tossed his beer bottle in the trash.

Obediently, he came back. "Thanks for a fun party," he said, giving my shoulder a little squeeze.

I had to act fast. Grabbing his arm, I led him through the thinning crowd to the little nook where my bed hid behind the bureau. "What're you ..." he asked, but I pulled him down on the bed, tossed my pillow over his lap, and slipped my hand beneath it.

Of course, I'd never done anything like that before, but I'd fantasized plenty about messing around with Bruce in the back seat of a car, so I felt reasonably experienced. The healthy tan seemed to fade from Andrew's face as I looked him straight in the eye and allowed my fingers to meander around under the pillow. One bump at a time, I explored his curious landscape: the tight thigh muscles, the various protruding areas, the snap at the top of his fly, the hair on his belly. His face remained frozen, his small mouth pinched together like a letter *O.*

Which I assumed was a good thing. I mean, he was a guy, and I'd listened to enough rock & roll to know how much guys loved sex.

Moving my hand back down, I felt his penis growing hard. *Yes!* He was ready. Ready to prove it all night. My crotch grew damp and my breathing faster. Sex with Andrew would be *exciting.* Not nearly as exciting as it'd be with Bruce some day, but I was moving in the right direction.

I took hold of his zipper and pulled. It was tricky to maneuver with just one hand, but I managed to get it down far enough to feel the warmth inside, the humidity, and the baby-soft skin. *Toni would be so proud of me,* I thought. Sure, she hated Bruce, but I was scooping a guy. A really cute guy.

Andrew still hadn't made any noise, and I did my best to be quiet too, because a few people remained on the other side of my bookcase. A cool drop of sweat from his forehead landed on my arm, and I smiled. The door opened again, and as the RA stepped back inside, a couple of people bid a hasty goodnight to Janet and Beverly and went on their way.

"Okay," said the RA. "Lookin' good. Who're you, honey?"

That question confused me, but then a woman I didn't know spoke up. She said she was Gillian, Janet's brother's girlfriend, and that she was helping with the cleanup.

"Cool," said the RA. "But Janet and Bev can handle this. You gotta go."

"Okay," said Gillian. "G'night, guys."

"Thanks, Gill," said Janet. "See you tomorrow."

"Hey, where's your third roommate?" asked the RA.

I pressed my face into Andrew's shoulder and tried not to breathe.

"I guess she went out somewhere," said Janet. "I haven't seen her in a while."

"All right," said the RA. "Thanks for clearing the place out so fast. And no more loud parties or I'll have to fine you. Tell your other roommate too, okay?" She walked out and shut the door behind her.

"Holy shit," said Beverly, sounding far more sober than before.

Janet sighed. "Well, it was fun while it lasted. But where'd Erin go? Another party?"

"I'm right here," I called from my nook.

"*What?* You little shit. You've been *hiding?*" Janet sounded like she wasn't sure whether to be angry or amused, but when she walked around the bureau and saw Andrew, she jumped back. "Whoa!" Then she saw where my hand was. "Oh man. What the fuck? Andrew?"

Andrew just sat there, unmoving, as Bev staggered up behind Janet. "Oh boy," she said. "This is weird."

Janet recovered first. "Bev, let's give these guys some *privacy*." She took Beverly's arm, led her away, and turned on the radio.

Andrew didn't seem interested in privacy, though. He just stood up, zipped his pants, and cleared his throat. He didn't look me in the eye, and his hands were trembling.

"Don't be embarrassed," I whispered. "It's okay. C'mon. Let's go to your place."

"No," said Andrew. "I ... can't. This is ... too weird."

Weird? How was it weird? Sure, we'd been interrupted, but that happened sometimes, especially in dorm rooms. I stood up and tried to kiss his cheek.

"Stop," he said, gently—but firmly—pushing me away. "I can't. It's ... Charlie."

"Charlie?" I repeated. Charlie, the baby-faced guy with the hawk eyes?

Andrew still wouldn't look at me. "Yeah. He's ... my friend. I'm gay, Erin. Or something like that. I don't know."

My guts caved in, and before I could think, I blurted, "No you're not."

Andrew leaned back against the wall and a tear rolled down his cheek. "Look, I gotta go. Really." Suddenly, he seemed much older. I noticed dark circles under his eyes, and a large purple vein pulsing in his forehead.

"But ..." *No.* Andrew couldn't be gay. He'd gotten an erection when I'd touched him, and that couldn't have happened unless he'd been attracted to me. Right? "I ... I don't get it," I said, moving closer to him and putting my hand on his shoulder. His breath smelled like grapefruit juice. "You were ... you were *into* me before. I could *tell.*"

Andrew's face turned bright red. "Stop it!" he hissed, ducking out from under my hand. "I never ..." But instead of finishing his thought, he turned and stormed out of my nook. Janet and Beverly were busy emptying ashtrays and dumping cups of beer into the sink, and he raced past them and out into the hallway.

Of course, I followed him. "Andrew! Stop! I just wanna talk to you!" I chased him down the stairs and out into the cool September air, but he wouldn't slow down, and when I reached the quad, I gave up. In utter confusion, I watched him until he disappeared: a tall, blond figure in white pants, bobbing across campus in the dark.

The next day, when we were both sober, Janet and I talked about Andrew. She told me that even though they'd gone to the same high school, they hadn't really become friends until their freshman year at Danforth. Andrew had a car, so he'd given her a few rides home to New Jersey for weekends and holidays, and they'd spent lots of time talking.

"But is he *gay*?" I asked. "I mean, he said that last night, but it seemed like he wasn't sure."

Janet shrugged. "That'd be my guess, but we've never, you know, discussed it. Mostly, we talk about Bruce, and school, and shit like that. And since he's been hanging out with Charlie, we don't see each other much anymore." She shrugged again.

"But how *old* is Charlie? He seems way too old for Danforth."

Janet rolled her eyes. "Yeah, he was a senior here when Andrew and I were freshmen. I guess they met at some party. I remember one Sunday morning, Bev and I were eating in the caf, and I looked over, and there was Andrew with Charlie Fuller at the next table. It totally blew my mind."

"Why?" I asked. "They were just eating, right?"

Janet shook her head and sighed. "Look, I really don't wanna get into all this. It's ... I don't know. It feels like gossip. But let me say this—Charlie was a *freak* at Danforth. He was, like, a militant gay guy, and Danforth's not a militant gay place, you know? It's like, the most conservative school ever. Meanwhile, Charlie used to dress up in purple all the time, and just be ... really flamboyant. And Andrew never liked calling attention to himself. So when they started hanging around together? It was strange."

My stomach hurt. "Okay," I said, "but just 'cause Andrew hangs out with Charlie doesn't make him gay. Maybe they're just good friends. I mean, I'm straight, and I live with you and Bev. Right?"

As soon as those words were out of my mouth, I wondered if I'd said the wrong thing. But Janet chuckled. "Trust me, Erin, it's different with Andrew and Charlie."

"How do you know?" I asked.

She knocked a cigarette out of the pack of Dorals beside her. "C'mon, Erin. I just do."

"Yeah, but ..."

"Yeah, but I'm pretty sure whatever happened between you two last night was an accident. And now he's embarrassed and ... yeah. I think you should leave Andrew alone for a while."

On some level, I knew she was right, but I couldn't just let him go. I mean, he wasn't just any guy. He had a direct line to Bruce.

Unfortunately, Andrew wanted *nothing* to do with me. I dropped a letter in his campus mailbox—telling him I was sorry for being so pushy—but he didn't write or call back. After a few more days, I called his dorm room, but another guy answered and took a message. Then I stayed in *my* room for the next fifteen hours—I even asked Janet to get me a sandwich from the cafeteria for dinner so I wouldn't miss Andrew's call—but the phone rang only once, and it was Mom.

Next, I asked Janet to intervene, but Andrew didn't want to talk to her about me either. The most he'd say was that he'd been drunk at our party, and that he didn't want to date anyone.

"You see?" Janet said to me. "It's not personal. He's just trying to figure himself out."

But every time I convinced myself to give up on Andrew, I'd think about the Stone Pony. Finally, I decided to approach him and ask if we could just be friends. So I waited for him outside his dorm building one morning, but when he saw me standing there, he literally turned around and went back inside. I was stunned. At first, I thought he must've forgotten something important, but after waiting half an hour with no sign of him, I knew it was more than that. There'd been a huge misunderstanding, and I needed to correct it. Fast. Andrew and I needed to start all over again.

It became an obsession. I tried sitting near him in the cafeteria, but he refused to make eye contact. I studied on the couches near the doorway of the campus library, but whenever Andrew showed up with his books, he'd walk right past me. I knocked on his door—multiple times—but he didn't answer. Ever. And when I called his dorm phone, both he and his roommate would hang up on me.

"You need to quit this crap," said Janet. "You're becoming a stalker."

She was right, of course, and my grades were suffering too. But in the grand scheme of things—in my mind—grades were a low priority. After all, I didn't need grades to get to the Promised Land.

CHAPTER 17

December 1993

On Friday morning, Luke was back at the intersection in his Range Rover, seeming much improved. He said his illness the previous day must've been a twenty-four-hour bug, and I agreed. *Drug addict, my ass,* I thought. I loved Claire, but she didn't know everything. A good night's sleep had done wonders for Luke.

But by Monday, his sickness had returned: his nose was running again, and he couldn't stay awake. Once again, I asked if he wanted me to drive, and once again, he handed me the keys. Then, for the second time, I left him to nap in the Don-Wash parking lot. But when I went outside to check on him—it was around 9:30 a.m., and Claire hadn't yet made it into work—Luke sat up straight and asked to use the office bathroom. He said he had diarrhea.

"Who the *fuck* is in *there*?" demanded Don, gesturing toward the bathroom door and ignoring his own rule about foul language in the office. The door had been closed for at least twenty minutes.

I explained to him that my friend—the guy who drove me to work every day—had the stomach flu, but Don showed no sympathy. "What the fuck, Erin?" he muttered. "Now we're all gonna get sick?"

A minute or two later, Luke emerged, pale and hunched over. His sunglasses sat askew on his nose, making him look even more pathetic.

"I'm Erin's boss," announced Don, before the stench from the bathroom found its way to him. "Oh my god ..." He withdrew the hand he'd begun to extend to Luke and recoiled in horror.

"Sorry, man," said Luke, sounding exhausted and guilty. "I think I've got food poisoning."

"Sure," said Don, turning on his heel and strutting out the door in his tight pants, probably to take a leak behind the building.

"I'm worried about you," I blurted on Tuesday. I hadn't planned on saying anything to Luke about his bizarre ailments, but I couldn't help it. I mean, illness doesn't just drop in and out on people like that. Besides, he was acting almost *too* healthy that day, almost *too* alert. Not to mention that he was chewing gum, which I'd never seen him do before.

"Thanks," he said. "But don't worry."

I studied my chipped nails. "Yeah, but, your health. It seems ... unstable."

His mouth twitched. "Yeah. It's not great. But I'm gonna get some help, okay? I'm leaving on my trip a week from today."

"A week from today," I repeated, trying to appear calm.

He pressed his lips together and nodded. "Yup. Not looking forward to it, but I got no choice. Three days on the road. Not fun."

"Wow," I said, in the most casual tone I could manage. "So you're really doing it."

"Uh huh. You didn't think I was lying, did you?"

"No! Of course not. But ... I'm surprised you're driving and not flying." I'd actually been desperately hoping he'd change his mind and stay in Massachusetts.

"Oh yeah," he said, opening the window and spitting out his gum. Then he reached into the pocket of his leather jacket, took out a big pack of Juicy Fruit, unwrapped another piece, and shoved it in his mouth. "Want some gum?"

I started to say okay, but he'd already returned the pack to his pocket. "I don't do planes anymore," he continued. "Too much bullshit. Last time I flew, they held me in the airport for two straight hours 'cause they thought I was carrying drugs."

Luke rarely disclosed personal information he didn't need to, and I knew if I got too nosy, he'd clam right up. "That sounds scary," I said cautiously. "What happened?"

He chewed his gum faster. "Long story. And total bullshit, by the way. I didn't have any drugs, but still had to reschedule everything. Fucking fascists."

"Wow." I couldn't think of anything else to say. His behavior was so untypical.

"Yeah. So did you find a car yet?"

I tried to sound positive. "Almost." In truth, I'd managed to save about six hundred dollars since the death of the Honda, and I'd talked to Mom about borrowing five or six hundred more from her.

She'd agreed to lend me the money, but had also made it clear that if she did, she wouldn't be able to cover my airfare to Texas for Christmas. In other words, I'd be spending another holiday alone.

Luke drove on, chewing his gum along with the Beastie Boys on the radio. He seemed extra tense.

"Aren't you ... a little worried about getting sick on the drive down there?" I asked.

He chewed more aggressively. "Sure. It's a concern. But I'll manage." He opened the window again, spat, and helped himself to yet another piece of gum. "Like I said, there's no way around this trip."

My throat tightened. It occurred to me that I'd spent more time alone with Luke than any other man in my life, aside from my dad. And now he was going away too. I didn't know how long he'd be in Florida, but it didn't really matter, because our days of riding together would end regardless. I'd get a new car and start driving to work alone again. Maybe I'd see Luke occasionally on the highway—and we'd beep and wave to each other—but that'd be it. I wouldn't need him anymore.

On the radio, the Smashing Pumpkins sang "Disarm" while angry December snow flurries blasted down from the gray sky. I thought back to the days when I'd considered winter beautiful, when I'd looked forward to Christmas and the holidays. As an ignorant little kid, I'd loved all that frenzied excitement.

"I'll miss you," I said, my voice breaking. I couldn't help it.

Luke stopped chewing, but kept his eyes on the road as he turned onto Route 128. He hadn't shaved in a couple of days, and there was a fair amount of stubble on his head and face. "I'll miss you too, Erin. Unless, you know, you come with me." He chuckled nervously.

I breathed in but couldn't breathe back out. I mean, had Luke really just invited me to go to Florida with him?

He started nodding his head, like he was agreeing with something I'd asked, even though I hadn't made a sound. "Yeah, what'dya think about that? I mean, I understand if you have other holiday plans, but I was thinking it'd be good for me to have a backup driver, you know? In case my stomach flares up." He spat another piece of gum out the window.

"Um," I couldn't speak, but of course, I'd have to say no. After all, Don-Wash was open during the week between Christmas and New Year's, and I had zero vacation time left. Besides, I couldn't go all the way to Florida with a stranger. I didn't even know Luke's last name.

"It's really nice of you to ask," I finally said, as he folded another piece of gum into his mouth, "but, you know, I've gotta work."

"Oh," answered Luke in his normal voice. Then, his tone turned more abrasive. "You mean your asshole boss won't give you a couple weeks off?"

Luke hardly ever swore like that. "Don's not an asshole," I said quickly. "It's just a small company, and he relies on us. Besides, I can't afford to get fired, especially now that I'm buying a car."

I'd expected him to understand that, but I felt his body tense up against the seat of the Range Rover. On the radio, Billy Corgan went on singing about the killer inside him, and I wished I could mute the music. I mean, I loved Smashing Pumpkins and all, but the lyrics of that song were kind of creepy. I was also having trouble interpreting Luke's signals. Luke, who seemed to be on a different type of drug that day. *A speedy drug. Like cocaine or something.*

"So what would happen," he asked, "if you did get fired?"

I spoke more slowly. "Well, I wouldn't have a job."

"And you couldn't find another one?"

I didn't like that edge in his voice. "I don't want another job, Luke. I like what I do. And I love working with Claire."

His hands gripped the steering wheel tighter. "You mean that girl who looks like Violet Chasm? The one who hates me?"

"Luke! She doesn't hate you. She's my best friend."

"Hmm. And what about me? Aren't I your friend too? Don't I give you a ride every single day?"

I got a little scared. I mean, what the hell? Luke had consistently claimed to enjoy having me as a passenger—his alleged reason for never accepting my gas money—and I'd never asked him to go out of his way for me. So why was he making me feel guilty now? "I can't just quit," I said. "I mean, Don depends on me and—"

"Don? That fucking ... that fucking ..." Luke slammed the directional lever upwards, as if he was going to make a right-hand turn, but we were already in the right lane and our exit was miles ahead.

Oh shit. The skin on my arms prickled. *Now I'm in trouble.* All of Claire's warnings about Luke flash-flooded my brain. *He's a psycho! A serial killer! He probably makes snuff movies!*

Luke glanced over his shoulder, then swerved as far into the breakdown lane as he could without landing the car in the woods. Then he thrust the gearshift into park and ripped the key out of the ignition. My heart pounded; my legs were paralyzed. I expected my life to flash before my eyes, but all I saw were trees, pavement, and cars whizzing by.

No one will hear me if I scream. And they won't pay any attention to a Range Rover on the side of the road, either. It was deer hunting season in Massachusetts, so it was common to see SUVs parked along that stretch of Route 128 in December. My only hope would be to run. *Up the highway,* I decided. *Not into the woods.* I popped the lock button and reached for my door handle, but Luke was faster. "No, Erin! No!" he shouted, grabbing my arm. His grip was surprisingly firm. I tried wrenching away, but couldn't.

"Let go of me, you fucker!" I hissed.

His sunglasses fell off, and I saw the hysterical tears in his eyes. "Please, please," he said, still holding my arm tightly. "I swear I won't hurt you, Erin. I promise. I just need to talk to you."

"Let go!" I shouted back. I remembered that woman, the one who'd told me to kick or punch an attacker in the balls, and I did my best. It wasn't easy—since I was sitting beside Luke—but I lifted my right leg as high as I could and slammed my boot into his groin. He groaned and slumped backwards in pain, dropping my arm and bumping his head against the window. Tears began to pour from his eyes as he sat there, sobbing. I flung my door open, but stayed in the vehicle.

"I'm sorry, Erin," he muttered through his pain. "I'm sorry. I'm sorry. I didn't mean to scare you."

I wasn't sure what to do. Common sense told me to get the hell out of there, but Luke looked so pathetic, and I felt terrible about hurting him. He no longer seemed dangerous or violent. And with his sunglasses off, he looked more familiar than ever.

"Go," he said. "It's okay. Go out there and flag down a cop. Have me arrested. It's all right. I need help anyway. The cops can probably get me to rehab faster than I can get myself there." He began to clench and unclench his fists in sync with his heavy breathing.

"What're you doing?" I asked.

He opened his hazel eyes wide and looked straight at me. "Trying to calm down. Trying to get a grip. I'm not a bad person, Erin. I swear. The only creature I've ever hurt is myself."

"Well, you *definitely* need help," I said. But just then, I saw something that stopped me short. His sunglasses remained on the floor, and the stubble on his head and face were just long enough for me to imagine him with a beard, mustache, and full head of hair. "You're ..." My mouth froze.

He nodded, his eyes still reflecting the pain I'd inflicted on him. "Yeah. I'm an addict. That's why I'm going to Miami. There's a rehab down there where they know me well. Extremely well." He let out a sad little chuckle. "I was hoping you could help me with the transportation, but I understand. You gotta work. I get it."

"No," I blurted. "I'll do it. I'll quit my job."

He sat up slowly, his hand over his groin. "No. Don't. Seriously. I'm sorry for being a dick. Come on, let's get you to work. You're gonna be extra late today."

But I'd made up my mind. "I don't care, Luke. I'm not going back to Don-Wash. Ever. I've got some money saved, and I'll find another job after the trip to Florida. In Boston or something. So I won't need a car. This is what I wanna do."

"Listen, Erin," he said, wiping a smudge off one of his sunglass lenses. "I'd be psyched if you came, and I really do think your boss is an asshole, but you should give this some thought." His pupils were pinpricks as he replaced the glasses on his face, but everything had changed during the moment or two they'd been off. I'd finally figured out where I'd met him before.

"I'm quitting."

His face brightened, even though I could tell he was still in pain. "That's awesome," he said. "And, you know, I can help you out with cash. Not now, but when we get to Florida. There's a guy down there who owes me, and ... yeah, I can probably give you about five grand. As payment for helping me out, you know."

I nodded. I heard everything he was saying, but it was registering in some foreign part of my brain that I don't normally use. The normal part had gone totally numb.

Luke went on talking. "I can cover expenses too. Gas, food, hotels, whatever. You won't have to spend a dime."

"Okay," I said. It occurred to me that I was being too agreeable, but I couldn't help it. I was working so hard to act nonchalant, because he obviously didn't want me to know his true identity. Not yet, anyway.

It was *him,* though. Lenny *Weir.* I'd been riding in Lenny Weir's car for almost a month. And it all added up. The guitar, the drugs, the secrecy, the way he'd freaked out the day he mistook Claire for Violet. I had no idea why he was in Massachusetts when everyone in the world thought he was dead, but that didn't matter. Because Lenny was alive, semi-well, and part of my life again. And we were going on a road trip together. To Miami.

Chapter 18

September 1983

Janet always kept her clock radio tuned to WBRU, the Brown University radio station that played new wave bands like the Cure, Talking Heads, New Order, the Smiths, and the occasional "classic" progressive artist like Bowie. So it shouldn't have been an immense shock to wake up one sunny September morning to the old Bowie song "Quicksand."

Nevertheless, it caught me by surprise. Lying there on my narrow dorm bed, my mind skipped back to a more innocent time, when I'd been a virgin in so many ways. I'd graduated from high school less than eighteen months earlier, but felt like I'd aged ten years since then. I mean, had I really been naïve enough to believe that an international rock god like David Bowie—whose *Let's Dance* album was selling by the millions—would even look at a girl like me? And when I dyed my hair blond and shaved off my eyebrows—which, by the way, had never grown back properly—did I actually expect David to be impressed?

But wait. *Wait.* The DJ was saying something about Bowie in *Massachusetts.* I jumped out of bed and turned up the volume. At first, I thought the dude was discussing an event that'd already happened, but it soon became clear that the *Serious Moonlight* tour was coming to Sullivan Stadium in Foxboro—where the New England Patriots played—in *one week.* Foxboro, which was less than an hour from Providence. "Tickets are still available at Ticketron," said the DJ, "but they're selling fast. The good news is that it's a general admission show. Meaning anyone can have front row seats if they arrive early enough."

"Janet!" I shouted, banging on the bathroom door in my oversized t-shirt. Beverly rolled over in her bed and moaned, but I barely noticed. "Bowie's coming to Foxboro! Sullivan Stadium! Next Sunday!"

"Yeah, I heard about that," called Janet from the shower. "But it's gonna suck. It's a *Let's Dance* tour."

What's wrong with her? David Bowie, an hour away? "Who gives a shit?" I yelled through the door. "It's Bowie! He can play 'Jingle Bells' or 'Happy Birthday' the whole time for all I care. We gotta go!"

Janet turned off the water. "Chill out!" she called. "How much are tickets?"

"I don't know! Who cares? Janet, we need to be there. It's general admission."

Janet opened the bathroom door and walked out, dripping wet and wrapped in a towel. "Great," she said. "So there can be another stampede like at the Who concert?"

I wanted to shake her. "Think, Janet! We'll regret it forever if we miss this."

She glanced over at Beverly, who was rubbing her eyes. "Whatdya think, Bev?"

"I'll go," said Bev. "But we need a ride."

The van had no muffler, but I barely noticed the noise. Wearing the same borrowed denim mini-skirt I'd worn to the dorm party a few weeks earlier, I sat awkwardly on the vehicle's rusty metal floor, sipping beer and trying to stay calm. Every few minutes, I'd check for the brightly colored ticket in my pocket, just to make sure it was still there. Sure, it'd cost $13.50, but I'd soon be breathing the same air as David Bowie! It no longer mattered that his new album sucked. Everyone made a few mistakes in life, right?

Suddenly, Bowie was back at the top of my rock star list. I mean, nothing against Bruce, but getting to New Jersey would take some serious time and effort—Andrew still wouldn't acknowledge me—and Bowie was less than an hour away. Everything inside me quivered and twitched. I wanted to stand up and scream, but the other seven people in the van were acting pretty unfazed. Clearly, they'd all been to concerts before, but not me. Bowie would be my first.

"I'm definitely getting in the front row," I said to no one in particular.

Janet smiled the way a preschool teacher smiles at a child discussing the tooth fairy. "Sullivan Stadium holds sixty thousand people," she said. "And we're totally late. None of us are gonna see more than a little dot on the stage. If even."

The lateness wasn't our fault. The concert started at eight, so the plan had been for Neil, the owner of the van, to meet us outside our dorm at five o'clock. But by six-thirty, he still hadn't shown up. Neil, a part-time Danforth student who sold drugs to supplement his tuition payments, had agreed to drive us if we paid for gas *and* bought him a ticket to the show. Janet swore Neil was a sweet guy, but he seemed shady to me. I'd suggested we hitchhike to Foxboro, but Janet and Bev weren't into that. Instead, they'd invited a few other people to join our group and help defer the expenses.

Janet sat between Bev and me on one side of the van's floor while across the way, Janet's younger brother Tommy and his girlfriend Gillian snuggled. And leaning against the back door—which struck me as dangerous—were Spike Walker and Jimmy "Strings" Healey, both members of the heinous Springsteen-wannabe band Spike and the Asbury Rockers. In any other situation, I would've complained about going *anywhere* with people like Spike and Strings, but I had other things on my mind. Namely, getting to the show and making a run for the stage.

But apparently, Spike and Strings were into the journey as well as the concert, and had come prepared with drugs. My roommates and I had pitched in for a case of Miller—which we gladly shared with everyone—and Strings sparked up a joint shortly after we left Danforth. Then, as we passed that around, Spike pulled out a plastic baggie full of something that looked like leftovers from the cafeteria salad bar.

"Shrooms!" said Janet.

"Help yourself," said Spike.

Janet quickly gobbled a mushroom, but Beverly shook her head, saying hallucinogens made her sick to her stomach. Strings helped himself to a small handful. Tommy and Gillian paid no attention to any of us.

"You want some, Erin?" asked Spike.

"Uh, I don't know." Pot and alcohol were the only drugs I'd ever tried, and I already felt buzzed.

Spike raised his eyebrows. His eyes were kind, and he looked much cuter up close than on stage. "First time?"

"Yeah." I wanted to like him, but how could I respect the leader of such a terrible band?

"Don't worry," he said. "Just take it slow."

"Thanks," I said. "I guess I'll try one."

It tasted like the shell of a sunflower seed, and I washed it down with beer.

I knew Jim Morrison had used "magic mushrooms" before some of his best concerts—supposedly, they gave him the courage to totally let loose—so I hoped they'd work some magic on me too. Because although I'd never been to a rock show before, my goal was to get backstage and talk to David.

But when we pulled into Sullivan Stadium—after taking two wrong exits—magic wasn't exactly in the air. Sweaty people wearing pink t-shirts with Bowie's face on them milled around everywhere, and Bowie music blared from what seemed like a thousand car windows. "Are *all* these people going to the show?" I asked.

"Uh huh," answered Spike. "And this is just the parking lot."

"Yeah. You ain't seen nothin' yet," said Strings, lighting another joint.

As Neil drove around looking for a good parking spot, my stomach shrank. I mean, where had all these Bowie people come from? During my freshman year at Danforth, the only Bowie lovers I'd met were Janet and Bev, and that was on the very last day of finals. But seeing so many in one place, I felt only anger and disdain. In a pissed-off little epiphany, I realized I didn't *want* to share David. I wanted him all to myself.

"At least they're all wearing *Let's Dance* shirts," I commented.

"And why's that a good thing?" asked Janet.

I felt a little confused and definitely kind of drunk. "They're not real fans," I said. "They're morons."

Janet gave me a funny look. "They're concert shirts. They sell 'em here."

"Yeah, but the album sucks," I said. "You know that."

Gillian, who hadn't spoken to me all day, looked really hurt. "I like the record," she said. "And the shirts."

"Okay," I replied. "Whatever." I barely knew Gillian, and wasn't up for arguing with her about music or anything else. My brain was growing fuzzier by the moment. How would David recognize me?

I had an idea. I ripped off one of the cardboard ends from the case of Miller and grabbed a pen from the van's floor. *Dear David,* I wrote, shielding my note from the others. *I love you. I've loved you forever. Please bring me backstage. My name is Erin Reardon.* Then I folded the thing in half and shoved it down my bra. In my altered state, it seemed like a foolproof plan.

"Guys," I said as soon as Neil parked and opened the van's back door, "we gotta run. Now." I checked once more for the ticket in my skirt pocket, then jumped down onto the pavement.

Janet stared at me like I was on drugs. Which, of course, was accurate, but I resented the judgmental look in her eyes. "Erin, it's too late and this place is packed. Let's just stay here in the parking lot. It'll be way more fun and chill."

"Yeah," agreed Beverly. "We'll hear him just as good from out here. Hey Spike, you guys got any more weed?"

The air around me thinned, and I actually gasped for breath. Surely Janet and Bev weren't serious. But there was Spike telling Bev he had plenty of weed. "I'm with your roommates, Erin," he said, laying a hand on my shoulder. "I heard on the radio that people were lined up here at six this morning."

"Can you imagine people doin' that for *us*, Spike?" asked Sticks Healey.

"Some day," said Spike. "Hey Erin, you ever heard The Asbury Rockers? We play lotsa parties around campus."

I couldn't even answer that. All around us, people headed for the stadium gates. "Fuck it, Janet, we came here to *see* Bowie, not *listen* to him. Come *on*! We gotta try!"

Janet glanced over at Bev, who shook her head and mouthed the word *no*.

"It's not a good idea, Erin," said Janet.

"She's right," said Spike, pushing back his greasy hair. His leather motorcycle jacket made him look like an idiot, especially since it was about seventy degrees outside. "Plus, the security guards are probably brutal."

I had no one. Tommy and Gillian didn't care, nor did Neil, who was rolling a joint. My mouth felt too big for my face, and my tongue seemed extra heavy, but I didn't have time for that shit. Not when David was about to go on stage. I don't remember if I spoke any more words; all I recall is running away from my group. I imagine they called me and maybe even chased me, but they definitely didn't catch me.

Once I got past the ticket takers, I realized how far away the stage was. Probably about a quarter mile. But the problem wasn't so much distance as density. Viewed from behind, the crowd was a writhing, impermeable mass of arms, legs, and sweaty bodies. Still, I had to try. It was Bowie.

Shyly, I tapped the shoulder of a guy in front of me. "Excuse me," I said, "my boyfriend's up there, and I need to get through." The guy looked annoyed, but stepped aside.

I thanked him, then did the same thing to the next person blocking my way. And the next. And the next. I needed to pee, but that was impossible, and each person who let me pass seemed a little surlier than the previous one. Some even shoved me a bit. I felt guilty, but also couldn't stop. Bowie had possessed me. At some point, he actually took the stage, but I was so focused on my task that I didn't see it happen. I just heard the crowd explode; then the band started playing "Let's Dance."

Right around then, things started feeling surreal. My sense of right and wrong weakened as the music filled me with new resolve. "Let's Dance" may have been the worst Bowie song ever, but hearing David sing it live changed everything about it. And I was there with him, goddamn it! That figure onstage in the glowing white suit was *my destiny*. What choice did I have but to keep moving forward? I felt like a woman in childbirth, pushing through the agony. "I'm coming, David!" I howled, tugging at my denim skirt in a lame attempt to keep my butt covered.

Of course, no one else understood or appreciated the critical nature of my mission, and the security guards only patrolled the perimeter of the crowd. In other words, martial law ruled in the middle. A woman scratched my arm with her fingernails and drew blood, and a guy elbowed me so hard in the ribs that he knocked the wind out of me. For a split second, I thought about the kids who'd been crushed at the Who concert and freaked out. Then someone kicked me in the ankle with a heavy shoe or boot, and I resumed my struggle.

I'm not sure how long the pushing and bashing went on, but David made it through a bunch of songs. I remember "Rebel Rebel" and that cool song from *Cat People* about fires and gasoline, and one of my all-time favorites, "Life on Mars." But my body was getting battered so badly I couldn't enjoy any of it. If not for that beautiful blond angel on stage, I would've quit for sure. But every time I looked up, I vowed to press on.

Each stab of pain brought me closer. And closer. I may have been numb from all the physical and verbal insults—not to mention the alcohol and drugs I'd ingested—but after a few more songs, I made it—sweaty, bloody, and drenched with beer—to the front row.

That's when the true bodily torture began. Being a moving target had been one thing, but as a sitting duck, I couldn't escape. And everyone around me despised me. Rightfully so, by the way. They'd been out there all day in the sun, waiting for Bowie, and I'd just clawed my way into their area. I'd stolen what they'd worked hard for, then acted like it'd always been mine. But damn it, it hurt. The guy directly to my left—a smelly bastard with curly brown hair and acne—kept shoving me and calling me a slut and a whore, while the surging masses behind me repeatedly bashed my ribs and hips against the stage. Had I been fully conscious, I would've been terrified, but I was about as far from consciousness as an upright person can be.

Pain, alcohol, mushrooms, marijuana, and adrenaline combined to form an interesting cocktail in my brain, anesthetizing certain parts of me, but also unleashing aggressions I'd never felt before. Meanwhile, Bowie's razor-sharp cheekbones shone under the stage lights less than fifty feet away. I *needed* to touch him, or at least give him my note.

Then the lights dimmed, and everything changed. At first, I thought my imagination had gone bonkers, but it was real: the band began playing the introduction to "Station to Station" that'd been imprinted on my DNA so long ago. *This was meant to be.* Kismet. As the drums and piano intensified, peace filled my heart.

But not for long. Since the song was older and lesser-known than others, many people used it as an opportunity for a breather, and began chatting amongst themselves. And I couldn't allow that. If they were going to attend a Bowie show, they'd need to appreciate David's work. Just as David needed to know that he had one true fan in that pathetic mass of losers and wannabes. He needed to know *someone* knew his history and loved *all* of him, not just the 80s pop star.

So, I began singing along—loudly—and waving my arms around to attract his attention. My body grew tired and my throat ached. Still, as the melody shifted and the song got jazzier, I did my best to keep up. "David!" I cried. "I love you!" The curly-haired guy beside me elbowed me in the ribs.

David smiled out at the audience, singing about the side effects of cocaine, and I gasped, stunned by his proximity. Then the most amazing thing of all happened: he looked down and straight into my eyes. *Straight.* I wasn't hallucinating. For one split second, I had a direct link to Bowie. He saw me, and he was happy. But before I could respond, he was off, jogging toward the other side of the stage.

I reached under my bra and pulled out the folded scrap of cardboard from the case of Miller. By that point, the stage was littered with all kinds of crap other people had thrown up there: clothing, paper airplanes, flowers, plastic cups, baseball caps. "David!" I screamed, tossing my note onto the platform. "Read this!"

"Cut it out, you fuckin' idiot!" yelled my curly-haired "neighbor," his breath reeking of booze. "Security!" He waved his arms in the direction of a security guard in the aisle. "This lady just threw something at Bowie!"

The guard glanced in our direction, then looked away.

"Fuck you!" I yelled at the guy. "I know David. Personally."

The guy laughed an evil laugh, but suddenly, I had an idea: what if I told one of the security guards that David was my friend? And that he was *expecting* me backstage? It was such a simple plan, yet so unique—or so I thought. I just needed to get to the end of the aisle and speak to one of those guards. And if I spoke in a British accent, I'd sound even more authentic.

"Excuse me!" I yelled at Mr. Curly Hair. "I gotta get past you." I couldn't believe how British I sounded.

"Fuck you, cunt!" he screamed back, his face awash in sweat. "Go fuck yourself!"

No one had ever called me the "c" word before, and even after all I'd been through, its crassness shocked me. Especially since I was trying to *leave.* I mean, didn't the guy want me out of his hair?

"Let me out! Now!" I shouted in my new accent. Bowie had begun singing "China Girl," and people were going nuts. "Please!"

But the guy snapped or something. Maybe I'd underestimated his potential for cruelty, or maybe he'd just been drinking in the sun for too long. All I remember is him grabbing me, lifting me off the ground, and—I think—trying to toss me backwards into the crowd. I found myself suspended in the air in a vertical position; the only thing keeping me from going on my head was the density of the crowd. Then things got blurry. I recall tasting blood, hearing someone scream, seeing blood, and finally being carried by two large security guards who wouldn't listen to reason. My British accent was *perfect,* but they ignored me. Completely.

I told the guards how the curly-haired man had tried to kill me, and that I'd grown up in Bowie's neighborhood, and that he'd invited me to visit him backstage after the show, but they simply carried me all the way to the parking lot and dumped my ass there. They also instructed the ticket takers not to let me back inside the concert under any circumstances. People averted their eyes as they passed.

"Don't you understand? He tried to murder me!" I protested, unable to shake the British accent, even when I tried.

One of the guards got a call on his two-way radio and darted back into the stadium, but the other one squatted beside me and looked me in face. "Little girl," he growled, "you're a fuckin' mess. No one tried to kill you, okay? *You're* the one who hurt someone. And if you don't shut up, we'll have you arrested. Is that what you want? How old are you, anyway?"

"Nineteen," I said. "But I didn't hurt anyone. That guy—"

"The one whose shoulder looks like hamburger thanks to your teeth? He'll be lucky if he gets away with ten stitches. And *you're* lucky he doesn't know your name, or you'd be hearing from his lawyer tomorrow."

"What? I didn't do anything!" But when I spat on the ground, blood came out, and I didn't seem to be bleeding. Had I *bitten* the guy? "I'm sorry," I said, choking up but still unable to shake the British accent. "He shoved me and called me names and picked me up and ... oh just lemme talk to David. He's an old friend and—"

"*Do not* start with that bullshit again!" interrupted the guard, "or I'm callin' the cops. Listen, I know that guy was a jerk, so I'm lettin' you off easy. But you need to go home. Now. How'd you get here tonight? Where are your friends?"

I shrugged.

"You don't know? Do I have to call your parents?"

The guard was in his forties, probably about the same age my dad would've been if he were alive. "I don't have any parents," I blurted.

Just then, a siren blasted nearby, and I turned to see an ambulance stop about fifty yards from us. A bunch of people who'd been hanging out in the parking lot crowded around it, and I heard someone shout, "Give these guys some space! C'mon! Give 'em space!"

"Alcohol and drugs," muttered my security guard pal. "I don't know why you kids all gotta abuse 'em."

I didn't know how to answer that, so the two of us just watched the commotion in silence for a couple of minutes. Then the ambulance's door slammed, the siren blared again, and the car inched its way toward the exit. A moment or two later, it wailed off into the night.

"I'm okay," I told the guard in a temporary moment of clarity. "You can go back to work now." Finally—and miraculously—the British accent had vanished.

"Not so quick," he said. "You can't just sit here all night."

"Don't worry," I said with a shrug. "I'll find my friends." *Or figure out another way backstage.*

But right then, I looked up and saw Beverly walking toward the row of porta-potties. "Bev!" I shouted. "Bev! It's Erin."

"Ohmigod!" cried my roommate. She looked like she'd been crying. The security guard stood up and crossed his arms over his chest as she approached. "What *happened* to you, Erin?"

Before I could answer, the guard asked Bev if we had a sober person to drive us home. "Of course," she said. "We're not stupid."

"Right," said the guard, patting me on the shoulder as his two-way radio barked some sort of request. "Well, take good care of this one, would ya? She's had a rough time."

"Thank you," I said to him, my head reeling.

"Just doin' my job," he answered. "Stay safe, girls."

"Did you see the ambulance?" asked Bev when the guard was gone.

"Yeah ..."

"It was Spike. He stopped breathing."

"What? Oh my god."

"Uh huh. I think he'll be okay, though. They put him on oxygen."

"That's good," I said, and my head spun again. "Bowie smiled at me."

Beverly squinted. "Is that *blood* on your mouth?"

I wiped my lips and saw red on my hand. "I think so."

"Erin! You need help!"

"Nah. I'm fine. But Bowie. We gotta get backstage."

"Erin!" shouted Bev.

I have a vague memory of puking on the ground while 'TVC 15' played in the background, but that's about it. The remainder of the night has been forever blacked out in my mind.

Around ten the next morning, I awoke alone in our mini-suite, dressed in the same clothes I'd worn at the show. My ribs ached; the denim skirt was hiked up around my waist like a belt; my underwear was wet and filthy. Apparently, I'd peed myself at some point, because I smelled like urine. The biggest surprise, though, came when I dragged my ass off the bed and looked in the mirror.

My entire torso—shoulders to thighs—was black and blue. No flesh-colored skin could be seen on my breasts, stomach, back, or butt. None. My arms and legs were bruised too, as was my face, in multiple places. When I spat into the sink, my blood-stained saliva tasted metallic.

"Bowie wounds," I said, my throat so ravaged from screaming that the words came out like a whisper. My left hip, which had taken the most severe thrashing against the stage, was entirely black—not even blue—and so tender that touching it felt like torture. Later in the day, I learned that I'd chipped the bone there. But I was alive. And Bowie had smiled at me.

Yes. That flash in his eyes, the sincerity of his dimples. Lowering my damaged body back onto the bed, I allowed that sweet, dazzling memory to momentarily numb my pain.

I'd been so close. If only I'd been sober and had arrived earlier. Going in Neil's van had been my fatal mistake. Next time, I'd have to be smarter. Slowly, slowly, I was learning.

The phone was ringing. Or maybe it was a dream. I closed my eyes tighter and willed it to stop. And it did. *Phew.* Then it started again.

Fucker! I thought, sitting up in bed. The pain had worsened—all my joints and muscles hurt now—and my brain felt like it was being simultaneously stretched and burned. I couldn't see straight. "Hello?" I whispered into the phone.

"Erin Reardon?" said a very official-sounding voice. "Did you forget about our meeting this morning?"

It was the dean of students. Oh lord, I'd been scheduled to meet with him to discuss my grades. As far as I knew, I was passing all my classes, although I *had* skipped a bunch of them the previous week due to my excitement over going to see Bowie. "I'm sick," I said.

"Hmm. Sorry to hear that. Have you been to the infirmary?"

"No. I ... I'm in bed."

The dean cleared his throat. "I see. Well, it's three in the afternoon. What are your symptoms?"

"I don't know." What could I say? The pounding of my heart made my bruised ribs hurt more. "Just ... sick. I think I have a fever."

"Well, you'd better get checked out. Can you make it to the infirmary ..."

I was about to say no, but the dean wasn't finished.

"... or should I send a nurse to you?"

Oh god, I couldn't let an adult into the suite. The place was trashed, and it stunk like alcohol, piss, and cigarettes. Janet and Bev would be mortified if a nurse came in. "Um ... I can probably be there in a while. I need to shower first." The thought of water on my bruised skin made me cringe, but I smelled so bad. And what would the nurse do when she saw me?

"All right. Feel better, Erin. I'll call the infirmary now and let them know you're coming."

"Thanks," I said, not feeling very thankful.

"Sure. I'll be in touch soon to reschedule our meeting."

Chapter 19

December 23, 1993

"Richmond. Cool city."

Startled, I glanced over my shoulder and saw Luke sitting up and looking out the car window. A few minutes earlier, he'd been crashed out on the back seat, snoring.

All day long, I'd been driving south on Route 95. Luke had shown up at my apartment at around seven that morning—hey, if I trusted him enough to accompany him to Florida, I had to trust him with my home address too—looking sickly and pale. He hadn't even bothered to make an excuse about his condition; he just handed me the car keys, climbed into the back of the Range Rover, and curled up on his side. Throughout the day, he'd barely spoken at all and had exited the vehicle only twice, both times to use the bathroom and buy stuff from vending machines. He'd also picked up a pack of Marlboros in Connecticut, saying he liked to smoke on the road.

He confused me, this Luke. The day I'd agreed to take the trip with him, I'd been a hundred percent convinced he was Lenny Weir. But as we headed into unfamiliar territory together, some doubts crept back into my mind. He'd re-shaved his head and face, and once again looked nothing like the sloppy, hairy Lenny on my bedroom wall. And while Luke wore the same *style* of clothing as Lenny—faded jeans and t-shirts—he wasn't nearly as pathetic or scrawny. It was only when I concentrated *really* hard on the way Lenny's eyes had looked that night at the Middle East that I could relax again. Of course, I'd searched all over the place—even gone through countless back issues of music magazines at the library— for a photo of Lenny Weir without sunglasses, but came up dry. Colin's friend Mark had been correct about Lenny's shyness.

Which was why it made perfect sense for him to fake his own death. I mean, how else could he escape his obsessive, adoring fans? And now, he felt safe with me. An honor, for sure, but wow, how exhausting. And I resented being treated like an employee.

"Hey, Luke, we just passed a sign for a Quality Inn on the next exit. That sound all right to you?" I was trying hard to be upbeat, despite the nine hours of driving I'd just done. Not bad, considering I'd never driven more than two in a single day before.

"Sure," came Luke's weak voice from the back seat. "Gotta love quality."

In the hotel lobby—where silver tinsel letters spelled out SEASON'S GREETINGS on the wall—we waited in the reception line behind an overweight man having trouble with his corporate credit card and a woman with a Southern accent who kept insisting that since she was a nurse, she should get a "medical discount." At first, I thought they were a couple, but soon realized the receptionist was trying to help two people with separate issues at the same time. Luke, meanwhile, acted edgy and irritable. He cleared his throat about a hundred times, and kicked repeatedly at his duffle bag.

"What time were you thinking of hitting the road in the morning?" I asked, hoping he'd suggest sleeping in. I'd studied his map, and Miami was another nine hundred miles from Richmond. Meaning that if we got an early enough start, we could conceivably cover the entire distance in just one day. With me doing the driving, of course. I much preferred the option of spreading it out over two.

Luke kicked his bag again and shrugged. "Depends on how I feel in the morning." His sunglasses remained on his face, even though we were indoors and it was nighttime.

I nodded, pissed at him for being so self-centered, but also at myself for allowing that. Maybe I shouldn't have left Don-Wash and Claire.

Claire. She and I had met for dinner in the North End the night before the Florida trip, and we'd both cried into our pasta and wine. She'd made the decision to move—at least temporarily—out of Bobby's apartment and back home with her mom so she could think about what she really wanted. She also admitted she'd been working on her resume, and planned to start looking for a new job after the holidays.

"That's awesome!" I said as we walked to the T. "Maybe you and I can even work together again. In a normal office, with no skeevy boss."

"I was thinking the same thing," she said, hugging me goodbye. "But for now, Reardon, just be careful of yourself. I'll be sending positive energy your way every day. And remember, don't let that Luke dude behind the wheel for one *second*. And call me if you ever feel scared. Any time of the day or night."

"Don't worry," I replied. "I'll be fine."

Miraculously, the overweight man's corporate credit card eventually went through, and the receptionist handed him a key while signaling for Luke and me to step forward. The Southern nurse continued to stand by, waiting to hear the verdict on her "medical discount," and we all watched the big man shuffle off to his room, grunting obscenities. I felt bad for the poor receptionist, and wished Luke would remove his stupid sunglasses.

"Tough night?" I asked the woman.

"Typical," she answered. "How can I help you folks?"

"Two rooms, please," muttered Luke, extracting a bulging wallet from his back pocket and pulling out an American Express card. I couldn't help staring at the bills jammed into the thing; I couldn't see their denominations, but there were *lots* of them. Even more surprising, though, was his request for two rooms. I'd assumed we'd share.

The receptionist nodded and seemed relieved when Luke's credit card cleared quickly. "All right, could you sign here, Mr. Walker?"

It was the first time I'd heard Luke's last name—or at least the last name he used. In my head, I'd been referring to him as *Luke Weir* for a while, so the name *Walker* threw me for a second. Although it made perfect sense. I mean, if illegal immigrants can get fake IDs, how hard could it be for someone as wealthy and famous as Lenny Weir?

"Luke *Sky*walker?" I asked, making a bad joke.

"No," he said humorlessly, and the receptionist clicked her tongue, as if to emphasize that she hadn't found my comment funny either.

"Sorry. Just goofing around," I said.

She raised her eyebrows. "Two smoking or non-smoking rooms?"

Both Luke and I answered at the same time; he said "smoking," and I said "non."

"Smoking," said Luke again, this time with more authority. "Definitely smoking."

"All right," said the receptionist. "Smoking it is. I've got two adjoining smoking rooms on the eighth floor."

"Is there a lock between them?" asked Luke.

The receptionist assessed me again while I stood there speechless. I mean, was Luke afraid of me? Or did other people know—or suspect—that he was Lenny Weir? Was he protecting himself from the public? Or did he just want to get away from *me* for a while?

Back in Massachusetts, we'd agreed that after we reached Miami, he'd meet with his rehab doctor and get an estimate on the length of his treatment. But in typical Luke fashion, he'd only been sharing information on a need-to-know basis. In other words, I knew he had "a long history of problems with various drugs," and that there was only one doctor, at one particular rehab hospital, who *really* knew how to help him. Which struck me as bizarre. I mean, if this doctor was so great, then why had Luke ended up in rehab so many times? But I was no authority on treating addiction. And I didn't want to say anything that might upset him again. I'd seen Luke angry once, and had no interest in a repeat performance. I wasn't worried about getting physically hurt, but didn't want to get booted off the trip. After all, Luke was *most likely* Lenny Weir, and I couldn't bear the thought of losing Lenny a second time.

Not that I had any viable explanation for how Lenny and I had ended up *together* a second time. Could he have been searching for me ever since our meeting at the Middle East? That would explain why he'd called me *Erin* the first time he drove me to Gloucester. But when I really thought about that, I'd start freaking out and would have to grab my head with both hands and squeeze to avoid losing it completely. There's a big difference between *believing* you're destined to be with a rock icon and hanging out with him on a daily basis.

Anyway, Luke assumed he'd be in rehab a few weeks. So we had a tentative plan for me to hang around Miami—in a hotel he'd pay for—until he got released. Then we'd drive home to Massachusetts together. But as a backup, he'd also give me the five thousand dollars he'd promised—the money his friend in Florida owed him—*before* checking in. That way, if he ended up staying in rehab longer, I could buy a plane ticket home, pay my rent and bills, and start looking for a job. I didn't expect that to happen, though. He and I had been through so much, and this stint in rehab was just the final lap of a long race.

"Luke?" I asked as we trudged down the hallway toward our hotel rooms. "You wanna get some food?" It was nine o'clock, and our last stop had been McDonald's at three that afternoon.

"Eat? Now?" He looked at me as if I'd suggested we go square dancing. "Uh-uh. Good night."

"Sleep well," I said as he entered his room. The door closed behind him, and the deadbolt slid home with a loud click.

At around five in the morning, I awoke famished. Apparently my "dinner" of Raisinettes, pretzels, and Sprite—purchased from the lobby vending machines—hadn't been enough to hold me over until a normal breakfast time. Since I couldn't sleep any longer, I decided to shower, then ask the person at the front desk where to find good coffee and bagels.

Tiptoeing across the rug to the door that separated my room from Luke's, I pressed my ear against it and heard no evidence of movement inside. Yay! I'd slept fitfully and was in no hurry to hit the highway again.

I stepped into the shower and tried to relax, but the fickle nozzle tortured me by sending out random strong bursts of lukewarm water followed by a burning hot trickle. I'd also forgotten my hair conditioner, and the hotel didn't provide any, so my hair would be an unruly mess until I got to a drugstore and bought some. On the other hand, my complexion actually looked way better than normal. I'd been so busy preparing for the trip during the week leading up to it that I'd had no time to puke, and the raw, red patches around my mouth had healed and faded significantly. Maybe this trip would help me quit for good.

I smiled at that thought, turned off the water, and reached for a towel. But right then, I felt a familiar stabbing pain in the right side of my abdomen. My doctor had told me not to worry about it—she said it was probably just caused by ovulation—but it freaked me out. Not only did it hurt a lot, but it made me dizzy too. I needed to lie down. So I pressed my ear against Luke's door again, heard nothing, and climbed back into bed.

I must've fallen asleep, because I remember thinking someone was wheeling me down a hospital corridor on a stretcher while a loud male voice shouted about an emergency. Then I opened my eyes in my hotel room. *Phew. It was all a dream.* But why was that same voice still yelling, "Emergency!" I sat up straight. I heard a ton of commotion in Luke's room, and a young woman was sobbing loudly.

"No move! He like dead!" she cried.

Dead?

"Take it easy, he's breathin'," declared a man. "He's gonna be okay."

I froze as a woman with a strong Southern accent yelled for everyone to back off. Immediately, I recognized the voice of the nurse we'd seen at the reception desk the previous night, the one insisting on a medical discount. My empty stomach seized with all kinds of pain and anxiety as I pulled on my t-shirt and sweats and quietly left my room.

Luke's door was ajar, and from the hallway, I could see several people standing around the bed. I ran in and gasped. My traveling companion lay sprawled, face down on the bed and perfectly still in a pair of blue plaid boxer shorts. The nurse's puffy blonde head was pressed against his bare back.

"What's wrong with him?" I asked, darting over to the bed. "He was fine last night."

A skinny, brown-skinned girl dressed in a housekeeping uniform seemed to be trying to blend in with the curtains while a man wearing a nametag that said *Assistant Manager* just looked exasperated.

"I dunno," said the girl, dropping her eyes to the floor. "I knock, but no. Nothing."

"Would you please shut up?" demanded the nurse. "I'm trying to check his heart rate over here."

The assistant manager turned to me and spoke in a professional tone. "The gentleman's breathing, ma'am, and we've called a doctor. I assume you're travelling with him?"

But before I could answer, Luke's arm started to twitch. Then his whole body jerked wildly, and he made an attempt to roll over. The nurse jumped back, looking disappointed. Perhaps she'd been hoping she'd have to resuscitate him.

"Whathefuck?" Luke mumbled.

"Sir," said the nurse sternly, repositioning her small hands on Luke's shoulders and directing him to lie on his back. "I'm a nurse. And lucky for you, I happened to be walking down the hall a few minutes ago when this cleaning lady here thought you were dead." She cut her eyes at the girl in the curtains before continuing. "Can you tell me your name and today's date?"

"Yeah," said Luke with a groggy sniffle. "I'm ... Luke Walker, and it's ... right before Christmas ... like ... a day before. You can all go away now."

The nurse stood up. "Slow down, Lukey boy. You need to be examined by a doctor. Probably hospitalized too."

"What?" said Luke, suddenly sounding much more awake.

The door burst open, and everyone turned to see a short, heavyset man carrying a canvas gym bag rush into the room. "Sorry I'm late," he apologized. "Holiday shoppers. Traffic's a mess. What's the situation here?"

"Looks like a drug OD," declared the nurse. "Completely unresponsive until a minute ago. I recommend a full workup at the nearest hospital. Blood work definitely."

The doctor sighed. "Why don't I take a look?" he suggested, squatting next to the bed and laying a hand on Luke's forehead. "No fever. That's good. Sir, can you tell me your name?"

Luke looked defeated. "Luke Walker," he said.

"Nice to meet you, Luke," said the man. "I'm George Klein, a physician from the area. Why don't you tell me a bit about yourself."

Luke yawned nonchalantly, but his hands were shaking. "There's nothing to say. I just need coffee."

"Oh no," said the nurse. "Doctor, this man wasn't sleeping. He was *completely* unresponsive."

The doctor glared at her. "No pulse? No heartbeat?"

The nurse rolled her eyes. "He had weak vitals, but his skin was clammy, and he didn't stir when I shouted at him. The housekeeper thought he was dead."

"Hmm," said the doctor, taking a little flashlight out of his gym bag, "maybe he doesn't like shouting." Then, methodically, he began shining the light into Luke's eyes.

I was freaking out, of course. About Luke, but also about myself. I mean, what would I do if he ended up in the hospital? I'd be stuck in Richmond with the eighty-five dollars I had in my purse. Meaning I'd probably end up calling my mom for money. Mom, who thought I was enjoying a traditional Christmas in Vermont with Pete's family. She'd be so upset and disappointed, and I hadn't even told her about quitting my job. And what would happen to Luke? Would the people at the hospital figure out his true identity? I knew he trusted the rehab staff in Miami, but I couldn't let him be carted off to some anonymous hospital in Virginia.

"All right, Luke," said Doctor Klein. "I've gotta ask you a few questions. First of all, have you taken any medication in the last twelve hours?"

"No," replied Luke without the slightest hesitation.

The doctor scratched his dark, curly head. "Look, Luke, I'm a medical doctor. I need the truth in order to treat you properly." He turned around and assessed the rest of us. "Why don't you people take a walk down the hall so Luke and I can talk privately. Thanks."

"Erin can stay," said Luke. "She needs to know what's goin' on."

"Erin?" asked the doctor.

"That's me," I said.

"All right, everyone else out," ordered the doctor. "There's free coffee down in the lobby. Doughnuts too."

The assistant manager took the cleaning woman by the arm. "C'mon, Zoraida," he said. "Let's go have a talk in my office." The girl looked scared, but the manager smiled at her. "It's okay. You did the right thing, honey." The nurse, on the other hand, was clearly pissed. Smirking, she told the doctor she'd like a word with him later on, then stormed off in a huff.

Once they were gone, Luke's hands got even shakier, and his nose started running. "I've got a heroin problem, doctor," he admitted. "A bad one."

Dr. Klein nodded and sat back on his heavy haunches. "Well, Luke, you've gotta get help for that."

"I know," said Luke defensively. "That's why I'm going to Miami. There's a rehab down there where I've been before. A few times."

The doctor, who looked about thirty-five, pursed his lips and nodded. "And you're happy with the care they provide at this rehab?"

"Oh yeah," said Luke. "A hundred percent. You can ask around. They do great stuff. They understand people like me. Musicians, artists, you know."

"And you're an artist?"

"Musician."

The doctor drew a deep breath. "All right, Luke. I think you're doing the right thing. But *I'm* responsible for you at the moment. Medically and legally. And I don't feel comfortable sending you off on the road, for obvious reasons. Especially with it being Christmas Eve."

Luke sniffled, wiped his nose, and started to sob. I wanted to give him a hug, but in all the time I'd known him, I'd barely even touched the guy.

"Well, I'll be doing all the driving, Doctor," I said as confidently as possible. "So Luke won't be alone. We're planning to get into Miami tomorrow."

Dr. Klein regarded me with genuine interest for the first time. "On Christmas Day?" he replied. "Do you folks celebrate Christmas?"

Luke shrugged and I said, "Sort of."

"I see," said the doctor, looking at me. "And you're Luke's ... friend?"

"She's my sister," cut in Luke. "I asked her for help when I knew I couldn't do this alone."

"Really?" asked Dr. Klein, his eyes zipping back and forth between the two of us, trying—I'm sure—to glimpse some trace of physical resemblance between my blunt features and Luke's sharp, delicate ones. I considered saying I'd been adopted, but didn't want to further convolute the story.

"Uh huh," said Luke with utter conviction.

"Hmm," said Dr. Klein. "So how'd you get access to the opiates you used last night, Luke? Because a guy on his way to rehab shouldn't have access to opiates. Your sister couldn't have been watching you very well."

"I didn't know he had drugs with him!" I blurted. "I'm so sorry!" But as soon as those words were out, I felt angry. I mean, how dare this man blame me for Luke's problems?

Dr. Klein turned to me with a critical glint in his eyes. "Well, why was he left alone in a hotel room?"

"Hey," said Luke. "Hang on a minute. This had nothing to do with Erin. Erin's just here to help. She's no druggie. She doesn't know how we operate. I'm sorry, Erin," he said, looking me straight in the eye. "I lied when I told you I was clean."

The doctor shook his head while I tried to process it all. Luke hadn't actually said anything to me about being clean; in fact, he'd done nothing to hide the fact that he'd been on something in the car the previous day. The guy had a huge drug problem, and I'd pretty much assumed he'd be using until we got to the rehab. But I hadn't expected him to *overdose*.

"It's okay," I whispered. "I should've taken better care of you."

Dr. Klein sighed. "Erin, it's like this—your brother's a very sick man and he can *not* have access to drugs. Any drugs."

"Yes."

"And if I'm gonna send him off to Miami with you, you'll have to be a better babysitter. And Luke, I need it all. Every single pharmaceutical the two of you've got, including aspirin."

Luke and I both agreed.

"That means now," said the doctor.

Luke reached under his pillow and pulled out a Ziploc baggie containing some brownish powder, which Dr. Klein held up to the light. "All right. This is a good start. Now where's your works?"

"Nowhere," said Luke, holding out his bare arms in front of him. "Honest. I hate needles. Check my whole body if you want. No marks, no tattoos. Needles terrify me."

"So you snort?" asked the doctor.

"Uh huh."

"Hmm. Okay, what else you got? I'm gonna search the room and all your bags anyway, but it'll be a whole lot easier for us all if you hand it over first. Because if I find anything hidden, the cops'll be here in a heartbeat. I don't care what holiday it is."

This soft-spoken guy wasn't screwing around, and Luke seemed to understand that. "Look in that black duffle bag over there," he said. "In the front pocket."

The doctor unzipped the pocket and pulled out another plastic baggie, this one filled with little white pills. "What's this?"

"Ritalin."

Dr. Klein sighed. "Speedballing? Not a smart idea, Luke."

Luke shrugged.

"All right, keep 'em comin'," said the doctor. "What else we got?"

"Look in that same pocket," said Luke, "for an envelope with a few Valiums in it. But that's it. That's the end. Seriously. Dump everything, strip the bed, call the Feds. Do what you need. You won't find anything else."

The doctor retrieved the envelope with the Valium and looked inside. "How 'bout in your car? Can I take a look out there?"

Luke managed a tired smile. "Go for it, dude. You might find a few M&Ms, but that's it. Erin, give him the keys."

"Okay," I said. "I'll be right back."

But as I moved to exit the room, Dr. Klein told me to stop. "No," he said tersely. "I've got patients waiting. I believe you're telling the truth."

We both nodded. "We are," I said.

"Now Erin," he said. "Listen carefully. Your brother is *not* to be left alone for a second. For his safety, but also because I can be held liable if he has an accident. Understand? In other words, it's your job to follow him everywhere, even into the bathroom, which is one of the most dangerous places for a junkie to go alone. Sleep in the same room with him, preferably in the same bed. I know that might be awkward, but he's your brother, and he needs you close to him for a couple of days. Can you do that?"

"Yes."

"You're sure? Because if it's a problem, I need to bring him to a hospital here in Richmond for evaluation and treatment. The only reason I'm letting him go at all is because I know things will work out better at a familiar rehab facility."

"I promise I'll do my best."

"No. No, no, *no*. Not your best. You need to follow my instructions to the *letter*, or your brother could die. I can't tell you how many people lose loved ones while they're doing their best. Especially over the holidays."

I nodded again. "Okay."

"Where's the rest of your family, anyway?"

I turned to Luke for help, but he appeared to be sleeping again. "Well, we don't have much family," I said.

"Are your parents alive?"

I decided to tell as much truth as possible. "Um, our mom is, but she's in Texas with her boyfriend."

"I see. Any other siblings?"

"No. Just us."

"Hmm. Well, the last thing I need's the name and phone number of the rehab in Miami. I'll call down there when I get back to my office and let them know what's happened here. They *are* expecting you, right?"

"Yeah. Of course."

He kept his eyes focused on me. "What's the name of the place?"

"Um ... wait a minute." I shook Luke gently. We were so close to freedom. "Luke," I said. "What's the name of the rehab? The doctor needs to know."

"Sunnydale," he muttered. "Look in my pants. In my wallet. There's a card in there somewhere."

It felt almost criminal to take his faded jeans off the floor and go through his wallet as if he really was my brother. But the doctor was watching my every move. I left the money in the billfold section, but pulled everything else out and let it fall on the bed: a few credit cards (all registered to Luke Walker), a bunch of business cards from record stores and radio stations, a few old receipts from hotels, and lots of little scraps of paper with names and phone numbers written on them. I was almost ready to give up when I noticed a wrinkled blue business card that said:

Sunnydale Center
Sensible Solutions for Substance Abuse

"Thanks," said Dr. Klein, taking the card from me and jotting down the contact information on a piece of hotel stationary. Then he handed it back, along with one of his own business cards. "Mind if I take a look in your bags as well, Erin? For pharmaceuticals?"

"Oh ... sure," I said. "Feel free. All I've got's a little bottle of Advil and some Xanax from my doctor. I get anxious sometimes."

"Um hmm. Well, I'm gonna need all that. On second thought, you can keep the Advil."

I ran back to my room and returned with the orange plastic container from the drugstore. I also had about seven emergency Xanaxes in my purse, but decided not to mention them.

"Can you live without Xanax until you get home?" asked the doctor after thoroughly examining my prescription bottle.

"Sure," I said. "I hardly ever take 'em anyway." That was an outright lie. In truth, I took one almost every night before bed, and occasionally during the day when I felt nervous or panicky. But I didn't want to give Dr. Klein any reason to detain us in Virginia. The seven pills in my purse were probably more than enough to tide me over until I could call my doctor back home and refill the prescription.

"All right then," said Dr. Klein, slipping the orange container into his pocket. "And I'm expecting a call from Sunnydale tomorrow night at the latest. I wanna hear that Luke's been checked in safely."

"Yes," I assured him, "I'll remind them to call."

"No excuses. If I don't pick up after five rings, have me paged. And if you run into trouble along the road, call from a pay phone. Any trouble at all."

"I will. Thanks."

"You're welcome. Happy holidays. And be safe."

After he left, I sat tentatively on the bed beside Luke. It felt strange being close to him like that, even though we'd spent so much time alone together in his car. "How're you feeling, brother?" I asked with a shy smile.

"Oh man," he sighed, his chin quivering. "I'm such a fuckup."

"No you're not," I assured him. "You just need ... treatment, like the doctor said."

"But I've *been* treated," he answered. "Treated and treated and treated. And look at me. I'm a fucking mess."

I thought about my puking. "Well, I don't have a sickness like yours," I said, "but I have a different problem, and ... well ... I sorta know how you feel. I think we should both try to get better. We owe it to ourselves, you know?"

He wriggled into a half-sitting position. "Oh yeah? What's wrong with you?"

I'd never told anyone about my puking before. I'd never even said its real name out loud, even though I was pretty sure I had bulimia. "I have ... well, it's like an eating disorder," I admitted, instantly feeling my cheeks heat up. And not only because I was embarrassed—which I was—but also because an eating disorder sounded so trivial compared to full-blown drug addiction. And yet, both Luke and I had problems that controlled our lives and prevented us from being productive. We both looked fairly normal, but were obsessed with abnormal things. And we were both in danger of dying way too soon.

Still, when Luke broke down and began to cry for real, I was shocked. He threw his arms around my waist and hugged me, his knobby shoulder pressing against my hip, his whole body convulsing.

"It's all right, Luke," I said, not sure where to put my hands. "You're gonna get the help you need."

"I know," he rasped. "It's just that my sister was anorexic. My *biological* sister." He continued to sob, but more softly. "She had a heart attack and died at twenty-two."

Holy shit, I thought as his tears and drool soaked the thigh of my sweats. He continued to hold onto me in that awkward manner. *We lied to the doctor about being siblings, but Luke's actual sister died of an illness like mine.* I shivered in the warm room and imagined what she may have looked like. A female version of Luke, with hollow cheeks and limp hair, her clothes hanging off.

Suddenly, the song "Weeds" began to play in my head, and I remembered the violent way Luke had reacted to it in his car.

Tangle children, tangled gardens
Cripple horses, mangle monsters
Crumble lightning, mangle blackness
Tangle thunder, cripple madness

Could it be that the mysterious weeds were eating disorders? I handed Luke a tissue and felt a tear slip out of my eye.

Two hours later, we were at a gas station. While I shopped for snacks and bottled water in the convenience store area, Luke used the bathroom. I knew I wasn't supposed to leave him alone for even a second, but when I'd suggested going into the men's room with him, he'd laughed out loud.

"Erin, I know you wanna do the right thing, but I draw the line at letting you watch me take a shit."

So I let him go alone. When Dr. Klein told me to accompany Luke in bathrooms, it'd seemed like a simple task. But in reality? Out in public? Well, that was different. Not to mention that Dr. Klein hadn't provided instructions regarding gas station men's rooms. I wasn't even sure women could legally go in there.

Luckily, Luke returned after only a few minutes and joined me at the checkout counter. "I fucking hate paying for water," he said, placing a carton of orange juice next to my two plastic water bottles. "Water should be free."

I shrugged. "Yeah, but it costs money to put it in bottles, right?" We had a long drive ahead of us, and I didn't want to get dehydrated.

"Whatever." But as he paid the cashier, his tone softened. "Oh and Erin? Here's that card for Sunnydale." He took the crumpled blue business card out of his wallet and handed it to me.

"Thanks," I said, with a twinge of anxiety, "but why don't you hang onto it until we get there?"

"Eh," he said, with a shrug. "I guess I'll feel safer if you have it. I'm a little spacey these days."

CHAPTER 20

November 1983

It had to be death.

I felt dizzy, my heart was pounding, my lungs constricted, my vision blurred. Clutching my chest, I stood panting on the sidewalk, but no one else was around. *A heart attack,* I thought, leaning against a tree and easing myself down into a sitting position on the cement. *I'm gonna die right here on the street where I grew up. One of the neighbors will eventually come out and check on me, but it'll be too late.*

My poor mother. I'd been booted out of Danforth a week earlier—she'd been so shocked and devastated—and now the Winthrop police would have to call her at work and tell her I'd been found dead. How would she handle that? And to make it worse, it was all my fault. I'd known about the dangers of bulimia, and had ignored every warning.

I prayed for another chance at life, but felt hopeless. "Help!" I called out. A squirrel stopped and stared, probably wondering why a human would sit on the ground on such a chilly day. Every house within earshot had its doors and windows closed. "Help!" I called again, but nobody heard and the squirrel ran away.

But wait. Was it my imagination, or did I feel a little stronger? I certainly had nothing to lose, so I decided to try standing. Using the tree as a helper, I pulled myself to my feet. I took a shaky step. And then another. Maybe I could get to a phone and call 911. My head still reeled, but my heart had stopped beating so wildly, so I staggered home and crashed on the couch. I knew I should call an ambulance, but what would I tell the paramedics? Especially since I was feeling a lot more like myself.

Was there such a thing as a *minor* heart attack? Or a *slight* stroke? I had no idea, but some sixth sense told me I might not be in immediate danger. Maybe I *was* getting a second chance. Not to mention that I hadn't eaten a thing all day. (I'd actually been on my way to the convenience store to buy food for puking when I'd been stricken.)

Slowly then, I got up, drank two glasses of water, and made a peanut butter sandwich. It tasted wonderful.

I chewed each bite carefully, relishing the flavors. *This is what life's about. Taking care of yourself, eating healthy food, helping other people, appreciating each minute.* Yes. I needed to quit the bullshit and pull my life together. I'd stop puking and start exercising. Stop drinking so much alcohol and drink more juice. And water. Maybe even that fancy Perrier stuff. Live a clean lifestyle, read good books, go back to college. Volunteer at a hospital or nursing home. Eat steamed vegetables and tofu. Write poetry. I could do it all, if I didn't die. I could be a better person. I just needed another chance to live.

Eventually, my heartbeat and breathing returned to normal, but I couldn't take that for granted. The memory of my near-death experience less than an hour earlier convinced me to call a doctor. The medical people would probably figure out I'd been bulimic, but that was all in the past.

Dr. Mateo's office was a tiny renovated beach cottage with a porch for a waiting room. The carpeting on the floor was the indoor/outdoor type, and the windows facing the ocean were shuttered for privacy. But there's only so much you can do to make a drafty old beach house look professional.

I sat in a wicker chair with a clipboard and a bunch of forms, updating my personal information while the Eagles sang "Hotel California" on the office radio. And I was doing all right until I got to the section about my medical history. Then my heart started pounding again, almost like it had the day before. Because what if Dr. Mateo said I was dying? How could I prepare for that?

I checked the *NO* boxes next to most of the major illnesses listed—diabetes, cancer, liver disease, muscular disorders—but wrote *possible* next to "heart disease," and scribbled a shaky *dizzy/heart problems* on the line that said "reason for today's visit." Then I handed the clipboard to the receptionist and returned to the prickly wicker chair to await my verdict.

Could a few months in one of those eating disorder clinics cure me? I wondered. Or am I past that point? Have I damaged my heart so badly that I'll need surgery? Maybe even a transplant? Or is it too late for any medical help at all?

Finally, a chubby nurse led me into the exam room to take my blood pressure and pulse. I cringed and shivered as she pumped air into the Velcro thing on my arm, but she just smiled and said, "Great! Very low. Are you an athlete?"

An *athlete?* Couldn't she see the sickness in my eyes? Had she even read the form I'd filled out? "No," I answered.

"Well, you've got the heart rate of an athlete, so you're doing somethin' right. Let's check your height." I didn't understand how any part of my health could be good, but I stood there and let her measure me. I was 5'10", the same height I'd been in eighth grade.

"Step on the scale, please."

With a grunt, I slipped off my shoes and did as she asked. "Oh well," said the nurse. "Three pounds more than last time, but don't feel bad. I know all about the college life. Pizza and beer. My daughter's over at UMass."

I nodded, completely freaked out. I mean, she was treating me like a normal, healthy person. And she seemed to have no clue about me being kicked out of school, despite the fact that I'd written *living at home for a while* on my form.

"All right, time to change." She pointed to a folded green hospital gown on the exam table. "Underwear only, no bra. Leave it open in the back. The doctor'll be in soon."

I waited until she was gone, then undressed, my bones rattling with cold and terror. Luckily, Dr. Mateo—whose hair was much grayer than I'd remembered—knocked on the door a few minutes later. "Hi, Erin," she said kindly, shaking my hand and setting her clipboard down next to the sink. "How're you doing? It sounds like you're concerned about your heart?"

Tears filled my eyes. The knowledge that my entire future would be revealed in this pitiful little office overwhelmed me, and I trembled harder than ever.

"Yes," I whispered. "I think I had a heart attack yesterday."

She nodded noncommittally. "Hmm. Well, why don't you lie flat on the table—on your back—and think of something relaxing. Can you do that?"

"Sure." I tried to get comfortable on the narrow table, but couldn't come up with a single relaxing thought.

"I'm sorry the stethoscope's cold," she said as I squirmed. Then she looked in my mouth and ears, and asked me to describe my "heart attack." I did my best, although just hearing the words coming out of my mouth felt terrifying.

At the end of my story, she made a few notes on her clipboard, then grabbed a gray plastic chair from the corner and placed it about three feet from the exam table. I felt my breathing accelerate, but she touched my shoulder reassuringly and sat down, leaning forward as she spoke. "What's happening in your life, Erin? School, family, that sort of thing?"

I hadn't expected any more questions at that point; I just wanted to get the fateful diagnosis thing over with. "Well, I was, um, asked to leave school because of bad grades, but I'm hoping to go back soon. If I'm healthy enough, you know."

She nodded. "To the same school? Danforth?"

Spit it out! I thought. *Cough up the bad news. Quick!* "No, I'll probably go somewhere else next time. If there is a next time."

"Hmm. And how's your Mom? How're you guys managing without your dad?"

Oh my god! She was nice to be concerned, but come on! "We're fine. Mom's got a new boyfriend named Edward, and I think she really likes him. He's got a gas station over in Medford."

The doctor jotted something else on her clipboard. "Nice. And what about you? What do you think of Edward?"

What the fuck? Did Dr. Mateo wanna become a shrink or something? And what did Edward have to do with my heart? "Um, he's okay, I guess. I don't see much of him." I had huge goosebumps on my arms.

"All right. Now tell me more about this school situation. How do you feel about being back home?"

I wanted to wrench the clipboard out of her hands and throw it against the wall. "I don't know. It's all right. I'd rather be in school, but, you know." My freshly-shaved armpits stung from nervous sweat. "Dr. Mateo," I said, sitting straighter, "please tell me what's wrong with my heart."

She stood up and gave me a wry smile. "Well, Erin, your heart sounds pretty good to me. The rate's a little slower than normal, but it's steady and regular. Are you an athlete, by any chance?"

I stared at her in shock. I mean, if my *doctor* couldn't tell I was diseased, then who could? I'd been puking for four years and had finally sought help, and this was the best I could get? Two medical professionals in a row, asking if I was an athlete?

"No!" I practically screamed. "I'm not athletic at *all.* I'm telling you, I think I had a heart attack yesterday."

I started to describe all the things that'd happened to my body again, but Doctor Mateo took my clammy hand in hers and interrupted me. "Erin, I'm certain you didn't have a heart attack. But I do think you suffered a panic attack, which is a very scary thing. It's quite common for people to confuse the two."

"No! I wasn't panicking about *anything*. I was just walking to the store."

"Think about it, Erin. Think about your life recently. You've lost a parent, your mom's seeing someone new, and you're having difficulty adjusting to college. I think you're dealing with a lot more stress than you admit to yourself."

Well, she was right about the stress, but I also knew I should tell her about the puking. It was my big chance. I just needed to say a few words, then everything would change. But I couldn't do it. "Yeah ..."

"Listen, Erin. Here's what I recommend. I'm gonna write you a script for Xanax, and I'd like you to take one pill every morning for two weeks. Xanax is a sedative, and I'm giving you a very mild prescription. Just enough to take the edge off your anxiety. Will you try that?"

"Um ... I think so. But ..." *Tell her! Tell her about the bulimia.*

"But what? Erin, is there something else?"

"No."

"Okay. Good. I want you to call me in two weeks and tell me how you're feeling. My guess is that the medicine will help a lot. But if you're having more panic attacks, we'll reevaluate. Sound good?"

I thought about that. She'd said my heart sounded fine, and I *had* read about people mistaking panic attacks for heart attacks. And I *really* didn't want to be hospitalized for bulimia. I'd just have to stop vomiting on my own. "All right," I said. "I'll try it."

"I do have one question for you though, Erin, and it's about your teeth. You seem to be losing a good deal of dental enamel, and I saw some cavities in there too. When did you last visit the dentist?"

I had no idea, but my teeth had definitely been sore for a couple of years, especially when I ate or drank cold things. "Um, a while ago."

"Yeah," she said. "I think you're overdue for an appointment. You don't want to let those cavities get any bigger. Otherwise, though, you seem pretty healthy. Why don't you get dressed and I'll write up that script? Sound good?"

Chapter 21

December 24, 1993

I drove until I didn't feel safe driving anymore. The sun was setting in the distance, and the shadows on the road were playing tricks with my eyes. My stomach also felt queasy, probably due to another lunch at McDonald's.

"Quittin' for the day?" asked Luke, sitting up in the back seat as I chose one of the exits for Jacksonville, Florida. Miami was still three hundred miles away.

"Yup. I'm toast."

"Me too," he said, his voice groggy. I couldn't help feeling irritated because he'd done nothing but sleep for the past two hours. Then again, he'd had a rough morning.

The first motel we came across was a generic, gray, two-story building with a name like "The Willows" or "The Pines." Not fancy at all, but the sign on the lawn said they had vacancy, so I pulled into the driveway.

In the office, a pretty woman about twenty years old sat behind a desk, playing solitaire and eating chips out of a bag. The neckband had been cut off her loose black t-shirt in a way that exposed a good portion of her large breasts.

"Hi," said Luke, taking out his wallet. "We need two single rooms."

"No!" I said quickly and much too loudly. Both Luke and the woman focused their attention on me.

"C'mon, Luke," I said. "We gotta share. You know that."

The woman's eyes were lined cat-style in black, and her blond hair was pinned loosely on top of her head. "I think your man wants a night alone," she said.

"He's not ..." I shook my head and turned to Luke. "Luke," I said more calmly. "Please. We promised Dr. Klein."

He rolled his eyes. "Okay, okay. One room."

"Aw," said the woman, "what a sweet guy. But I'll be here in the office 'til midnight if you wanna come visit." On the counter in front of her was a little ceramic lamb with its butt sticking out and a slogan on the base that read:

Spank Me! I've Been B-A-A-A-A-D Today.

Luke handed her his American Express card without a word.

"All righty then," said the woman, pushing her lips out in a classic pout. She made an imprint of the card and handed him a slip to sign. "I'm putting you guys in number eighteen."

"Thanks," I said.

The woman dangled the room key in front of Luke. "I'll drop by in a while to make sure you've got enough blankets and all that."

"Don't worry about it," I said. "We'll be fine."

"Oh, I'm not worried," she replied, handing Luke the key with a wink. "But I check on all the rooms anyway. Just in case."

I waited until Luke had gone outside, then turned to the girl. "Please leave us alone," I said.

"Well, the room's on *his* credit card," she answered. "And *he* might want something."

I looked hard at her, trying to figure out what she was after. I mean, did she simply hope to make a new friend or perhaps have sex with Luke? Or did she have some reason to suspect that he was Lenny Weir? "Listen," I whispered, "that guy's my brother, and he's got a *serious* medical condition. A highly *contagious* one, if you know what I mean. So if I were you, I'd stay the hell away. In fact, you might wanna wash your hands before eating anything else."

The girl's mouth fell open and she dropped a potato chip on the desk.

"Just a suggestion," I said before walking out.

I parked the car in its designated spot, then opened the door to room number eighteen where Luke sat on the miserable-looking double bed. The smell of mildew hung in the damp air, and the walls were painted the exact same shade of gray as the building's exterior. Compared to this place, the Quality Inn in Richmond was the Ritz.

"Should we go somewhere else?" I asked. "I'll bet we can get our money back if we leave right now."

"No," said Luke, rubbing the fuzzy hair on his chin. He hadn't shaved his face or head since we'd left Winthrop, and he looked more like the guy I'd met in the Middle East bathroom every day. "This is cool for one night. Just kick me if I snore."

"All right," I agreed with an uneasy laugh, my stomach flipping over. I mean, surreal as it seemed, I was about to spend Christmas Eve in bed with Lenny Weir. But was I the luckiest woman on earth or the most doomed? It would all depend on how the night went.

Because if Luke got really sick again, I wouldn't have Dr. Klein to help me. I'd be forced to call 911 and hope for the best. I imagined the headline story on Christmas morning: *Rock Star Lenny Weir Dies a Second Time; Massachusetts Woman Questioned by Jacksonville Police.*

On the other hand, if I could help Luke rediscover the man he'd been *before* fame destroyed him, I could become his everything. I thought about Patti Scialfa, and how she'd turned Bruce Springsteen's life around by saving him from depression. *And I can do even more than that,* I realized. *I can bring Lenny Weir back from the dead!*

"I don't mind snoring," I said. "Just promise me you don't have any more drugs on you."

He raised his eyebrows and scratched his beard some more. "Look, I have a little methadone. I couldn't get through the night without it. I'd die."

"Methadone? Luke, where'd you get *methadone*? You told Dr. Klein you were totally clean, and he *believed* you. *I* believed you. I even gave him my Xanax. We're supposed to be drug free."

His eyes brightened, and I thought he was getting ready to smile. But no. "Shut up, Erin," he snarled. "You don't get it. Methadone's not a drug, per se. It's an *anti*-drug. It stops people from taking bad drugs. I got it from a doctor at a clinic back home, and I *need* it to survive. So please stay off my ass." Then he opened his bag, extracted a little carton of orange juice he'd bought at McDonald's, marched into the bathroom, and locked the door.

I stood there, terrified, wondering what to do. I knew he was right about methadone being helpful in some cases, but also knew it could be quite dangerous. Just recently, I'd read an article in the *Globe* about a homeless man who'd overdosed on it. Damn it, why hadn't Dr. Klein searched Luke's bags?

"Luke!" I called, knocking on the bathroom door. "I need to talk to you. Now."

"Leave me alone, Erin," he called back. "I know what I'm doing."

A Xanax would've helped me feel better, but I didn't want to waste the few pills I had. So I checked the phone to make sure it was hooked up, and paced around the room.

Eventually, Luke came out of the bathroom. "Hey," he said, sounding fairly normal and calm. "Can you call Domino's and order a pizza?"

"You want pizza?"

"Sure. Maybe a couple beers too. I'm not supposed to drink, but you can. It's Christmas, after all."

The greasy pizza box served as a centerpiece for what I realized was my first official dinner with Luke. I was starving and ate several slices quickly, while Luke picked at one and avoided the crust. For an extra ten bucks, the pizza delivery guy had been happy to stop by a liquor store and get us a six-pack, and as I cracked open my second bottle of Bud, Luke leaned against the wall and closed his eyes. Since there were no chairs in the room and the rug was stained and dirty, the bed was the only safe place to sit. "Wanna play a game?" he asked.

I eyed him warily. With the methadone flowing through his system, he seemed much better. Still, I couldn't help feeling guilty and scared because we'd both broken our promises to Dr. Klein. "What kinda game?"

He wiped his nose with the back of his hand. "You know, like Truth or Dare. Or something."

Truth or Dare? With a person who'd never even given me a straight answer about where he'd grown up? "Are you serious?" I asked.

He cleared his throat. "Yeah. I mean, no. I mean, I don't really wanna play *that* game. It's just that, well, I feel like there's some stuff I should tell you. There's ... stuff about me you should know."

"Oh. Okay." Goosebumps rose on my arms and legs, and my face began to burn. At that moment, I realized I was terrified to learn the truth. It was easier knowing his secret and pretending I didn't.

"So back in the day," he said, "a long time ago, I was sort of a successful musician."

Those words—the words I'd waited so long to hear—sliced through my veins like knives, and blood gushed wildly through my inner organs. My extremities went limp.

"No. Seriously," he said, perhaps mistaking my numb facial expression for doubt. "I'm not kidding. I was actually sorta well known. I even met *you* once."

My head felt tethered to my neck by a single thread of skin. "I know," I said, unable to hold back any longer.

"You *do*?"

"Yes," I whispered.

Blinking a few times, he frowned. "Do you know *everything?*" I couldn't tell if he wanted me to say yes or no.

"I think so."

"Oh wow." He drew his head back. "But when? I mean, how? How'd you figure it out?"

I stared into those beautiful hazel eyes. "Well, I knew something was up that first day you picked me up hitching—when you called me Erin—and then you took off your sunglasses one day and ..."

"Wow," he replied again. "So ... you remember that *night*? At the *show*?"

"Yeah. Of course."

He looked at me with a combination of wonder and relief. "You know, I knew you were a cool girl then, but there was so much shit going on, and I was *so* fucked up." He sighed. "I ended up in the hospital, you know. But it's funny, because when they were taking me in the ambulance, I kept wondering if I'd ever see you again."

I studied the broken ceiling fan and tugged hard on my frizzy hair. Then I wiggled my toes and dug my fingernails into my palms. *Pain. Movement.* Yes, everything functioned. I was fully conscious. "It's so crazy," I finally said.

He laughed humorlessly. "Yeah." Then, for what felt like five minutes—although it was probably only about ten seconds—he stared down at the brown bedspread. "I'm sorry I wasn't honest with you sooner."

"I understand—"

"No. Let me explain. My rehab doctor advised me to leave the past behind. He said to start over again completely, become a totally new person. 'Break all the old ties,' he said. 'Make new friends, lose the stage name, everything.' But then I saw you out there that day hitching, and I ... I just had to stop."

"It's okay," I said. I was so freaked out that I didn't feel capable of handling any more information. My stomach quivered like a person's arm after carrying a heavy suitcase for miles. "Thank you for trusting me."

He looked up in surprise. "Oh," he said, twisting the cap off a bottle of beer and handing it to me, "I still haven't told you the important part. You better have a drink for this one."

My eyes felt like they might fall out of my face. I definitely wasn't ready for whatever he was about to say next, but how could I stop him? I wished we could just go to sleep and talk more in the morning, but he was on a roll. "So you've probably heard that Winterlong song 'Weeds,' right?"

"Yeah," I said nervously. "Of course."

He tossed his pizza crust into the open cardboard box on the bed. "Are you done eating?"

"What? Oh, yeah."

"Good." His voice faltered as he pushed the box onto the floor and moved closer to me, his eyes shiny with tears. "Well, you know how that song has all those lyrics about someone getting tangled up in underwater weeds and someone else following?"

I nodded.

"Well," he continued, running his thumb over his dry lips, "remember that first day I gave you a ride? That snowy day?"

"Yeah ..."

"Well, I was on my way up to Gloucester to kill myself."

He watched my face intently, apparently searching for signs of emotion, but I felt blank. I knew all about sadness and failure, but that level of intimacy was entirely foreign to me.

"It's true," he continued. "I'd been clean all summer and doing well, but then ... well, some really bad stuff happened to me in September, and I started using again. Mostly heroin, but some other stuff too. Then I got even more depressed and ..." He sniffled and blew his nose into a napkin. "I told you yesterday about my sister who died, right? Well, I guess I felt like it was time for me to go join her, to follow her into the weeds, like in the song. I mean, her death was at least half my fault."

Suddenly, I felt confused. "Why do you say that?"

Luke's eyes flashed, but he took a deep breath and blinked a few times. "'Cause I was so fucked up on drugs when she was sick, and I did *nothing* to help her. All I did was get high every day."

"But I don't think you could've ..."

"She wouldn't eat, Erin. Nothing. She was starving herself. And my parents kept telling me how her doctor was losing hope, but I just kept getting high and listening to old Springsteen records. How pathetic is that?" His shoulders began to heave, and he wept into his hands.

"Luke," I said, leaning forward and putting my arm around his shoulder. "You really couldn't have helped her." The conviction in my voice surprised me; I hadn't realized what an authority on eating disorders I'd become. "Trust me, I know. She didn't *want* help. It's totally fucked up, but ... people with eating disorders use their disease to hide from life or ... something. They can't be helped 'til they're ready. Maybe you could've gotten your sister to eat a little, but she probably would've figured out a way to puke it up anyway. Or she would've taken laxatives or something. Like I said, eating disorders are fucked up things."

I paused for a second and thought about how good I'd gotten at hiding my own illness. How skilled I'd become at tucking it away when other people were around. Even Dr. Mateo hadn't spotted it, and when I'd had the perfect opportunity to tell her, I'd stayed silent. "Eating disorders are bitches," I said. "They're actually a lot like drug addiction. Or alcoholism. So you can't blame yourself for your sister's illness, any more than you can blame her for yours."

A glint of optimism flickered in Luke's eyes, and for the first time in years, I felt hope for myself too. At that moment, it occurred to me that I couldn't have helped my father with his drinking either, because he hadn't wanted my help. Even if he'd stayed home the night of his car crash, he would've crashed some other time, and maybe taken someone else to the grave with him. Despite my love for him, he'd been a drunk, and he drove drunk a lot.

"Luke," I whispered, "you and I aren't responsible for what our family members did. But if we don't get the help we need, we'll end up killing ourselves."

He took the beer out of my hand and placed it on the floor, then took both of my hands in his. "Well, you saved my life that day on the road, Erin. You really did."

"No, I didn't."

"Yeah. You did. I had a whole plan. I was gonna play guitar on the beach for a while, then get on my raft and paddle out as far as I could into the ocean. I had a fifth of Jack Daniels with me, and when I got drunk enough, I was just gonna slide off. I'm a bad swimmer, and the ocean's freezing cold up in Gloucester. I wouldn't have made it to shore. But then I saw you standing there on the side of the road in the sleet and ... I could tell you needed a ride. I know that sounds corny, but that's how it was. You gave me a reason to live, at least one more day."

"Wow," I said, tears welling in my eyes. Everything in my head was spinning like dead leaves in a snow squall, creating little sparks of pain in the corners of my skull. *So I'd saved Lenny Weir from death, after all.* "But ... why'd you go back up to Gloucester again the next day?" I asked. "And again, and again?"

He shrugged. "I was definitely still thinking about dying, and I went down to that beach plenty of times thinking about ... you know. But ... I liked being with you. Talking to you. Helping you. You kept me off the raft, if you know what I mean. Some days, I'd get so depressed, I couldn't stand the thought of being alone in my apartment. But I'd give you a ride up there, then go see a movie or two, and I'd end up feeling better. And those days I made you drive—I'm sorry about them, Erin. I'm a selfish prick sometimes. But like I said, I enjoyed your company. *Craved it,* actually."

I had nothing left. I just stared at him.

"But ... I wanna do better," he continued. "There's stuff in this world I care about, and I wanna stop screwing up. For real." He chuckled darkly. "Let's hear it for the power of rehab. Yeah."

I nodded. "You can do it. I know you can, L—" I almost said *Lenny,* but caught myself just in time. "Wait," I said, "what should I call you now?"

"Call me? You mean, what name?"

"Yeah."

He looked slightly torn. "Um, I think you should keep calling me Luke, if you don't mind. It's ... well, I'm more comfortable with that." He laughed. "It's also my legal name."

"Oh, okay then."

"Hey, come 'ere," he said, wrapping his arms around me and massaging my back with his strong fingers. Wild, warm emotions pulsed through my body: happiness, pride, lust, love, relief, disbelief. They coiled and knotted around each other like vines in a jungle, growing much too fast. A little cry escaped from my mouth.

Luke kissed me on the forehead. "Is this cool?" he asked, pulling off my shirt.

"Yeah." I felt his hands on my skin—hands that'd played guitars in the world's biggest arenas, hands that'd written some of the most stunning songs in rock history—but that night, they existed just for me. They moved slowly and gently over my body, and when our mouths came together, I felt something I'd never come close to feeling with Don. Luke was mine. This scrawny, dirty-haired man loved me. And I loved him. What more could anyone ever want?

Chapter 22

1983/1984

The day after the visit to Dr. Mateo, I called Joe, my boss at the Sand Dollar, to ask if he had any job openings. I still felt shaky, but since I was no longer in college and apparently not in any immediate danger of dropping dead of a heart attack, I figured I should earn some money.

Fortunately for me, a waitress named Diane had just quit to spend a year with a cousin in Europe, so Joe hired me right away. But when I showed up for work a few days later, I discovered that the Sand Dollar in winter was nothing like the Sand Dollar in summer. No one employed there during the winter months had been to college or even aspired to such a thing—unless you counted the middle-aged dishwasher who supposedly dreamed about the swell education he'd get if he ever won the lottery. They were all Winthrop townies, and after I'd been there a couple of weeks, they started accepting me as one of them. For the first time ever, I felt like I *belonged* in Winthrop. And that only made me want to escape more.

"Maybe *you* should go over to Europe, like Diane," suggested Wendy, a fifty-year-old waitress who was helping me set up the tables early one Saturday morning. Wendy was incredibly beautiful and energetic, and she had no wrinkles at all. She attributed her good health to eating vegetarian and smoking only hand-rolled cigarettes, but I think she just had good genes. Her mother had been a fashion model in the 1950s. "Diane sent me a postcard from Italy and it sounds like she's havin' a blast. She met a wicked cute Italian count at a party."

"Hey Wendy! Don't you go plantin' bugs in Erin's head!" said Joe as he hustled by with a crate of eggs. Joe had a huge crush on Wendy, and he flirted by yelling at her all the time. "Erin's doin' great right here. She's a waitress, not a world traveler."

But I wasn't doing great at all. I'd quit puking for exactly three days after my doctor's appointment. Then, I'd relapsed. Hard. I'd even started vomiting at work on slow days. It helped pass the time, and I loved the food at the Sand Dollar.

Wendy must've sensed my misery. Maybe she even knew about the puking. After all, the Sand Dollar was a small restaurant. In any case, she kept pushing the idea of me taking a trip to Europe; she said her mom had sent her to France one summer when she was young, and it'd changed her life. The museums, the gardens, the wineries, the handsome men; according to Wendy, Europe was paradise for girls my age.

"That's because you're gorgeous, Wendy," I'd say with a laugh. "All guys are in love with you."

But one muddy spring day when the breakfast rush ended, she sat me down "for a serious talk" at a table near the back of the restaurant. I'd just finished vomiting, and had brushed my teeth with the last bit of toothpaste I had in my purse. But it hadn't been enough, and I covered my mouth with my hand each time I spoke to avoid offending her with my raunchy breath.

"Honey, remember when I told you my mom died of cancer last year?" said Wendy.

"Yeah. That so sucks. I'm sorry."

"Thanks. But that's not why I'm talking to you now. You see, the old girl had a little money saved, and since she wasn't speaking to my brother anymore, she left everything to me. Not a lot, unfortunately, but a little."

I nodded. "That's cool."

"Uh huh. But here's the other thing. About a month before she died, she asked me to donate some of her savings to a charity that helps sick kids. She'd seen children with cancer at the hospital, and it broke her heart. She wanted to be part of the solution."

"Cool." I blinked hard. I was starting to see where the conversation might be headed, and I didn't like it.

"Erin," said Wendy, leaning across the table as I covered my mouth again. "You don't seem very ... healthy to me. I'm thinking you could use some help."

"What?" I said, sliding my chair back and smiling as confidently as I could. "I'm incredibly healthy. I had a checkup in November and the doctor said I was fine."

"Uh huh," said Wendy. "Well, doctors don't know everything."

My body heated up and my palms got sweaty.

Wendy raised her eyebrows. "So here's what I've decided. I'm givin' you three grand, but *only* to use for a trip to Europe. Nothin' else. And you can't go during the summer either, 'cause it's way too crowded over there. I'll help you book a trip for the fall. That way, you can save some cash on your own too."

"No, Wendy. I don't wanna—"

"Too bad," she said. "I'm gonna make you do it. One way or another. I made a promise to my mom, and this is what she'd want. I know it."

"But Wendy ..."

At that point, she stood up and banged the table with her hand. "Fuck it, Erin. You need to get your goddamn life in order. Look at you. You're a mess. A wicked big mess." She sat down again as Joe came out of the back room with a scared look on his face. "Leave us alone, Joe," she said, without looking at him. "Everything's fine. I got it all under control."

As soon as I found my seat on the airplane, I popped two Xanaxes. I'd left my giant backpack at the luggage counter, so all I had with me was a khaki shoulder bag I'd bought at the Army/Navy store, and it was crammed with stuff I'd need if the airline lost the backpack: my passport, a two-month Eurail Pass (Wendy had helped me buy that), a bunch of travelers cheques, a notebook and pen, a bar of soap, some deodorant, four tampons, two pairs of clean underwear, my Walkman and tapes, the book *Let's Go: Europe* (which contained the addresses and phone numbers of all the American Embassies on the Continent), a two-month supply of Xanax, and a little makeup. But although I'd packed carefully, I still felt like I was blasting off naked into outer space. I kept rifling through the shoulder bag, checking to make sure I hadn't forgotten something important. As if I could do anything about it at that point.

The pills were taking their time kicking in too, so I forced myself to focus on some stuff I'd learned about Europe from Wendy and the various travel books I'd read. I knew there were plenty of payphones in most places, and that almost everyone spoke some English. But most importantly, I'd heard about celebrities roaming around freely, as undisturbed as pigeons. In other words, Bowie could go out to clubs like a normal person; Springsteen could have a beer in a pub without being badgered for his autograph; Bob Dylan could wander the streets of Paris in peace. Hey, for all I knew, Jim Morrison was hanging out in some café over there too, completely incognito. And if so, *I'd* recognize him.

All the tip money I'd saved over the summer—plus Wendy's amazing gift of three grand—had been earmarked for the trip. *You will not fuck this up,* I promised myself, again and again. *You screwed up high school and you screwed up college. If you screw up this up too, you'll have nothing. Plus, Wendy will think you're a total loser.*

I couldn't wait to get going, but the plane's takeoff had been delayed. Apparently, we were waiting for a passenger experiencing a family emergency. People grumbled and complained, and I wished the Xanax would just put me to sleep. Finally, a distraught looking thirty-something guy with a red face clamored into the cabin—apologizing profusely in French—and collapsed into the empty seat beside me. *So much for that extra legroom,* I thought. The guy smelled like some sort of sugary alcohol, possibly rum.

In spotty English, he introduced himself as Jean-Pierre. He said he'd been traveling in the States on holiday when he'd received word that his father in Paris had suffered a stroke and would most likely die soon. I expressed my sympathies, and he blew his nose loudly into a handkerchief. Then he ordered a bottle of red wine and two glasses, one of which he handed to me. And how could I say no to that?

The wine tasted good: heavy and smoky, and I really wanted to sleep, so I took a couple of big sips. But I could feel the Xanax starting to work too, so I put the glass down for a few minutes. Unfortunately, Jean-Pierre's drinking was just getting started, and with each glass of wine he poured himself, his English devolved. More and more of his monologue was coming out in French, and keeping up with him got harder and harder for me. But he didn't seem to notice at all as he talked—with plenty of spittle flying—about the Beatles, then the Clash, then Elvis Costello.

"*Paris Match* say Elvis imitate Dylan," he practically shouted through wine-stained lips, foamy saliva accumulating at the corners of his mouth. *"Mais non! C'nest pas vrais. Oui?"*

I told Jean-Pierre that my French was limited to the *petit* amount I'd learned in high school, and that I only knew one Elvis Costello song—"Pump it Up"—but that made little difference to him. *"L'angst avec la tristesse ... Dylan est fantastique, oui, mais Elvis, il est différent ! Plus original! Plus superior!"*

I knew he was saying that Elvis was somehow better than Bob Dylan, but had neither the energy nor desire to get into a discussion like that. "I think I need some rest," I replied. Of course, I felt bad about his dying father, but also couldn't keep my eyes open.

"Oui. Moi aussi, peut-etre," he said sadly, half to himself. "Merci. You are very kind." Then he took my face in his rough hands, kissed me lightly on the forehead, and told me to sleep

The flight attendant kept calling my name, and when I opened my eyes, I saw that I was the only passenger still on the plane. Apparently, we'd landed about fifteen minutes earlier, but I'd been in such a deep sleep that the attendant had wondered if I was comatose. I apologized profusely, but she clearly considered me a source of irritation.

"Your ... companion, he leave this for you," she said when I became more cognizant. In her hand, she held a small plastic box with a picture of elephants on it. The sunlight streaming through the window made my head ache, and my tongue felt like sandpaper. "He apologize for your jumper," she said, pointing to my shoulder. "He must leave to his family." I looked down to see a large wet spot on my shoulder that appeared to be drool. Gross. Then I examined the box more carefully and saw that it was an Elvis Costello cassette called *Armed Forces.*

"Are we ... in Paris?" I asked.

"Oui," she said. "Now up, *s'il vous plait.* Please." She clapped her hands twice, and I grabbed my bag, just as the pilot appeared in the doorway of the cabin and barked something in French at the attendant.

At six in the morning in Charles de Gaulle Airport, there were hundreds—maybe thousands—of people flowing through the terminal, speaking every imaginable language. The one thing they all seemed to have in common was their weight—I didn't see any obese ones—and most seemed quite relaxed too. Which only increased my anxiety level. The Xanax had pretty much worn off, and the crisp October air laced with cigarette smoke tasted decidedly foreign in my dry mouth.

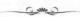

If it weren't for the new cassette tape in my bag, I might've had a full-on panic attack. My heart was beating much faster than normal, but thinking about the tape—and Jean-Pierre, that nice man who'd kissed me—kept me from focusing too much on my fears, and allowed me to

keep following signs to the train. I bumped lots of people with my backpack, but what could I do? *I've got a friend in France already,* I kept reminding myself, *and he gave me a gift.*

Bravely, then, I stopped at a kiosk to buy a bottle of Perrier, some bread, and a chocolate bar, then took the train into Paris—Wendy had written down some directions for me, so I wasn't at a complete loss—switched over to the Metro, and used the map in my *Let's Go* book to locate one of the cheap hotels near *Saint-Germain-des-Pres* that Wendy had circled. But I must say that the city—on first impression—disappointed me. It was older and dirtier than I'd expected, and heavily polluted with tobacco smoke.

Around ten o'clock, I washed my face in the sink of my tiny hotel room, used the toilet down the hall—a real toilet, thankfully, and not one of those holes in the floor—then sat on my bed with the bread and water, watching Paris from my third floor window. People always say it's such a romantic place, but where were the artists and celebrities? And the glamorous people in beautiful clothing? Everyone looked well put-together—I'd never seen so many scarves—but the entire city was painted in shades of gray. Even the Eiffel Tower in the distance was gray. I felt incredibly alone, and that sweet man Jean-Pierre hadn't left a phone number.

Don't judge it yet, I told myself. *It's gotta get better.* So I finished my bread, popped a Xanax, and crawled under the covers for a nap.

I awoke around two in the afternoon feeling scared, anxious, and needing to pee. But when I made it down the hall to the bathroom, someone else was in there with the shower running. In the room beside the bathroom, men spoke loudly in German, a language I'd never studied. A chill ran down my spine.

My mother's in her cozy house with her own bathroom, I thought. While I'm here, in a place where no one speaks English, waiting for a toilet in a dark hallway. And I spent over three thousand dollars for this privilege. I might've cried right then, but a small, dark-haired woman wrapped in a towel popped out of another room and headed my way. She didn't acknowledge me at all, though; she just opened the bathroom door and joined the other person in the shower. I could hear the two of them talking and laughing in Spanish or Italian under the water. It all felt so European, but I wasn't yet ready for the cultural immersion. I decided to go back to my room and wait.

Now, for years, music critics had been praising the "angry young man" who went by the name "Elvis Costello." Jean-Pierre on the plane was far from the first person to compare Elvis to Bob Dylan, but as I'd told him, the only Elvis song I knew was "Pump it Up," and that didn't sound very Dylanesque to me. Not to mention that I didn't like "Pump it Up" either; it sounded punky and aggressive and not very accessible. I'd never doubted Elvis's talent, but he didn't strike me as my kind of musician.

What a surprise then, to pop *Armed Forces* into my Walkman and hear that its first tune, "Accidents Will Happen," was fun and catchy. It sounded almost like an Abba song, but with better words. The next song, "Senior Service," didn't do much for me—it actually reminded me a bit of "Pump it Up," but the third, "Oliver's Army," was another sweet-sounding pop song. The lyrics confused me because they seemed to be about war and killing, but I was beginning to understand what Jean-Pierre meant when he'd referred to Elvis as *plus original*.

My poor bladder forced me back out to the hallway at that point, and luckily, the bathroom was free. But when I returned to my room, I put the headphones right back on. I found it fascinating that a twerpy little guy like Elvis—with those big glasses and tight suits—could expose himself so honestly in his music. And although I couldn't figure out what most of the songs were really *about*, they'd obviously come directly from his heart. And his rhymes and phrasing were so unique and clever. Did he seem angry? Perhaps, but not in a scary way. He struck me as a man who'd been treated badly by women because of his looks, and I could relate to that.

Then came "Party Girl," the final song on side one, and I did actually cry. It's slower and more direct than any of the other tunes on the album, and incredibly romantic. In the song, Elvis meets a girl at a party, a girl he's been told is only out for a good time. But Elvis can tell that's not true, and he desperately wants to get to know her better. Unfortunately, he can't, because he doesn't have enough time. So he dreams about her, and imagines the two of them running away and hiding from the world. To me, it was the antithesis of Cyndi Lauper's "Girls Just Wanna Have Fun," and I loved it immediately. I mean, Cyndi Lauper's great and all, but I'd always had trouble relating to her big hit. Because I wanted so much more than fun in this life.

After a hot shower, I went outside to explore the neighborhood. I was hungry, but too shy to go into a café alone, so I retraced my steps to the *Gare du Nord,* which bustled with people and food vendors. I decided to buy a loaf of bread and eat it on a bench while pretending to wait for a train.

But when I sat down, I immediately noticed a red-haired guy about my age playing guitar over by the tracks. He appeared to be trying to grow dreadlocks—or maybe he just hadn't combed his hair in a while—and on the front of his gray sweatshirt were the letters *UNH.* I tore my loaf of French bread in half and watched him tune a couple of strings; then he started playing the Eagles' song, "Desperado." A tall woman walked by and dropped a coin in his open guitar case, and the red-haired guy thanked her in a clear American accent. If I'd seen him on the streets of Boston, I wouldn't have looked twice. But on my first day in Europe, he was an angel. He glanced in my direction, and I smiled.

"Hey there," he said, coming over to talk on his break. "You American?"

"Yeah. How'd you know?" He smelled sweaty, but not in a bad way, and there was something very earnest about his thick red eyebrows, pale freckled skin, and light blue eyes.

He pointed to my New Balance running shoes. "People from here don't wear sneakers," he said, brushing the hair out of his face and lighting a European cigarette. "Only Americans and Canadians."

I looked at his worn-out Nikes and nodded. "So you're American too?"

"Oh yeah." He pointed to the *UNH* logo on his sweatshirt. "When'd you arrive?"

My travel books had warned me about sharing personal information with strangers, especially strangers in airports and train stations. Apparently, those places were prime hangouts for pickpockets and creeps. "A while ago."

He raised his eyebrows and took a puff on his cigarette. "Is that a Boston accent I detect?"

I wasn't used to cute guys being so friendly to me. "Sort of," I said, trying to sound cool.

"Sort of? What's that mean?"

I had no idea. "I mean, you know, I'm from New England." I decided to change the subject. "Do you go to UNH?"

He shrugged. "I did for two years. Then I quit and came over here. My parents are all pissed off. I wish I never had to go back."

I'm not sure why I felt a sudden urge to get away from him; I think it was too intimate for me, too fast. But I stood up quickly and shoved the rest of the bread into my shoulder bag. "Well, good luck," I said. "I gotta go."

The guy looked surprised. "What's the hurry?"

"I'm catching a train to Italy. Rome." It was the first thing that popped into my head.

"Really?" he asked, his eyes narrowing. "Now?"

"Uh huh."

"No you're not. Tell the truth."

My stomach tensed. What did this guy know that I didn't? How could he tell I was lying? "That *is* the truth," I said. "Bye."

But as I started to leave, the guy stopped me with a sharp, "Wait!"

"What?" I replied, unable to hide the fear in my voice.

"Look," he said, "I'm not a stalker. I'm just trying to help you. The sleeper doesn't leave 'til like seven or eight tonight. And it leaves from the *Gare de Lyon*."

"What?" I said again. *What the hell was a sleeper?*

He nodded and sighed as if to say, *I knew it*. "You haven't been here long, have you?"

I opened my mouth to talk, but he cut me off. "Here's the deal, there's only one train a day from Paris to Italy, and it's a sleeper train. Do you have a Eurail Pass?"

"Yeah ..."

"Okay," he said, smiling that earnest smile. "Here's what you do. Hang out for a couple more hours—maybe check out a museum or get a good meal—then catch the sleeper tonight from the *Gare de Lyon*. I have a schedule somewhere, but you can get your own at the station."

"And you sleep on the *train*?"

He nodded. "Yeah, it's a little weird, but they have sleeper compartments, and it saves you the cost of a hotel. Everyone does it. I haven't paid for a room in weeks."

"But ... how do you shower?" I tried to envision a sleeper compartment, but couldn't.

The guy smiled a little wider. His teeth were large and very white. "Oh, you know. Sometimes friends let me borrow. You don't happen to have a room around here, do you?"

I stared at the guy, unable to imagine bringing him back to my hotel *for a shower*. "I really gotta go," I muttered. Then I turned and walked away as fast as I could, looking over my shoulder from time to time to make sure he wasn't following me.

Luckily, I was better prepared for the next young American I met in Europe, and even better for the next. Soon, I figured out the special set of social rules for people like me on the Continent. Because even though there were thousands of college-age Yankees traveling around over there—the US dollar was the highest it'd been in years—we were still a tiny minority, and not particularly popular with most Europeans. Some, in fact, considered us quite vulgar.

Which made sense, I guess. I mean, we dressed like slobs, we talked loudly, and some of us were wealthy. And as a whole, we knew very little about European culture and history—at least compared to what Europeans know about ours. Hence, we often got treated snottily, and many of us found safety in numbers. And that worked terrifically to my advantage. The autumn weather that year wasn't spectacular—it was colder and rainier than normal—but I barely noticed.

And the sleeper car system, which had first been brought to my attention by the red-haired guitarist, became my favorite way to make new friends. I didn't like skipping showers, but all the trains sold beer and wine, and you could drink legally in most European countries at age eighteen. Therefore, a sleeper car filled with young Americans often became a forum for late-night, alcohol-fueled discussion.

And we always had so much to talk about; we went on so many amazing adventures and saw so many cool things. Canals in Venice, cafés in Amsterdam that sold marijuana and hash, castles in Austria, beer halls in Munich, ruins in Rome, art and leather in Florence, more art in Paris, cathedrals everywhere. Sometimes our conversations got a little heated—especially when politics or religion was the topic—but in the morning, everyone would hug and make up. Then, I'd often get invited to tag along and sightsee with the people I'd befriended during the night. I should also add that I never saw or experienced any sexual activity—other than a little kissing—in the sleeper cars. The doors didn't lock, so random people would enter and leave throughout the night, and the train conductors made a habit of stopping in on a regular—and noisy—basis to check tickets and make sure nothing funny was going on.

Of course, I didn't want any of my new pals feeling bad for me—or thinking I was a loner—so I told them I was a student from Danforth, taking a semester off to explore overseas. "I broke up with my boyfriend," I'd say casually, "and I needed a change of scenery." But I didn't have to tell many other lies. Most Americans I met in Europe were living in the moment, and they accepted my words with few questions.

Even better, my puking problem pretty much went into remission, as it'd done when I'd lived in the dorm at Danforth. It wasn't that I didn't *want* to binge and purge, but finding privacy as a budget tourist wasn't easy. Most of the hotels and hostels wouldn't let you check in until late in the afternoon, and the bathrooms were usually communal. And as for the bathrooms on trains? Well, let's just say that when you looked down into the toilets, you could see the tracks whizzing by underneath, and the one time I tried puking into one of those things, I got extremely dizzy. Not to mention that the running water on trains wasn't clean enough for drinking or tooth brushing.

But here's the most important part: no matter who I traveled with—and I never stayed with any group of Americans for more than a few days—Elvis Costello was the only guy allowed on my Walkman. All my other tapes—which I'd once believed I couldn't live without—had been exiled to the bottom of my backpack, along with the bikini and sandals I'd packed for the Greek Islands. Wendy had told me I *needed* to see Athens, but all the Americans I met said they were waiting until spring—when the weather was warmer—to go to Greece.

I'd also vowed not to buy many items on the trip. My backpack was already stuffed, and I wore the same black-and-white checked wool scarf every day because it was warm, and—in my opinion—stylish. But I made an exception for Elvis tapes. In other words, when I grew tired of listening exclusively to *Armed Forces*, I sought out secondhand music stores in various cities, and hunted for his other cassettes.

At that time, he'd released eight albums, and Jean-Pierre had given me one. So it wasn't all that difficult to obtain the other seven, and those eight tapes became the soundtrack to my European tour. Even now, it's impossible for me to think of the Leaning Tower of Pisa without hearing "The Long Honeymoon" in my head, and every time I see a picture of the Sagrada Familia in Barcelona, I remember buying the album *This Year's Model* on a nearby side street.

I learned quite a bit about Elvis from his songs too. I came to know the things he wanted (to fall into someone's human hands); the things he worried about (common decency and grand larceny); the places he didn't want to go (Chelsea); the things he wasn't (a telephone junkie); and the things he didn't want to be (a ventriloquist or a puppet).

Then, one day, I came across a magazine article—I think it was in *Blender*—that provided much more specific and detailed info. For example, Elvis was newly single because he'd cheated on his wife with a model named Bebe Buell. Before that, I hadn't even known he'd ever been married. The article also informed me that he'd been having issues with his band—the Attractions—and that his most recent album, *Goodbye Cruel World,* was selling poorly and had been panned almost universally by critics.

Now, I owned a copy of *Goodbye Cruel World* and didn't love it as much as I loved his other albums. The songs didn't hit me with quite the same punch; they seemed almost mellow. Some actually bored me. But I'd assumed the problem was mine, that I didn't understand the album well enough to appreciate it. The article, however, made it clear that Elvis was depressed and unable to function well in his current mental state. Even he knew it: he'd actually written in the liner notes for *Goodbye Cruel World* that it was his worst record ever.

Wow. The man obviously needed a positive force in his life, a new woman who'd understand his troubles and help him regain his strength. And after reading the article, I knew *exactly* how to become that woman. Because he'd be playing the Palladium Music Hall in Geneva in just one week.

As the train pulled into the station, I popped a Xanax and strapped on my giant backpack, my most essential and irritating possession. I'd awakened that morning dehydrated and hungover in Milan, and had spent several hours dozing and recovering on the train ride to Geneva. I'd been stupid to drink so much wine the night before, but one of the Americans I'd met at the Milan youth hostel was celebrating her birthday at a nightclub, and had invited me to join in. Of course I could've declined, but after missing so many high school and college parties, I always felt like I needed to make up for lost time.

Anyway, as the sky darkened, I started feeling better. Hungry too, and optimistic. A guy on the train had told me the Palladium was a good-sized music hall, but he didn't think it'd be difficult to get near the stage if I arrived early enough. Which was good news, because I couldn't afford another disaster like the Bowie show. My money and Xanax were running low, and my Eurail Pass expired in two weeks. I'd been having a blast and meeting lots of new people in Europe, but it was time to get serious.

First, though, I needed food. Stumbling through the drizzly Swiss evening, I did my best to calculate the amount of time I had to grab a quick bite before the show. First and foremost, I wanted to locate the Palladium, but Geneva—with its ancient stone buildings, twisty alleyways, and confusing system of bridges crossing the Rhone—didn't cut me any breaks. Nor did the sky, which spat out so much cold mist that I was soaked to the skin when I finally reached my destination at 6:45 p.m., fifteen minutes before the doors opened.

Luckily, I spotted a restaurant right across the street, and only about twenty people waiting in the line outside the music hall. An American singer named T-Bone Burnett—a guy I'd never heard of—was opening for Elvis, and based on the lack of enthusiasm on the faces in line, I felt confident in my ability to get up front after dinner. Those Euro guys weren't gonna elbow me in the ribs or kick me in the shins. I could tell.

Still, I wasn't thrilled when the maître de at the restaurant took one look at my sopping hair and sweatshirt and directed me straight to the bar. The dining room, he said, required formal dress. Which was insane, since the place was deserted, but the Swiss are rule-oriented people. It also occurred to me that if Elvis wanted a drink before the show, he might choose that bar too, so I settled my wet, hungry body on a barstool, and ordered a *croque monsieur.* Then the handsome blond bartender informed me that the bar served no food. Just drinks.

What? I mean, why wouldn't he want to help a drenched, starving woman? In my faltering French, I inquired if perhaps I could get a bowl of soup, or maybe some bread. Anything.

"Non. Pas ici." I'd learned just enough of the language to know that meant *not here.*

What a jackass, I thought. But I couldn't go back out in that rain to search for another restaurant. So I swallowed and regrouped. All right. I'll get through the night on alcohol and adrenaline. Elvis is more important than food.

"Une Cardinal, s'il vous plais?" I asked, proud of the fact that I could order myself a Swiss beer in French.

But once again, the man shook his head. *"Pas de bière,"* he said, pointing to the shelf of bottles behind him.

No beer in a *bar?* Only in Switzerland. *Ugh.* I scanned the liquor bottles with their European labels—Cynar, brandy, Ouzo, whiskey, various types of kirsch, and lots of fancy wine—and drew a blank. Meanwhile, the bartender eyed me impatiently, as if he had a hundred other customers to wait on.

Then, just like in the movies, a sudden flash of insight shot through my weak, famished brain: *Tanqueray and wine.* In a Springsteen song, a guy named Ralph gets drunk after mixing Tanqueray and wine. And although I wasn't quite sure what Tanqueray was, I'd always liked the *sound* of Tanqueray and wine. It sounded like a cool drink to me. Sexy.

"Je voudrais un Tanqueray avec vin," I said confidently, butchering the lovely language with my poor grammar and harsh accent.

The man raised his eyebrows. *"Mélange ensemble?"* he asked.

I was pretty sure *ensemble* meant *together* so I said, *"Oui,"* as firmly as possible. It was beginning to dawn on me that perhaps Springsteen's Ralph hadn't mixed his two liquids in the *same glass;* maybe he'd drunk some Tanqueray first, then had wine later on, or vice-versa. But I was determined not to backpedal. Not with this guy.

"C'était dégout," the bartender warned, turning down his lips. When I looked confused, he switched to English, "Disgusting."

"C'est okay."

"D'accord," he agreed haughtily. *"Comme vous voudrez."*

An hour later, feeling far worse than before, I stumbled out into the rain and across the street to the Palladium. I'd downed a second Tanqueray and wine—just to prove to the bartender that I knew my cocktails—but that'd been a mistake. I mean, was it possible for two drinks to burn a hole all the way through a person's stomach lining? And if I started bleeding internally and had to leave the show on a stretcher, would Elvis visit me in the hospital?

But those thoughts quickly dissolved when I heard muted, country-rock music pumping out of the building, followed by an American voice shouting, "All right! We got one more song for you!"

"Is that T-Bone Burnett?" I called to a group of Euro guys smoking cigarettes out front. I tried to run, but my backpack was too heavy. "Did he already play?"

The men regarded me with a blend of curiosity and amusement. "*Ja*," answered one, while his friends smiled smugly.

But I didn't care about them. Visions of the botched Bowie concert flashed through my head as I hobbled past the dudes and handed the doorman my ticket. The wet straps of the backpack cut into my shoulders.

Inside, though, I breathed a sigh of relief. The Palladium looked more like a nightclub than a concert hall, and although lots of people milled around, none seemed particularly psyched about being there. A few audience members acted startled and a bit miffed when I barged past them with my giant backpack, but no one tried to stop me. *Okay,* I decided, *no more complaining about the Swiss. They may be uptight, but they don't like conflict, and that's a good thing right now.*

T-Bone Burnett, a tall, thin guy with a long face and intense eyes, was just finishing up a song, and the crowd clapped respectfully when it ended. He, in turn, thanked them very much and promised that Elvis would be out soon.

"Yay!" I screamed, because that's what people do at concerts, right? Wrong. At least not that night at the Palladium.

T-Bone smiled down at me in the front row. "All right!"

"Yeah!" I cried, the oddness of the moment increasing my lightheadedness. I mean, I'd just arrived, and was already chatting with the opening act. So what if I'd never heard of him before? He was on tour with Elvis Costello, and he was talking to me. *Tanqueray and wine forever,* I thought.

But T-Bone had nothing more to add to the conversation; he just ambled off the stage. I wriggled out of the backpack and dropped it on the floor, then looked around the room. Pretty much everyone was wearing the European winter uniform of 1984: tight jeans, bulky sweaters, and woolen scarves wrapped artfully around their necks. And, like well-behaved clones, they all smoked and talked quietly, without the slightest hint of restlessness.

There was nothing to do but wait. Again. The pain in my stomach returned, and I wondered if I might be developing an ulcer. *Maybe a shot of Bailey's would help,* I thought. *A little cream and sugar.* I thought back to the days when I drank my mom's Bailey's at home in Winthrop and nodded. It also seemed perfectly safe to abandon my front row spot long enough to grab a quick drink.

But just as I started heading toward the bar, a tall woman in a short black dress and shiny red boots breezed past me and slipped through a metal door beside the stage. Her dark hair was tied back in a tight chignon, and her blood-red lipstick made her mouth look like evil candy. She would've turned heads anywhere, but on that wintry Swiss night, she stood out like a polished nail on a lumberjack's hand.

A groupie! A beautiful groupie! No! I couldn't let her get to Elvis before me. If I did, she might steal him away. But when I gazed down at my damp sweatshirt and blue jeans hanging around my legs like wet newspaper, my heart sank. How could I compete with a gorgeous person like her? Then I took another look at my giant backpack and got an idea.

Women turned away, and some men actually laughed as I maneuvered my half-naked self out of the bathroom and through the crowd. My skin glowed pasty and white, and I knew I was at least fifty pounds heavier than any self-respecting Swiss woman would ever allow herself to become. But I sucked in my stomach and held my head high, aided by Xanax, alcohol, and the unflinching belief that Europeans are incapable of understanding the American spirit.

The metal door the groupie had used opened effortlessly, but once I'd gotten through and closed it behind me, I thought perhaps I'd made a mistake because I couldn't see a thing. Was I in a broom closet or something? But then I saw a dim light ahead, and heard people talking. I could smell food too, so I felt my way through the darkness.

Soon, I found myself in the entranceway to a small room filled with cigarette smoke and about thirty people, most of them standing around talking, like at a cocktail party. T-Bone Burnett—easy to spot due to his height—loaded food onto a plate at a buffet table near the back, and a few feet away, three attractive women, including the one in the red boots, laughed quietly over glasses of white wine. But I saw no sign of

Elvis anywhere. My eyes searched anxiously for a shy, skinny guy in oversized glasses, but no. No one like that was in the room.

Maybe I should try talking to T-Bone. He looked approachable, all by himself at the buffet. But something held me back. I looked down at my heavy breasts in the blue bikini top, and smoothed the wrinkled denim miniskirt Beverly had given me when I left Danforth. *Don't lose your nerve now. And don't worry about your weight. You're a genuine American woman, like Jane Russell and Mae West, not an emaciated European. You're voluptuous and sexy and ...*

The woman in the red boots interrupted my internal pep talk by darting toward me. Suddenly, her evil candy mouth was inches from my face, and her sharp eyes flashed. "Pardon me," she snapped in a British accent that surprised me. "May I help you?"

Marveling at her speed and grace in such high heels, I pointed a shaky finger at T-Bone. "N-no," I stammered, "I'm a friend of his."

Everyone in the room, including T-Bone, noticed the commotion, and the musician's mouth fell open.

"Do you know this woman?" Evil Candy asked him.

T-Bone blinked hard and assessed me carefully. "I don't ... believe so."

"All right then," said the woman, shaking her head and gripping my upper arm with her bony fingers. "Ma'am, you need to leave *now*." Apparently, she wasn't a groupie, but some sort of official. Perhaps a band manager, or someone who worked for the Palladium. "Unless you prefer that I call security."

Oh no. Not security. Tears welled in my eyes. "I'm sorry," I blurted, trying to shake her grip from my arm. "I just wanted to talk to Elvis." My chin quivered with sadness, embarrassment, and cold.

The woman regarded me with obvious distain, but everyone was watching us. "Dear," she said, loosening her grip a little, "are you all *right*?"

"Yes," I said. "Just let me go. Please."

She dropped her hand from my arm and took a step back. "Fine," she agreed. "But get out of this backstage area and don't come back. Or you'll *really* be sorry. Is that clear?"

I nodded.

"Good," she said. "And would someone please make sure that door stays locked in the future?"

Making my way back to the front of the concert hall felt anticlimactic after all that, and I stopped at the bar only to ask for a glass of water. The jeering glares of the audience members stung much more sharply than they had earlier. I desperately wanted to change back into normal clothes, but there was no time for that; the Elvis part of the show was clearly about to begin.

Then a bloated man strolled unceremoniously onto the stage, muttered a curt hello to the crowd, and took a seat behind the piano. A few other guys with instruments joined him onstage, and the next thing I knew, they were playing a song while the bloated guy sang. It sounded like country music, and the words weren't very nice. I don't remember most of them, but one line was about wishing someone would get run over by a train.

I stood there, confused as hell, until I realized I *knew* that voice. It was *Elvis's* voice. And the bloated man was Elvis! But everything else about him was ... wrong. His suit looked like it'd been slept in, and he was sweating profusely. His hairline was receding, and he wasn't wearing huge glasses—just regular ones. But the saddest thing of all was that he seemed *miserable*. He appeared depressed, and possibly drunk.

And the audience didn't give a shit. Once they'd assessed the situation, most of them simply shrugged and went back to chattering in French and German. Elvis may as well have been a singer in a bad wedding band.

I watched him closely as he finished the first song, and a brief look of annoyance crossed his face. He signaled to the band, and they played the hit "Girls Talk," but once again, the audience didn't engage. The noisy crowd just got noisier. I could hear the irritation in Elvis's voice increasing, and felt so bad for him. I mean, the poor guy's life was already in shambles. He needed me even more than I'd imagined.

"Elvis!" I screamed as loudly as I could. "I'm here for you!"

He didn't hear me, though, or didn't appear to. He played three other obscure tunes in a careless manner while the audience went on talking. Then he slowed down and played a really sad song called "Kid About It," and I almost cried when he sang the line about wishing he could be a child again. *This is torture for him,* I thought, as someone tossed a plastic beer cup onto the stage. The cup didn't hit Elvis or even get close to him, but the thrower's intent was clear. Suddenly, the band stopped playing, and the room got very quiet.

"Elvis!" I cried from the front row as he stood up and assessed the audience. "I love you! I understand you!"

The girl next to me giggled, and a few other people glanced dubiously at my bikini top and rolled their eyes. But a flicker of a smile passed over Elvis's lips, and I braced myself. I thought back to the Bowie show, and my naïve attempt at getting a note to David onstage. But this was so much better! Now, all I needed to do was let Elvis know how much his music spoke to me. Then, he'd welcome me backstage later on. My life was finally about to get *good.*

"All right, I'm gonna play an old song now," Elvis announced in his soft Irish voice. "For you old fans."

I sucked in my breath and gripped the edge of the stage, my fingernails digging, clawlike, into the wood. "'Party Girl!" I screamed. "Please, Elvis, play 'Party Girl!'" I knew the crowd was staring, but I didn't care. I could feel Elvis's love flowing into my body.

His eyebrows arched, and he ran his fingers through his thinning hair. Standing perfectly still, I waited for the perfect, magical moment that would go down in rock & roll history.

"No," he answered. Then he picked up a guitar, took a gulp of his drink, and started playing "Red Shoes."

I guess I went into some kind of shock after that. I mean, I couldn't handle it. I'd gotten my hopes up so high, and he'd denied me. Rejected me. To my face. Elvis Costello had rejected me to my face.

"No!" I screamed. "No!" It couldn't be real. It was a dream.

But the band was rocking, and the audience finally seemed to be having some fun. My head blurred, my ears felt blocked, and I'm not sure what happened during the next minute or two. I think maybe my nervous system shut down or something.

Eventually, though, my senses returned, and I heard Elvis playing "Alison"—a song I'd always liked—but I couldn't listen to it that night. I *hated* it that night. I recall turning my back on him, pushing my way to the bathroom, changing into semi-dry clothes, and walking out into the cold. If I'd had enough Xanax in my bag to guarantee a quick suicide, I probably would've swallowed them all. Luckily, I didn't.

I wandered around Geneva in the mist for hours, sobbing. Pathetically, I still hoped to run into Elvis somewhere, and I gazed into the face of every man I passed on the street. Then, around five in the morning, I laid down on one of the docks on the Rhone and fell asleep for a short time, using my overcoat and backpack for warmth.

But it wasn't long before the sun rose over me, beaming with unwavering clarity. I had nothing left. Nothing. Not even tears.

On the way to the train station, I caught a glimpse of my reflection in a bank window and knew the truth. I was a fat, desperate girl who'd never be anything more than that. Certainly, I'd never be with a rock star. I was ugly, stupid, and messed up. I had been since high school.

What was wrong with me? I mean, if a guy like Todd Eldridge wouldn't date me, what chance had I *ever* had with Elvis Costello? Or Bowie, or Springsteen, or Jim Morrison? I was crazy. Delusional. And my teeth hurt. I needed to see a dentist. I needed to go home.

I used my Eurail Pass to catch the next train to Paris, then transferred over to the Metro, and went straight to the airport. Almost two weeks of use remained on the pass, but my traveling days were over. I just wanted to be back in my bedroom, eating my mother's food and puking to my heart's content. I knew I couldn't return to the Sand Dollar—in fact, I'd need to figure out a way to avoid Wendy for the rest of my life—but I'd find a way to support myself. Some of the students I'd met in Europe had mentioned something called *temp work,* which required no commitment to any one company. They said you could move around from office to office, trying out lots of different things. Plus, you could quit any job you hated.

All of which sounded perfect. No obligations, no plans. And definitely no more rock stars.

Chapter 23

December 25, 1993

With an aching head and bladder, I got up at around three in the morning to pee and take Advil. Swallowing two pills, I examined my naked body in the mirror. The belly fat, the cellulite on my butt, my heavy breasts. But it was all me, and Luke had kissed me. Everywhere. I could still feel his skin against mine, but it already seemed like a fantasy. *How will I ever tell Claire?* I thought. *What sane person will ever believe I made love to Lenny Weir?* I could barely believe it myself. I was actually grateful for the rash on my face from his whiskers. At least I had some fleeting physical evidence.

When I got back into bed, he was snuggled up, naked, like a child, and I tried not to look at him as I slipped under the blanket, afraid my gaze might wake him and break the spell. If only my head didn't hurt so much. That part didn't make sense. I mean, how many beers had I drunk the night before? Two? Maybe three? Certainly not enough to cause such an epic hangover.

Just then, Luke rolled over and pulled me close, his lips brushing my shoulder, and I realized he'd be in rehab in less than twenty-four hours. We'd finally slept together, but there was no telling when—or if—it would ever happen again. Only one thing was certain. I loved him. I'd loved him since the Middle East, and that love had only grown stronger. Even when I'd thought he was dead, I'd loved him. And now we'd have to separate again.

And who knew what would happen in rehab? I imagined hallways filled with insomniac women in flowing white nightgowns—models, actresses, prostitutes—all tragically beautiful and searching for comfort as they struggled together to get sober. Would Luke be able to resist them? Would he even try? My fragile, scared Luke?

Oh, take a Xanax and stop thinking crazy thoughts, I chided myself. *Luke's an addict. He needs help.* Besides, I had to drive in the morning, and I hadn't gotten nearly enough sleep. And my head was killing me.

Luke opened his eyes as I tiptoed across the room to get a pill out of my purse. "What're you doing, Erin?" he whispered.

"Need a drink of water," I answered, darting into the bathroom before joining him again in bed. Luke smiled peacefully.

"Hey, I've got an idea," he said. "Let's skip Sunnydale tomorrow."

"Yeah, right." I forced myself to chuckle.

"No, I mean it. Let's go visit my friend Carlos. He's the one who owes me money. Just for a few days. You'll like him. I know you will. He lives near the beach."

"Luke," I replied, propping myself up on an elbow and pushing the pillow against my breasts in an effort to keep them covered, "you know they'll take good care of you at the hospital."

His voice came out dry and scratchy. "Yeah, but it'll be hell. I'd rather hang out with you."

I thought about all the girls in the world who were lying in their beds at that very moment, listening to Winterlong and imagining themselves with Lenny Weir. Young, pretty girls with soft hair and slender bodies, girls like the ones I used to envy on the Winthrop seawall. But they had no idea what it was like to actually *be* with this man. They'd invented a magical, supernatural genius named Lenny Weir, and idolized him as if he was a god. But I knew *Luke.* I knew the real guy, the person who existed *before* Lenny, the one who lived on. He was lying next to me. In bed.

Tears stung my eyes as I took his hand. I was sad, and angry too. "Damn it, Luke," I said, "I wish you didn't have this problem."

Instantly, he deflated. "Yeah, well, don't you think I wish that too? Don't you think I'd like to snap my fingers and make it all go away?"

"Yeah, but—"

"Erin, I wake up every morning saying I'm gonna quit. But then ... I don't. Because you know what the truth is? I hate drugs, but I love 'em too. And honestly, I don't know if I'll ever get better. You wanna know something? If someone told me right now that they'd invented a heroin that could keep you high forever, I'd take it. I'd stay high *eternally* if I could. So what's rehab gonna do for me?"

"Luke, that's crazy talk."

He relaxed and kissed my hand. "Yeah, well, crazy's the best I got right now. It's not so bad."

I looked down at his bony ribs and watery eyes. I saw his yellowing teeth and sallow skin, and smelled something like decay on his breath. Then I ran my tongue over my own teeth, which puking was slowly destroying. I felt cavities in many of the molars, and my whole mouth ached when I ate ice cream.

"Luke," I said, "let's try to get some more sleep. We'll talk again in the morning."

At sunrise, though, Luke was retching in the toilet. *Merry Christmas,* I thought, the brightness of the room making it almost impossible to open my eyes. My head throbbed, and I shuddered with cold under the thin blanket.

This can't be a hangover. It's gotta be some kind of virus. The flu had been rampant on the East Coast for weeks, so it made sense that I'd catch it. But the timing couldn't have been much worse. I needed to get out of bed.

Not that I wanted to stay in *that* particular bed. The motel room stank like Luke's vomit, and if I didn't get some fresh air soon, I'd be puking too, and not by choice. So while Luke showered and hacked in the bathroom, I threw on some clothes and went outside to sit in the car.

In the rearview mirror, I checked his whisker rash on my face again, but it'd faded considerably. Then Luke came staggering out of the motel with his duffel bag, a lit cigarette already in his mouth.

He grunted a greeting and planted himself in the back seat. "Open the windows," he barked. "I can't breathe in this fucking car."

Shivering with cold, I turned the key in the ignition and opened all the windows, then stepped out of the vehicle. "Luke, I'm sick," I said. "Really sick. Like with the flu. I'm going inside to wash up, but when we start driving, these windows are getting closed. I've got a fever or something."

He grunted again in reply.

Luckily, he'd crashed in the back seat by the time I was ready to hit the road. Turning on the heat, I peeled out of the parking lot, wondering if I'd make it to Miami without fainting behind the wheel. My teeth wouldn't stop chattering. But half an hour later, Luke sprang awake and declared that he was sweating to death. "Get off right here," he said, pointing to a sign for an upcoming exit. Based on his tone, I could tell that some bodily fluid was getting ready to explode from his mouth or his ass, and when I pulled into the first gas station available, he jumped out of the car and ran for the bathroom before I could even shift into park.

Holy shit, I thought, freezing in the driver's seat, *this guy spends more time in bathrooms than me, and I'm bulimic.* We were down to a quarter tank of gas, but I was too cold to get out and pump. Meanwhile, the thermometer on the side of the building claimed it was seventy degrees outside, and the sun sat high and bright in the sky. I found a second sweatshirt in my bag and pulled it over my head, then tugged it down so it covered my knees. But I couldn't get warm.

Luke stayed in the bathroom for at least twenty minutes. "What the *fuck* is he doing in there?" I shouted out loud to nobody. If I felt better, I would've gone and knocked on the door. Instead, I assumed he was using more methadone, which had helped him the previous night. And we'd most likely be at the rehab before dark. Then, it'd be the doctors' job to deal with him. I rested my head on the steering wheel and wished I could nap for a while.

But a few minutes later, I looked out and saw Luke leaning against the brick building, a payphone pressed to his ear. *What the hell?* Who could he possibly be talking to? And why was he smiling? Could he have called some old girlfriend? Violet Chasm, perhaps?

"What was *that* all about?" I asked when he finally returned to the Range Rover. He was in the back seat again, but looked way more alert than he had earlier.

His tone of voice had changed too; it'd gone from bratty and whiny to edgy and defiant. "Well, you know, Erin, I've done some more thinking."

"Oh yeah?" My body had been warming up under the double sweatshirts, but it was a sick, feverish warm. "About what?" I asked.

An impish smile twisted his lips, and I clenched my clammy hands together in an attempt to fend off panic. All my muscles ached. "Well, you know it's Christmas, right?" he said.

"Yeah?"

Opening a new pack of Marlboros, he shook the box until a cigarette slid out. "So." He tapped the butt against his fist a couple of times, then stuck it in his mouth and lit it with a match. My stomach retched and I opened my window. "Erin, I need a little more time. Just a week. I need to get through New Year's in the free world." He laughed nervously. "You know what I mean. I know you do."

"No," I said. "I mean, yeah, I know what you mean, but it's a bad idea. You might not survive another week."

He frowned and his mouth began to twitch. "Listen, Erin, I'm not saying I won't go. Okay? I'm just saying I need a week. That's *my* decision. This is *my* car. It's not up to you."

I stared at him and tried to make my sick, overtired brain think faster. "So ... where would you go? If you didn't go to rehab?"

"Carlos's," he said more calmly. "The guy I mentioned to you. That was him on the phone back there. He said you're welcome to hang with us too, if you want. He's got a big place. Plenty o' room. He's an old friend, Erin. A really good friend."

"But what about that doctor?" I said. "Dr. Klein, remember? He's gonna call Sunnydale *today*, and we'll be in huge trouble. He'll send the police after us or something."

"Fuck him!" shouted Luke. "Erin, I don't owe that guy a thing! This is *my* life, not his."

A tingly feeling, sort of like déjà vu, came over me. It may have been flu-related, but I didn't think so. All I knew was that Luke turned fuzzy in front of me, and everything got dark. Suddenly, I saw my dad in our old kitchen doorway, drunk and struggling to shove his foot into a flip-flop. Then I looked to the left and saw myself, sprawled on the living room couch, a chubby kid in gym shorts and a t-shirt, eating Lay's potato chips. *Love Boat* was on the TV.

"Dad, you shouldn't drive," I called, my eyes fixed on the screen. Captain Stubing and the rest of the crew were shipwrecked on an island, and I couldn't imagine how they'd escape.

"Leemeealone, Erin," my dad replied, grabbing his car keys. "I know what I'm doin'. Don' worry. It'll be fine."

I swallowed hard and rubbed my eyes, and then I was looking at Luke again. "What'd you say?" I asked.

"I said don't worry. It'll be fine."

Vomit shot up my throat, and I pushed the car door open just in time to puke all over the pavement. It tasted disgusting—much worse than bulimia vomit—since the food had been digesting in my stomach all night. I felt like I'd just rid myself of toxic waste.

"Better now?" asked Luke when I was done. Clearly, he'd seen his share of puking people.

"Yeah," I sniffled, blowing my nose into an old McDonald's napkin I found on the seat. "I'll survive."

"Here, have a drink," he said, passing me a half-empty bottle of water from the floor of the car. He was still smoking his cigarette, and his hand trembled. In the sunlight, his grinning face looked almost skeletal.

I sipped the warm water—which tasted vaguely of plastic and spit—and a plan began to form in my mind. "Hey, Luke," I said,

"I'm gonna go brush my teeth in the bathroom. Then, if you want, I'll drive you to your friend's house. But I'm not going inside. I'm sick and I wanna go home. To Winthrop. I just need you to give me enough money for a cab and a plane ticket. Okay?"

Luke looked surprised, but he nodded slowly. "Okay. That's cool. I'm sure Carlos'll be good for the cash he owes me, in, like, a day or two."

But I didn't have a day or two. "No. You're not listening. I need money *today*. You promised me five thousand dollars, but I'll take five hundred. I just need enough to get home."

He nodded again. "You really can't stick around?"

"No. I'm sorry. I'm dying."

"No you're not. It's probably a twenty-four-hour thing. You'll be better tomorrow."

"Luke, I'm not fucking around. I'm dropping you at Carlos's and taking a cab to the airport."

If he were paying closer attention, he might've noticed that I couldn't make eye contact with him as I spoke. But he just cleared his throat and handed his wallet to me. "Okay then. Take it all. There's a couple grand in here. I'll mail you more when I get it."

I felt like crying as I took the heavy wallet from him and removed the bills. "You sure?" I asked, starting to count.

"Yeah. Like I said, Carlos owes me."

There were lots of hundreds and even more fifties, so the counting went quickly. "Two-thousand, three-hundred forty dollars," I said.

"So take twenty-three hundred. Just leave me forty."

I hesitated, but he nodded. "Really. I want you to have it."

"Okay," I said. "But that's enough. We're even. Don't mail me any more."

He shrugged as I shoved the money into my purse and zipped it. Then I climbed shakily out of the car.

"Wait!" he said. "Where're you going?"

I smiled. "Don't worry, Luke. I'm not ditching you. Like I said, I'm just gonna brush my teeth and buy some more water. I'll be right back."

We rolled into Miami as dusk descended on the city. The air was warmer and more humid than it'd been in Jacksonville, and the Christmas lights everywhere were somehow disturbing. Thanks to the

Advil, my fever had subsided, and my headache had been temporarily replaced by fear and sadness.

"Luke," I whispered, "are you awake?"

His breathing came hard and heavy from the back seat.

I reached over and poked his shoulder, but he didn't stir. The three Xanaxes I'd crumbled into his water bottle had served their purpose well.

Everything went far more smoothly than I'd expected. Once Luke was asleep, I stopped at another gas station, and called Sunnydale from a payphone. The doctor on call was extremely helpful.

Yes, he assured me, Luke should be brought in immediately. A crew would be waiting outside the hospital to welcome us. *Yes,* he understood why I'd needed to sedate Luke, and *yes,* they could pump his stomach if necessary. And *no,* they wouldn't call the cops, despite the fact that I'd given Luke drugs prescribed for me. The doctor understood that I only wanted to help my friend, and stressed the importance of getting him there as quickly as possible. Because if he woke up in the car, we'd have a real problem.

And although most people probably wouldn't consider strapping a guy to a stretcher and snapping him into restraints much of a welcome, the staff at Sunnydale was certainly prepared for Luke's arrival. By the time he got around to resisting, his wrists and ankles had been tied down. "Erin!" he shouted. "What'd you do? You fucking bitch!"

But his words paled in comparison to the ugly, angry terror raging in his eyes. All the beauty, all the kindness, all the trust those eyes had once reflected were gone. And Lenny Weir, the gentle, lost soul I'd met at the Middle East, had vanished too. The person writhing on the stretcher was a stranger to me.

"Your cab should be here soon." A nurse came up behind me and rested a hand on my shoulder. I'd already surrendered the keys to the Range Rover, and had been sitting on the rehab's front lawn for close to an hour. With the help of Sunnydale's receptionist, I'd managed to book a late flight to Boston. "Do you need money or anything?" asked the nurse.

I stared at the large, unglamorous woman in white, wishing I could trade places with her. My eyes stung from crying. "No. But I'm not sure I should really leave. I'm thinking maybe I should get a hotel room near here, so I can stay close to Luke for a while, and ..."

"You're sweet," she said, squeezing my arm, "but he won't be allowed contact with the outside world for months. He won't even have phone access. You need to go home. Get back to your life."

My life. What life? According to the plastic tag pinned to her chest, the nurse's name was Maggie, and she was an RN. "No, he said this'll be a short stay," I informed her. "He's hoping to be out in a week or two."

Maggie winced. "Honey, Luke's an old friend of ours. And an eternal optimist. But even he should know better than to say stuff like that."

I stared at her. "Are you saying he lied?"

She shook her head and smiled. "Like I said, an eternal optimist. I'd never call Luke a liar. But you did him a solid, hon. I talked to that doctor in Richmond, and he was glad to hear you both arrived safely. Oh, and he said to wish you a happy holiday."

"Great."

"Sweetie, I'm telling you, Luke'll thank you for this someday." She raised her thin eyebrows. "Maybe he'll even write a song for you."

My eyes filled with tears. "Maggie?" I asked hesitantly, not sure if I should call her by her first name, since we hadn't been formally introduced. "Have you ever heard Luke ... sing?"

She nodded. "Yeah, but I can't talk about that. Patient confidentiality, you know. But between you and me, I love his voice. I really hope he gets it together and figures things out. He's got ... a complicated situation."

"Yeah."

Suddenly Maggie withdrew from me a little. "Well, that cab had better get here soon, huh? I don't want you sleeping in MIA tonight."

"MIA?"

"Miami International Airport."

"Oh yeah. That'd suck."

"You okay?"

"Yeah. I've got the flu or something."

She felt my forehead and nodded. "You've got something, all right. Hey, you know what? Wait here a second while I run inside and talk to my supervisor. I'll cancel that cab and drive you to the airport. One good deed deserves another. And trust me, honey, you did a good one tonight."

CHAPTER 24

November 2009

The old Helen Reddy song, "Angie Baby" haunted me almost every night. I'd be changing into my pajamas, or waiting for LB to get home from basketball practice, when, for no apparent reason, the song would start playing in my head. First, I'd hear the groovy, 1970s keyboard and bass intro; then the story of the "insane" girl who somehow turns her evil boy neighbor into her secret lover. Sometimes I'd wonder if "Angie Baby" had been buried and preserved in the deepest layers of my brain tissue, like crude oil beneath the earth. Which kind of made sense, but why was it bubbling to the surface now?

And I wasn't insane. That much I knew for sure. No insane single mother could've raised a kid as great as LB. Nor could she have handled all the stuff I handled over the years: borderline bankruptcy, childcare, homework, teachers, bullies, landlords, neighbors, friends, sports and coaches, dentists, doctors, and so much more. I'm not bragging, by the way. I realize that LB and I never would've survived without lots of luck and *tons* of help from my mother and Claire. But the truth is that by 2009, my son and I were doing okay. We were happy, and considered normal by most people. Maybe that was the craziest part of all. People thought I was normal.

Of course, being a single mom is never a bed of roses. (I like using that cliché because it reminds me of Freddy Mercury in "We Are the Champions.") But early in 1994, when I saw those two blue lines on the drugstore pregnancy test, I felt like I'd been offered a mission I couldn't refuse. I mean, I had rock & roll royalty growing in my uterus. I had no idea if I'd be able to care for a baby, but didn't I owe it to the world to at least *deliver* the kid?

Luckily, I'd gotten over my Florida flu fairly quickly, and had been seeing a therapist for over six weeks by the time I took the pregnancy test. The trip with Luke had convinced me that I needed help, so I called Dr. Mateo the day after arriving home, and asked her to recommend a psychologist who was good with eating disorders.

Then the weirdest thing happened. After so many years of being terrified of mental health treatment, suddenly, I couldn't wait to see a therapist. And once I started talking to Deb, my shrink, I felt like I was draining a wound that'd been filling with pus for almost fifteen years. I'd step into her office and the words would just ooze out of me. And Deb, an eating disorder survivor herself, totally got it. She listened carefully, and never made me feel odd or freaky. I told her everything too. Or almost everything. The only information I omitted from our sessions was the part about Luke being Lenny Weir. That was *my* secret and I wanted to keep it that way.

By our second meeting, Deb was giving me pointers on getting healthier, and talking to me about finding a new job. She also shared lots of facts and statistics, and told me that eating disorders have the highest mortality rate of any mental illness. But most importantly, she informed me that bulimia doesn't have to be a lifetime plague. She said that unlike drugs and alcohol—which often lead to chemical dependency—bulimia's more about *psychological* dependency. In other words, I could control it. It wouldn't be easy, but I could get better if I really wanted to.

So I did. I know that sounds simplistic, but after everything I'd been through, I was ready. Plus, I had Deb on my side, and she was a great inspiration. Then I found out I was pregnant, and she—along with my OB/GYN—helped me make good food choices and keep my mind focused on things that would keep the baby and me healthier.

But even after LB was born, and I no longer had another life depending on my body for nutrition, I never puked again. Not once. I thought about it a few times after overeating, but always reached the conclusion that gaining a pound or two was way better than heading back down that dark road. I could make it all sound poetic and say that rock & roll saved my life, but it didn't. In the end, I saved myself.

As for money, I relied on government assistance for a while. I'm not proud of that, but I couldn't see any other way of surviving, and I was determined to keep my baby happy and healthy. And when LB started preschool at age three, I found a part-time job as a receptionist at a software company, and enrolled in a business course at UMASS Boston. The state of Massachusetts continued to supplement my finances for about six more years, but when I finally earned a bachelor's degree in marketing—with Claire and Mom clapping and cheering from the bleachers—and accepted a full-time job, I was able to stand on my own for the first time. I was thirty-eight years old—and LB was already in third grade—but it felt amazing to be able to provide for our little family. And LB always knew he was loved. By his mother and everyone else who knew him.

I waited until I was three months pregnant, though, to call Sunnydale. My doctor had warned me about the high risk of miscarriage during the first trimester—especially for a woman with a history of eating disorders—so why tell Luke, then disappoint him?

I checked the calendar about ten times to make sure I had the date correct. Then I took a nice warm shower, ate some oatmeal and an orange, and made a cup of decaf tea. I'd already gained five pounds, and Jeff and Pete kept telling me I glowed. They knew about the pregnancy, of course, and were helping me find my own apartment, because their place was far too small for four people, especially when one of them might be inclined to scream all night long.

I'm going to hear Luke's voice, I thought as I dialed the phone. Thanks to Deb, I'd prepared myself for a variety of reactions. She'd warned me that Luke might get angry or express disbelief—he might even accuse me of lying—but he needed to know the truth. My hope was that the baby would help with his recovery process, but Deb had stressed that things didn't always work out that way.

I certainly wasn't prepared, though, for what actually happened. When I got through to Sunnydale, the receptionist informed me that Luke was no longer a resident at the facility.

"Oh," I replied, my throat catching. "Well ... I'm the person who brought him there in the first place. And I'm pregnant with his child. So ... do you ... have his phone number?"

She said nothing for a full second; then her voice came back, almost as perky as before. "Um, well, first of all, congratulations, ma'am. But I can't give out any patient data. If you'd like, though, I can try to get a message to him."

I was stunned. "No, you don't understand. I need to speak to him *right away*. The baby's due in six months."

"I'm sorry, ma'am. All patient data's confidential. But if you give me your contact info, I'll do my best to pass along your good news."

I slammed the phone down and called back the next day. A different receptionist answered, but she said pretty much the same thing as the other one. So I started calling on a regular basis, at all times of the day and night. But none of my tricks worked, and eventually, I gave up.

Of course, I talked to Deb about it a lot, and she advised me to have faith in human nature. "He knows where you live, Erin, so maybe he'll come back to you someday. But if he doesn't, that's okay too. You're doing great on your own, and I have faith in your ability to make good choices.

"Ma, do you want cream cheese on your bagel?" called LB from the kitchen.

I'd been awake in bed for about an hour, listening self-indulgently as my handsome, green-eyed son sang along with his new Foo Fighters album. I'd always loved the tone of LB's voice, and his eclectic taste in music was truly impressive. Not only was he into straight-ahead rock, but he also liked more progressive bands like Radiohead, rootsy guys like Jeff Tweedy, classic country artists like Johnny Cash, some hip-hop, and all kinds of other stuff. One day, I borrowed his iPod Shuffle when I went out for a walk, and heard a Talking Heads song from the 80s, then a new Kanye song, then a classical piece by Bach, then Marvin Gaye's "What's Going On?"

But the night LB came home from Newbury Comics with an old Winterlong CD, I'd been speechless to the point where I could only nod and run off to my room before the tears started flowing. *Gosh, I wish he could meet his dad,* I thought. But although I'd searched the Internet countless times for *Luke Walker,* I'd never seen anything about *my* Luke. All I'd learned was that Luke Walker is a fairly common American name.

"I didn't hear you, Ma," called LB from the kitchen. "Cream cheese or no cream cheese?"

I reached into the glass I kept on the nightstand, took out my dentures, and popped them in my mouth. Almost all my teeth were fake, thanks to bulimia. My dentist had recommended at least a few dental implants, but they were way too expensive, especially since I was saving for Luke to go to college. "No cream cheese, thanks," I answered, marveling at how lucky I was to have a fifteen-year-old who still made me breakfast on Sunday mornings. "I'm trying to cut back a little before the holidays." His full name was Luke Benjamin—after his father and grandfather—but I'd started calling him LB the day he was born, and it'd stuck. And that was a good thing, because for the longest time, I couldn't say the word *Luke* without getting emotional.

Of course, LB had been asking questions about his dad almost as long as he'd been able to talk, but pretty much everything I knew about Luke was stuff I didn't want to share with him. I mean, how do you tell your son that you met his dad hitchhiking? Or that you haven't spoken to the guy since the night you dropped him off at a rehab hospital, kicking and screaming? How do you tell your kid that his father's last words to you were *you fucking bitch*? And what intelligent child would believe that his mother was impregnated in December, 1993 by a rock god who'd supposedly died in August of '92?

So I kept things vague, implying to LB that I'd had a fling with the wrong guy. "Your dad was a kind man," I'd say. "He was sweet and gentle, but honestly, I was just getting to know him when he left me. I didn't even know I was pregnant until he'd been gone a few weeks." Sometimes LB would wonder where his dad was, and I'd tell him honestly that I had no idea. And once, after a big glass of wine, I told him his father had been a musician. But when the kid pressed me for details, I simply said he'd never played for me. Which was at least partially true.

"Um, your bagel's getting cold, Ma."

"Okay, honey. I'll be right there." But the bed was so comfy, and I didn't feel like getting up. Especially not for a dry bagel.

Although I'd been managing my weight pretty well. I didn't look like Nicole Kidman or anything, but I was between a size ten and a twelve, and felt much healthier than I'd ever felt in the 90s. I had a good job too; I worked in the marketing department at a company that made music software, so I was on the periphery of the music business. Every once in a while, some famous musician who used our products would stop by the office to meet with the bigwigs, but I never got worked up the way my coworkers did. I mean, I'd been Lenny Weir's lover. What celebrity could fluster me?

Climbing out of bed, I pulled on my chenille bathrobe and glanced over at my computer. *Maybe I'll Google Luke before breakfast*, I thought. I did that every couple of months, but each time, I found the same dudes: a chemist and a software engineer on LinkedIn; a whole bunch of guys on Facebook; a former soldier who blogged about his experiences in Afghanistan. But on that particular Sunday, the first thing that popped up when I typed "Luke Walker" into Google was an obituary from the *Boston Globe.*

No, I thought. This can't be him.

"Ma, should I pour you a coffee?"

"No! Hang on, LB!"

"Jeez, Ma. Take it easy."

Normally, I'd apologize if I snapped at LB, but as I read the text, I felt like someone was pumping Novocain through my veins.

WALKER, Luke M, 45, suddenly, at his Revere home on November 5th. Beloved husband of Mandy Bartilotta, and devoted father to Leo M. Walker, both of Revere. Cherished son of the late Joseph A. Walker and Marie (Zani) Walker, both formerly of Orlando.

Mr. Walker, a native of Orlando, Florida who resided in New England for most of his adult life, graduated from Danforth College in Providence, Rhode Island, in 1986. A musician and songwriter, he was best known as the lead singer for the band "Spike and the Asbury Rockers," a Bruce Springsteen cover band. Spike and the Asbury Rockers also scored a Top Forty hit in 1990 with an original song penned by Walker called "City of Decay," and they toured briefly with the Violet Chasm's band, Funspot. "City of Decay" has been featured in several television commercials and a few independent movies. Mr. Walker also enjoyed writing and co-writing songs for his son Leo's band, "Grenadine," which was a top contender in last year's WBCN Rock & Roll Rumble.

Due to serious issues with drugs and alcohol, Mr. Walker took an extended leave of absence from performing in 1991, but was attempting to bring the Asbury Rockers back together for a reunion tour at the time of his death.

Mr. Walker often told his wife Mandy that his proudest achievement in life was kicking heroin addiction and learning to enjoy each day without drugs. The couple separated legally in 1990, but reunited in 1994, after Mr. Walker returned from a Florida rehab hospital, drug-free. He remained sober for the remainder of his life.

In addition to writing and playing music, Mr. Walker dabbled in photography and taught guitar lessons in his home studio. A memorial service was held on Revere Beach November 9th. In lieu of flowers, contributions in Mr. Walker's memory may be made to the Sunnydale Substance Abuse Center in Miami, FL.

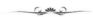

"Ma, are you okay?" LB stood in my doorway looking concerned.

"Leave me alone, LB," I said doing my best to show no emotion. I closed my browser and covered my face with my hands.

"Ma, what's wrong?"

"LB, I mean it. Go away!" I got up, slammed the door, and collapsed on the bed.

All week, I stayed home with a migraine. At least that's what I told my coworkers. But LB knew better, and he kept asking what was up. He knew about my history with bulimia, and was clearly worried. I was sleeping late every morning, then hanging out in my room all day in sweats, trolling the Internet for stories about Luke, and reading his obituary over and over again.

But no matter how much I read, I still couldn't accept it. *Luke had never been Lenny Weir. All along, he'd been Spike Walker from the Asbury Rockers.* I'd been so proud of myself for getting my act together and facing up to the real world, but the last sixteen years of my life had been based on a giant fantasy. I was more like Angie in "Angie Baby" than I ever could've imagined. For sixteen years, my secret lover had been keeping me satisfied. I'd been happy, yes, but also delusional.

The nights were worse than the days. My body desperately needed rest, but I'd stay up super late, watching TV and falling asleep on the couch. Meanwhile, my diet had gone straight to hell: I was living on Doritos, Chex Mix, and Lay's potato chips. I wanted to be mad at Luke for lying to me, but he'd never lied. I'd been the liar. I'd added all kinds of imaginary details to his stories, hearing and seeing only what I wanted to.

"Ma," LB finally said on Friday night around eleven o'clock. "You're not puking all this food you're eating, are you?"

"Oh no, honey." After at least three glasses of boxed wine, I was pretty buzzed and moved to tears by his concern. "I'm done with puking forever. There's just ... well, I found out last Sunday that someone very special to me died. I'm sorry I've been acting so weird."

"Was it my dad?" asked LB.

Damn, he's perceptive. "Um ... yeah. Yeah, it was. I'm so sorry. But ... I can't really talk about it now because I don't ... I don't understand it." I sighed. "I guess the bottom line is I didn't know him nearly as well as I thought I did."

LB did his best to smile. "You've always said that, Ma. He didn't even know you were pregnant, right?"

I nodded. "Yeah, but ...that's not the half of it. It's ... well, I'm pretty confused right now."

Now, most kids probably would've asked a lot more questions at a moment like that, but not LB. He just gave me a hug, and said he loved me. "But Ma?" he added as he headed off to bed. "I *would* like to talk about this sometime. When you're ready, I mean."

Down on Winthrop Beach, only a few brave souls were out. On that sunny November Saturday, the chilly breeze signaled that winter was rolling in fast. A girl wearing earbuds and a Fall Out Boy t-shirt sat on the seawall, messing around with her phone. She regarded my giant boombox with suspicion.

LB was obviously embarrassed. "Ma, you gotta tell me what we're doing now," he said.

"Wait and see," I said calmly. "Just be patient for another half hour."

He said okay and decided to take a walk on the sand, but I opted to stay put and sit. I hadn't been to Winthrop in several years—LB and I lived about forty minutes away, in Arlington—but it was easy to remember how it'd looked in the late seventies. Mainly because it hadn't changed very much.

In fact, if I squinted hard, I could almost see the surfers down by the rocks, the willowy girls lounging near them, and the burnouts a bit further up the beach. *Where are they all now*? I wondered. *Do any still live in town?* I figured some were probably very far away, and at least a few must've died. But I preferred not to think about that.

A boy driving a rust-colored Scion pulled sharply into one of the parking spaces, and rolled down his window. I expected music to come blaring out, but then noticed an earbud in one of his ears. In his own car! What a strange and dangerous thing to do.

Checking my watch, I saw that it was ten minutes before twelve. I'd been hoping for a little more activity, but a small crowd was better than none. "Excuse me!" I called to the girl in the Fall Out Boy shirt. "In ten minutes, tune your radio to WBCN!"

She gave me a weird look. "I don't have a *radio*. This is an iPhone."

"Okay," I answered. "Well, then, you can listen to mine." But she just shrugged and went back to playing with her phone.

"What's up?" called the boy in the Scion. "What's happening on 'BCN?"

Now *that's* what I'd been hoping for. A little buzz. I raised my eyebrows mysteriously. "Tune in and you'll see."

"Okay, whatever," he answered, unplugging the iPod from his dashboard.

It was time for LB to join me, so I called to him. Then I jogged down the wall to where a girl and boy were eating sandwiches from Kelly's Roast Beef. The boy wore a maroon sweatshirt with a giant white rhinoceros printed on the front, while the girl, whose eyebrow was pierced, was dressed in a pink velour sweat suit with a large "J" embroidered on her left thigh. "Hey, if you guys have a radio, tune it to 'BCN in eight minutes," I instructed them.

The girl ignored me, but the boy seemed slightly curious. "Is that an XM station?" he asked.

I couldn't believe it. I mean, how could a kid his age—probably seventeen or eighteen—not know his local radio stations? "No," I said, trying to keep the irritation out of my voice. "It's an *F*M station. 104.1. Trust me. Just turn it on and you'll understand why in a few minutes."

He took a bite of his sandwich. "I don't think I can," he said. "My car's all the way over there." He pointed to a shiny new red Jeep parked across the street. If Johnny Palmese could've afforded such a vehicle back in the seventies, he would've been the envy of every kid at Winthrop High. Of course, Johnny would've tricked it out with speakers the size of microwave ovens too. But the new Jeep looked refined, almost classy. I could imagine a young businessman driving it.

"Yeah," agreed the girl. "Besides, someone'll post it online later if it's good."

I shook my head. "No," I replied, trying to pique her interest without giving anything away. "It's not that kinda thing."

LB climbed up on the wall, and I could tell he was trying hard to look supportive. "Come on, buddy," I said. "Let's go talk to some *other* people. We'll let these folks enjoy their lunch in peace."

But the only other person around was an elderly woman walking a dog, so LB and I headed back to where I'd left the boombox. Then, just as we were sitting down, LB whispered, "Ma, don't look now, but those kids are packing up their food."

It was true. The girl didn't look happy about it, but she and the boy in the rhinoceros sweatshirt were up on their feet and making their way toward the red Jeep. "C'mon," the boy said to her. "It might be cool."

Meanwhile, the Fall Out Boy girl watched intently as I tuned in the station on my boombox, and the boy in the Scion started fiddling with his stereo too. From across the street in the Jeep, the rhinoceros kid called out, "Hey! You said 104.1, right?"

"Yup!" I replied. "It should be on in a second."

I turned the volume knob on my boombox as far to the left as it would go, and heard the voice of an unfamiliar DJ. "... and everyone's wondering if the Celtics can do it again this year, with Rondo and the Big Three all looking so good. But we'll talk sports later on. Right now, let's get back to playing some music."

Oh please, I thought. Please. Play it now.

"So listen up, folks," continued the DJ, his deep voice emanating from all three radios in the salt air. "As you probably know, we don't usually take requests here at 'BCN, but I got a call from a woman a while ago who said it was *very* critical that I play this song at noon today. She said it's got something to do with history, some ... event that happened in 1978. To be honest, I didn't quite catch the significance, but this lady wasn't screwing around. She sounded a little scary, to tell the truth. So Erin, you crazy bitch over there on Winthrop Beach, this is for you. At least you picked a good song, a timeless classic from Queen."

"Bohemian Rhapsody" started the same way it always does: the *a cappella* voices, the quiet piano, then Freddie's operatic voice, rising above it all, as magnificent as ever. Then the segue into power chords. The cymbals, and Brian May's edgy but smooth guitar work. I felt the molecules in my brain heating and expanding, and I might've even levitated a bit. Nothing like that first time, but still. My skin prickled with excitement.

LB, however, just sat there, staring out at the ocean. I could only see the left side of his face, so I had no sense of what he thought.

Unfortunately, the kids in the Jeep made their opinion quite clear. About a minute into the song, they turned off their radio, started the engine, and sped off. The girl flipped me the bird and yelled something unintelligible.

The Fall Out Boy girl continued to play with her phone—apparently oblivious to the rest of us—her earbuds firmly in place. But the kid in the Scion wasn't giving up. Clearly, he wanted to understand. "Is this what we're supposed to be listening to?" he called. "Queen?"

"Yup," I answered. "Amazing, isn't it?"

The boy nodded, then rolled up his window. But I didn't care. At least he was trying, and maybe he just wanted to listen in private.

Meanwhile, Freddie pleaded with someone not to throw stones at him or spit in his eye, and I couldn't help it. I started to cry. *How can anyone not be moved by this song?* I wondered. *Has the human race lost its* soul?

But LB turned to me with a shy smile. Normally, he reminded me of Luke, but that day he looked more like his grandfather. My dad.

"You're nuts, Ma," he said, throwing an arm around me. "You know that, don't you?"

Panic struck me as the guitar solo started to burn. *Nuts? Does my kid really think I'm crazy?*

But then, his whole face softened. "That's why I love you," he said.

Freddie was winding things down by then, saying goodbye one last time, and trying to convince the world—for better or for worse—that nothing mattered.

But he was wrong about that. Definitely, absolutely wrong. "It all matters, LB," I whispered. "I don't understand a lot of things, but I know everything matters. Every little bit."

A tear rolled down my son's face, reflecting the blue of the ocean and the sky. "Damn straight it does, Ma."

What a kid, I thought. *What an amazing kid.* I rested my graying head on his shoulder and all I could do was smile.

THE END

Book Club Guide

1. Erin is clearly a misfit among her peers for most of the story. Do you believe her mental health issues and social awkwardness are the result of nature, nurture, or both?

2. Fantasy plays a large role in Erin's life, although she also functions every day in a real—often harsh—world. Do you think her fantasies protect her or add to her troubles?

3. Why do you think Erin is so obsessed with male rock stars? What do they offer her that non-celebrity men (and women) don't?

4. What's your favorite part of the story, and what parts do you wish hadn't been included?

5. Many of Erin's attempts at meeting her heroes in person end in disappointment. Have you ever met an idol of yours? If so, how did it turn out?

6. Describe Erin in five adjectives and explain why you chose these five.

7. Near the beginning of the story, Erin's father chides her—a young teen at the time—for eating too much. Do you think this relates to the eating disorder she later develops? Why or why not?

8. How do you feel about Erin's various peers (high school pals, college and post-college roommates, work associates, etc.)? Which of them do you think have her best interests at heart, and which ones don't?

9. Erin's method of getting to a distant job when she no longer has a car is clearly dangerous. What would you have done in her situation?

10. Do you find the ending of the story satisfying? Why or why not?

A Personal Note from the Author

As a currently healthy person who struggled with anorexia, bulimia, and—to some extent—body dysmorphia for almost twenty years, I'm happy to report that good therapy, supportive family and friends, and a sincere will to get better were the keys to my recovery. Eating disorders, however, are extremely complex entities that manifest differently in different individuals. No two cases are identical, but seeking help is critical. If you or someone you know suffers from an eating disorder, please contact a local hospital or health care center, or go to the website below.

www.NationalEatingDisorders.org

Acknowledgements

What a thrill it is to be writing acknowledgements for *Leaving the Beach* a second time. I wasn't sure it would ever see print again, but here we are.

For that reason, I must first thank the wonderful team at Evolved Publishing for resuscitating this work after my first publisher shut down in 2016. Dave Lane (aka Lane Diamond), thank you for inspiring me to dig deeper into each sentence and craft what I hope is an improved version of something I once considered finished. Jessica West, what did I do to deserve an editor as patient, thorough, and all-around terrific as you? And Kabir Shah, I'm not sure if the story of *Leaving the Beach* can possibly live up to the gorgeous cover you created for it.

April Eberhardt, agent extraordinaire, thank you for continuing to believe in me and stand beside me through the storms. I've learned the hard way that the writing business is more unpredictable than New England weather, and its winters can feel interminable. Which only makes me appreciate your optimism and expertise more.

To my writing buddies who keep me afloat, thank you for understanding, listening, and sharing your hearts with me. Since I've been at this thing for twenty years (!) now, I'd need several pages to name you all, but I hope you know how much you mean to me. Special thanks to my resolute writing group (Terri Brosius, Karen Harris, and Sheila Moeschen). I'd also like to thank Sheryl Kaleo, who's always there with encouragement and words of wisdom when I need to hear them.

Friends, I treasure you. Each and every one of you. Even though it seems cheesy to bunch you all together like this.

And family, of course. Mom, Dad (watching over us from the Other Place), Steve, Chris and Beth, Marilyn and Jerry, Sandra and Chris, Tim and Joanne, all the kids. I'm blessed to be part of your world.

Mike, Walter, and Maggie, you're the reason I get up every morning and live. I'll love you unconditionally forever.

-- Mary

About the Author

I'm drawn to stories about women facing and overcoming challenges at various stages of life, so I love reading and writing women's fiction. Music, musicians, and music fans tend to find their way into my work too.

Other interests include feminism, body image issues, parenting, and current events. I blog about that stuff and more whenever I can. My essays have been featured on numerous sites and blogs, including Mutha Magazine, Feminine Collective, and Huffington Post.

A graduate of Providence College, I was raised in the Massachusetts Merrimack Valley, and live in the Boston area with my family and pets.

For more, please visit me online at:
Website: www.MaryRowen.com
Goodreads: Mary Rowen
Facebook: @MaryRowenAuthor
Twitter: @MaryJRowen
Pinterest: @MaryRowenAuthor

What's Next?

LIVING BY EAR

(Scheduled to Release in the Fall of 2019)

Singer-songwriter Christine Daley hit the streets of Boston and became a minor celebrity – with a local radio hit – in the 90s, but a "brief" career break to marry and start a family changed all that. Now, sixteen years later, she's a frustrated suburban housewife, struggling to reestablish her sense of identity.

After filing for divorce, forty-six-year-old Chris quickly learns that the challenges she faces are even greater than anticipated. Her two teenage children suddenly seem to need their mom more than ever, and neither of them is thrilled about her getting back on the music scene. Meanwhile, her soon-to-be-ex-husband is throwing every possible obstacle in her way.

Adding to the stress is technological progress, which has radically changed both the music industry and the dating world. Is there room in this new mix for Chris?

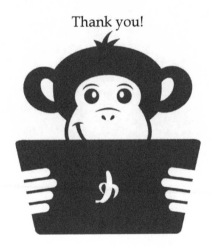

CPSIA information can be obtained
at www.ICGtesting.com
Printed in the USA
BVHW041147270619
552124BV00002B/35/P

9 781622 535804